To my Brother Jimmy—
with love

Destiny
Lingers

May you find a destiny
that's sweet and a love
that's strong! Thank you
for still being such a
positive light in my
life! DRo

ROLONDA WATTS

"Time moves on … but destiny lingers."
What would you do for a second chance at your first love?

DESTINY LINGERS

iUniverse books may be ordered through booksellers or by contacting:

iUniverse
1663 Liberty Drive
Bloomington, IN 47403
www.iuniverse.com
1-800-Authors (1-800-288-4677)

ISBN: 978-1-4917-6862-4 (sc)
ISBN: 978-1-4917-6864-8 (hc)
ISBN: 978-1-4917-6863-1 (e)

Library of Congress Control Number: 2015909009

Print information available on the last page.

iUniverse rev. date: 10/27/2015

I dedicate my novel to my beloved father, Roland Smith "Sonny" Watts ... to my beloved great aunt, Florence "Flo" Smith, and my beloved grandparents, Maurice Love and Garnelle Smith Watts who all gave me their unconditional, unyielding, and undying love -- and Tranquility.

Chapter ✬ One

THE THOUGHT OF ANOTHER WOMAN IN MY BED MAKES ME WANT TO vomit. But I cannot deny that my wrenching gut is screaming something's afoul. I lie here on this glorious May morning, sun now streaming through my bedroom window, its sunbeams expecting to find happiness stretched across my face. But instead it finds me staring at another long strand of red hair—this one, at eye level, stretched across my husband's bed pillow, as if it belongs here.

Against the backdrop of stark-white 800-count Egyptian cotton, this auspicious find is impossible to ignore and is quite shocking in itself. But my alarm and curiosity are only compounded by the fact that this is the third long strand of red hair that I have found in as many weeks right up here in my personal space—up in my husband's and my special space, up in our very sacred space where no redhead has ever gone before. Not to my knowledge. Not until now.

The first strand of long red hair introduced itself to me on another recent bright spring morning from the hollows of my bathroom sink. I stared down at it in my sleepy haze as I brushed my teeth and leaned over to spit the minty toothpaste froth into the basin. How do you not notice long red hair in your white porcelain sink, especially when your own hair is short and chestnut brown? I spat and moved on. I was late for work.

The second strand of red hair caught my attention a couple of weeks later as I turned on the shower and waited for the water to heat up. I was in a melancholy mood that day, and my thoughts drifted as I watched little droplets of water racing down the sides of the tub in mad neck-to-neck dashes and darts to join the curling stream below. A little squiggle of red dancing for survival near the drain snapped me back to reality. "Another one?" I asked myself.

And just like that, it was gone, gulped up by the thirsty drain.

But it is still emblazoned here in my brain right now, racing like the little droplets of water.

These morning strands of long red hair seem to have taken root in our home—a home Garrett and I have cherished since we first found this beautiful Harlem brownstone three years ago, right after our wedding. It's only a one-bedroom rented apartment, the second floor of a five-story brownstone, but to us, just starting out in our marriage and television careers, it is our mansion—the beautiful, stately, and historic home of Mr. and Mrs. Garrett Theodore Nelson. In one fleeting spring moment, dressed in a long, white lace gown, tears streaming down my face, and surrounded by a thousand people, I became Mrs. Garrett Nelson. I'm still getting used to it. Destiny Newell Nelson. A mouthful for TV, so I just keep my maiden name for the news.

Our living room is accented with twelve-foot ceilings and intricate crown molding running along the tops of the walls. Our favorite feature is the big bay window that overlooks Hamilton Terrace, with its rows of exquisite brownstones. The elderly couple across the street in this historic landmark district of Harlem always proudly keeps their window boxes flourishing with bright pink geraniums at this time of year, so there's always a delightful view. You can actually forget you're in New York.

On Saturday mornings, I have a ritual with our big bay window. While Garrett piddles around the apartment, reads the newspaper, or disappears for a game of golf, I grab a bottle of Windex, a roll of paper towels, and crank up Marvin Gaye as I sit on my big bay-window ledge, crooning to and escaping in my favorite hits, from "What's Going On" to "Let's Get It On." Sometimes I play Marvin so loud that I draw a small crowd of Marvin-lovin' neighbors outside my window. I caress her until she sparkles clean clear through.

But it doesn't take a bottle of Windex to see through the dirt I seem to have uncovered this spring morning in our beautiful brownstone home.

I struggle to maintain my composure as a sordid rush of truth overcomes me. I know what I know, and I know things are not ever going to be the same at the end of this day that has not yet begun.

I lie here and ponder my morning shock, predicament, and rage. I shudder as I realize that the only person we know with long red hair is one of my best girlfriends, Eve Havaway. In fact, Eve is the only real redhead I have ever known. The only real redheaded black girl I have ever seen. Along with her smooth mocha skin, hazel eyes, freckles, dimples, and that brilliant red hair, Eve also sports the kind of body that makes the boys in Harlem yell, "B-*dam!*" It's as though she casts a wicked spell on them as they shake their heads, lick their lips, lean to the side, and grab their hardening crotches, gawking in speechless awe at her curvy hips, her slender waist, and those big perky breasts—and, of course, her red hair.

"Hey, Red!" they catcall as she floats down the avenue. But she ignores them. Eve is a brick house on legs—the black Marilyn Monroe, conducting herself like a strategic tigress, using her poignant feminine power profusely.

I haven't seen Eve in a while. She keeps canceling on our girls' nights out, claiming that Fritz, her boyfriend of five years, is in one of his "Big Daddy" funks and doesn't want her hanging out so much. I know how much free rent, fur coats, and lavish gifts of jewelry mean to Eve, so I haven't questioned her a lot about it. I try to stay out of her business because I don't understand why she doesn't think more of herself than to be with a Harlem hustler.

On the surface, Fritz Salese is a really nice guy, but he is also one of the biggest drug-dealing gangsters in Harlem and the Bronx, so who knows how nice Fritz *really* is?

All I know is that Fast-Footed Fritz has spoiled the shit out of Eve over the past five years, keeping her latest Louis Vuitton full of cash. She is always donned in the top and most expensive fashions, from Gucci to Pucci to Fiorucci and a bunch of other haute couture names I can't even pronounce. I figure most of her prize possessions could melt steel they're so hot.

Eve is such a bright girl that it bothers me to see her settle for less than what I know she could achieve on her own. She has a college degree from Brown University and speaks fluent Spanish—even studied in Spain. She has dreams of a career in television, and I have promised to help her by seeing if I can arrange an internship in our news department.

Garrett says he's disappointed in Eve too. He's known her longer than I have. He also went to Brown, and he says that while she has always been smart, she also loves the fast life. He remembers that in college, they called her "the red-hot chick from Queens."

"Eve wouldn't give me the time of day back then," Garrett scoffs. "I was a dumpy bookworm, and she was 'big city.' She gave me no play at all!"

They certainly are good friends now, thanks to my meeting Eve on my own. We actually met in the bathroom one ladies' night out at the House of Jazz, a popular westside club. I was talking with my girlfriend Kat McCullough in the next stall about how Garrett and I wouldn't be around over the weekend because we had planned a Connecticut bed-and-breakfast getaway with two other couples. I told her we'd probably also head up to Providence, Rhode Island, and visit Brown University, where all the guys had originally met in college.

"Girl, too bad your ass is married," Kat teased, "'cause there are some f-i-i-ine men in here tonight!" Kat had dumped her husband a few months before and was now on the prowl.

"Go for it, girl," I yelled back over the sounds of toilets flushing, faucets running, and women chattering. "Don't hurt nobody now!"

Kat let out a loud hoot.

"Are you guys talking about Garrett Nelson?" A strange voice from outside the stalls suddenly interrupted our girls' conversation.

"Who is that?" a defensive Kat wanted to know.

"Yeah, you know Garrett?" I chimed in.

Our toilets flushed at the same time as more women piled into the bathroom.

I moved my way out of the stall and into the crowd of restless women waiting for their turn. I squeezed my way to the sink ... and there she was, decked out in a big red-fox coat, a charming dimpled smile, and a tube of Russian Red Mac lipstick in her hand, the one Madonna made famous. I could not help but notice her shiny, bouncy, red hair as she pointed a long red acrylic fingernail my way.

"You can't be married to Garrett Nelson," she exclaimed.

"And why not?" Kat demanded. She was always so protective of me and did not like, much less trust, most other women.

A couple of heavyset sisters waiting for a stall darted their eyes our way. They were grinning as if preparing for some fierce feline fireworks.

"I know Garrett," Eve shot back. She turned to the mirror and started slowly applying her lipstick, carefully making sure to stay within the lines of her plump lips.

"And just how well do you know her husband?" For some reason Kat was going head-to-head with Eve.

One of the big sisters listening in couldn't hold it any longer. "Ooooo!" she exclaimed. "I gotta hear this." She moved her big body up to the sink.

"Me too, girl," her friend said, moving in closer too. "How do you know her husband? Sound like you know him *well!*"

The big girls nudged each other and exploded into hearty laughter. Kat crossed her arms, scoping Eve's big fur from top to bottom. I wanted to sink into the floor.

"Why don't you ask Garrett? We knew each other at Brown." Eve then turned, directing her dimpled smile at the two big girls. "We were just *friends.*"

Eve turned back to the mirror and wiped any residual redness out of the corners of her mouth with her fingertips. So seductive in her mirrored movements, she seemed to be making love to herself.

"Then you must know his best friends, Reggie and Rick, too." I had to know more about this startling woman.

"Ah … yes—those nuts? Of course! They were all runnin' buddies back in school."

"They were Garrett's best men in our wedding. We had a thousand people." I felt stupid adding that note.

"A thousand people!" wailed one of the big girls. "Gi-i-irl, you *good* and married!"

We all burst into laughter, finally breaking the ice.

"Why don't you join us for a drink," I offered Eve.

"Okay," she replied with a bright smile.

We said our good-byes to the big loud girls and made our way through the bar crowd and back to our table where our girl, Hope Linton, was keeping an eye on our big down coats.

"Where have y'all been?" she demanded. "This fine brutha asked me to dance, and I said no cause I was watchin' y'all's coats! Now, he's out there dancin' with that crazy Wall Street girl. Ooo—I can't stand her!"

"Easy, girlfriend." Kat slid into her seat and swooped up the vodka martini she'd left waiting. "We got sidetracked meeting Miss Eve Havaway here, who says she knows Garrett."

Kat took a long, dramatic, wide-eyed sip of her martini without taking her eyes off Hope, who, as if on cue, perked up with sudden interest and curiosity.

"Oh, it's nice to meet you, Eve." Hope extended her long arm across the table in a how-do-you-do shake and then asked, "How do you know Garrett?"

"School chums," Kat blurted with a wry smile before Eve had a chance to speak.

"Ah, I see." Hope knew Kat was up to no good. But perhaps, so was this Eve.

"So ..." Eve abruptly eluded the conversation and turned to me, exuding a big smile. "What a small world. Now tell me, what is Mr. Garrett up to these days?"

"He's an overnight producer at ABC network news," I proudly explained. "He's doing so well over there. We're thrilled—"

"Oh, I bet you are! ABC network news? A big overnight producer!" I could almost see Eve salivating. "I had no idea! Oh, please tell Garrett I said hello."

"I will," I promised.

The four of us ended up having a ball on what turned out to be our first of many ladies' nights. Kat filled our ears with jaw-dropping stories about some of the well-known celebrities she'd dealt with as an event planner. Hope held Eve's hand and soothed her concerns about flying, as Hope's a top flight attendant at a big airline and has a calming way about her anyway. I offered tons of details about murder, mobs, and mayhem from my many hours covering gruesome crime reports in New York City. Eve gushed about her growing collection of designer bags and shoes—she called them "make-up gifts" from her naughty boyfriend. I felt no need to rush home to our empty brownstone, as I had called Garrett, and he had already left for work on the overnight shift. He wouldn't be home until the next morning, long after I had left for my day job as a reporter at NBC. So feeling free and adventurous and in love with New York City and the people one might meet along the way, I hung out with my girlfriends until about three in the morning. After exchanging hugs, numbers, and promises to hook up again, I made my way home, alone, up to Harlem in a big Yellow Cab.

But that was a year ago, and so much has happened since then.

I think of Eve now, and a shiver catches me off guard. A mixture of nausea and dizziness overwhelms me. My throat goes dry, and I begin to pant. "Get through this—you can get through this."

My heart pounds against the walls of my chest like a big fist trying to break out. I struggle to breathe in the midst of this howling storm in my head and this pain in the pit of my stomach. I throw back the sheets and bound from bed to vomit.

That bitch! I bet if I call Fritz right now and tell him this shit, those two motherfuckers would be dead by midnight!

Still panting and wiping spittle from my mouth, my investigative eye begins a stealth survey of the bathroom. I can't help it. I am in a masochistic hunt for another red hair. My squinted eye cases the white porcelain sink, down to the tub, its drain, its faucet handles, and then sweeps its stellar vision across the little white hexagonal tiles of the cold, hard marble floor. I am in a sick and desperate search for any other trace of my newfound enemy.

I shake myself out of what I fear could be a delusion and try to bury my thoughts in my career responsibilities of the day. The old cast-iron tub's faucet handle squeaks and groans as I twist it to release my morning shower. The hot water and steam feel soothing against my skin. I duck my head underneath the heavy shower fall, disappearing into its white sound, where all other noise is blocked out by the rhythmic pounding of water onmy head.

I wonder if Garrett and Eve left my bed and showered here.

I turn off the water, grab a towel, and tiptoe my way through the bedroom and out to the kitchen. I open the refrigerator in hope of finding at least a morsel of something to nibble on before work. There is nothing in there but the light and an almost-empty carton of orange juice. Garrett always complains that I never grocery shop, never have time or energy to cook him a home-cooked meal—I guess, like his mama. Sometimes I think Garrett is just plain jealous of my career and the time it takes right now to make it. But what else am I supposed to do? I'm just starting out, just like him, and he's working just as hard as I am, except people don't stop *him* on the streets of New York City—a growing number of viewers are stopping me to express how much they like my work. I think that really bugs Garrett, and I wonder if an unemployed hussy like Eve might make him feel more like a man. I swig down the last gulps of juice and slam the empty carton into the kitchen trash bin.

I peek into the mirror and find myself dressed in my conservative navy blue Ann Taylor pantsuit, starched white blouse, my sapphire blue-faced Rolex watch (a graduation gift from Daddy), and Mother's white pearl necklace and matching earrings—I don't even remember getting dressed. And while I may be ready for work, I am not quite readied for life. Particularly not the life I may find after this day.

The thought of taking the A train to Rockefeller Center is more of an intrusion than I can handle on this particular morning. So instead, I call a local gypsy cab, since Yellow Cabs aren't as readily found cruising the streets of Harlem. The dispatcher answers in a deep, husky Dominican accent and then, in a loud, booming voice, assures me that the cab will arrive in fifteen minutes.

As I wait, I stare out of my big bay window. The glorious vision of my elderly neighbors' flower boxes fills my eyes with tears, and my vision blurs as I lose sight of Garrett and me together, filling flower boxes at that age. I quickly remind myself that I cannot cry. I cannot afford to have swollen eyes on the six o'clock news. No time for any kind of emotional baggage today. I have ignored all signs up to this point. One more day won't hurt.

The harsh blast of the gypsy cab's horn startles me back into reality. The impatient cab driver lays on his horn again and again. I curse him as I grab my Coach leather satchel and reporter's notebook and dash out the door. Whatever I am feeling—whatever I am going through—it will have to wait; it's time to put on my game face and get to work.

I double-lock our front door and dash down the stairs. I am shocked when I see what looks like a souped-up pimp-mobile waiting on the street before me. I am almost embarrassed to ride to work in this shiny-rimmed, baby blue, horn-blaring vehicle. The driver, with a big, thick black mustache, ducks his head below the gaudy white tassels dangling from his side window and looks up at me with a glare of impatience.

I slip down the steps and into his big car. It smells like Opium perfume.

The cabby barrels down the avenue in a mad, reckless race to beat the lights. Between the earsplitting blasts of salsa music and his loud radio transmissions in Spanish, I can barely hear myself think. The gypsy cab plows its way downtown, dodging potholes and early-morning pedestrians. I look out of the smudged window and see New York City carrying on her business as usual.

With a quick turn, the cabby makes a dramatic swerve up to the curb of 30 Rockefeller Plaza and screeches to a halt underneath the awning. The cabby has the nerve to overcharge me, but I am too distraught to argue, and I let him slide this time. He hands me a makeshift business card—as if I'd call his lame ass again. I grab my stuff and slide out of the cab.

I make my way through the revolving door and to the elevator that will take me to the fourth-floor newsroom. An overly nice security guard, clad in his gray uniform, greets me at the elevator bank with his usual big smile and a warm "Good morning!"

I wonder if he can tell my heart is broken.

The newsroom is bustling this bright spring morning as reporters congregate around the assignment desk, hungry for a meaty assignment. Tom Mack, the grouchy assignment editor, is busy barking out marching orders to crews scattered around the city, gathering news.

I grab a *New York Times*, the *Post*, the *Daily News*, and a *USA Today* and slip into my cubicle, hoping to dodge Tom's hawk eye. He probably has one of those dreadful rookie assignments cooked up for me—another hospital teddy bear drive? Another Good Samaritan award? Or another subway delay? The big, juicy lead stories of murder, mayhem, scandals, and politics are usually saved for the news veterans or Tom's favorites. Today, I am neither.

It seems it'll take an act of God for a big story to finally land in my lap. The only lead story consuming me today seems to be that of my own life.

Who else knows about this? *What* will I do? *When* did it start? *Where* do I turn? *Why* didn't I speak up when I got the first inklings long ago?

I want to call my mom, cry on her shoulder, and feel the sacred comfort of motherly advice, but I know that's not what I'd get if I called home. I know Mother and Daddy'll join forces and in unison chime: "*We told you so.*"

My folks have despised Garrett from the first day they met him. They were not at all happy about my even talking about marriage at twenty-one, much less to Garrett Nelson, whom they found arrogant, rude, and downright shady. They wouldn't be at all surprised if Garrett hurt me.

"That Garrett is just so full of his wee little self!" Mother has been on an anti-Garrett campaign ever since he basically told her and Daddy to mind their own business and butt out of our marriage. To my folks, Garrett might as well have told them to go to hell.

All of this family drama still comes as a tremendous shock to me. I thought for sure my folks would love Garrett. After all, he came from "good stock." The Nelsons were featured on the cover of *Ebony* magazine as the first black family to integrate the upper-middle-class, traditionally white Shaker Heights community of Ohio. Garrett's dad was a lawyer and his mom a schoolteacher, who baked big, fat Virginia hams just so her three beautiful black preppy sons could have fresh ham-and-cheese sandwiches with homemade potato chips after their football practices.

His little sister was my age and the only black girl I ever knew named Jenny. She was a daddy's girl who spoke in a baby voice and craved constant attention. Jenny would have normally gotten on my last nerve—in fact, under any other circumstance, I would have just downright despised the girl—but I desperately wanted to be a part of her family. So I bit my lip, behaved myself, and worked harder to get along.

The Nelsons were a beautiful family. Garrett's dad adored me and would spend hours holding court in the kitchen of their ranch-style suburban home, acting out his latest joke or sharing another one of his many golf adventures. He would have me doubled over with laughter, while Mrs. Nelson smiled on, her gregarious husband's stories getting longer and more elaborate with each telling.

Thanksgiving at the Nelson home was amazing. As many as thirty family members lovingly gathered around one long, exquisitely set table full of delicious food, including as many as three turkeys—and of course, a nice, fat, honey-baked ham. Coming from a forever-fighting family of four, I was amazed at how much unconditional love, laughter, joy, and unyielding support was around that table. When Garrett and I announced our engagement, they all clapped and whooped and hollered. They jumped up and down. They hugged and kissed us and told us how happy they were. I never ever wanted to lose that feeling of unconditional love and acceptance. Not ever.

Yet on this bright spring morning, I apparently have.

It's nine in the morning, and Garrett will be getting off the ABC news desk soon. We have to talk—today. I cannot pretend any longer. I pick up my work phone, fingers trembling and cold, and begin punching in Garrett's number, nervous and still not sure what to say.

"Yeah, Nelson." His abrupt I-am-very-busy-and-even-more-important news voice snares the phone.

"Garrett?" My voice does not sound like my own.

"Hey, baby, what's up?"

I feel like an interruption. "I ... we ... we need to talk, Garrett. Can we talk when I get home?"

"What's wrong?"

I can't get the words out of my mouth. It hurts too much to speak. "We just need to talk." There's silence on the other end of the phone. "Are you there?" I ask.

"Yeah ... I'm still here ... I'll see if I can go in late tonight so I can spend some time with you, okay?"

"I'd appreciate that, Garrett."

We sound like two people who don't even know each other, not the loving couple we used to be. Not the two people who met the first day of journalism school and watched their close friendship and deep admiration and respect for each other blossom into a passionate and bona fide love.

"I'll see what I can do." Garrett's voice drops. "Call you later." And with that, my husband is gone. I wonder just how far gone he really is.

"Hey! *You!*" I am startled by a loud, barking "Tom the assignment editor," now standing over my desk, pointing his fat finger at me. My heart pounds furiously as he urgently rattles out orders like bullets.

"I'll call you back, baby," I say into a dead phone. "Yeah, Tom. What's up?"

"We got a hostage situation developing up in Harlem. That's your neighborhood, isn't it? Perp's holding a kid, maybe three or four years old. He says he'll kill him unless he gets to talk to a reporter. You're all I got right now. Need you to hightail it up there and check it out." Tom turns and heads back to his assignment desk, marching as if off to war. "If it's something, it's yours!" Tom yells over his shoulder as he flips on the radio mike to find out the estimated time of arrival of the closest camera crew.

Cameraman Fred Robinson and his audio guy, Butch Mason, say their ETA is seven minutes.

"Where the hell is my reporter?" Tom yells like an animal at me across the newsroom. "Let's *move!*" He emphasizes the order with a Jackie Gleason swerve of the neck.

I grab my papers, my Coach satchel, my reporter's notebook, and my Mont Blanc pen and am out the door.

I guess I'll have to put off meeting with Garrett until later. After all, this big, breaking story could be the big "get" of my budding career—with a live shot for the five, six, and eleven o'clock newscasts, advancing my visibility and credibility in the number-one news market. I'll spend the night preparing video packages for the early morning news and perhaps even a network news break-in.

Forget the story of my life right now.

Again, my life will have to wait.

Thank God for my career.

Chapter Two

By the time I make it down the elevator and out to the Fiftieth Street awning, I can see the Channel 4 news van accelerating up the street. I can also hear the pulsating boom-diddy-boom-diddy-boom of reggae music blasting out the window as my news crew gets closer. Cameraman Fred and his soundman, Butch, are both bobbing their heads to the funky Caribbean beat but are also looking very serious behind their dark shades. Fred swerves up to the curb with immediacy as Butch jumps out and slides open the news van's roaring door and helps me hop in.

"Sounds like we're going to be up there a while," a concerned Butch reports. "Cops've been negotiating with this guy for more than three hours now and looks like he's not lettin' up."

"Yeah," Fred chimes in from the driver's seat. "They say the guy's pissed off 'cause the city took his kids. Now, why he thinks holdin' his kid hostage is going to help his case with the city, I do not know."

"Yeah, that fool could actually kill his kid on the six o'clock news." Butch blows a swift puff of air through his lips and props his big, booted foot up on the dashboard with a thud. "People are nuts today, ya know?"

"Tell me about it," I reply with an air of calm, but inside, my heart is pounding like crazy as another adrenaline rush kicks in. I am excited, thrilled, prepared, and in shock. I am ready for anything.

The van continues its wobbly way up Amsterdam Avenue into Harlem, where police say a man is holding a machete to his three-year-old son's throat, threatening to kill the terrified child unless the city's Social Services Department restores him custody of his son and four other children. The agency reportedly took the kids after the man was ruled unfit to raise them. Officials say he became delusional after his wife was killed in a recent arson fire, and he was left to raise their five children alone. The weight of all the mounting family pressures clearly took its toll on the man, as well as a disastrous turn for his offspring.

As I stare out the window, wondering what in the world could drive someone to such madness, I feel my own growing anger at the thought of someone taking my loved one away. I imagine holding a machete to Eve's throat as she tearfully begs for mercy—if what I most fear is true. I am somewhat glad this big hostage story broke now, granting me at least a bit more time to think about what I am going to say to Garrett.

Do I just come right out and say what I suspect to be true—that my husband is fucking my best friend? Or should I wait for more evidence? Ha! More evidence? How much more evidence do I need? Does God have to draw me a picture before I finally realize what even Ray Charles can see? I must be an idiot not to have noticed—or to have pretended not to. There comes a time in every woman's life when she has to be truthful to the things she is pretending not to know. That time has apparently come for me.

I must now admit the horrible truth: that somewhere deep down inside, I have always known there is far more than just an innocent friendship between my husband and my best friend. They grin in my face as they smile at each other, laughing about old times and how they go so far back that they consider each other as brother and sister.

I shudder as I remember how many times I thought I caught a glimpse of some far deeper familiarity and knowing between them. It made me feel insecure and uncomfortable. Did I see what I think I saw, or am I imagining things? Is this betrayal drama playing out only in my head? I saw the way their hands brushed that day as Eve joined us in our kitchen to help us prepare for a party. I see the mysterious way their spirits seem to commingle—and so naturally. I can actually feel the energy and heat between them, and whenever Eve is with us, I often feel like an outsider in my own home.

I see a touch here, or a too-long lingering smile there, or that surprising and way-too-thoughtful gift that Eve gave Garrett last Christmas. It was a dull beige pullover sweater that on any other day, or from anybody else, would have surely been a return or regifting item, but Garrett cherished that damn sweater from Eve as if she had woven it herself with strands of gold. But it wasn't gold; it was a drab beige sweater, and I hated it as it sat there all stunningly hand-wrapped, right under my nose, right under our Christmas tree. Garrett's eyes lit up when he read the gift card: "To Santa—From Eve."

"Wow, this is *beautiful!*" he exclaimed like an excited little boy that bright Christmas morning. The big gold satin and mesh bows on Eve's gift had little nutcracker soldiers entwined in them. Sweet little keepsakes for Christmases to come, we thought.

"Cool sweater." Garrett rubbed the wool. "It's an Eddie Bauer."

"Well, that was nice." And while I put it off, one of my mother's warnings started clanging loudly in my head: *"Respectable women don't give men clothing as gifts; it's far too personal."*

"Give him something for his desk or a good book to read," Mother had suggested. *"Clothes imply intimacy."*

I thought my mother was nuts—until that Christmas morning as I watched my husband smiling from ear to ear over another woman's gift of a wheat-colored sweater that he would wrap himself in just about every other day. This, to me, was a fleeting but strong sign that my mother might be right.

I hated that damn sweater.

And then, just this week, I get this urgent and awkward call from my hairdresser, Maxine Johnson, who also styles Eve's hair. Maxine, a gruff ghetto girl who snaps gum while she back-curls and blow-dries hair, asks if I could stop by her apartment after work sometime this week because she has something very important that she needs to talk to me about concerning Garrett, and it can't wait. Maxine's tone sounded so severe that out of concern, I asked if everything was all right. She told me she'd feel a lot better if we could speak in person—and the sooner the better. She also made me promise not to mention our meeting to Eve or Garrett. She spewed out her address and abruptly hung up the phone. I found her phone call odd but figured it must be something awfully urgent for her to sound so strange.

After work, I caught a cab down to the Chelsea projects and made my way to Maxine's apartment, past some old men talking smack and laughing loudly over a game of dominoes.

As I passed a group of youngbloods hanging out on a park bench, listening to rap music, one of them yelled out in my direction, "Hey, ain'tchu that news lady?"

I nodded my head and kept stepping toward Maxine's building, cautious but happy that these homeboys were at least watching the news.

"Whatchu doin' down *here*?" They guffawed.

"Just seeing a friend," I shouted back over my shoulder as I also picked up my pace. "Just seeing a friend."

"I'll be your friend!" one of the youngbloods said, flirting. "I wanna date the *news lady*!"

The boys burst into cackles of laughter, busting chops and slapping fives.

But it seemed my friend Maxine was the one delivering the breaking news that day.

I finally entered her building, darted into the big clunky elevator, and pushed the button to the nineteenth floor. The elevator car smelled like piss, and I wondered why anyone would pee in their own elevator.

When I got to Maxine's nineteenth-floor apartment, she seemed relieved to see me. "Come on in, girl," she said. "Rushion, get your stuff, and go on in your room now." Rushion is Maxine's lazy-ass seventeen-year-old son who still cannot read. He made a disgruntled face, mumbled something under his breath, scratched his fat stomach, and slowly headed back to his room, where he slammed the door.

"Don't make me have to come in there, boy!" Maxine yelled at Rushion and then turned to me. "Girl, I don't know what I'mma do wit' dat boy. He gittin' worse all the time—thinkin' he a man and all that shit. Humpf! I'll show him some man all right!"

Maxine constantly worried and complained about Rushion, often to his face, which I am sure didn't help him with his sad plight of stupidity and low self-esteem. "I don't know why dat boy don't go back to school or get a job or somethin' and get outta my house."

What Maxine failed to realize was that she must have raised the boy that way.

I just sat there at Maxine's kitchen table, waiting for one storm to clear as another one felt like it was brewing.

"Can I getchu somethin'?" Maxine asked as she shuffled over to the refrigerator. Her once-fluffy pink bedroom slippers now were matted and dirty. They made a shush-shush-shushing sound as she shuffled back and forth across the dingy, greasy linoleum floor. She grabbed a Miller Lite out the vegetable cooler unit of the fridge and offered me one with a big broad smile, sporting a gold front tooth. The beer looked refreshing and cold, and I felt the need to calm my frayed nerves, so I nodded yes. The room was stuffy with the stale smell of Maxine's Newport cigarette smoke, and I felt trapped. I had no idea why I was there, and I really didn't want to hear any bad news that day.

Maxine twisted off the bottle top and handed me the beer as she plopped down on a chair she pulled up to the kitchen table. She slapped her hand down and dragged a crumpled pack of Newport cigarettes to her and took a peek inside.

"Damn, almost outta cigarettes," Maxine snarled with grave disappointment. *"Rushion!"* she yelled at the top of her voice. *"Go to the store and get me a pack of cigarettes!"*

We heard some bumbling around in the bedroom and suddenly the door burst open and out bounded a bouncing Rushion—a teenager jumping at any chance to get out of the apartment and into the streets with some money.

"Mama, can I get some potato chips too?" he pleaded like a little boy.

"Yeah, but you better get a small bag!" she warned. Rushion sprang out the door like a puppy. "And don't be out there all night!" Then Maxine turned to me. "Good. Now we can talk."

I took a deep breath.

"I'm just going to get straight to the point," Maxine said with a squint in her eye. "I think you need to talk to your husband." She sucked her teeth and rolled her eyes with all the brash and bold attitude of an angry black woman living in the projects.

I was stunned. What on earth could she possibly mean? What in the world had Garrett done to Maxine to raise such ire?

Stunned, I stuttered, "W-w-why ...?"

Maxine rolled her eyes until they met mine. "Eve told me she's startin' to feel uncomfortable around your husband. Says Garrett keeps givin' her all kinds of gifts and things, and she feels ... *uncomfortable."* Maxine emphasized the word to further stress the point.

"Well, what kind of gifts?" In my daze, I didn't know what else to ask.

Maxine shrugged as she lit up a cigarette. "I don't know. Sweat suits and shit, she told me—oh, and some lingerie too one time. A couple of months ago, I think."

"What?" I didn't stutter that time. *"Lingerie? A couple of months ago?* What the hell are you saying here, Maxine?"

"That's what she tells me!" Maxine crossed her arms. "Maybe I shouldn't be telling you this, but you my girl, and I think you should know."

I sat there, stupefied. I knew in my heart that Maxine wouldn't lie to me. She was too gangster and too street. But even her loyalty didn't make me feel any better.

Lingerie? Wait a minute ...

"Was it black and red?" I heard myself whisper.

"What?" The question caught Maxine off guard.

"The lingerie Garrett gave Eve," I said quietly, head down. "Was it red and black?" I couldn't even look Maxine in the eye. I was too afraid and too sure of her answer.

Maxine took a slow, deep drag off her cigarette. As she exhaled the long plume of smoke, she looked at the ceiling as if it were a movie screen of her memories. Then, slowly, she looked at me, nodding her head in remembrance. "Yeah, a little corset number. How'd you know?"

"I think I saw it," I replied.

Three months ago, just before Valentine's Day, all the girls were excited about what and who we were each doing for the big day of romance. I had no idea what Garrett was planning for the two of us, but I was hoping it would include roses, champagne, a heart-shaped box of chocolates, and loads of great sex. I was naïve enough to believe that was all it took to make one happy on the day we celebrate love.

Each of us gals had our own plans, excited about what surprises the night had in store. Kat had just met a tall, gorgeous, chocolate-brown engineer from Fort Lee, New Jersey. She was thrilled about his modern high-rise apartment with the breathtaking view of Manhattan out of the bedroom window. I knew I wouldn't hear from Kat for days.

In total contrast, Hope was having a quiet evening with her live-in boyfriend. The two had been together since high school and were already acting like an old married couple. She was probably making him his favorite meatloaf tonight.

Eve said she was getting with Fritz and couldn't wait to see what fine piece of jewelry he'd picked out for her this year. We were all excited, living vicariously. The day before Valentine's Day, I stopped by Eve's apartment on my way home from work. She seemed awkward and surprised to see me.

Eve immediately dashed over to a brightly colored gift box sitting on the easy chair next to the fireplace. With her back to me, as if blocking my view, she scrambled to collect the box and its belongings. What looked like a Valentine's Day gift had apparently just been unwrapped, perhaps even moments before I got there, as the tissue paper, the shiny red gift-wrapping, the frilly white satin ribbons, and heart-shaped card were still freshly strewn about the floor. Eve chuckled nervously as she gestured toward the couch across the room. "Oh, take a seat."

I thought Eve was acting really odd, so I asked her what in the world was in that box.

"Oh, girl …" She chuckled again, scrambling to pick up the guts of her gift. With wads of paper in one hand and the partly opened gift box under her arm, she made a quick turn and was just about to dash into her bedroom, when a beautiful slip of red and black silk slid from the box and onto the Oriental rug.

We both looked down.

The exquisite red-and-black silk was garnished with black lace and four little hanging garter belts. It was a hot little corset, made for a naughty night.

I was amazed at the look of sudden shock and embarrassment that spread across Eve's face. She stared at me, paralyzed. I had never seen her like this.

Nervous myself, I started to chuckle. "Well, well, well," I teased as I bent over and swept up Eve's little secret off the floor. I dangled the sexy lingerie in front of her, balancing the exquisite silk on my index finger. "Well, look … what … we … have … here. All I can say is Fritz has great taste!"

Eve snatched her teddy off my finger and shoved it back into the box. "Girl, you are just too much," she snapped and quickly retreated into her bedroom.

We were girlfriends who shared everything, especially delicious news about new Valentine's Day lingerie. I remember wondering then why Eve was suddenly so coy, nervous, and super-secretive with me. Perhaps now, the answer is all too clear.

After speaking with Maxine, I went straight to Eve and asked her point-blank if Garrett was doing anything to make her feel "uncomfortable" in any way. I reminded her that we were girlfriends and could talk about anything and always be honest and open with each other. I prayed she would tell me the truth. I deliberately asked her again, "Is Garrett doing anything that makes you feel uncomfortable in any way?"

Eve looked me dead in the eye and coolly replied, "No."

"Are you sure," I pressed.

Eve maintained her cool. "Yes."

I didn't want to press any more. Maybe I wasn't ready for the truth. Maybe I didn't believe it. Maybe everything stopped after Eve talked to Maxine. Then again, maybe not.

Another eerie recollection still haunts me in much the same way. In our group, Eve is the "sex therapist." Often, at Sweetwater's, over several after-work martinis, Eve leads us in one of her marathon discussions concerning the "how-to" and the "gotta try" of incredible and irresistible sex. One night, she had us practically rolling on the floor with giddy girlish laughter after she revealed that she had a thing for getting her elbows and kneecaps sucked.

"*Ew-w-w!*" we all reacted in unison, thinking the girl had truly lost her mind. But Eve kept insisting we should try it, explaining that the knees and elbows have all kinds of sensitive nerves running through them and that we haven't experienced a sexual sensation until we have experienced somebody sucking our kneecaps and elbows.

I didn't think much more of that wacky conversation until Valentine's night when Garrett and I were making love, and his sexual pattern suddenly changed. To the sensual crooning of Will Downing in the background, Garrett flicked his tongue down the curve of my ear, continuing down the crest of my neck, nibbling his way around my breasts, and down the curve of my side. I arched my back as my husband's hot and hungry mouth nibbled, licked, and sucked its way deep into my flesh, lost in its sensual journey. As his large thick hands grabbed my ass, pulling me closer to him, he thrust his big, wet tongue into my belly button. I squealed in the sheer delight and newness of it all as he wound his way down, down, down. I spread my legs and closed my eyes, smiling and ready to receive my husband's desperate and yearning kisses in my deep, dark, and secret places. As he continued to tease, I panted wildly. My eyes rolled back, and I released a deep, passionate moan to the gods. I rolled my hips, around and around, churning out my impatient wanting and desire. I felt his quick and heavy breath on the insides of my thighs as his hunger grew more ferocious, along with mine. Then, suddenly, up he moved ... flicking his large eager tongue up the inside of my thigh ... and ... yes ... yes ... yes ... oh, no! *Not* my *kneecap*!

Garrett was locked in a mad, sexual frenzy. He licked and sucked my right kneecap and then moved to the left one, while all the time moaning and gasping for air as if he had fallen into some kind of deep, sexual, kneecapped trance. He wound his head and thick, fat tongue around and around the outside of my kneecap, moving faster and faster and moaning louder and louder as he opened his big, wet, drooling mouth and sucked my kneecap right there in front of my shocked face!

I was stunned. Dumbfounded. Confused.

My sweaty husband panted with a lecherous smile across his face. "Do you like that, baby?" He wiped his mouth with the back of his hand. "Wait'll I suck your *elbows*. Happy Valentine's Day, baby."

Garrett then lifted my arm, moving his greedy mouth toward my elbow as I stared at the ceiling, wanting to die.

Chapter ★ Three

"HEY! HEY, YOU!"

I snap out of my blinded visions and see Fred's curious eyes staring at me in the rearview mirror of the news van as we barrel our way up to Harlem. "You're awfully quiet today, lady. Got a lot on your mind?"

"If you only knew, Freddy." I shake my head and go back to staring out the van's back window.

"Well, whatever it is, just remember this," he offers. "It could always be a lot worse. Look at this guy we're about to see in Harlem."

Outside the news van window, the neighborhood is changing as it flashes by in a blur before me. The majestic bay-windowed brownstones and wide tree-lined avenues of the beautiful historic landmark district of Harlem I know, love, and call home now give way to the dingy, dirty, drug-infested streets of an embattled neighborhood filled with embattled people. Abandoned, burned-out buildings—many used as crack and heroin dens—line these littered streets. There is no color here, except for the splash of emerald green in the Kool cigarette ads on the bus-stop bench or those splashes of silver and blue on the many Schlitz Malt Liquor billboards dotting this impoverished area.

Just up ahead, we see the chaos. Streets are blocked off and at least twenty emergency vehicles are scattered about the area. Cops are communicating on two-way earpieces and walkie-talkies as they race around in a frantic pace. A child's life is on the line. I start my mission by looking for the top cop.

We drive slowly past a gawking crowd of onlookers huddled behind the police tape. Some of them point at our news van, smiling and waving at the crew, mouthing "Hey, Mom!" and poking their chests, yelling, "Put me on TV! Put me on TV!"

Some elderly women gather and stand whispering among themselves on the corner. One woman slaps her hand over her mouth and shakes her head violently, as if she is about to scream out for mercy, as her friend rattles off in Spanish about the little boy taken hostage and how his own daddy is threatening to kill him. I wonder if she knows the boy or the father on the verge of murder.

This neighborhood reeks of death. Destitution and prostitution seem to have become the institution up here. Even the old buildings tell the story of decades of decay, abuse, and neglect. They, like the people, look forgotten and uncared for.

Fred careens into a self-made parking spot up on the sidewalk, and the guys bolt from the van and quickly gather their equipment. I hop out and dart through the crowd in hopes of getting a head start on some of the legwork. I move closer to the building and flash my New York City press credentials, swinging from the chain around my neck, as I slip underneath the yellow police line tape. A few of the cops recognize me and nod a professional yet warm hello as I move in closer to the building, where I pray the little boy is still alive. I need to find out who's in charge, and if and when the cops are holding a presser to update us on the latest developments, and what the hostage team's next move is going to be.

I see the familiar face of David Chan, the City Hall press agent, and squeeze my way through the sea of emergency officials until I reach him. Maybe there's a statement.

"Hi there, David. Any change?"

"Hey, Destiny. No change at all. He's still holed up in that rattrap." David squints up at the building with a grimace. "The guy's not giving in. We've tried to reason with him, but SWAT is on the way. So is the mayor."

If the Special Weapons and Tactics Team is heading here, and the mayor is on the way, this is not looking good.

I wave my hands, motioning to my camera crew across the field to hurry up, hoping I can get a quick on-camera sound bite from David, but somebody abruptly pushes his way through and rudely steps in front of me, thrusting a microphone into the press agent's face. It is that asshole from Channel 7, Walt Windsor. He's referred to in the field as "Walking Walt," because he is always walking in his stand-ups. Nobody knows why or where Walt is walking, and it seems Walt doesn't know either, but every stand-up that Walt does, Walt walks. I don't trust Walking Walt. I think he would sell the soul of his own dear mother to the devil if he could beat the next guy on a story. And surely today will be no exception.

"Are you rolling?" Walt snaps at his camera crew and then gruffly clears his throat. He stoops down to catch his reflection in his cameraman's lens and adjusts his tie before pompously wielding his microphone in David's face as he charges into a barrage of questions. "So, Dave, what can you tell us? What's the latest? What's going on?" He continues booming away in his oh-I'm-so-important baritone voice. His bushy blond left eyebrow is pushed up into a dramatic arch of "deep interest," while the right one dips into a furrow of "deep concern." This is Walt's big moment.

I count to ten and wait patiently for him to finish, despite my strong urge to strangle him. Good news; I know that we'll all be here for a while, and I also trust that Dave will hook me up with my own personal one-on-one interview whenever something breaks anyway. It helps to have made friends in City Hall. And besides, the last thing I want to do is share an interview with this idiot, the infamous "Walking Walt."

Just then, a crowd of police officers pours out of the building, led by a red-faced and extremely agitated Police Chief Joseph Pulaski.

"He says he wants to talk to a goddamn *reporter*!" Chief Pulaski screams. Then, turning on his heels, he points right between my eyes. "You! Channel 4! You're a woman and you're black. Maybe you can talk some goddamn sense into him. Get in there!"

Before I have a chance to feel insulted or even refuse, I am swept up by a group of police officers who rush me into the building. I swear they've lifted me off the ground.

It is dark and cold inside the abandoned building. Paint peels from the graffiti-splattered walls. Windows are cracked and shattered. Trash is strewn about, perhaps left behind by temporary visitors stopping by to hit the needle or the crack pipe. Hushed voices and snippets from crackling radio transmissions now echo throughout the old, beaten, and winding stairwell.

"We don't know what he wants," the now-even-more-agitated chief continues, "but we think we might have a chance by getting a reporter in there. At least we can buy some time and maybe win some points here."

I realize that I am in the greatest danger I have ever faced in my life, and I am now incommunicado—cut off from the rest of my world, stuck with some maniac who wants to kill his kid and possibly himself … or even worse, me.

"You ready?" Chief Pulaski gives me a hard atta-boy pat on the shoulder, but before I can answer, he turns, crosses the building lobby, and darts up the stairs. "Follow me."

We climb up at least six flights of filthy marble stairs until we reach the floor where police officers are lying on their bellies, negotiating with the deranged man and trying to calm the terrified boy. Speaking in soothing tones through a twelve-by-twelve hole kicked in at the bottom of the apartment door, it looks as if the hostage-negotiating team has exhausted every psychological effort.

"You'll get down there and talk to him, okay?" the chief whispers to me.

My heart is pounding wildly as I slowly move down the hallway toward the police gathered outside the apartment door. I hear the muffled cries of a child and what sounds like moaning and wailing from the man inside. I pray we are not too late and that God will be with me every step of the way. "Please use me, dear Lord, to save this child and make a difference here today," I pray.

I hear the creaking and wincing of wood, as if the man is pacing on the old hardwood floors or rocking on a wooden crate or chair. I smell the body stench born from nervous sweat, mixed with the heat, the adrenaline, and the fear of men. What if I can't stop this guy, and he kills that poor child right in front of me? What if he kills me?

The cops surrounding the door speak in hushed tones and whispers. Chief Pulaski motions to one high-ranking officer and then points at me.

"Send her in," he orders.

The officer motions to me to move closer. "You will have to approach the subject by getting down on your knees and remaining there with your hands up where he can see them. Understood?"

"Understood," I respond.

"Good."

"Want me to go now?"

The officer gives me a serious look and then nods me toward the hole in the bottom of the door, through which we can see and hopefully successfully communicate with the man.

Slowly crouching down on the floor, I crawl the rest of the way down the roach-infested, dusty hallway and up next to the officers who have been negotiating.

"We got that reporter you asked for. She's from Channel 4." After the officer delivers the news to the deranged man, he swiftly crawls away, glancing over his shoulder at me as if to say, 'You're on your own now, lady.'

I crawl closer to the hole and peer in. There, sitting in a big empty room, backlit by sunlight and clouded by particles of dust swimming in the air is the unhinged father in a tattered rocking chair. Tears are streaming down his black face. His frightened little boy, who looks about three years old, squirms in his lap. He clenches the child's fragile upper arm in one hand while gripping a huge and ominous-looking machete in the other. The boy squeals in pain through his tears and mucous-covered face as he tries to pry himself out of his father's strong grip. His soft cotton hair is unkempt and full of lint. He is missing a sock, and the one hanging half on his other little foot is deeply soiled to a dark gray. There are no baby shoes in the room. The man, exhausted, scared, and sweating profusely looks at me through swollen eyes—through the hole in the door—like a scared animal.

"You really from Channel 4?" he asks. I am surprised by his meekness and the timidity in his voice, particularly considering the man's huge size. He has a muscular build, with smooth skin the color of midnight. Big beads of sweat pour from the man's brow. In torn and dirty overalls, the distraught man looks more like a farmhand from my home fields of North Carolina than a baby murderer.

"Yes, sir, I am a reporter for Channel 4 News," I reply, "and I am here to listen to whatever you have to say, sir."

I hope Fred and Butch are not far behind. I glance at the crowd of authorities crouched down behind me. The looks on their faces say this is grave, and the outcome is far-reaching, not only for the kid but for the mayor's office too.

"*I want the city to gi' me back my kids!*" The man starts to wail uncontrollably. He rocks back and forth, swinging the boy from side to side like a rag doll. The boy sends out another high-pitched squeal of pain. "Lemme go! No, Daddy, no," he pleads to his father, who doesn't seem to be here anymore.

"*Gi' me my kids!*" he screams.

"Sir … sir, I'm here to help you, but you have to calm down." I feel the officers behind me restlessly stirring. I press on. "Why don't you let the boy go, and we can talk about how we can get yo—"

"*No-o-o-o!* It's a trick! It's a trick it's a trick it's a trick!"

"No, sir, I am not here to trick you. I am here to help you. But you've gotta let your little boy go. Your problem is with the city. Your little boy shouldn't have to pay any more than he already has, sir."

The giant of a man starts to weep, then cry, and then begins to wail uncontrollably; his haunting voice is thunderous as it bounces off the walls of the vast and empty room. He rocks back and forth harder—the terrified child lost in confusion; the father, lost in madness. I fear he will rip the poor child's arm right out of its socket.

"Please, sir," I beg. "Let your little boy go. That's what a good father would do, and everybody knows you want to be a good father."

"Yes … yes, I do," he sobs.

"Then let your boy go. We'll get him something to eat, and then we can talk."

The man suddenly stops his savage rocking, staring at me in openmouthed disbelief, clearly amazed that someone finally cares enough to listen to his story.

Chapter ★ Four

I AM NOT SURE HOW MANY HOURS HAVE PASSED, BUT THE STINGING PAIN shooting down my thighs lets me know that we have been crouched here in this long dark hallway, negotiating with the crazed man through the hole in the bottom of the door, for quite some time now. Emergency crews, cops, and news crews across New York City are calling him "the perp." The distraught father of five tells me his name is Thomas.

Holding his own three-year-old child hostage at the glistening and deadly point of a two-foot machete for several hours has indeed earned Thomas the role of horrid perpetrator in this story. But Thomas argues that the city also perpetrated when officials snatched his kids two weeks ago. More than a perp, Thomas is also a father of five in a family in crisis.

He tells me that he's been a night watchman for various midtown corporations for almost thirty years, but earlier this year he had to take a sudden sick leave. "I had to take time off 'cause of my sugah," he explains. "I have too much sugah in my blood, see?"

"Diabetes?"

"Hm-mm. Yes, ma'am. Di-beetis." Thomas leans over and slowly lifts his pant leg, exposing a horribly grotesque open wound. The festering sore is located just above his ankle, which is swollen to the size of a cantaloupe. Thomas shakes his head. "See there. The sugah won't let my sore heal. Doctor say he want to cut my whole foot off."

Hospitalized when an arsonist set fire to his apartment building three months ago, Thomas has yet to forgive himself for not being at home to protect his family at the time of the fire. His wife, Irene, was trapped inside the burning building when it collapsed, burying her in flames.

Fire officials say that initially, Irene and all five kids had escaped unharmed along with dozens of other residents, but when Irene couldn't find three-year-old Malakhai, who had gotten lost in the melee, she ran back into the burning building in a desperate search to save her baby boy. She never made it back out alive.

Firefighters later found little Malakhai wandering lost in the crowd.

Sadly, today he is lost in a hostage situation.

"I shoulda been there to help Irene take care of them kids." Thomas rocks back and forth, clutching his son and shaking his head downward in shame. "I shoulda been there!"

"But it wasn't your fault," I offer with compassion, leaning deeper inside the hole.

"I shoulda been there to help her," Thomas sobs, beating his fist down on his bum leg, cursing his powerlessness on his disability.

Thomas has no insurance, no job, no home, and no kids after Social Service officials deemed him physically and financially unfit to father his five children alone. It's one thing to lose your foot; it's a whole other thing to lose your family.

"Seems like the city could at least try to help a po' cripple man like myself. I don't want to jus' gi' my kids away. Don't nobody understand *that*?"

I remain crouched here, unmoving and still kneeling on numb knees in this filthy hallway because I really do care about what happens to Thomas and to his children. I hear the echo of the thump-thump-thump-thump-ing of helicopter blades circling above, and I know police are buzzing about everywhere, having long surrounded the area. All of New York City continues to be held at bay, waiting for Thomas to surrender, as more news teams flood the Harlem hostage area.

While I've lost all track of time, I seem to have somehow found a connection with Thomas. At this point, it seems, I'm all he has to the outside world, where millions of people are right now waiting to hear his story on the evening news.

"Thomas, would you like some water? Something to eat?" I keep my tone soothing, calm, and supportive. It's like gently coaxing a small, scared animal out of its hiding place with a tiny morsel of food between your fingers.

"I'm all right." Thomas nods my way. "Thank you for askin', though." He blinks.

"What about your boy?" I press on. "He looks hungry. Why don't we get him something to eat?"

Thomas looks down at his son. Both are trembling, exhausted, and covered with fear. I feel it won't be long before Thomas finally surrenders.

I look back to see the cops have allowed Fred and Butch through. We are a team in these mean streets, especially on days like today. Fred catches my eye, winks, and gives me a solid thumbs-up. He then leans over, swooping up his camera on his shoulder with the agility of a true pro. I know by the courageous look in his big brown eyes that Fred fears big trouble on the other side of that door.

The cops open up a human alley for my guys to move through with their heavy equipment. Butch slips his headphones around his neck and wraps his audio cable around his hand a few times to make their two-man band more compact. He grabs his audio unit and checks the levels as the two continue to head my way down the darkened corridor.

I slowly turn back to the hole where Thomas looks even more worn out and weary. He wipes the sweat from his brow with the back of his dingy sleeve. The sharp blade of his machete sweeps dangerously close to his child, and I gasp involuntarily. An officer swiftly crouches down behind me, gently placing his steady hand on my back out of concern, but I motion to him that I'm okay.

"You gotta camera witchu?" Thomas's voice has dwindled down to a deep and hoarse whisper now, due to his many hours of ranting and wailing. I pray he is too depleted to be any more of a threat to his child, to me, or to himself. Still, madness has an uncanny way of pumping enough adrenaline through a man's veins to turn him into an animal. So I continue cautiously as I wait for surrender.

Separated from the phone back in the van, I'm disconnected from time and a newsroom that may be sending up smoke signals by now. After all, we have the biggest story of the day, but we also face a looming deadline, and our asses are on the line. I know our news director, Barry Grossman, is already gunning for a lead story and a live shot at the top of WNBC's five o'clock local news. This guy runs our newsroom like it's World War III. He is one of the most brilliant newsmen in the business, but he is also a relentless and demanding bully.

I have to think fast. I continue to reason with Thomas. "Everybody sees how important your family is to you. I'll help you get your message out, so people also understand your side of the story. Maybe we can get you and your family some help."

Thomas slowly nods, not taking his eyes off mine.

"Maybe your story will help people understand what happened to you. Millions of people watch our newscasts—lawyers, city child-care officials, the mayor, regular people … everybody. Maybe we can drum up some help for you, Thomas."

Slowly, Thomas bows his head.

"I want to tell my story … but only to *you*." He looks back into my eyes, searching my soul for a promise.

"Only me," I agree. "Only me."

"Tell 'em I don't want my chil'ren growin' up in different homes all over the city," Thomas continues. "One over here, one over there—*no!*" he yells with a frenzied passion growing in his wild eyes. "*We's a family!*" he shouts. "My wife and me—we works real hard to have a *family*. These chil'ren deserves that. And won't *nobody* downtown listen to me!"

The boy screeches a high-pitched squeal.

"I'm listening," I quickly interject, deeply concerned about the boy. "My cameramen, Fred and Butch—two *good* brothers—are here. We want you to tell us your story. It might make a difference."

And again, I pray.

Thomas hesitates, and then … "All right. Bring 'em in."

I don't know whether to jump for joy or head for the hills. After all, this could be Thomas's last-ditch ploy to take more hostages, for all I know. While the risky idea of entering the same room where a man is holding his child hostage seems awfully dangerous, I am the only one who has built a rapport with Thomas. I seem to be the only one he trusts right now. Whether we like it or not, it looks like it's up to me.

"Hey, hey, wait a minute! You can't go in there."

I am startled by a young, muscular sergeant as he steps in front of me, blocking my way to the door, through which Thomas waits for me.

"But Thomas wants to talk to us," I explain, motioning to Fred and Butch.

"Well, *Thomas* ain't runnin' this show," the officer snaps back as he shields the door with his strong arm, "and *you* ain't goin' in nere."

I take a deep breath and look at the officer straight in his eye. "Officer, with all due respect, Thomas *is* running this show right now, and looks like *I'm* all you've got. Plus, Chief Pulaski sent me here."

The officer and I continue locking eyes like rams' horns for what seems like an eternity.

"Move outta the way! Let her in!" The chief's voice booms as he marches down the hallway, swinging a huge NYPD bullhorn.

Heart pounding, I kneel back down to the hole. "We're coming in, Thomas. You okay with that? No problems?"

"Yeah, yeah …" Thomas's breath is hoarse and heavy as he clings to the machete and to his son. His huge, broad shoulders are slumped; he seems deflated and defeated. Thomas's boy desperately holds fast to his daddy's dungaree suspender strap with one hand, while desperately sucking the thumb on his other hand. His tiny, tear-filled eyes show his inner terror.

Chief Pulaski moves past the sergeant and kneels down, nudging me out of the way with his big burly elbows. He carefully peers through the door hole at Thomas as he lifts the ominous police bullhorn to his mouth.

"Sir, before you talk to this reporter, you must first drop the machete and release the child. If you create any further disturbance—if you try to harm your child, this reporter, her cameramen, or yourself—we remind you that you are surrounded. My officers will shoot to kill. Do you understand that, sir?"

I'm not sure if this really helps, but it certainly startles Thomas. Surprisingly, he drops the machete on the dull, dusty wooden floor and then kicks the huge blade across the room. It twirls across the floor until it hits the bottom of the opposite wall with a loud clunk. The once life-threatening weapon, used for hours to hold a small child and a big city at bay, now lies there, lifeless.

"I don't want to hurt nobody! I won't hurt no-body," Thomas promises as he cries uncontrollably in deep, heavy, heaving pain, while still dangerously gripping and jerking about his small child. "I just want to tell my side of the story."

The child reaches for his father and whimpers. My gut tells me that no matter how deep a threat Thomas may appear, he would never hurt his own baby boy. But how can anyone be sure?

I approach carefully, opening the abandoned apartment's door so as not to further startle Thomas. We move in slowly, keeping our distance, just in case. Fred's camera continues to roll, capturing all the drama on videotape. I can feel Fred's breath on the back of my neck as he sticks close to me, one steady eye through the viewfinder, his other sharp eye alert, protective, and targeted on the unpredictable perp, Thomas.

"It took a lot of guts to do what you did today, Thomas," I say in a soothing tone, moving in closer, inch by careful inch.

Thomas nods his head and looks down at his son. He seems to recognize the child's distress and gently releases the boy, who crawls into a corner and curls up in a fetal position, sucking his thumb and whimpering. It is a shame that this child has had to endure so many traumas in only three years of life. What effect will all of this have on his future? What will happen to little Malakhai and his siblings after the authorities surely take Thomas away at the end of this day—either in handcuffs or a body bag. Either way, it's not looking good for either of them, no matter what Thomas has to tell me.

Then, suddenly, for no apparent reason, Thomas leaps to his feet in a big burst of energy, thrashing his huge black arms up in the air. He looks like a looming, angry giant. He must be six foot eight, far larger than I had imagined. He is flailing his massive arms, swaying back and forth, and yelling. "I want my kids! Tell them people down der wi' the city to gi' me my kids!" Thomas pounds his heart with his fists, stomping his feet in a marching motion as he screams, *"I want my chil'ren! Tell dem peoples I want my chil'ren!"*

"Get back! Get back!" Fred and Butch are yelling. I don't know if they are talking to me or to Thomas or the cops. Everything is happening fast and furious.

"Sit down, Thomas," I say. "Please … sit down!"

"Get back!" yells the chief.

Malakhai starts to wail.

I hear the crash of breaking glass and three pops. Thomas jerks and then turns into a wild animal. His eyes dart back and forth until they finally roll back in his head. With a look of shock and pain etched on his face, Thomas makes a gurgling sound, takes two steps forward, abruptly stops, and then falls flat on his face on the hard wood floor with a loud thud. From across the room, Thomas looks like a big felled oak tree. Blood begins to seep from three bullet holes in Thomas's back.

I scream in terror and disbelief as the room explodes with a flood of police officers and SWAT teams from every direction. All I hear is Malakhai's high-pitched screams and cries for "Da-da-a-a-a!" and the stomp-stomp-stomping of the troopers' boots across the creaky wooden floor as they storm in and take over. One, a gruff-looking Asian woman, takes a quick glance at me from beneath her helmet and then swoops up little Malakhai under her jacket and into her bosom. She darts off through the sea of officers and disappears out the door.

"Malakhai!" I scream as I feel a set of strong-gloved fists wrap around my upper arms and lift me off the ground. They rush me out of the door and down the darkened stairwell behind their big plastic bulletproof shields that clank and clap against each other loudly. The SWAT team, protected underneath bulletproof gear, maneuvers me out of what they have determined is harm's way.

I felt much safer with Thomas.

"No-o-o-o!" I scream as the officers manhandle me through the lobby and hurry me out the building. "You shot him! I can't believe they shot Thomas! He wasn't doing anything! He didn't even have a weapon!" I cry, desperately grabbing the shirtsleeves of officers and paramedics scrambling by, but no one is listening. They are sweeping me out of the building and onto the front sidewalk, where they leave me in the hands of street cops who hustle me to a waiting ambulance. Everything has gone crazy.

"Are you okay? Are you okay?" a Puerto Rican paramedic with a long braided ponytail keeps asking me, but I look at her in a daze. My whole world is falling apart. Everything around me seems to be dying—or on the verge of it: Thomas … my marriage … even pieces of me.

"She's fine."

I turn and see Fred and Butch rushing up to the ambulance.

"She's our reporter, and she's got a live shot to do." Fred proudly smiles my way. "If we hustle, we can still make the top of the five. Here's that lead story you always wanted." Fred takes off toward the van. "I'll get on the horn and tell 'em what we got."

I am still dazed.

I pray that those cops didn't kill poor Thomas. I feel a powerful rush of tears coming, and I try hard to control my emotions. *A reporter is not supposed to get emotionally involved*, I remind my Columbia University-ed self, but the human being in me does not want to hear it.

Despite the whirling confusion in my head and heart, I still have to make the lead live shot at the top of the evening newscast. I have to break this story, burying myself so deep inside it that the howling in my head will go away.

"Where the hell have you sons of bitches been?" Grossman is screaming over the radio when I get back to the truck.

"What an asshole." Fred shakes his head and then flicks on the radio mic. "Uh, yeah, we've been negotiating a hostage situation, man." Fred almost laughs at of the absurdity of it all.

"Well, it better be a damn good one, or all of you people are fired. We've been trying to reach you for three fucking hours!"

"Can't this motherfucker get fined by the FCC talkin' like that over the radio?" Fred asks us and then flicks on the mic. "Roger," he replies. Then again to us: "What an ass."

While the guys set up the live shot, I take out my reporter's notebook and scribble out my dramatic lead story of how a father of five on the edge took his own baby son hostage and is tonight clinging to life after police officers shot him three times in the back. I track the voice-overs that will lead in to some of the most compelling sound bites we videotaped from our many exclusive hours of negotiations. Butch will then feed the information back to the newsroom via satellite, where an editor will take the material and chop it all down into action-packed two-minute packages for the top of the five, six, and eleven o'clock news broadcasts and then rehash fresh stuff for the early morning network news breaks. We are sure to beat every other station across the nation on this story. And it comes right on time for the crucial May sweeps, when the networks eat their young for that almighty advertising dollar.

I will wrap our pieces live from Harlem all night and stay on the horn, trying to find out if Thomas, my marriage, and my soul will survive.

Chapter
★ Five

THE PHONE RINGS, AND I AM STARTLED AWAKE IN THE MIDST OF A dream that Thomas is entering the gates of heaven and city officials have deemed me Malakhai's new mother.

I wake up in a sweat, panting. It is a new day. The sun's not even up yet.

I fumble in the darkness to answer the phone, and it's Garrett on the line, calling from his overnight job. I worked so late last night that I missed him before he left for his overnight shift. We figure it's a small price we have to pay for such great opportunities straight out of grad school.

"Wake up, babe. You are *every*where!" Garrett sounds ecstatic. "You made the front page of every local newspaper—the *Daily News* and the *New York Post*. Way to go, babe. You really nailed 'em in the ratings with that one."

"What?" My brain is mush. I am struggling to shake myself awake and make sense of Garrett's exuberance.

"NBC should be kissing you in the *mouth* today," he continues. "Look, gotta go. Hey, I'm really proud of you, babe."

And with that, Garrett is gone.

I am still trying to bust out of my fog of exhaustion, worn to shreds from the dramatic and terrifying events from the night before. I am so tired that my eyes feel like they're peppered with sand. My whole body aches. My head is pounding. My heart's racing. I desperately need a glass of water or my husband's proud voice again, telling me he wants to come home, hold me close, and reassure me that everything, including our marriage, is going to be okay.

The phone rings again. Could it be Garrett calling back? I grab the phone. Instead, it's my news director's executive assistant. In a nervous and harried voice, she tells me that Grossman, my boss, wants to see me in his office—pronto. It is twenty minutes before six o'clock in the morning, and big, bad Barry is already barking out intimidating orders. Maybe I'll be lucky enough to fall off his shit list today after my big "get" last night.

Then again, maybe not.

A sudden rush of shame and loathing overcomes me as I have a flashback of my emotional live shots during last night's newscasts. Burned out after several hours of negotiating on my knees and still freaked out from my hostage-situation-turned-shooting and the fear that my marriage has turned mirage, I lost it, bursting into tears and uncontrollable sobs during my eleven o'clock live report on Thomas. I had gotten through the five and six o'clock newscasts with all the professionalism I could muster, but by the eleven, I was an emotional wreck, and it showed. It was as if every distressing thing I had ever experienced in my life suddenly came rushing in on me all at once. The dam that held back years of pain opened up like a thundercloud, and the tears came running down my cheeks like rivers.

I am in severe emotional overload. For the first time in my life, I am weak.

I flick on the television for the latest at the top of the six o'clock morning news. I am eager to see how our early morning producers will spin my story.

Da-dadadada—Da-dadadada … The urgent and majestic sound of the six o'clock morning newscast theme snaps me out of my sleepy haze, and the camera zooms in on a very serious anchorwoman.

"Good morning, everyone. A father of five is clinging to his life this morning after police shot him three times in the back during a dramatic hostage situation in Harlem. Our reporter was there …"

I suddenly feel sick to my stomach as I hear my shaky voice broadcast over the morning airwaves. I recall the horrid image of Thomas's face slamming down on that dusty hard wooden floor. *Please, dear God, let Thomas live*, I pray, knowing that while Thomas made a bad decision, he is not a bad person. Thomas deserves to live.

The anchorwoman wraps my news report with an update on Thomas's condition: he is still clinging to life.

My phone rings again. Garrett must have just seen my news report and is calling me back.

"Yo!" I blare into the receiver.

"Is that how you answer your phone?"

It's my mother. Mrs. Barbara Codrington Newell, the glory and bane of my existence.

"Hi," I say, startled. "You're up early. What's up?"

"'What's up?' Really, Dee. You tell me. You were the one all over the news this morning. You even made the *network news*, my dear. Something about a hostage situation and a shooting up there. Are you okay?"

"Yes, yes, I'm fine." I try to sound strong because I know Mother is listening carefully in hopes of reading any tone of weakness in my voice.

"Your father and I are just worried sick about you. Why in the world didn't you call us, for heaven's sake?"

"Well, I've been rather bus—"

"Destiny, this is your father." Daddy's deep voice booms through the line.

"Hi, Daddy." I try to sound cheerful, suddenly feeling like his little girl again.

"What's this about a shooting and you talking to some deranged man—in *Harlem* of all places? I have tried to tell you how dangerous that area is, Dee. It's a *ghetto,* after all! And I swear I don't know for the life of me why that deranged husband of yours still insists on the two of you living there. 'Getting back to your roots,' he says—pshaw! I'm telling you, it is dangerous up there, Dee."

"Daddy—"

"No, Dee, your daddy is right," Mother chimes in. "Your husband *is* deranged!"

"*Mother!*"

I cannot believe that I am a grown woman with a big New York City job, covering news stories that can change peoples' lives, maybe even save some. Yet here I am, standing in my underwear, getting blessed out by my parents like I'm seventeen and stayed out past curfew. Some things never change.

Daddy tries to lighten the conversation, now that he's assured his baby girl is okay. "We're just worried about you, Diddle-Dee, that's all, honey."

"Be proud of me too, Daddy?" I ask, in desperate need of more support and less scolding right now.

"Oh, we're proud of you all right," Mother interjects. "Just promise us you won't get yourself killed up there. Why don't you come home this weekend anyway? It's Memorial Day. We're heading to the island. Your aunt Joy has been asking about you an awful lot. She's getting older, you know, and she thinks you forgot all about her and the beach house since you got married to that lunatic."

Mother is conjuring up her feel-guilty brew, but I do love my aunt Joy and hold some of the most sacred life memories from spending summers with her at Tranquility, our family beach house on Topsail Island, North Carolina. Now, well into her eighties, those same memories and spending time with her only niece may mean even more to Aunt Joy today. Maybe I should start going home more often—but it's always so problematic.

"Now, DeeDee." Daddy clears his throat. "I want you to make it down to Topsail this weekend, like your mother says. We're counting on you."

"But, Daddy," I try to reason, "you know that you guys and Garrett don't get along. He's never been crazy about the beach anyway. It's just not that easy."

"Well, *make* it easy, for goodness' sake!" Mother snaps. "Can't you control your husband? Can't we all just make a special effort this time and stop all the fussing?" Mother's offering is quite surprising, particularly since she's usually the one doing most of the fussing. "Life is too short. Your aunt Joy is not going to be around forever, Dee. Plus, we all miss you desperately. We're worried stiff!"

"And it's a holiday, sweet pea," Daddy coos.

"Daddy, news knows no holiday. But I'll talk to Garrett and see how he feels."

"Well, just don't let him talk you out of it, Dee," warns Mother. "You know what an ass he can be."

"Okay," I sigh. I don't have the energy to get into it with her this morning. "I love you."

"Love you back, and be careful!"

"I will."

"Go get 'em, Tiger!" I can hear Daddy's pride beaming through the phone.

I take a quick shower and race to get dressed, noticing for the first time in a long time that I have not even thought about scoping out my home for another red hair. Life-or-death situations have an uncanny way of putting everything into perspective. In the greater scheme of things, the thought of another red hair seems, at least at this moment, trivial and minute. Another day of work, no matter how hard I have to push, is probably the best move I can make right now to keep my mind busy and off red hairs and lying lovers. It's also better than staying home alone in this apartment, where apparently both have been.

The long walk across the WNBC newsroom through the sea of reporter cubicles to Grossman's glass office on the other side of the room seems to take forever. Along the way, several of my colleagues give me a pat on the back for a job well done last night, but I can still feel a bit of tension in the newsroom air and wonder if it relates to my embarrassing emotional outburst that did not get past Grossman—or is it Garrett's infidelity that did not get past me?

I can see Barry's face turning red the moment he sees me through his glass walls. He motions for me to come in.

"Yeah, so what's this with the fucking tears—lead story—live shot— last night's eleven o'clock newscast? What we gotta do, huh? Send your ass outta here with a big box of Kleenex?" Grossman's collar looks like it's about to explode from all the pressure bulging out of his fat neck.

"I ... I was just really touched by the story, Barry. I'd spent a lot of really intense time with the guy and ... and ... the ba-baby ... and I'm still freaking out over him getting shot like that—and right in front of me."

"Fuck that shit! You see reporters covering death and destruction every fucking day, and you don't see 'em boo-hooing like fucking sissies— *not on* my *news, you don't*! Take the long Memorial Day weekend to get your head together."

"Barry, I appreciate that, but ... I really don't want to lose my story. I just—"

"Just *one* day. You're not going to lose your story. City Hall's not making a decision over the holiday, and the perp's in a fuckin' coma anyways. You need it. You just saw a guy get shot, remember? Go get yourself together and then get back here."

"Okay ... Okay ... I will. Thank you ... thank you, Barry."

By the end of the day, our news team has covered every possible angle of Thomas's follow-up story as city officials begin the grueling process of determining Thomas's fate. I sit here at my cubicle, my head and heart still buzzing, and I'm not sure whether I've lost my job or lost my marriage, and I pray I don't lose my mind.

My phone rings. *Please be Garrett, calling to see if I'm okay and to say he loves me and is taking the day off to stay home and hold me, so we can finally talk—so we can finally work things out, put my suspicions to bed, and save our marriage.*

"Hello," I say with a voice full of emotion and hope.

"Thank God we gotchu! It's us, girl—you okay?" It's my best girlfriends, Kat McCullough and Hope Linton, on a three-way call with an avalanche of questions. "Are you all right? You didn't get hurt, did you? You haven't answered any of our calls!"

"Yeah, I'm fine. Still in a daze, that's all. My news director just told me to take some time off. And y'all, I really think I need it. There's so much going on right now. I don't think I can keep it together much longer."

Hope's voice trembles into the phone. "Girl, we heard the news and freaked out when we saw you right there in the middle of it. Everybody's talking about it. You poor thing."

"Were you actually there when they shot that man?" Kat asks. "You saw the blood and that baby and everything?"

"Yeah ... yeah ... I was ... it was a trip."

"Jesus," Hope whispers.

"Where's Garrett?" Kat asks. "Has he been home long enough to take care of you?"

"No," I whisper into the phone. "To tell you the truth, I think he's taking care of somebody else these days."

The phone goes dead silent for a moment, and then ...

"Say *what*?" Kat and Hope spurt out at the same time. "Whoa, now. Wait a minute, Dee. What are you talking about? How do you know this? Oh my God ... Are you sure?"

"Yeah ... I ... I'm pretty sure. I think he is. No, I know Garrett's having an affair. I just know he is."

"They say a woman always knows deep in her gut when it's happening," says Hope. "But, honey, please be wrong."

"I don't think so, Hopey," I sadly admit. "I think I have enough proof. There're lots of things that make me wonder."

"Proof? Proof like what?" demands Kat. "Who is this bitch? Do you know her?"

How am I ever going to tell my girls that I suspect "this bitch" is one of our closest friends?

"Well, look, y'all, I'm at work. I can't talk right now. We'll talk about it later."

"You need a martini and your girlfriends, girlfriend. That's what you need! Meet us after work at Hurlihey's for happy hour."

"I just might do that," I surrender. "I could sure use a happy hour 'round about now. I don't know what to do."

"Don't worry," Kat reassures me. "We're on the way. See you there."

Chapter
★ Six

THE BELLS JINGLE AS I SLIP INTO THE BIG GLASS DOORS OF HURLIHEY'S famous Irish pub. There is the familiar and warm sound of laughter and gaiety inside this happy hub, known as the network watering hole. We always have a grand time here, with reporters, anchors, producers, camera crews, and friends often meeting to hobnob, talk shit, and blow off some of the steam of our stressful days covering city streets full of death, destruction, crime, and politics. I guess today's topics will also include my shaky marriage after fears and suspicions about Garrett and Eve.

Patrick O'Malley, the burly Irish bartender, greets me with his lilting Irish brogue and his big, broad smile. Patrick remembers everybody's drink. Today is no different.

"There's my martini girl!" he bellows as I walk through the pub door. "This one's on me, muh lady. I been watching you out there wit' that hostage thing. That's some kinda story they got you on."

"Yeah, Pat, they're wearing me out," I say as I slip up to the bar. "But nice to finally have a good lead story for a change."

"Well, take a load off, girlie." Patrick smiles as he flips up a martini glass by the stem between his thick index finger and thumb. He plops the glass on the bar in front of me and pours in ice-cold water to the brim, giving the glass a nice chill. Then Patrick proceeds to conjure up my spirits. Like an artist in his studio, Patrick twirls a couple of bottles and then dips them upside down, pouring their prized liquids into the mouth of a silver shaker—just a splash of vermouth from one and quite a generous pour of fine vodka from the other. He grabs the shaker like a man on a mission and rattles it back and forth like a maraca. Patrick dumps the icy water out of the martini glass and then slowly opens the top of the shaker and gently pours out the liquid gold into my open glass. My mouth waters, as I cannot wait to kick off my long weekend by savoring the first sip.

Patrick proudly smiles as he pours out the last drop. He then carefully places my perfect martini in front of me with a flourish.

I giggle.

"Extra cold, extra dry, extra olives—just like my girlie-girl likes 'em, right?" Patrick winks my way.

I laugh, shaking my head in awe. "You know me, Paddy. You really know me." I am happy to feel at home.

"*That's* my girl," Patrick says as he slaps his big hand on the oak bar. "I'll have Marty grab you a table."

"Thanks, Pat," I say and take my long-awaited first sip of my martini. It is just what the doctor ordered. The icy vodka goes down smoothly, like liquid air. My throat feels its blossoming warmth move down to my chest as I feel a relaxing calm melt all over me.

At last …

"Right this way, sweetheart." I turn from the bar and see Marty, the skinny maître d''s smiling face. "Got your favorite table waiting. Let me carry that martini for you."

I almost don't want to let it go, but I hand over my delicious martini to Marty anyway. I figure it looks more ladylike for him to carry my drink through the crowded restaurant on his tray than for me to spill my way across the floor. As we pass by the happy-hour food bar, I take advantage of my free hands and grab some free treats. I fill up a small saucer with meatballs and fried chicken drumettes. These freebies are sure to be my dinner tonight, so I gladly help myself.

I make my way to the table, and Marty pulls out my chair.

"Thanks, Marty," I say as I juggle my happy meal and slip him a five.

"Hey …" Marty twists his mouth to the side in deep confidence. "You ain't gotta do that there, ya know."

"I know, Marty," I reply. "I just appreciate you for always taking good care of me."

Marty winks, swiftly pockets the bill, and then dashes off to take care of the next Hurlihey's regular.

I take another long sip of my martini and a deep breath. I watch the crowd. I wonder how many men in this bar are tonight being unfaithful to their wives.

The doorbell jingles again and by the combustion, chatter, and burst of energy, I can tell—my girls have arrived. I wave my hand to catch their attention.

"There she is!" spurts Hope. She and Kat bustle over to the table.

"Hey, girl, are you okay? What in the world happened up there in Harlem? How close were you when they shot him?" My girls are whirling in a frenzy of concern.

"I'm okay, I'm okay, really," I assure them. "I just feel so sorry for Thomas and his family. I just—"

"Oh, so you know this fool on a first-name basis? Seriously? Girl, you meet some strange people on your job!" Kat shakes her head. Like she doesn't meet strange people on her job as an event planner for a vodka company.

"Well, I know Garrett must have been worried," Hope surmises as she takes a quick sip of my martini. "How's he handling his cowgirl of a wife these days?"

I think for a second. I can't even remember the last time I actually saw Garrett. We're so come-and-go, fly-by-in-the-night these days.

"To tell you the truth, I really don't know what Garrett is thinking – whether he's worried about me or not. If he is, he hasn't said anything to me. He was happy my story made the papers, though."

"Always after 'the big story'—just like you." Kat rolls her eyes. "But do you guys ever see each other? I mean, I know you work different shifts and all, but I never hear about you doing anything special on the weekends or holidays like you used to."

"Well, you know how Garrett got bitten by that golf bug. He got those new clubs, and he can't wait to hit those greens every Saturday morning. I figure it's not much to ask after he's worked the graveyard shift all week."

"I don't know how y'all do it," says Hope. "Garrett's off covering war stories in the middle of the night, and you're up in some abandoned building in Harlem getting shot at in the middle of the day. Y'all need to be on prime time, honey."

Marty swoops up to the table and smiles.

"Two more—same way," I order.

"Coming right up!" Marty scurries back into the crowd.

"So now what? You gonna be okay?" Hope looks worried. "I mean, what you just went through is more than a notion, honey."

"Why does everybody keep asking me if I'm okay?" I snap.

"Because you don't look okay, that's why!" Kat cuts to the chase. "You look like a rabbit under the ax. You seem scattered, and you are very much on edge these days, my dear."

"Jesus." I cover my face with my hands. "Am I that bad?"

"You've looked a lot better, D." Hope sympathetically rubs my back. "And who can blame you. Look what you've been through."

"You look a hot mess!" Kat quips. "You sure everything's okay with you—I mean, you and Garrett? It's more than that hostage story, girlfriend. You've been a bit frazzled for a while now."

"Yes ... I mean, no ... I mean ..." I have never been able to lie to my best friends.

"What?" Kat and Hope ask in unison.

"Okay." I blow out a deep breath. I have to talk to someone about this. Get it off my chest. Who else can I confide in but my best girlfriends? "Well, I have this strange feeling ... that ... well, I'm not sure ... but I swear—"

"Here ya go, ladies—two martinis, extra cold, extra dry, extra olives."

"Go on; drink up," I urge them. "You're gonna need it for this one."

Kat and Hope look at each other and then throw a quizzical look back at me. As if on cue, they both sip their martinis at the same time.

"Okay, let's hear it," Kat commands. "What's going on?"

I look at my two best friends sitting across from me, with the look in their eyes of care, concern, and willingness to kick somebody's ass if they have to. It breaks my heart to have to tell them something so repulsive as 'I have this feeling our friend Eve is fucking Garrett.' How do I tell them *that*? I stare into my half-empty martini glass and begin to play with the olive.

Kat grabs my hands and squeezes them. "Girlfriend, are you sick or something? You can tell us anything."

I chuckle. "No. ... Heartsick, maybe ... but—"

"Oh my God, I thought I'd never get here!" We are interrupted by a shrill and breathless voice. I look up, and there stands Eve, all aglow in a red formfitting sleeveless dress. "Traffic was a mess! Hey, girls!" She plops down into the fourth chair, her breasts bulging with every deep breath she takes, as she tosses her newly done and bouncy red curls back and forth, rattling on and on as she explains how she left Frankie's early, with all good intentions to get here on time, but ... well ... you know that New

York traffic! Then Eve oozes what I fear is feigned concern. "And I was *so* worried about you all day, Destiny! Are you okay?"

There's that damn question again. I really want to answer, "Hell no, bitch. As a matter of fact, I'm not okay, because I think you're fucking my husband! My life is feeling like shit right now, thanks to you and that fucking red hair of yours!" But I decide instead to maintain my composure, as Hurlihey's—and in front of my colleagues and friends—is not the place for a girl-fight over a man, not even if it's over my husband with a woman I thought was my best friend.

"Glad you made it," I struggle to say.

"Oh, *honey.*" Eve scoots her high-heeled way around the table to the seat next to me, leans over, wraps her arms around me, and squeezes my neck. She smells of Chanel No. 5. "You could have been killed! We are so glad you're okay." Eve pats my back. It seems a bit much, coming from her. Was she really that worried? Maybe she really wanted me dead. "So what did I miss?" Eve darts a look at each of us.

"We were just supporting Dee, that's all," says Kat. "Girl, where has your ass been, all dressed up in scarlet?"

"Oh, you know." Eve tosses her long red hair over her shoulder. "Just shopping and stuff. I am *so* in love with the new Missouni resort collection I had to stop by for a quick peek."

Kat rolls her eyes. "You're in love with some new designer collection every year, girl."

"Gotta keep it lookin' good for my man!" Eve responds with a sly smile. I wonder which man she's talking about as I scope her shiny red head, missing at least three long hairs left in my home—one in my bed.

"So how is that Frankie?" Hope asks.

"He's fine. Got big plans for me this weekend. Gon' get some of that good stuff, and I don't mean Dolce and Gabbana this time!" Eve leans back with a lusty laugh.

"Yeah, I could use some of that good stuff too," says Hope. "I think Dan and I are staying close to home. What about you, Kat? What—or should I say, who—are you doing?"

We all laugh as Kat winds up to bat.

"*Well*, since you asked … I'mma be up under this fine dreadlocked French man. Ain't that some shit—a French man with dreadlocks. Mm-mm-mm."

These special moments between us girls have always brought us closer together. I adore these special moments, and I feel like a real shit, believing that one of us wants to destroy all of this and so much more. How can I believe that one of us would try to annihilate the other's marriage by bedding her husband? Is that not the worst betrayal?

Dear God, please let me be wrong.

"So what are you and Garrett up to this weekend?" Eve asks me. "Staying home? Is Garrett playing golf, as usual?"

"Uh ... well, I think ..." I stumble. "I'd like to get out of town—get away, to tell you the truth."

"Now that's what I'm talkin' about!" Kat slams her hand down on the table as if marking a done deal. "That's exactly what you two need to do."

"Out of town? *This* weekend? You and Garrett?" Eve is looking at me with the most incredulous look on her face. "When did you guys decide that?"

"Well, we ... ugh ... you know, I really need to get home. Garrett'll be up soon, and I want us to start our weekend." I start to gather my things.

"Yeah, girl, get home to your man," Kat urges. "And please get some rest this weekend. Chill. Do something nice for yourself. Get out of town. You and Garrett go someplace nice."

"Yeah," Eve chimes in. "But maybe you should take some time just for yourself—you know, go away all by yourself for some—what is it they call it? Oh—some 'me' time."

"Uh-huh," I respond as I keep gathering my belongings and my wits about me, feeling as if I am about to suffocate in one of my favorite places with someone who used to be one of my favorite friends.

Could Eve really be my newfound foe? Could my husband really be fucking my best friend? I take one last look at her, dead in the eye. I throw back the last gulp of my now-warm martini and then turn and flee Hurlihey's as if my hair is on fire.

Chapter ★ Seven

SLIP THE KEY INTO THE DOOR OF MY BUILDING AND, EVEN FROM THE front atrium, can hear Garrett talking loudly on the phone in our apartment on the second floor. I can tell that he is agitated because I can also hear him pacing back and forth on our squeaky wooden floors. He is in a heated conversation, and I hope it's not with work. I pray he doesn't have to go back to the newsroom and spoil the time we have to be together this Memorial Day weekend. I am counting on this holiday to have that long talk with Garrett in hopes of saving our marriage. This long holiday weekend comes just in time. For two short hours a day, Garrett and I see each other between jobs, and when we do, it's only in passing, heading in different directions, living different lives.

"I'm not saying I don't want to come down there, I'm just sayin' I had other plans for this weekend, and she may not want to go anyway. Oh, don't put this on me, Barbara!"

Oh, no. Garrett is not loud-talking a fellow producer; he is loud-talking my mother—*again*. I pick up my pace in hope of stopping what could quickly turn into World War III.

"*What?*" I hear Garrett exclaim. "Oh, *don't* go there, Barbara!"

I bang on the apartment door, hoping to interrupt this long-distance battle between Harlem and North Carolina.

"Hold on a minute, Barbara—*just hold on!*" Garrett shouts, and I hear him storm over to the door. He swings it open with such an angry force that I feel a cool breeze. I stand in the doorway, frozen.

"Hey, baby." He blows a deep sigh of exhaustion as he greets me, shaking his head. "It's your *mother*. That witch is *crazy!*"

I grab the phone from Garrett and cover the receiver in my chest.

"Don't call my mother a crazy witch!" I snap, even though I know how difficult she can be. In fact, both she and Garrett can be difficult, stubborn, and proud.

Garrett throws his hand in surrender to me, and still shaking his head in disgust, he storms off to the bedroom.

I take a deep breath. "Mother?" I speak into the phone.

"You tell that son of a bitch you married to go to hell!" Mother barks.

"Mother, what's going on?"

All I hear is her heavy breathing on the other end of the phone. I wait as she tries to compose herself.

"We are worried sick about you, and for some reason that idiot husband of yours just can't see that. Does he have one bit of concern for you? It could have been *you* who took that bullet! We want you to come home, DeeDee!"

It isn't often I hear such desperation in my mother's voice. I can tell she and the rest of my family are truly worried. There's nothing more my mother wants to see than my winning that Emmy or going network one day so she has even more to brag about in her social circles—but not if my life is threatened in the process.

I also know deep in my soul that there is no place else I'd rather be right now than my beloved Topsail Island. I am emotionally shot, my marriage is hanging on a loose hinge, and I miss my aunt Joy and our special time at the beach together more than I ever realized. I need my family right now.

"We'll catch the first thing out tomorrow morning," I say to Mother.

"Good." Mother has rested her case, finally satisfied. "Your father and I are driving down to the beach house to meet Aunt Joy tonight. She'll be thrilled to hear that you are finally coming home. I'd beg you to leave that jackass you married in New York and just come yourself, if Joy hadn't insisted the whole family be together so much. She is getting old, Dee. She has this urgency about everything."

"Well, you know how she is about keeping us all together," I reply. "She just wants us to be one big happy family."

"We all want that, as difficult as it is—"

"Yes, Mother, I know—*with that man I married.*"

"Well, yes. *You* said it."

"Good-bye, Mother. See you in the morning."

"Get in by brunch time," she adds. "I'm cooking salmon croquettes."

"Mother, you know Garrett doesn't like croquettes."

"Yes," she replies. "I know."

I hear the click of her receiver and then turn to see that Garrett has been listening to the conversation at the bedroom door. He does not look happy.

"Did you just tell your mother that we are going to Topsail Island tomorrow morning?"

"Yes. I did," I confess. "I really want us to be there with the family. They sound worried about me. Plus, believe it or not, Garrett, Grossman actually gave me the time off. I need it, baby. We both do."

"How could you make the decision without talking to me first, Destiny? Jeez! I promised the guys I'd play golf with them tomorrow, and then I thought we could figure out something to do."

"*Figure out something to do?*" He's so insensitive tonight. "Well, I just did, Garrett. Golf can wait. This is a special time—a whole long weekend—for us, for our family. And it's been forever since we've been to Topsail."

"How the hell is this weekend going to be 'for us' with your whole family down there?"

"Garrett—"

"I'm serious, Dee. Your mother hates me. Your father barely speaks to me. Your aunt Joy's okay, but—"

"But what, Garrett? What now? What's wrong with Aunt Joy?"

"Well, you know how she's all into you, like you're the baby girl she never had or something."

"And? Come on, Garrett. Aunt Joy practically raised me. She was there for me when my dad was struggling to become a doctor and my mother was more interested in becoming a socialite than a mother. As a child, Aunt Joy was all I had, the only one who understood me and made me feel important, encouraged, and loved. She was my mother figure. I spent so many wonderful summers with her on Topsail. I have to admit—I miss her very much. I didn't realize how much until now."

"Well, you guys are just into that whole beach scene, and you know I'm from the Midwest, Destiny. I'm not into all that sand and water and shit. We didn't have all that craziness in Ohio."

"So … what? You feel left out? You can't find something to do to be happy? C'mon, Garrett. Try something new, just for the sake of it? Okay?"

"Naw, I just hate going down there," Garrett snaps. He's done with this conversation.

"Baby," I say, walking over to Garrett. I wrap my arms around his waist, nestling my head under his chin. "Please try to understand. I need this. We need this. Think of it as a time for us away from it all—time out for our marriage."

Garrett stiffens. "Wh-what's wrong with our marriage?" He frowns down at me.

"Honey, I just think we need time together, that's all. I'm really worried about this distance I've been feeling between us."

"*Distance?*" Garrett looks surprised and shocked by my admission. "What *distance?*"

"Sometimes I wonder if you still love me, Garrett."

Garrett's face turns red. He runs his big hand over the top of his forehead and back over his hair. He seems to be searching, either for words, an excuse, or an exit.

"Do you love me, Garrett?" I feel at this point I have nothing to lose, and I don't want to lose my marriage.

"Do I love you? What are you talking about, Destiny? You're my *wife.*"

"Yes, but something's happened to us, Garrett; something has changed. Haven't you felt it too?"

Garrett stands there looking at me with a blank stare. He blinks. We are both exhausted. Two award-winning journalists, at a loss for words.

Finally, I ask, "Are you having an affair, Garrett?" My heart can't wait any longer.

"Wh-what? An affair? Of course not!" Garrett looks incensed.

"Tell me the truth, Garrett." I hold him tighter, looking up into his eyes. "Please tell me the truth. You can be honest with me. Is there someone else?"

"Destiny, look …" Garrett calms his voice, takes a step back, and places his big hands on my shoulders. "Baby, you have been through a lot of stress in the past couple of days. You're under a lot right now, and it's got you imagining things. Plus, you've been drinking a little bit there, haven't you?" Garrett tickles his finger underneath my chin. I cannot deny martinis at Hurlihey's, but I also cannot deny those three red hairs in our private living space either.

"Yes, but Garrett—"

"Hey, hey, hey! Sh-h-h-h. I got you, baby." Garrett pulls my body back into his. "I will take you home, if that's what you want. Now, c'mon, go pack your bags, pretty girl, and I'll call about our reservations to Topsail."

"Oh, Garrett, really? Really?"

Garrett nods.

"Oh, honey, thank you—thank you so much!" I gush, knowing how hard this is for him. "I really appreciate it. I really do."

"Yeah, baby, don't worry about it. I'll do it if it makes you happy." Then Garrett looks deeply into my eyes. "I do love you very much, Destiny. I hope you know that. You just a little crazy right now, that's all. My baby's been through a lot."

"I love you too, Garrett," I say, and even with so much swirling doubt, I really mean it.

Garrett gently kisses me on my forehead, my eyelids, my temples, and my cheeks. He caresses my hair and begins to press his strong, hard body against mine. He becomes aroused, his muscular thigh rubbing in between mine. He dives his hot tongue into my mouth, and I am so hungry for my husband's kiss that I nearly swallow it. I give up the fighting and the questions and surrender myself to him as we make our way to our bed. Thrashing back and forth, rolling over once neatly folded laundry, we make wild love. I am so starved for everything to be right between us that I squeeze him as tightly as I can—as tightly as I am squeezing my eyes shut right now, trying to hold back the tears and the traumatic truth I feel. I desperately try to suffocate the vision of that long strand of mysterious red hair stretched across my husband's pillow, right here in our bed, where we are fucking like never before.

Chapter
★ Eight

THE TWO-HOUR JET FLIGHT BETWEEN NEW YORK AND GREENSBORO, North Carolina, goes without a hitch this early Saturday morning. It's the little puddle-jumper between Greensboro and Wilmington that's now got my stomach churning. The sniffling toddler behind us, kicking my seat, doesn't help. Nor does Garrett's constant complaining about the high cost of our last-minute tickets from New York to North Carolina.

"Fasten your seatbelts, please. We are about to take off," chirps the perky blonde flight attendant standing in the aisle in front of us and the other dozen or so passengers at God's mercy aboard this tiny, toy-like plane. The young woman standing there in the position of saving our lives looks more like a college cheerleader than someone with in-air crisis training.

"We should arrive in Wilmington in … oh …" She checks her dainty gold bracelet watch with a happy smile. "I'd say about forty-five minutes." She pops her head sideways with a bounce of one of her shoulder-length curls. She's beaming with pride, as if she's just guessed the right answer on a TV game show. I almost want to jump up and pin a gold star on her pumped-up chest, which I notice Garrett is admiring.

"Can I get y'all something?"

Well, okay. I forgive her. At least she's attentive.

"Sure. Some water, please."

"I'll have a stiff Bloody Mary," Garrett interjects.

"Honey, are you sure? This early in the morning?" I whisper. But Garrett seems convinced that a strong drink will help calm his nerves. It's Garrett's dang nerve after a few drinks that concerns me right now, especially fearing how he might react if provoked by my parents.

"Oh yeah, I'm sure." Garrett motions to the flight attendant. "Make it a double." He then turns his eyes out the small plastic window of the tiny plane.

"O-kay ..." The happy hostess smiles brightly. I take a second look at this cheery young lady with the big smile stretched across her face, who just moments ago was simply a southern belle waitress in the sky. But somehow, all of a sudden, as she smiles down at me, with Garrett's back to us both, she feels like an ally. It's as if she knows my story, senses my sadness, and feels my confusion, my pain, and my desperation for everything in my world to be back to what it used to be when everything was good, and I felt loved. She may forever hold my secret, as she has probably sensed and seen so many times before on this short and bumpy flight.

"How 'bout some *peanu-uts*?"

"Oh, no, thank you." I smile.

"You suuure?" she drawls.

"Yes, I'm sure. Thanks so much."

Garrett shoots me an incredulous look.

"You turning into a little southern belle too now?"

"What?" I shoot him back a menacing look that says, "Do not even try."

But things certainly have changed from the bustling streets and hustling lives we share in New York City. Here, in the not so bustling South, there are men on this plane wearing checkered shirts and polyester pants. One old man even wears overalls.

"Hey, baby." Garrett nudges me with his elbow. "You think ol' grandpa over there might be married to one of those gals who wears a housecoat and curlers to the grocery store?" He cracks up at his own joke. "Welcome back to backcountry USA!"

I try to defend my home state. "Well, at least most people are sweet and hospitable down here. I mean, down here, a smile really does mean a smile."

"Yeah, *right*," Garrett says with a smirk. "They smile when they cut you! Then they come visit you in the hospital, bring you a pie, and ask how your mama and 'nem is. And that big ol' smile never leaves their southern faces. Yeah, welcome back to the South, baby! Come *hang* with us!" Garrett laughs at his own joke.

Nuthin' could be finer than to be in Carolina in the mo-or-or-ning, is all my heart sings.

The little plane suddenly dips and swerves a bit, caught momentarily in a strong gust of wind. I instinctively grab Garrett's arm, and he comforts me, even though the concerned look on his face lets me know he is as startled and caught off guard as I am. My heart is skipping as I pray we'll reach home safely. I take a long sip of my cool water, hoping it will help me chill. I am comforted by the lush green fields and miles of pine trees down below.

On the horizon, the deep green fades into an even deeper blue, and I know it is Mother Ocean not far away. The little houses dotting the fields of crops on the farms below make the land look like a Monopoly game board. The plane's motor continues its loud humming as we glide over the miles and miles of pine trees and fertile earth toward the deep blue Atlantic Ocean. I can't help but admire God and His works as I marvel at this bird's-eye view of my rich Tar Heel state. It's hard to believe that I spent so much time and energy trying to run away from this southern land. I was the only one of all the generations of my family to ever "flee North." Now, oddly enough, I find myself fleeing right back home again to find tranquility—not only a safe, calm, and peaceful feeling, but Tranquility is also the name my grandfather gave our family beach house three generations ago. It was one of the very first black-owned beachfront properties in North Carolina. Before it was built in 1948, establishing the Ocean City section of the island, blacks weren't allowed on the beach. The oceanfront was reserved by the law just for whites. But my grandparents joined some other wealthy black families in helping change that.

Garrett and I finally arrive in Wilmington, where we grab our luggage and rent a car to make the thirty-mile trek to the island, where I cannot wait to see my parents and Aunt Joy, who I know is going to be, as she calls it, "tickled brown" to see us. I smile to myself as we make the turn out of the airport driveway and hit the old familiar Route 50 East, the little two-lane highway to Topsail Island.

Garrett is still grumpy, despite his double Bloody Mary. "I hate that you guys live so far from the airport," he whines.

"Aw, c'mon, G," I tease. "Hell, getting to the Hamptons in all that New York traffic is a lot worse. Here, you get to enjoy the quaint uniqueness of the southern countryside along the way. Honey, just look out the window, please, and try to relax." I gently rub Garrett's hand.

The southern scenes are serene and beautiful. I get a big rush as we drive past some fruit-and-vegetable stands. Most of the hand-built wooden structures are set up on the very land on which the fruit and vegetables are grown, manned by farmers and their families right there in their own front yards. I am comforted by the gentleness of humanity down here as I watch barefooted children bagging fruit and helping old ladies to their cars. Country kids can run across anything barefooted—tobacco fields, gravel driveways, hot asphalt, and seashelled beaches, just as I did as a kid growing up here, at the beach and in the country in the summertime.

"Oh, Garrett, let's stop at one of those stands. We can bring home some fresh fruit and vegetables for the house."

"Now, Dest, you know good and well that your mother has already packed that fridge with enough food to feed an army."

"I know, but it's tradition—we have to stop and shop. *Please?*"

Garrett finally surrenders, continuing down the little country road until he spots another fruit-and-vegetable stand, this one situated in the parking lot of an antiquated gas station. He pulls over and parks under a shady tree in the gravel drive.

"Okay, southern belle. Here're your plantation fruits and veggies. Shop till you drop."

"C'mon, sweetie, we won't be long," I say as I get out of the car. I can already smell the sticky sweetness of fresh cantaloupe, ripe peaches, and watermelon.

"Get some of those big-ass tomatoes too, babe," Garrett calls to me.

"You got it," I call back in my excitement and the hope that maybe Garrett is finally coming around.

"And how about a bunch of those wildflowers for Aunt Joy too."

"I will!" I blow a great big kiss to my thoughtful man and then busy myself with the produce, enraptured by this beautiful display of God's natural glory. I will do everything I can to make Garrett feel at home and loved and not like a fish out of water this weekend.

I fill my brown paper bags with peaches, okra, string beans, and corn, which will all go perfectly with one of these huge, beefy tomatoes. A gigantic one catches my eye, and I know it will make Garrett's mouth water. I can't remember when I last saw a fresh tomato this humongous, certainly not in Harlem.

"Take a look at this one, Garrett," I squeal, turning slowly to reveal the enormous red tomato cradled in the palm of my hand. "How'd you like me to slice this one up on your fresh little salad, Big Daddy?"

But Garrett is not there. Instead, there stands an old, snaggletoothed white man, grinning at me as he picks through the plump peaches.

"Oh, I'm so sorry, sir. Please forgive me," I say, totally embarrassed. "I thought you were my husband. He was just standing here—I thought."

"If you're talking about that young colored fellow, I seen him over there by the station on the pay phone." The old man nudges his head in that direction.

"Thank you, sir," I say. Why in the world would Garrett be using the pay phone way out here in the middle of nowhere? After adding a few more tomatoes to our basket, I realize my purse is locked in the car, and Garrett is still nowhere to be found. Who could Garrett be talking to all this time?

Worried, I make my way over to the station, and I finally spot Garrett on the pay phone, waving his hands emphatically as he carries on in a heated conversation. My poor husband never stops working, even on a Saturday during a holiday weekend. But enough already—we promised we'd leave our jobs in New York and enjoy this free time together. So I march across the gravel drive, determined to hold my precious press prince to that promise if it's the last thing I do.

As I get closer, Garrett's voice gets louder. He does not notice me, as he is in deep conversation and his back is turned.

"I'm sorry ... Look, I said I'm *sorry.*" I hear him pleading into the phone. "I know. I *know,* but it was a last-minute thing ... I didn't have a choice ... No! I *couldn't* get out of it. ... I know you're upset, but Evie, please!" Garrett slaps his forehead and runs his thick fingers through his freshly cut hair. He suddenly spins around in midsentence. Garrett locks his eyes with mine, with a look of complete shock on his face.

"*Stevie,*" he says into the phone but in a much-different tone this time and still not taking his eyes off mine. "Stevie, let me call you back later, man. But as I said, I'm sorry. I'm not available this weekend." Garrett places the receiver back on the hook. "Can you believe those bastards? They actually thought I would work today. I tell ya—that Stevie!"

I look at Garrett with a blank stare. I could have sworn I just heard him say "Evie," not "Stevie."

"Who's Stevie?" I ask. "I've never heard you mention that name before."

"Aw, he's the new guy," Garrett explains. "A real punk on the assignment desk. Always trying to get me to work overtime and weekends. And now, the holiday."

"Ah, I see," I say, but I don't.

"C'mon, babe, let's grab our stuff and get out of here. Everybody's waiting for us, and we don't want to be late for Barbara's *big brunch*," Garrett teases.

I smile. "You're right about that."

Maybe I did mishear Garrett. Maybe I am mistaken. Maybe I'm just too sensitive right now, overwhelmed with stress and jumping too quickly to an unfair conclusion. But I swear I'm not mistaken about the name I heard Garrett say. Still, all I know is that whoever was on the other end of that phone is very clear that my husband is with me this weekend, and that makes me glad. This long weekend on Topsail may very well change everything.

Just a few miles away from the little drawbridge that takes us across the intercoastal waterway and onto Topsail Island, I get a whiff of the fresh salt air as it boldly eases its way through the dank scent of the dark Tar Heel soil. The sides of the road have now given way to sandy banks, dunes, and tall blades of sea grass swaying in the gentle ocean breeze.

I roll down the windows as I did as a child. I close my eyes and take a deep breath, with the wind and afternoon sun in my face. I thank God for this feeling of freedom. Garrett takes my hand and squeezes it tightly.

"We're here," he says with a smile. The lines in his face seem to have relaxed a bit. Perhaps peace is beginning to find us here. At least, that's what I hope comes out of our dream vacation as I pray we also come out of our nightmare and finally find tranquility.

Chapter
★ Nine

$\mathcal{T}$HE BEACH HOUSE IS JUST AS I REMEMBER IT, LOOKING LIKE A LITTLE white matchbox with a black shingle hat atop four long toothpick-like legs. But there she is—Tranquility, standing tall, simple, and proud against the baby-blue sky and Mother Ocean's deep blue-green. My eyes sting with tears, engulfed by this sudden rush of emotions. How could I possibly have been away from Tranquility and Topsail for this long?

"Well, here we are." Garrett tries to sound as if he's not tense as we pull into the cracked-shell driveway, but I know he is. I lean over and give my husband a reassuring kiss on the cheek.

"Thank you, baby," I say tenderly. "You know this means the world to me. We'll have fun—you'll see. Just try not to fall into Mother's old traps, okay?"

"Okay, baby." Garrett smirks. "Let's go."

Excited, I honk the horn in our traditional way of letting family know we're home.

Da-da-da-dada-dada.

The first thing I hear is a big squeal from inside and suddenly, Aunt Joy comes bursting out of the screen porch door at the top of the beach house steps. She has a huge smile on her plump face and a red plastic shrimp deveiner in her hand.

"Praise God, you got here in one piece!" she exclaims to the heavens with her arms raised in the air. "Come here, kiddos. Let me get a good look at you! Praise God!"

I dash out of the car, up the steps, and into my aunt Joy's big open arms. I love her so much, and she still smells as fresh as the ocean breeze, with a hint of lavender—and of course, shrimp. In fact, whenever I see my aunt Joy, there's probably a plump shrimp around somewhere. If she's not baiting one on a fishing hook, she's deveining a couple dozen for a family feast.

"I love you, Aunt Joy." I hug her again tightly, just so I can inhale her scent one more time.

"Well, kiddo, I love you too." Aunt Joy giggles and squeezes me back. "And I am so happy you and Garrett have finally come home. It's been way too long, my dear."

"I know, Aunt Joy, I know." I feel ashamed for having been away from Topsail for so long. I've always blamed that on my busy career, but I know it's also been because of Garrett's disdain for sand, sea, and family friction. It's a shame he doesn't enjoy that big beautiful beach out there. I can see in my aunt Joy's dewy eyes that she has missed me. And I promise myself never to be away from this special place and this special lady for as long as I have been.

"Whatcha got cooking, Aunt Joy?" I ask as we move into the house, arms still wrapped tightly around each other's waists. "It's smelling mighty good in here."

"Oh, just a little of this and a little of that," she replies with a wink and a squeeze. "Your mother's in there cooking up a big ol' batch of salmon croquettes, but as I recall, your hubby doesn't eat salmon croquettes, does he?"

"No, Aunt Joy, he doesn't," I whisper.

Aunt Joy chuckles and shakes her head. "Your mama is somthin' else, I tell ya, somthin' else. That's why I'm fixing up some of my famous shrimp salad so the poor boy doesn't go hungry."

"Oh, we love your shrimp salad, and that's awfully thoughtful of you, but, Aunt Joy, Garrett can take care of himself."

"Well, we might have to help the poor boy out every now and then." Aunt Joy nudges me. "Now, go on in there and speak to your mother and daddy. They're worried sick about you. We all are."

"Hey, who's that fine lady?" Garrett teases Aunt Joy as he enters the house with our weekend duffel bags slung over his shoulders.

"Aw, Garrett, you are too many things!" Aunt Joy giggles, arms outstretched. "Get in here and let me look atcha, boy!"

Garrett kisses Aunt Joy on the cheek as she pats and gently rubs his cheek.

"So good to see you, Garrett," she coos. "Where've you been?"

"We've been really busy, Auntie JoyJoy," Garrett says. "But we're here now."

"And I'm so glad!" Aunt Joy beams. "Now, I know you two must be hungry. Garrett, put your bags down in the back bedroom and wash up for brunch, honey."

"You got it, Aunt Joy!" Garrett happily moves on.

I am overwhelmed by all of the happy memories in this house—the tall wooden hallway shelf my late grandfather made to hold our newfound beach treasures of sand dollars, driftwood, and exotic seashells. I still hold precious memories of the screened-in back porch that kept the hungry mosquitoes out and our good times with friends and family in as we marveled at the sun setting over the sound while enjoying grilled oysters and cold beers and lots of good old stories.

"Well, you made it in time for brunch!" I hear Mother calling out from the kitchen.

"Hey, where's my Diddle-Dee?" Daddy walks into the room, arms outstretched. I rush to him and hug him tightly. "How was your trip, baby girl?"

"Oh, it was fine, Daddy. Nice to be home."

"Well, we're glad you made it," Mother says as she enters, wiping her hands on her apron. She gives me an air kiss while pitter-pattering her long bejeweled fingers on my back, never daring to get to close. "I'm glad you two got here in one piece."

I find it interesting how I hug and kiss my dad and air kiss and pitter-patter with Mother. She has never been the warm and fuzzy type. Never a hugger. In fact, Mother has never kissed me. I feel she's more concerned about catching germs than giving affection, even to her own child. Mother seems to believe that providing strict rules, private education, social status, and special privilege is enough love for one girl. She doesn't need to be touched too.

"So, now tell me, Dee, do you think that exclusive hostage report will get you a better job or an Emmy?" Mother probes. "I mean, that's the least they could do after putting your life on the line like that, don't you think?"

"Yes, DeeDee." Daddy rubs my back. "We were very worried about you, but we are very proud of you too. We know you have the right stuff to shine. And you did."

"Thanks, Daddy." I blush. Nothing makes me happier than hearing my daddy's praises.

"Yes, but are you okay?" Aunt Joy's soft eyes are full of concern. "I mean, what in the world happened up there in Harlem with that man getting shot, right there in front of you and that poor little boy, for God's sake. What in the world was he thinking?"

"He just wanted his kids back," I reply.

"Mm-mm-mm." Aunt Joy shakes her head. "What's this world coming to? I sure wish you didn't live in such a dangerous city."

"I'm all right, Aunt Joy. I love New York, and I hope my stories'll help make our city better. I'm still a little shaken up, but I'll be okay. I really do care about what happens to Thomas, though."

"Care what *happens* to him?" Mother snaps. "Why in the world would you care about what happens to him? Let him rot in jail with the rest of the insane criminals of New York."

"He's not a criminal."

"Destiny, he held a machete to a three-year-old's throat!" Mother argues. "What part of being a 'criminal' don't you understand?"

Daddy frowns. "And it could have been you shot, DeeDee, if not killed."

"Oh, leave her alone, you two!" Aunt Joy interrupts. "The poor child's exhausted. She's been negotiating for hostages and traveling for hours. Give her a break. Come on; let's eat."

"I'll be okay, you guys. It's my job."

"That's right. And you are destined to win that Emmy and move on to be a big network news correspondent one day, just like Carol Simpson. I can just feel it. Don't forget; you are pedigreed. You come from something. You were groomed for success, young lady!"

"Did somebody say 'groom'?" Garrett stands at the door, holding a bouquet of flowers and two big brown bags full of produce, like a shield and armor.

"*Hey!*" Everybody resounds a warm welcome to Garrett.

"Hello, Garrett. Ready for brunch?" Mother is wearing her smile like an apron. "You got my daughter home just in time for some delicious, golden-brown salmon croquettes!" Mother is obviously proud of herself—and her ploy.

"*And* your choice of a scrumptious 'Full of Joy' shrimp salad too!" Aunt Joy giggles at her quick save and catchy impromptu name and then darts a sharp look at Mother. "Why, I even whipped up some southern-fried hot-water corn bread and fresh butter."

"And we bought some delicious fruits and vegetables." Garrett smiles as he places the bags on the kitchen counter in front of Mother.

"How thoughtful of you," Mother remarks.

"I bet you brought some asparagus too." Daddy chuckles as he shakes Garrett's hand in welcome. "I've never seen anybody eat more asparagus than you, Garrett." Daddy dislikes asparagus as much as he dislikes Garrett.

"What's wrong with asparagus?" Garrett asks in a playful yet defensive way.

Daddy just shakes his head.

We sit down and enjoy our brunch, chitchatting about what we've been up to and the latest news about the neighbors. Mother's salmon croquettes are delicious, as usual. It's one of my favorite recipes. I've forgotten how delicious they are. I realize that because Garrett doesn't like them, he and I never eat them, like the beaches we never see. Instead of the croquettes, he's busy gobbling up Auntie's "Full of Joy" shrimp salad atop a piece of hot-water corn bread. He seems satisfied just being satisfied, munching away.

I can't wait to take a long walk on the beach and dip my big toe in the warm waters of the Atlantic. It's my special ritual to say hello to Mother Ocean. Perhaps this will also be a good time for Garrett and me to rebond. Maybe we'll enjoy a romantic Topsail sunset later in the day and finally unwind from our incredibly busy and separate lives.

Mother insists on doing the dishes and sprucing up the kitchen for the summer season, while Daddy settles in front of the TV for a long afternoon of old western movies. Aunt Joy grabs her favorite Sidney Sheldon novel and looks ready for a long stint of heavy reading on the porch. Garrett goes to our bedroom and starts to unpack. I enjoy flipping through an old family photo album filled with snapshots of days gone by, when I was a little girl who dreamed of mermaids and played with porpoises and passing schools of fish in the sea.

After a bit, I go find Garrett, who seems to be hiding out in our bedroom, watching a game on TV. I crawl into bed and lie next to him, nestling up against his big body, my head on his chest. His arms remain behind his head as he is totally engrossed in sports and seems not at all interested in me. I try to warm things up.

"Hey, baby ..." I start. "Wouldn't it be nice to take a long walk on the beach together?"

"Aw, c'mon, Dee." Garrett rubs his head and sighs. "I'm tired. Damn! We've been traveling all day."

"I know, but, honey, we're at the beach, and it's so beautiful. Don't you want to watch the sunset?"

"There'll be another one tomorrow."

"*Please*? C'mon, Garrett, we can relax on the beach … and … maybe …" I look up at Garrett, giving my husband a coy look.

"Oh, hell naw, baby. You know I ain't gettin' down in no sand! No way; plus, I'm just tired, Dee. Maybe tomorrow." Garrett gives me his puppy-dog look.

I lie here wishing I had a husband, not a puppy, who would enjoy long walks on the beach with me in the sunshine and the sunsets of Topsail Island as we share long romantic talks about our promising future together and all the dreams we will build as one. But I don't. I instead have a husband who despises the beach. He hates his feet touching sand and has apparently lost his appetite for conversation, sex, and me as well. So I decide to take my long walk anyway. When Aunt Joy gathers that I'm walking alone, she puts down her novel and insists on joining me.

"I can't go as far as I used to, kiddo," she says, "but I'll walk with you just a bit to feel the warm sand beneath my feet."

"Wonderful." I smile, remembering the many long walks and talks Aunt Joy and I have shared. We head down the beach, as we have done hundreds of times before, and I am startled by how much our little island has grown. New, modern homes seem to be popping up everywhere. Our little Topsail Island is indeed changing.

"Now, Dee, you are just going to have to tell me why you haven't been back to Topsail in so long. That's not like you." Aunt Joy keeps a close sideways watch on me as we slowly stroll down the long stretch of beach.

"Oh, I don't know, Aunt Joy. I guess it's mainly because Garrett has never really been into the 'North Carolina beach thing,' as he calls it. He says he wants to try more exotic places in the world, like Jamaica, St. Bart's, or Puerto Rico."

"Well, what do they have that we don't have, Destiny?" Aunt Joy looks incredulous. "What? What do they have?"

"Golf courses," I reply.

I feel a sudden rush of shame, feeling that, like a fool, I gave up one of my favorite places on earth—a most sacred gift from my family—and for what? Love in a concrete jungle? Love that I now find myself suspicious of and fighting for? How could I have given up so much of myself and what means so much to me for a love I'm not even sure of? Love is not giving your family, friends, and foundation away.

I look up and down the shore, and as far as I can see, there is not another soul around. I don't want Aunt Joy to sense my sadness or witness my tears, so I suggest we walk with our faces to the sun, and we turn right, toward the pier—one bare foot after the other in the warm, powdery white sand beneath, as we have done time and time again. Except this time, only halfway down the beach, Aunt Joy appears exhausted. Her breathing is heavy and labored.

"Well, I guess I'd better take my happy self on back home now," she announces. "You go on and enjoy your walk, honey."

"You okay, Aunt Joy?" I ask, concerned at how peaked she looks.

"Oh, I'm fine—just old," she says, panting. "You go on, kiddo. Whew! Don't worry about me. I just want to get back to my juicy romance novel, that's all. Go on, now."

I give Aunt Joy a kiss on the cheek. "You sure you'll be all right?"

"Fine as a Georgia pine!" Aunt Joy winks and turns to head back to the beach house. I watch her as she slowly waddles her way back home. For the first time, she looks small and frail against the wide stretch of our white-sand beach. Aunt Joy looks vulnerable and aged. I keep a close eye on her as she slowly disappears over the dunes.

I think about the audacity and tenacity it took for my grandparents and Aunt Joy to build our family beach house here on Topsail Island back in 1948, smack dab in the middle of the horrid Jim Crow era. At that time, there were still "colored" waiting rooms, drinking fountains, and separate swimming pools. The idea of a "summertime beachfront sanctuary" for North Carolina's black upper-middle-class—doctors, lawyers, and funeral home directors—was indeed an unheard-of vision. I still feel my grandfather's rooted pride as I walk the same sands he walked decades ago.

The summer sun feels amazing as its heat bakes my face. I close my eyes and inhale the ocean mist and salt air deep into my lungs. I see nothing but brilliant orange behind my closed lids. I hear the sound of the ocean waves pounding the shore. I can actually feel the earth rumble as the waves continue their mad and thunderous crashes. A little playful wave runs up the beach and zips around my ankle.

I look down and see the little sand fleas desperately digging their way back down into the sand as the water recedes back into the ocean. I had forgotten about these little insect crab-like creatures. Just when I think my whole world is gone, Mother Nature has an incredible way of making me stop, look, listen, think, and admire her awesome beauty—no matter how ugly my reality might seem. Mother Nature helps me believe in things I can't see or gave up on or have long forgotten about—like faith and God and love. But His stupendous things—like the sun rising and setting, the continual ebb and flow of the sea, or the constellation of the stars, are all the constant things in life. Some things, God says, I can count on.

"*Ah-gaaaaa! Ah-gaaaaa!*"

I look up and see a solo seagull soaring in the Carolina blue sky, and I smile a warm hello up to him and to the heavens. He reminds me that I am not the only solitaire being on the beach and, most important, that I am never alone. I remember when I was a child how Aunt Joy insisted I appreciate what she called "our little friends" in nature, like fireflies, butterflies, and bumblebees that would often hover right in front of our noses. Aunt Joy taught me that the bumblebee has no stinger, so she insisted I look that bumbling bee straight in the eye and instead of taking a big fat swat at him, take time instead to say good day. The bumblebee just hovers there, friendly, faithful, and unafraid. With that big, wide, hairy body, I wonder how he can even fly. I guess it's like Aunt Joy said: "Because he doesn't think he can't."

A good mile or two from home, I decide to turn around and walk back toward the beach house. The sun feels so good on my back. I see that the beach is now peppered here and there with fishermen preparing for a late-in-the-day lucky bite. The serenity found in the faces of fishermen is priceless. They look out over the ocean with a squinted once-in-a-while glance at the end of their poles in hopes of big drama and a great story to later share over a delicious fried fish meal. They stand there on the shore with their poles stuck in the sand for hours, displaying the patience of Job.

I pass one old man, and, knowing that any proud fisherman is going to open up his Styrofoam container and show off his latest catch, I ask, "Any luck today?"

The old man pops the lid, as protocol promised, and proudly points down at a few fish still flopping around in the water before becoming the fisherman's Saturday night dinner. Four medium spots and one big blue fish cling to life, when very soon hot grease and corn meal will be clinging to their gills.

"Gon' be good with some coleslaw, and Texas Pete, and a Pabst Blue Ribbon beer!" the old man exclaims with wide eyes and a toothless grin. "Gon' be mighty good," he reassures. We both laugh at the pleasure of sharing this wonderful, sacred life on the beach.

"Well, good luck!" I wave good-bye and start heading home again. Suddenly, I am frozen in my tracks by another human being on the beach. I see what looks like a vision of Adonis running toward me. In the late afternoon sun, this man looks like a dream. Orange and red sun rays beaming down on his bronzed skin and sun-bleached blond hair, make this incredibly beautiful man seem surreal. I feel as if I am watching a Coppertone commercial or witnessing a mirage in slow motion. His ripped stomach muscles glisten with sweat in the sunshine as he plows his way through the sand and surf. Big thighs; strong, shapely arms; and broad shoulders you want to cry on. He looks like a golden thoroughbred in motion.

Our eyes connect. They lock for what seems like an eternity as I continue my slow stroll, and he continues his steady run, both of us moving closer and closer, still locked in each other's gaze. I feel something weird, like a laser searing right through me. And as uncomfortable and as unnerved as I feel, I still cannot unlock myself from his gaze, nor from the oddly familiar warmth I find in the sparkling sea-green eyes of this beautiful bronzed being on the beach.

"Afternoon," he says with a bright smile as he pushes past me.

"Afternoon," I reply with a brilliant smile of my own.

We pass each other, yet I can still feel his electricity. I close my eyes, wanting to remember every aspect of this sudden and uncanny encounter. I smile to myself and turn to look over my shoulder for one last glimpse of Adonis, and as I turn, so does he. As he runs and I walk, moving in opposite directions, our eyes lock once again. He smiles like he knows me. I wave like I want him to.

He continues his run down the beach.

I keep walking home as the sun, in all of her amber splendor, begins to set over our Topsail Beach, preparing for nightfall and another day.

Chapter ★ Ten

I GET BACK TO THE BEACH HOUSE, FEELING GUILTY THAT ANOTHER MAN captured my attention, but the guy was beautiful—and attentive. That one moment of exchanging glances with a stranger was rather nice and innocent enough. I wish my husband's gaze was still that powerful. I know I should be fighting for the survival of my marriage right now, not looking over my shoulder at a beautiful bronzed boy on the beach, but for some reason, I couldn't stop myself today—and obviously, neither could he. It seems as if I know him from somewhere. Who knows? Maybe in another life.

As I reach the beach house and make my way up the stairs, I am determined to take this pent-up sexual passion to my husband—where it belongs—for a little late-afternoon delight. I pray he's still snuggled in bed, watching the game right now, waiting for me. I slip past my parents, both deeply engrossed in an old movie. Aunt Joy is sound asleep; her novel still nestled in her lap. I slip into our bedroom to seduce Garrett.

The lights are out. Shades drawn. Perfect. I slip out of my clothes and climb into bed with my husband, wrapping my legs around his, trying to ignite a bit of passion. My body is on fire, but Garrett just lies there, a lump of cold flesh, breathing deeply, with his back turned to me.

"Garrett," I whisper as I rub his back. "Want to mess around a little bit?"

No answer.

"Garrett?"

My husband's deep breathing turns into a snore. This is a long cry from the times when Garrett couldn't keep his hands off me. The sexual energy between us was undeniable, so much power in our longing for each other. We had to restrain ourselves in public. I miss those days.

Garrett chooses to sleep through dinner. I lie and tell my folks he's too exhausted to eat after our long drive and might be coming down with something.

We keep dinner simple. I nibble on a leftover croquette, some shrimp salad, and a piece of corn bread. My folks and I chat about the many new changes and booming real estate on our growing island. Night falls gently. The sound of chirping crickets are a pleasant change from New York City traffic. And I've forgotten how much I miss lightning bugs until I see them glowing against the black southern sky. I say my good nights and turn in early, climbing back into bed with my snoring husband.

I feel so small still lying here behind this big mountain of unmovable flesh, staring into the darkness, wondering where we are headed. I remember how I used to stare longingly at Garrett while he slept, feeling a sense of safety in his presence and sweetness in his slumbering soul. But I don't feel that serenity today. I feel Garrett's falling into slumber is yet another sign of his falling out of love with me.

I toss and turn as day turns into night, lying in this bed next to my husband, unable to rest or make love. The ocean crashes outside, and the house quakes inside. I hear the frantic brushes of the long stalks of sea grass, entwined and entangled in the ocean breeze. I wish my husband and I were entangled now.

As the sun rises over the ocean, I feel that I have finally found a friend in this vast darkness between night and day. I also feel sad, having spent another day and night alone, without Garrett, even though he's lying right here next to me.

While everyone else continues to sleep soundly, I feel an urge to get up and out of the house. Perhaps doing something traditional will make me feel better now that I'm back home. Ever since I saw that fisherman's fresh fish flopping around in that pail, I have had a craving for some fried spots, grits, and buttery biscuits, just like I enjoyed on so many summer mornings growing up here. I figure if I get to the fishing docks early, I can get a few fish to fry up for a big family breakfast. I know everybody—even Garrett—likes spots, and so, in hope of making peace this weekend, I'll head to the docks on this breaking dawn.

I slip out of bed and throw on some loose linen pants, a tight tank top, and one of Garrett's big button-down shirts. I slip into my flip-flops, being extra quiet so as not to wake Garrett or anyone else in the house. I love these early morning hours when no one else is awake, when there's no one else's agenda or energy to deal with—nobody but myself to please. Plus, every beach body knows that the best catches come in during the wee hours of the morning, after the fishermen have been out at sea all night. I am determined to make my husband, my family, and myself very happy this morning. And I believe frying up some fresh spotted gifts from the sea is sure to do it.

I arrive at the docks and drive up the gravel driveway. An old hound dog lying on the wooden storefront porch lifts his droopy head. Finding me not to be a threat, the old dog nestles back down into his sleeping position as I park the car under a weeping willow tree.

"Mornin'!" calls out one of the fishermen, cleaning out a large catch in an old free-standing sink. "Can I help ya today?"

"Yes, sir, looking for some spots," I say as I crunch my way across the gravel.

"*Well*, ya might be too late for them this mornin'. Young fella inside just asked for every spot we got in the house."

"What?" I exclaim. "Every single one of them? *All* of them? You sold them *all* to him?"

"Sure did. Fella wanted 'bout a hundred o' them spots."

"Can't he share—maybe like, a dozen?" In my disappointment, I sound like a whiny little girl.

"Well, now, you'll have to ask him that. But he's a real nice fella. I bet he'll share with you." The man squinches his sun-beaten face on one side up into a long, wise wink at me and nods his head. It's as if this old salt understands how much this is threatening my beach breakfast bliss.

"C'mon," he says as he rinses off his hands and wipes them on his towel. "Let's see what's going on in the fish house."

We walk into the fish house, which is more like an oversized ice garage. Workers are counting and wrapping up bushels and bushels of spots in brown paper and then tossing them into empty baskets before scooting them out to a waiting car—a *police car?* Why in the world are they putting all these fish in a police car? *So it's some greedy cop nabbing all the spots, huh? Figures.* And then I notice the words stenciled on the back of the patrol car: "Surf City Police Department: To Protect and Service."

Service? I muse. *Shouldn't it read "to protect and serve"?* I have to do everything I can not to burst out laughing. My cop buddies back in New York City would have a field day with this one. The fisherman notices me gawking at the police car.

"You notice anything funny about this car?" I chuckle, holding my inside joke.

"Yup," he replies. "It's filling up with fish."

We laugh.

"Yeah, your spots look like they're under arrest," I say as a worker puts another bushel of fish in the backseat.

"Yup, well, the police chief's the one's buying out the store!"

"What for?" I ask.

"There he is. Why don'tcha ask him." The old man motions over my shoulder.

I turn around, and the chief is walking toward me with his head down, his big, black patrol boots crunching through the gravel.

"You've got quite a lot of spots there, Chief," I say, my friendly tease bordering on perturbed sarcasm.

The chief looks up and squints in the sun. He pushes back his police hat. I cannot believe my eyes as they slowly reconnect with his, and we both smile. It is actually him—Adonis. Dreamy Adonis running down the beach is actually the *police chief*? I wonder if he can detect how stunned I am. He smiles that Adonis smile and removes his chief's hat.

"Mornin'." He gently nods my way and then turns his attention to his car. "Yeah, got quite a lotta fish all right. Gonna have to ride with all my windows down, I reckon."

"Maybe you oughta fire up your siren too so you can get there quicker," I reply. We share a neighborly chuckle.

"The lady's hoping you'll sell her a couple of them spots you got there, Chief," says the fisherman. "She looked all dreary-eyed after I done told her you done bought up every last one in the house."

"Well, I'd be most happy to share with the lady." The chief smiles that warm and charming smile at me again. "Better yet, why don't you just come to our big fish fry tomorrow, and you can have all the fish you can eat there, and you won't have to cook a one. Every year our island police department throws a big fund-raiser. Most of the money goes to our local battered women's shelter. We'll have hush puppies, North Carolina barbecue, baked beans, coleslaw, and plenty of fresh baked pies too." He smiles that smile again.

"Delicious," I say, knowing subconsciously I am referring to more than the food. "I'm a huge supporter of any efforts to fight domestic violence. Count me in."

"Well, I *thank ya*, ma'am!" he says. I find his inflection, with the emphasis on the "thank ya," both interesting and endearing. He seems to be such a southern gentleman. I forgot how special they are down here.

"You know something?" The chief squints those sea-green eyes at me. "You sure look darn familiar somehow. You from around here?"

"My family has a beach house here, but I live in New York."

"Woo-wee!" the chief spurts. "New Yawk City! Ain't that how y'all say it up there in the Big Apple?"

"Uh ... yeah, well, something like that." Even though the chief seems to be genuinely fascinated and cordial, I am still very aware of the animosity some of these southerners hold for New Yorkers, as if the Civil War is still not over. I didn't even know "damn Yankee" was two words till I left the South.

"New York City ..." the chief muses. "Now, I tell you, that is one fast place."

"Yes, it's nice to come home and slow down a bit."

"Well, you sho'nuff gon' slow down 'round here," interjects the old fisherman. "Nothing to do but enjoy the fat of the land and the fruit of the sea."

"You also saw me yesterday, out on the beach. You were running; I was walking ..." I suddenly sound silly.

"Oh, wait a minute. Oh, yeah!" The chief suddenly remembers with a bright smile. "You were hitting up some old man on the beach for his fish too, right?"

Totally busted, I blush.

"Dag, girl, what are you? Some kind of fish-nabber?" the charming chief teases.

Even the old fisherman, standing by observing us, snickers. "You gon' end up in his police car," the old geezer guffaws. "He's gon' arrest ya and throw ya in the back of that police car with all them smelly spots!"

"Hope I'll see you at the fish fry tomorrow," the chief calls over his shoulder as he heads back to his patrol car. "We'll start around four. Come comfortable and ready to eat and dance all night. Oh—and enjoy these on me." The chief tosses me a brown-papered bundle of spots. I catch it like a football. "Leave those poor fishermen on the beach alone, will ya?" he teases.

Chief "Adonis" starts his police car engine and slowly pulls out the gravel driveway. I can barely breathe as I cradle his package of fresh-caught fish like it's a newborn baby. *How nice*, I silently muse.

And on a cloud, I float home in my car, to enjoy my first meal on this new day.

Hail to the chief!

Chapter
☆ Eleven

I AM HALFWAY DONE COOKING BREAKFAST WHEN I HEAR THE FIRST sounds of the family starting to rise. I look up, and Aunt Joy is standing there with a big smile on her face.

"Whatcha got cookin', good-lookin'?" she teases.

"Something delicious that reminds me of home." I flip over a big spot, frying golden in the big cast-iron pan. "Can I get you a cup of coffee?"

"Please do," Aunt Joy happily accepts as she slides her round body into a chair and pulls up to the kitchen table with a hearty "Whew!"

"Feeling any better this morning?" I ask her, still worried about how she became so weak so fast while walking on the beach yesterday.

"Oh, I'm okay." She shoos away my concern. "Don't you fret over me now. Ooo! Boy, that fish sure looks good. Nice and golden brown, just like we like it. I sure do miss your breakfasts, kiddo."

"Yes," I reply with a sigh. "Everybody does."

I can't think of the last time I prepared a home-cooked meal for anyone. I forgot how soothing, therapeutic, generous, and loving it can be. Perhaps I'll cook more—prepare another special meal when Garrett and I get home, just for us, to express my love. But I know it will take a lot more than home cooking to save our marriage.

"Where's Garrett? Still sleeping?" Aunt Joy is nibbling on a crunchy fish tail she must have stolen when I wasn't looking.

"Yes, he's still asleep. He's been working really hard lately."

"You both have." Aunt Joy looks up at me. "Is he sensitive to how hard you've been working up there in that dangerous city, putting your life on the line while trying to save others?"

"I think so ..." I try to busy myself with my spatula, taking the sizzling fish out of the pan and draining it on a brown grocery bag.

"How are you two getting along?" Aunt Joy leans in. "Still enjoying newlywed bliss?"

I look at Aunt Joy, and she seems to have a look of knowing all over her face.

"We're struggling," I admit. "But we're trying."

"*We* are?" Aunt Joy asks.

"Yes, *we*. We're trying."

"Hmm. I certainly hope so. I just want you to be happy, Destiny," she says softly. "You are my concern. You deserve to be happy. You're my kiddo, and I care about you."

Aunt Joy winks.

I flip another spot.

"Well, well, well. What's for breakfast?" Mother suddenly flows into the room wearing one of her many colorful caftans as she carefully eyes my meal. Mother loves her caftans. They make her look and feel as regal as a queen. She also loves running the show. "I'll set the table," she offers. "I've been dying to use your grandmother's old china and linens for a special occasion anyway. And Destiny, your cooking breakfast is indeed a special occasion. What in the world's gotten into you?"

"Well, look here! It's our baby girl, cooking the family breakfast on this fine Topsail morning." Daddy sleepily saunters over and plants a big kiss on my forehead. "Oh, my word—look, Mother. She's frying spots!"

Mother makes a big fuss over setting the table. Every fork, knife, spoon, and seashell-embroidered cloth napkin is in its proper place. Daddy and Aunt Joy sit on the front-porch rocking chairs, sipping coffee, looking out over the ocean, and again talking about how much the island has changed with construction bustling everywhere and the beaches finally integrated today.

While the family moves in its natural order, there is still no sign of Garrett. Why does he not get out of that bed and come spend some time with the family? Is that really so hard to do?

"Wash up, everybody," I call out as I head back to the bedroom to wake up Garrett. I find him lying across the bed, reading.

"Well, good morning," I say, a bit of sarcasm leaking into my voice. "I didn't know you were up. Why don't you join us?"

"I'll be out in a minute." Garrett keeps reading.

I try again. "I fried some spots, and I have some grits and biscuits too—"

"I said I'd be out in a minute," Garrett snaps and then turns back to his reading.

I feel so rejected by Garrett right now that I could scream, but instead, I quietly back out of the bedroom. I take a deep breath and hold back the tears that are stinging behind my eyes before facing my family with a fake smile on my face. *Why does he insist on being so damn difficult? Is he purposely trying to piss off every member of my family—before noon?*

"Y'all ready for breakfast?" I ask.

Mother, Daddy, and Aunt Joy are already standing around the table, waiting for Garrett and me to join hands in prayer.

"Yes, DeeDee, everything looks wonderful." Daddy beams. "Let's eat. Where's Garrett?"

"He's coming," I say. We stand for a few beats, which seem like minutes. Still no sign of any movement from Garrett. "Well, let's just go on and say the grace," I say, trying to make light of the situation. "He's such a slowpoke. Don't worry; he's coming."

"Well, just how long are we supposed to wait for King Garrett?" Mother is clearly agitated, as she hates rudeness—and Garrett. "You work all morning on this nice meal for the whole family, and he can't even show his appreciation—much less respect—by just showing up for breakfast on time? It's not like he has to drive across town. He's in the bedroom, for God's sake!"

"Mother, I thought we were going to try to make this a peaceful weekend."

"Well, we could certainly use a bit more consideration from your husband," Daddy snaps.

"Pass the spots, and stop all this yapping," interjects Aunt Joy as she spoons a heap of hot grits on her plate. "Don't let nothing take your joy like this. Eat. Garrett will be out when he's good and ready."

We eat the delicious spots in silence. This is certainly not the joyous morning feast I had envisioned. Everyone is tense, seemingly ready to pounce on any sound or sign of Garrett. Finally, we hear the bedroom door open, and Garrett nonchalantly strolls into the room.

"Good morning," he announces.

"Morning," Mother and Daddy murmur without looking up from their now half-eaten meal.

"Grab a seat. You're missing these wonderful spots your wife cooked especially for you this morning." Aunt Joy motions to Garrett's place at the table.

"Thanks, baby," he says and squeezes my hand as he takes a seat. "Looks good."

"I hope you like them, Garrett," I say with a slight smile, still feeling sad and small.

"So when'd you go fishing, Dee?" Garrett attempts humor.

"I didn't go fishing, crazy. I got up this morning and went to the docks while you slept. I was lucky to get any. The funniest thing—the police chief had bought every last one of them for some big Memorial Day fish fry they're having on the island, but I convinced him to share."

"Oh, yes, the police department's big annual event that kicks off the summer. I tell you, that Chief Chase is a good fellow." Aunt Joy winks my way. "And a good catch too, if you ask me, just like these fine spots. Thank you, my dear."

"Anything for you, Aunt Joy."

I chuckle, as I know my spry aunt Joy has probably been flirting with that local police chief, but in this case, I know why. He is amazingly handsome and quite a southern gentleman, and he did provide our breakfast fish for free this morning. I blush at knowing how great he looks half naked, running on the beach in the Topsail sunset. I laugh quietly at how ludicrous it is that the back of his squad car reads *"To Protect and Service."*

"Baby, baby …"

I snap out of my musings to Garrett's nudging my elbow.

"Baby, pass me some hot sauce." He points across the table.

"Please," I tease.

"Please. Now, come on, baby. Stop playing around."

I reach over and pass the sauce.

My breakfast is obviously a big hit, as everyone has earned his or her membership into the Clean Plate Club. I am happy to have fed my family this morning. They all seem content. While they're still not speaking to Garrett, they're not trying to kill him either.

After the dishes are cleared away, we all retire to the front porch with another cup of coffee. We are screened in from the flies and mosquitoes and shaded from the sun. It is cool here, and the ocean breezes and the sound of the waves bring heaven to earth on my family's porch.

"So, Garrett, how's business?" My father is always asking Garrett about business. We are just starting out and not making a lot of money, so we live in Harlem, where we feel we get more for our money. For the first time for both of us, we live in a black neighborhood and are a part of our own community. Daddy does not understand, much less approve of that.

"I raised you in the suburbs," he often reminds me. "I worked hard to provide for you and your mother, so neither of you would ever have to worry about living in a ghetto. Now, this fool comes along and marries you, and where does he take you? Right to the ghetto!"

Daddy is always trying to give us money too, in his unsuccessful but repeated attempts to get us to move out of Harlem. Garrett refuses to take a dime. It assaults his pride. It's as if Daddy's offers make him feel impotent. We would starve on the streets before Garrett would take Daddy's money. Garrett says he'd feel owned. And although he knows my dad is just looking out for his baby girl, Garrett still resents the "how's business" question every single time Daddy asks.

"You making any money yet?" my father persists.

"Nope," Garrett answers frankly. "They're kicking my ass on the overnight desk. I mostly cover the wires in case anybody dies. If they do, I produce the obit by morning."

"How morbid." Mother rolls her eyes.

"Every once in a while a big story breaks, and I get to cover it," Garrett explains. "But no, I'm not making a lot of dough right now. Just trying to keep my foot in the door."

"Well, we shouldn't let that get in the way of your providing a safe home for my daughter," Daddy surmises. "I think we can all agree that after her life was in such danger up there this week, you need to reconsider my offer to help you get out of there. With the good advice of some of my real estate friends up North, I can help you find a suitable place much farther downtown. I will, of course, help you monetarily as well."

"Oh, no." Garrett shuffles in his chair. "Doc, I have told you time and time again, no. I don't want your money. We don't need your charity. We're fine."

"Oh, you're anything but fine. What if Dee wants to take time off from chasing ambulances to have a baby? Can you afford that?"

"W-wait a minute. What's a baby got to do with this? Look, Doc, you really need to back off me right now. I'm doing the best I can."

"*Romance* without *finance* is *nonsense* and a *nuisance*," Mother singsongs.

"I advise you not to look away so fast from a gift that's staring you right in the face, young man. Especially when it can also help you get my daughter out of the ghetto."

"Harlem is more than ghetto, Doc. We'll make good money soon enough. You'll see. But for now, we're cool. You can keep your money."

My father's jaw drops.

Mother glares at Garrett. "So … when do you think your midnight shift with dead people is going to end?"

Garrett rolls his eyes. "I have no idea, Barbara."

Daddy, apparently ignoring Garrett's brush-off, continues to press the issue. "I just wish you would take my advice—"

"I don't want your damn advice!" Garrett snaps. "Doc, I've told you. Stay out of our goddamned business!"

"Garrett!" Aunt Joy blurts in surprise at my husband's profane outburst.

"You watch your language in my house, young man!" my father booms.

"Then keep your nose out of my business!" Garrett retorts.

"Now, you wait just a minute, Garrett!" Mother struggles through her caftan to jump up from her rocking chair. "Don't you *dare* speak to my husband like that! Who do you think you are? Have you lost your mind?" Mother is so angry, she is red in the face, trembling, and looking as if she's about to explode into a million little pieces. "How *dare* you disrespect us!" she spews.

"Oh, dear," Aunt Joy gasps as she begins to fan herself and rock her chair faster.

A dead and deafening silence fills the air as the ocean waves continue their violent pounding and crashing to shore. I hear Aunt Joy's rocking chair squeaking against the wooden porch planks. I bow my head and close my eyes, praying this is all a bad dream. My parents are looking at each other in that silent language between them—a language only the two of them know, but everyone can see the looks of shock, outrage, and disgust on their hardened faces. I know they find Garrett's behavior unacceptable. He knows my parents consider any kind of cursing in their home as the utmost disrespect.

As if in slow motion, Mother and Daddy put down their coffee cups and, in suspended silence, head back into the beach house as smooth as ghosts. On the way out, Daddy stops and locks eyes with me. In a low, steady, and serious tone, he informs me that he and Mother do not at all approve of Garrett's volcanic behavior. Daddy speaks to me as if Garrett is not even in the room.

"This is a disgrace," he says. "Anyone who will disrespect your parents like this is just a heartbeat away from disrespecting you—if he hasn't already." Daddy scowls at Garrett. "My little girl may have been fool enough to marry you, but it doesn't mean I'm fool enough to let you disrespect her family or our home. If you don't like it here, can't stand us, and refuse to respect me and my rules, then you can pack your bags and leave my house right now."

"Fine!" Garrett spits. "I will."

"No, you won't, Garrett! Daddy!" I exclaim, trying my best to calm down the two men I love the most, but Daddy storms off into the beach house after Mother. Garrett angrily grabs the keys to the rental car.

"Garrett! Where are you going? Honey, wait! Sit down. Please!" I reach for Garrett's arm, but he jerks away from me.

"Get out of my way, Destiny, I gotta get outta here!" Garrett angrily storms past me and out the screen porch door. It slams with a whack behind him.

"Garrett, *please*!" I yell after him as he flees down the stairs, but he won't listen. He is fuming. Aunt Joy and I stand there on the porch of our beach house named Tranquility and see all but that playing out around us. We watch in disbelief as Garrett speeds off, swerving around the corner, and skidding onto the highway in a dusty haze of sand and seashells.

There is nothing but silence left amid the ocean's roar and the occasional squawks of hungry seagulls. And then, there is the squeak-squeak-squeak of Aunt Joy's rocking chair again. It is squeaking faster than usual now as she shakes her head and bites her nails while looking out over the boisterous sea.

"What in the world has gotten into this family?" she asks. "I just don't understand it."

"I give up," I say as I plop down in the rocking chair beside her. She takes my hand, and we rock in silence, not knowing what other surprises this day may bring.

Chapter ★ Twelve

I T IS WELL AFTER NOON, AND GARRETT IS STILL NOT BACK. HIS LUGGAGE and plane ticket are still here, so I guess he's coming back eventually. But I am getting stir-crazy, cooped up in the house, waiting for a husband who stormed off hours ago and still hasn't returned. I am also angry with my parents for pushing Garrett's buttons. I am pissed at him for letting them. And I am mostly mad at myself for believing that this would actually be a blissful holiday. What happened to our dream of a peaceful weekend at Tranquility?

Mother comes waltzing on to the porch, dressed in a pair of bright yellow linen knickers, matching top, and espadrilles. She holds a wide-brimmed sun hat with a long, flowing yellow scarf neatly tied around its crown. Her purse is embellished with seashells and an ornate bamboo handle. She looks like a resort fashion model.

"Come on, Diddle-Dee," she coos. "Let's get out of this house for a bit. You'll drive yourself and everyone else crazy if you stay here pent up and peeping off the porch like a sea widow all day. C'mon."

"Mother, I think maybe I should be here when Garrett gets back. I don't want him fighting with Daddy again. You know how they are."

"They?" Mother inquires with a raised eyebrow. "Hm. Well, your father is sound asleep. He'll be in dreamland for a while, thank God. You know how he escapes. Now, come on. Garrett needs to know that you're not just sitting around here moping all day, waiting for him."

Mother cocks the brim of her sun hat over her right eye. And then, and as if appearing before a crowd of fans, she cascades down the beach house steps, yellow scarf flying in the breeze, and gets in her car. She impatiently honks the horn for me to hurry.

"Go on," Aunt Joy says, nudging me. "It'll be good for you to get out and sightsee the island for a while. It'll also give me a chance to have a word or two with Garrett when he gets home. Maybe I can finally talk some sense into one of those men."

I give Aunt Joy a big kiss on her cheek. "I love you so much, and thank you, Aunt Joy."

"I love you too, kiddo!" She winks.

Mother and I tool around the island for a while, marveling at all the new houses and carefully keeping our conversation bright. Neither of us dares mention Garrett or the family's breakfast battle.

"I tell you, those damn Yankees are buying up everything down here," Mother says. "Who knew it would one day be so busy on Topsail."

While we're out, we decide to stop by Food Folks, the only supermarket on the island, where cross-sections of the different residents meet. We are pushing our shopping cart through the store when mother sends me off to get paper goods while she haggles with the butcher over a couple of whole fryer chickens.

I am standing in the paper section, trying to decide on the best deal on paper towels. I choose the big pack at the lowest price and drop the bundle into the shopping cart. I then turn to move down the aisle—and I surprisingly run into the police chief again. This time, he is off duty and in civilian clothes. He wears shorts, a brightly colored Hawaiian shirt, and flip-flops. Instead of the police chief of Topsail Island, he looks more like a Hawaiian chief of Big Island.

My heart skips a beat, and I have to catch my breath. He is at the other end of the same aisle with an older woman who is picking out dinner napkins. I struggle over whether to say hello but instead decide to turn my cart around and scram back to Mother as quickly as I can.

And then I hear his voice.

"Hey, you!" Chase calls out from the other end of the aisle. The chief starts walking toward me. "Hey, there. How you doin'?"

"Oh, just fine," I lie.

"I see you twice in one day—must be a lucky one." He grins wide, his teeth white and his eyes as pale green as the sea. "Did you eat all those spots yet?"

"Yes, yes, I did—I mean, we did. My whole family and me."

"Well, save some room for more tomorrow. You're still coming to the fish fry, right? Bring your whole family."

"I'll certainly try," I say politely. I don't know why I'm so nervous.

"Chase? Let's hurry on now." The older woman walks up with her shopping cart.

The handsome, sun-kissed police chief in the Hawaiian shirt turns to me. "Oh, I'm sorry. I didn't even get your name."

"Destiny," I say with a shy smile.

"I'm Chase, Miss Destiny," he replies. "And this here is my mom, Fern McKenzie."

"Nice to meet you, Mrs. McKenzie," I say and politely extend my hand to Chase's mother, who, to my surprise, doesn't take it. Instead, she busies herself rearranging the few items in her shopping cart. She does not even look at me, appearing to have no interest in meeting me at all.

"Destiny, why does it take you so long to buy paper towels?" My mother comes marching around the aisle with two big fryer chickens in her hands. I am relieved to see her.

"Mother, this is the Topsail police chief, Chase McKenzie, and his mother, Mrs. Fern McKenzie." I try to be as pleasant and polite as possible through my growing discomfort. I don't know why I want to impress Chase's mother so much when the woman doesn't even want to shake my hand.

My mother takes one look at Mrs. McKenzie and suddenly freezes in her tracks. Her face morphs into stone. "Fern McKenzie ..." she mouths in slow motion.

Mrs. McKenzie frowns at my mother and purses her ultra-thin lips. The two are locked in what appears to be a stare-down. No more southern niceties here. Abruptly, Mother takes the chickens she just picked up from the butcher and slams them down into the shopping cart.

"C'mon, Destiny," she snaps. "Let's go right now!" With one last hardened look at Chase's mother, she snaps her head under her wide brimmed hat and tornadoes away.

"I said, let's go, Chase," Mrs. McKenzie barks and marches her cart off in the opposite direction.

Chase and I stand here in the middle of the middle of the paper goods aisle, looking at each other in total shock, confusion, and embarrassing dismay.

"What in the world was that all about?" Chase seems just as dumbfounded as I am.

"I have no idea," I respond, feeling dazed, "but I'd better go. My mother's waiting."

"Yeah, mine too. But what the ...?" Chase shakes his head. "I swear that was the weirdest thing I've seen. What just happened there?"

"I have no idea," I again respond. "But something happened somewhere. I apologize, Chase, for my mother's rudeness. I don't know what's gotten into her. We had a long morning—and she's already a bit on edge. Just family stuff, you know?"

"No, no, no, I apologize for my mom," Chase insists. "She's just acts old and bitter sometimes. Let me go find her. Hope I'll see you later, Destiny." Chase dashes off down the aisle.

By the time I make my way through the checkout line, Mother is already sitting outside in the car, fuming.

"What in the world was that about, Mother?" I ask. "Don't you think you were a little rude to Mrs. McKenzie?"

Mother doesn't answer me. She stares out the car window with her arms crossed, breathing heavily with squinted eyes.

"Mother?" The more she refuses to answer me, the angrier I get. *"Why* do you always do this?"

"Do *what?*" she barks.

"Why did you have to make everyone so uncomfortable, causing a public standoff in the store like that?"

"They need to be uncomfortable—that *Fern McKenzie!*"

This shocks me, as my seething mother just spewed out the woman's name as if she actually knows her. "Mother, forget Mrs. McKenzie. Chase is my friend. I like him, and he has been very kind to me. And he's the *police chief*, for goodness' sake! I just don't understand why you'd react like that."

"Because they deserve it!" she spits. "And trust me—that man is no friend of yours. I can tell you that!"

"Mother, you don't even know them." I fear the incident with Garrett this morning has caused my mother to lose her mind.

"Oh, I know them all right," she says with evil-sounding gravel in her voice. "And trust me—what I know, I don't like!"

"How in the world do you know them, Mother? You rarely ever came to the Topsail. How can you make such judgments on people you don't even know?"

"Why don't you ask *them* about the judgments *they* make? I swear, Destiny! You are so naïve!"

"Naïve about what, Mother? You know, you are really scaring me now."

"Oh, no! What oughta scare you is the fact that that woman's child is now a *police chief*, of all things. They've probably brought back public lynching!"

"Okay, Mother! That's enough!" She is taking this drama way too far. "I think you may be wrong about Chase. He has been nothing but a kind and generous man to me."

"Oh, really? Well, watch your neck. The apple doesn't fall far from the lynching tree."

"Oh, Mother." I'm exasperated.

"Did your 'kind and generous' friend remind you about that time you two kids were fishing on your grandfather's beach. Just two little innocent kids, for God's sake, fishing, and in storms that white witch, Fern McKenzie, marching her nary ass across our property, yelling at that poor little boy to *'Git off that nigger beach'*? Huh? You remember that? That dragon nearly tore that poor child's ear off, dragging him across the sand like the trailer-park heathen that she is!"

"Whoa ... whoa, Mother. Wait a minute. You're talking too fast. I—"

"And what nerve! That was *our* beach. Her little trailer-park–trash son had no business in our neighborhood anyway, much less running his dirty little bare feet across our property!" Punctuating her point with a dramatic gesture of the hand, Mother swerves the car off the road before swerving it back on it again.

"Mother, slow down, please!" My head is whirling as fast as her red-lipsticked mouth is still running. She continues cursing and condemning the McKenzies with every breath in a determined litany. But I cannot hear her words for listening to my own inner voice and remembering scenes of a day and a boy long ago that I still wish I could forget. But that boy could not be my new friend Chase. No way. I remember the boy's name now. It was Chip, not Chase. My mad mother is mistaken.

But try telling her that. She is still fuming and running off at the mouth, while I am still confused and numb, stunned by all that I have just seen, heard, and suddenly remembered. But, surely, Police Chief Chase— that Adonis running in the sunset, that golden man with the sea-green eyes in the Hawaiian shirt, that kind cop who shared his fish and has a jacked up stencil on his squad car—that man could not possibly be that same little boy I was forever forbidden to see. Could it really be him? No, I remember—that boy's name was Chip. I don't remember a Chase back then, but I do remember that fateful day with a boy named Chip.

I was a child, and it was the first time I'd ever heard the "N" word. I never dreamed it was a thing a friend's mother would say. My family forbade me to ever play with Chip again. But that didn't stop us. We'd sneak and play anyway, deep in the marshes by the sound, hidden from the prejudiced eyes of a Jim Crow South. Every summer we would meet and together seek secret hiding places to play to avoid racial trouble. And as we grew, so did our secret love.

I remember the first time Chip kissed me. We were two preteens, madly in love. It was under a full moon and in the shadows of the marsh trees. He had been sucking on peppermint candy as he rode his bike to meet me. I still taste his wet peppermint lips as I remember kissing them to this day.

"I do have reason to be angry." Mother takes a deep breath and shakes her head. She grips the steering wheel and says, "There's just so much you don't know, Destiny. That boy's mother brings back so many hurtful memories for our family—our whole community. Memories that have made me hate this place as much I hate white folks. I couldn't stand coming here."

"I always thought it was the sand."

"No, it's the *crackers!*" she hisses.

"Mother, please. I hate that word, and I don't think—"

"Well, it's not only that you don't *think*, my dear; you just don't *know* all the things that your father and I have protected you from all these years. We never wanted to see you hurt by some of life's realities. Clearly, we're not doing a very good job of that anymore. But trust me; that Fern McKenzie would rather see you swinging by your neck from a tree than making it in this world, much less being all chummy with her police son."

Her words sting so badly that they bring tears to my eyes. I do not want to believe that my own mother is just as hateful and racist as Chase's. I can't fathom that the little boy I admired so much—the boy I was never allowed to play with, even speak with, and was told to forget—was actually a young Chase. Is Chip really there inside Adonis somewhere?

"Oh, your father and I protected you all right." Mother is relentless in making her point. "Like that time you couldn't go to Tanglewood Park. Do you remember that?"

"Remember it? *Couldn't* go? You wouldn't let me! I never forgave you for that. It was such a big deal—our class picnic. We were all so excited and couldn't wait to go to Tanglewood Park. And for some reason, you took me out of school that day to go visit Grandma and Grandpa instead. Do you know how much it hurt me the next day to have to listen to my classmates share all the good times they had at the park without me? I was the only one in the class who didn't go."

"Because you *couldn't* go!" Mother snaps. "You were the first and only colored child in that kindergarten."

"Yeah, and ...?" I hate it when she uses the "C" word.

"Well, do you also recall that little note your teacher pinned on your sweater the day before the field trip?"

"Yes, I remember how excited and proud I was when she pinned it on me. It was probably one of those reminders of what to pack, what I should wear, when to meet the bus—*if* you had let me go!"

"Ha!" Mother shakes her head and rolls her eyes as if I still have no clue. She stares off somewhere, where the memories still haunt her. "My darling, let me tell you exactly what that little note read." She leans in. "It said, *'Destiny will not be allowed to attend the class picnic tomorrow because Tanglewood Park's policy does not allow coloreds or Jews.'*"

"What?" I say in utter disbelief. "You're kidding me, right?"

But the look in my mother's eyes says she is not. She is telling the brutal truth, and I see that it hurts her as much as it does me.

"That's unbelievable, Mother. And all this time ... I thought ..."

"Yes, you thought your mother was an ogre, when I was only trying to protect you. Your father and I desperately tried to hide those terrible things from you. But it was a part of the times, and they were some dangerous times—and not much has changed. We were among the first of colored families to integrate the all-white schools and all-white neighborhoods, and a lot of times we had far more education and money than they did, which made it even tougher for us, because they resented that. But we persevered by knowing which side of the road to stay on and which kind of troubles to stay out of."

"So my being friends with Chip—or Chase, or whoever—is *trouble?*"

"Well, in times like that we just couldn't take a chance, Destiny. It could be a life-or-death matter. Racism ran rampant down here. It still does to this day, if you ask me. Remember that laws may change but some attitudes don't. So our family, along with the McKenzies, all agreed that the two of you could never see each other again. It was too much trouble, especially after that ugly day when his mother showed herself on your grandfather's beach like that! Oh, we vowed to do whatever it took to keep you away from that boy and that trash he calls family."

"Oh, Mother …" I am disturbed beyond words. "How could you?"

"Well, what did you want us to do? Feed you to the wolves? Just give our daughter away to a poor white trailer-park boy? Oh no. No way. Not under our watch. We did what was right."

"What? Being racist and classist? And so what do you want me to do now, Mother? Not be his friend because he grew up the poor boy of racist parents when he has been nothing in the world but kind and accepting of me? Yes, what his mother did was wrong—it was very wrong—but what you are doing is wrong too. Don't you see that? And sometimes attitudes do change, Mother. What you are doing to poor Chase after all these years is horribly unfair. If anybody's attitude should change, maybe it's yours. Really, Mother, why should Chase be held accountable for that? The past ignorance of his parents does not define who Chase is today. Why should either of us be punished for the ignorance of our parents?"

Mother shoots me a look like a dart. "Now, don't you go disrespecting me too!" she hisses as we pull up to the beach house. She slams on the brakes and comes to a skidding halt. Frustrated, she throws the gear into park and sits there, breathing hard and blinking.

"Mother, look, I'm not in kindergarten anymore. I'm a grown woman now. I can make my own decisions—right or wrong—whether you like them or not. I can make my own choices—"

"And *what*? You choose *Chip*?"

"*Chase!*"

"*Whoever!*"

"*Exactly!*"

I cannot muster the strength to argue with Mother anymore, as I am too distracted, noticing that the rental car is still not back, which means Garrett has still not returned home. Where in the world is my husband?

I look across the stubby brush leading to the highway in hope of catching a glimpse of Garrett heading home in the rental car, but all I see across the blades of blowing sea grass is the trailer park, where the forbidden boy once lived next to the shady marshes where we hid to play. I realize at this moment that the boy and the bittersweet memories of our forbidden love still live in my heart today. I somberly remember all I have long tried to forget.

"Well, looks like Garrett is still on the lam." Mother sucks her teeth and shakes her head as she grabs her bags and gets out the car. "You really know how to pick 'em, Dee. You really know how to pick 'em."

I hold my tongue and my bags and walk up the stairs to the house. Aunt Joy is inside watching TV.

"Hey, Aunt Joy. Garrett never came back, huh?"

"Yes, he came back," Aunt Joy says with a troubled look in her eyes. "But then he left again. Said they had an emergency at work, and he felt it better that he help out there than stay here with all the tension. He says he left you a note."

"Mm-mm-mm." Mother shakes her head again. "Well, I sure am glad your father slept through it all. He is not going to like this one bit."

"Well, Mother, he's the one who told Garrett he could leave!"

"Well, he didn't really *mean* it. I swear, I wonder about that husband of yours."

"You don't like my husband because he stands up for himself. You don't like my friend because he is white and was poor and grew up in a trailer. What *do* you like, Mother?"

I could not care less about the look of anger growing on my mother's forever unappeasable face. I could not care less about anything right now. I go to the bedroom that I was to have shared with my husband for what was to have been a wonderful, relaxing, and bonding holiday weekend. I fling myself across the empty bed that still smells like Garrett. There's a note stretched across the pillow that reads:

> Hey, baby—
>
> I couldn't wait for you any longer. Didn't want your Pops to be awake when I left. The new guy, Stevie, is freaking out on the desk and he really needs me, so I'm going to help out at work while you hang with your family. It's better this way. Take your time, and get some rest and beach time. Sorry for the way things turned out with your folks.
>
> Love you,
> Garrett

So much for that chance to talk about saving our marriage.

I roll over and cry myself to sleep.

Chapter Thirteen

GARRETT CALLS FIRST THING THIS MORNING TO LET ME KNOW HE MADE it back to New York safely and was already at work on the assignment desk this Memorial Day. He claims he worked the overnight shift last night and was back at it again today, as he was gathering footage of the holiday celebrations from across the country. I told him he should have stayed for the annual Topsail Island fish fry today. He found that quite amusing.

Mother and Daddy have gone to the mainland for antique shopping, while Aunt Joy is sitting on the beach under a big umbrella, shaded from the sun. She is totally absorbed in another juicy romance novel. I can always tell when she gets to the good part. She nibbles her nails. I decide to join her, as I could use a relaxing day to catch a few rays on the beach.

It is a beautiful afternoon. The sun's reflection sparkles on the ocean, dancing on the lazy blue sea. A few porpoises play just yards from the shore. I remember swimming right along with them when I was a kid. The pelicans soar above in Top-Gun formation. I appreciate the simplicity of life and nature down here, away from the madness of New York. I find I have sorely missed Topsail Island.

"I knew he'd find a way to get that gal!" Aunt Joy chuckles as she snaps closed her novel and moves out from under the umbrella to sit on the sand next to me. "Oooo—that was a good one."

"You love your romance, Aunt Joy."

"Yes, I do." She smiles and turns her face up toward the sun.

We sit here catching rays, not saying a word, just enjoying this peaceful moment by the sea, dreaming of romance. Finally, Aunt Joy breaks the silence.

"So … your mother tells me you ran into our fine police chief again."

"Yes, but try convincing her that he's fine," I say with a sneer. "Aunt Joy, Mother has this crazy idea that the police chief is that little boy on the beach that day—remember Chip? The boy I couldn't see? Well, I keep telling her the chief's name is not Chip; it's Chase."

"Well, he changed it," Aunt Joy interrupts matter-of-factly. Then, she turns to look me in the eye. "Chase *is* that little boy, Destiny. And no matter how much of a fool his mother may be, Chase is not at all like that. He's a good man. I don't care what your mother says."

"So it's true. It's him."

"Yes, Destiny, and unless you got hit by a bad case of denial, you know in your heart it's him. And I'm glad the two of you can finally meet again today, under different circumstances, when things aren't as … well, crazy, you know. You don't have to pretend you don't know each other anymore. It's a new day."

I feel my heart and head pounding as fiercely as the sea. A rush of memories and emotions come flooding back, set free by what I was pretending not to know. I also feel tricked by fate. Was it easier not knowing?

"He sure had a thing for you, kiddo," Aunt Joy says with a wink. "And I want you two to be friends, to stick together this time. He's a good man, and you never know when you might need a police chief on your side."

"Why?" I ask, even though my heart leaps at the idea.

"Well, one day I won't be here anymore, and I'll leave Tranquility to you. This will one day be your home to carry on for the family, and I want to leave here knowing you'll be okay. That you have a community of your own."

Oh, Aunt Joy …" I feel a sting of tears at the thought of Aunt Joy going anywhere. "Please don't talk that way. You're going to be here forever. Plus, the beach house should go to Mother and Daddy."

"Huh!" Aunt Joy scoffs. "Your parents would much rather sell this place for a king's ransom and a one-year tour of Europe. No, I want Tranquility to remain in the family, and only someone who loves it as dearly as you can do that. And I want you to have a good friend in Chase. I know he'll look after you and Tranquility."

"But we haven't known each other since we had to hide to play, remember?"

"Yes, but he still came 'round here every once in a while, asking for me but really looking for you. Your folks had a fit when they finally figured that out. Your mother told him to never come back and made me promise I wouldn't tell you he was looking for you. Well, now you're both grown, and I can tell you whatever I want, and you can do whatever you want. I hope you'll be friends."

I'm so stunned I can't answer. My heart's beating fiercely; I fear Aunt Joy might hear it. My head is in a whirlwind.

"Life is a funny thing, isn't it, Deedle Dee?" Aunt Flo muses, looking out over the ocean. "Time just keeps moving on. Hm. It's a new day, Destiny; it's a new day."

"I guess so," I respond.

"Well, I'm going in now, kiddo." Aunt Joy gathers her belongings. "Don't stay out here turning into a crispy critter all day. Don't you have a fish fry to go to?"

"Yes. Yes, I suppose I do," I say. "Don't you want to go?"

"Oh, no." She waves her hand. "I need to stay right here and rest a bit."

"You sure you're okay, Aunt Joy?" It's so unlike her not to want to join me to mingle at a good fair and hobnob with other island residents. "Can I get you anything?"

She shoos me away. "Naw. I got a brand-new novel, and I'm gonna start it tonight."

"I see," I say, yet still I'm suspicious. "Okay, I'll pack up and come with you."

We head back to the beach house to clean up as I wonder what in the world to wear to a country fish fry. I decide on a white sundress and flat gold sandals. Mother and Daddy are still not back from their afternoon of antique shopping. Daddy probably took Mother out to dinner on the mainland, so I decide to head over to the fish fry alone. I'm eager to find Chase. I have to talk with him. I want to hear his side of our story.

Chapter
★ Fourteen

I AM JUST ONE AMONG THE SCORES OF FOLKS WHO HAVE COME OUT TO support the local police department and its annual fish fry. Bands are playing, fish are frying, and the laughter of friends and families fill the air. I head into the crowd and smell the sweet aroma of fresh barbecue. Unlike in New York, here in North Carolina, "barbecue" is a noun, specifically referring to our finely chopped pork, cooked with a vinegar or tomato base, and usually served on a warmed hamburger bun with coleslaw, hot sauce, and a side of hush puppies. Now that's what I call home. We love to share our barbecue, even at a fish fry.

Organizers have set up tents of carnival games and pony rides for the children. A few old women sit underneath one tent, arguing good-naturedly over which one of their families has passed down the best pecan, peach, or blackberry cobbler recipe. Old men argue over the barbecue pit, where a huge pig on a rotisserie has captured the attention of some mischievous little boys—they seem to enjoy tossing pieces of straw into the flames and watching them curl and burn. The little girls love the ponies.

My hopeful eyes pan the crowd of happy islanders as I search for Chase—I can't wait to reconnect with him again. I don't know what it is, but from the moment I first met him—even as a child—there has been an indescribable electricity between us. He touches something deep inside my soul, as he always has.

"Hey, hey! Miss! You, over there!" A clown, sitting in a cage, is calling me. He is in a checkered outfit and has a big red grin painted on his face. He wears a foolish hat with a big yellow daisy and a bumblebee dancing around his head on a long spring wire. The crazy clown is perched atop a collapsible bench that will drop him into a pool of cold water if a ticket-buying patron can accurately throw a softball and hit the tin plate target that releases the apparatus. People are buying up the tickets, excitedly champing at the bit for their chance to "Dunk the Clown." In a booming character voice, the clown reminds passersby that the tickets are tax deductible, because the money goes to the local battered women's shelter.

The clown is also talking a lot of smack. He seems to be taunting everyone in the crowd, including the island's mayor.

"Mayor, we'll forgive you for everything if you can dunk me! *Awwwwww!*"

The comedic clown charms his captive audience. Folks are howling with laughter as he playfully picks on different local residents in the crowd.

"Harold Mitchell, is that you? When you gonna get that tractor in your front yard fixed? How you gonna dunk a clown when you can't even fix a tractor?"

The crowd is in stitches, leading me to believe that this is an ongoing story around here.

"Oh-oh, he-e-e-e-re comes *Junior!*" The clown has now targeted a tall and lanky teenage boy. The kid stops in his tracks. His face turns as red as the clown's big nose.

"Now, all y'all know this boy can throw a ball—baseball champ at Topsail High!"

The crowd applauds the kid. A few guys around him pat him on the back and ruffle his hair. A young girl in the crowd swoons. I smile, knowing a summer crush when I see one.

"But let's see if the champ can dunk a *clown!* Awwww!"

The clown seems to know everybody and their business. This may be why they're lined up to dunk him. I decide to move on; after all, I have a good-looking police chief to find and some finger-lickin' southern food to eat. Where are those spots? Where is that man?

"Yoo-hoo! Hey, little lady, you gon' buy a ticket?" I hear the clown calling out in a silly southern voice to some poor girl as I continue to move, head down, through the crowd.

"*You,* lady, *you!*"

People around me start to giggle. I look up and realize that that crazy-ass clown is actually calling out to me again.

"C'mon, sweetheart, lemme see whatchu got. *Awww*—you can't

throw no ball, sister. Go on back home!" He shoos me away with his hand. The crowd starts chanting, "Dunk the clown! Dunk the clown!" Then, one man steps up and surprisingly hands me three softballs.

"Dunk that clown!" he says.

The crowd cheers. The clown jeers. I look at the three softballs in my hand.

"G'wan now!"

"Poor little girl! She can't throw no ball! Where's my Barbie doll?" Waaaaa!"

Oh, that clown is going to pay now!

I step up to the plate as the crowd goes wild. I am trying to tap into any memory of softball anywhere in my life so I can remember how to throw this damn thing. The charity that protects and houses battered women and children gets the extra dollars when we dunk the clown, and so help me, God, for that cause alone this clown is going down tonight.

"Whatchu gon' do, little girl?" the blabbermouth clown chides. "Show me your big old muscles."

I focus, zeroing in on that tin plate, imagining it's the face of every man who has abused a woman. I think of Grossman and the cops that shot Thomas, but mostly I think of Garrett and Eve—and I rear back and throw!

The softball flies through the air as the crowd brings their excitement to a crescendo. It slaps against the back canvas of the pitching stand, missing the tin target by a long shot.

The clown is on fire, laughing and heckling and slapping his checkered knee as he taunts me into another try at victory.

I wind up, lean back, and throw!

Bam!

This time I almost cream the clown. The softball curves more like a hardball and careens directly toward the clown's head. Had it not been for his quick reflexes and that strong cage, that clown might have dropped all right—dropped dead!

The crowd utters a collective "Whoa!" in surprise and relief. The clown knows that I am serious, and he becomes even more obnoxious, even more grating with his whooping, and hollering, and clownish gesturing.

"C'mon, sister! Hit me! *Wi-i-i-ind* it up." He mocks a crazy pitcher on the mound.

"Dunk the clown!" The chanting crowd is hopeful. So am I.

I walk up to a face-down with the clown, final ball in hand. He is going nuts in that cage, and I want to shut his mouth so badly. I wind back with all my might and determination and throw.

The ball flies from my hand, whirling with high speed toward its tin target. Everything seems to be moving in slow motion and then ... *bing!*

The clown falls with a big splash. The crowd goes wild. Between that softball hitting that tin plate's sweet spot, that clown hitting the water, and the crowd's victorious roar, this is the best day I've had in I don't know how long.

Even the drenched and humbled clown is clapping, standing waist deep in cold water, with his makeup and wig dripping wet. His little hat with the dancing flower and spring-mounted bee floats atop the water.

"Good girl!" yells the clown. I wave good-bye and turn to walk away. Then the clown calls out, "I really *thank ya*, ma'am!"

My heart suddenly skips a beat. My skin tingles. I stop, spin around, and take another look. The dunked clown is climbing out of his water pit, with his costume clinging to his very fit swimmer's body. The clown is "Adonis"—it's Chase!

I make my way through the crowd and over to the pool where Chase is now drying off with a big towel. He has taken off his shirt, his skin glowing golden in the setting sun. I cannot help but take notice of his strong, cut, muscular arms.

"Hey!" I say as I approach him. "I had no idea that was you in that get up, Chief."

"Hey, yeah, it's me all right! And, boy, do you have one curveball," he says, laughing. "Almost as hard as your mom's." Chase extends his hand. "How you doin' today, Miss Dee?"

"Well, to tell you the truth, I'm still a little bit in shock right now," I confess. "First of all, I can't believe I actually dunked you." I feign a hint of guilt. "Then the situation in the grocery store earlier today, and then to learn—and to remember ... nuh ... but I ... I swear ... I didn't know. I had no idea at first ... that it was you."

The clown's bright red lips curl into a wide grin. "Well, I may not have recognized you either at first, Dee, but I swear I never forgot that little girl."

I feel a strong bolt of electricity surge through my body. I never knew until this moment how much I've secretly longed for those words and dreamed of this moment. I don't know whether to cry tears of anguish or joy.

"Miss Destiny, I gotta tell ya, you and fate can sure throw some mighty curveballs." Chase slides off his drenched clown wig. He is just as gorgeous as ever, even in a wet clown suit.

"I didn't hurt you, did I?" I ask.

"Hurt me? Pshaw!" Chase slings his towel over his broad, bronzed shoulder. "You don't know who you're talking to, girlie! I fight the bad guys, remember?"

Chase jumps into the same cartoonish crime-fighter pose that he did as a kid, back when he was Chip. It's even funnier now, with him in a white clown face, huge red nose and lips, and a stocking cap on his head. But those bright sea-green eyes still sparkle as he smiles down at me in the amber sunset.

"Hey, how 'bout you wait right here, and I go change into some dry clothes, and we go out there and find you your victory meal—some good ol' North Carolina chopped barbecue and some swaller-yer-tongue fried spots. How 'bout that? I mean, good golly, I *know* you like them. I betcha everybody on the beach knows that by now—this girl loves her some spots!"

"Are you clowning with me again?" I tease.

Chief Chase McKenzie winks at me and heads into the dressing tent to change. I linger here, waiting for him, blushing like a teenage girl with a summer crush.

Chapter ✦ Fifteen

CHASE AND I ARE BECOMING FAST FRIENDS AS WE TOOL AROUND THE fairgrounds, laughing and eating just about everything in sight. Oh, the savory taste of that North Carolina barbeque, the amazing freshness of the fried spots, and now, finally, our splurge on sweet caramel apples rolled in salty peanuts. Chase is so much fun. I enjoy being with him. He is a great escape—and a very attractive escape to top it off. Chase seems to know everybody, and everybody seems to know Chase. Even more, they seem to genuinely like him. He has an electric, country-boy charm about him, with a friendly one-liner for every soul he comes across—even when he's not dressed up as a clown. It's so refreshing to laugh.

"Now, this here young lady cooks the best chocolate pecan pie in the county. Isn't that right, Mrs. Jordan?" Chase gently pats the shoulder of an elderly woman who just grins up at him and nods, yet another woman taken by Chase's charms. "Mrs. Elynora Jordan's been baking those pies since I was a little boy." He leans over and kisses the beaming Mrs. Jordan on the cheek. "And I thank ya, ma'am."

"Aw, Chase, you go on now," the blushing old woman says with a chuckle and playful pat on his shoulder.

"Nice to meet you, Mrs. Jordan," I say.

"Pretty girl," Mrs. Jordan teases Chase in a loud whisper. "You be a good boy now, ya hea'?"

Can she detect this undeniable energy between us?

"Oh, I will, Mrs. Jordan," Chase responds. "Don't you worry about me."

Chase gently nudges me in a new direction, and we head toward a booth where two large black women in crisp white aprons are frying up batches and batches of golden brown spots in huge cauldrons of boiling grease. Hungry, wide-smiling onlookers gather, as they watch these proud women preparing their seasonal gifts from the sea.

"Ah, here we go. Time to make one clown-dunkin', spot-lovin' woman happy!" Chase leads me to a picnic table. "Dinner for two, this way!"

"C'mon, Chief," yells out one of the cooks. "Get in the front of the line. You get 'po-po privileges' 'round hea'." The two women laugh and wave Chase over.

"Be right back." He squeezes my elbow, winks at me, and then darts off into the crowd. This cop is quite a pistol.

I look at all the folks milling around the fairgrounds. There are very few brown or black faces, leading me to wonder if things really have changed that much since the segregated summers I lived here as a kid. Back then, Chase and I would not have been as comfortable hanging out in public together like this, not even as good friends. It's hard to believe that at one time it was against the law for us to be together.

"Hope you didn't get up there to the big city and forget your southern sweet tea." The chief has his hands full with two oversized Styrofoam cups full of what many call "Southern nectar." A big slice of lemon floats among the ice cubes.

"Are you kidding?" I ask, grabbing one of the sweet teas. "Gimme that tea!"

Chase grins at me and asks, "Hey, how'd you learn to throw a curveball like that anyway?"

"Oh, I don't know," I reply. "Just grew up a tomboy, I guess."

"Yeah, I remember; you sure could fish too." Chase chuckles. "Only girl I knew who wasn't afraid to bait a hook with a bloodworm."

One of the big lady cooks interrupts our conversation by calling out, "Two fried spot dinners for the chief!" We turn to find her holding two paper plates overloaded with mounds of golden-brown spots. I think I have died and gone to fish heaven.

"All right!" Chase claps his hands, rubs them together, and grins like a schoolboy. "Well, I thank ya, ma'am. Mighty nice of you, Miss Mary. You have made Miss Destiny here one happy lady. She's visitin' us from New Yawk City. Yankees don't eat like this!"

Miss Mary radiates her broad smile. "Well, hello there, Miss Destiny. How you doing today?"

"Just fine." I smile back.

Chase waves at someone in the crowd across the way. " Excuse me, ladies, I've got to say hello and maybe even apologize to the mayor over there. I'll be right back. Need anything?"

I laugh and answer, "No, I have plenty to deal with here."

Chase hops up from the table and moves his way into the crowd.

Miss Mary stands there, bright as sunshine. "Well, it sure is nice to meet you, Miss Destiny. Need some Texas Pete hot sauce for your fish?"

I chuckle. "Naw, I'm sure they're fine just like they are."

Miss Mary leans over and squints at me. "Why, now, you not li'l Miss Destiny, from Dr. Maurice Newell's family, are you?"

"Yes, that's me," I reply. "Dr. Newell was my grandfather."

"Well, lawd ha' mercy, chile! Let me look atcha. Lord, you done growed up to be a pretty li'l ol' gal. Only li'l girl I ever knowed named Destiny. Idn't that something." She clucks her tongue and shakes her head. "Well, just look at you. I used to love yo' granddaddy—and your grandmama, Miss Nellie, too. They was some good, kind people, and lawd, did yo' granddaddy love him some spots! Ha! Just like you!" The large-framed woman lets out a hearty laugh that seems to come from the depths of her round belly. "I'd cook him and your grandmama up some spots in exchange for a little teeth fixin' now and then, ya know. Well, antyway—I'm Mae Mae." She wipes her hands on her apron and quickly extends one.

"Nice to meet you, Miss Mae Mae," I reply. "Yes, my grandfather was a very kind man." I remember how much my grandpa also loved to fish. *"Always have two fishing poles,"* he'd remind me, *"just in case you meet a friend."*

"Nice to see you come back home, Miss Destiny." Miss Mae Mae radiates her southern warmth. "Y'all young folks enjoy yo'selves, hear?"

"Hey, let's eat these spots before they get cold," Chase says as he hops back into his seat next to me on the picnic table bench.

"God bless this meal! Amen!" I say to the heavens as we lunge into my favorite fish feast.

"A-men!" Chase takes a big bite of the crunchy seafood. "Mm-mm-good!"

Chase makes me laugh. I love the way his eyes twinkle; I love that he's curious and caring about everything; that he is so interested in so much outside of himself—including me.

"Hey, you like blue crabs?" Chase asks.

"Do I?" I reply. "I love them. I grew up catching them, using half-rotten chicken necks as bait, right back there in Stump's Sound." I point toward the intercoastal waterway on the backside of the island.

"Stump's Sound?" Chase asks incredulously. "I grew up crabbing in Stump's Sound too."

"Really?"

"Yep, started crabbing around six years old. A crab wasn't safe from us kids. Hey, how come I never saw you back there with us kids?"

And immediately, both Chase and I know the answer—it was only because of our differences in skin color. Black and white kids played separately growing up in these parts. My folks feared that with so much Ku Klux Klan activity in the eastern part of the state that it was downright dangerous for a black child to venture too far from home. In fact, my best friend, Macie, a nice Irish girl I grew up with, could never enjoy a summer vacation with me at our beach house, because my folks feared she might be called a "nigger lover"—or worse.

And it wasn't just white folks with prejudices. Some black folks down here had them too. They wanted nothing to do with the neighboring "trailer-park people," as they referred to the poor white families living in mobile homes behind this black, bourgeois community of doctors, lawyers, and morticians. Mother would stare out our kitchen window in disgust at the trailer park across the street. It interrupted her view of the sound. "All we need is one good hurricane to take away those dreadful trailers," she'd say. Did she ever think about what might happen to those poor families living inside them? Could they even survive a strong gust of wind in their flimsy little trailers?

I feel a sting of guilt that my own mother could be so mean. Chase must have been among those poor barefooted children across the street that my mother warned me to stay away from, claiming they were teaming with ringworms, lice, and all sorts of other horrid maladies. "Plus, they smell like wet chickens," she'd caution, much rather having me fear them than play with them. And their parents, reportedly describing us as "uppity porch monkeys," would rather their kids avoid us like the plague as well.

The more I get to know Chase, the more I see what a horrible shame that was. We are so much more alike than different. And as we share story after story, we find that we have enjoyed so many of the same pleasures on the tiny island we both love. Why could we have not openly shared this friendship all of our lives? Why were we not allowed to share love?

Bellies full, Chase and I join the crowd that is eagerly heading toward the beach, now that the sun has set. Country folks, with their plastic lawn chairs and quilts and blankets underarm, make their way to their favorite spots on the sand for what Chase describes as "one of the greatest fireworks shows on earth—country style."

"Every year, Farmer Jones floats out that big barge that he and his workers made, and they blow off fireworks that rival Gucci's up there in New Yawk."

"*Grucci*," I automatically correct. "It's actually Grucci fireworks, after the Grucci family."

Chase shrugs, unconcerned. "Gucci, Grucci—whatever, Farmer Jones's fireworks are spectacular—at least to us country folks. Just you wait and see." Chase looks up at the orange and golden sky in great anticipation. He looks so much like that innocent little boy again, so full of wonder and surprise—raw, real, and, as always, extremely charming.

I feel that even though time has moved on, I have known Chase all my life. I feel as if we are meant to be together. We fit. Just like from the very beginning, it feels right.

"C'mon, let's head this way." He nods toward a clearing in the crowd. He grabs my hand as we dodge our way toward the shore and over a big sand dune. His hand feels bigger than I expected and stronger; his fingers are thick, his palms callused. "I want you to meet some friends," Chase throws over his shoulder as he hastens his steps. I follow, admiring the back of the police chief's perfectly sun-bleached hair and tanned neck.

Across the beach, a group of young people gather around a huge quilt. They seem to be close friends; laughing and teaming with excitement as they glance at the darkening sky in anticipation of the big fireworks show ahead. Everyone is charged as day gives way to night.

"Hey! There's Chase!" a chubby girl in the group squeals. Everybody turns and bursts into a round of cheers. "Woooo-hoooo! Chase! Chase the clown! Chase the clown, and we watched him drown!" They whoop and holler and slap high-fives. They applaud and then chide a humble Chase, with pats on the back and congratulations for having the nerve to play that crazy, caged clown and getting dunked. Chase takes the friendly fire with humility.

One burly fellow turns to me. "Hey, aren't you the gal who dunked him?" he asks, his grin widening over his sunburned face.

"Well, yeah, that was me," I say, now feeling like the one on the hot bench.

"Hey, Chase," he yells out. "Arrest this woman for cruelty to clowns!"

Chase and his pals howl with laughter. It's so contagious that I cannot help but join in.

"Awl-right, everybody!" A fat man in a Lacoste shirt, plaid Bermuda shorts, Topsiders with no socks, and a straw plantation hat, holds a megaphone to his mouth. He is standing on a crude wooden platform, apparently built just for this special summer occasion. "It's time for the big show, y'all," he continues. "Farmer Jones is promising some mighty spectacular surprises this year, so sit back and relax and enjoy the fireworks! But first, I want to thank all of y'all for coming out with your families and friends—and hey, maybe you even got to meet some new friends."

Chase and I exchange a warm glance. He is my new old friend, for sure.

"Y'all having fun yet?" The man behind the megaphone eggs on the crowd, and the people respond with more whoops and hollers and whistles, removing any doubt that these country beach folks are having a blast as the local bluegrass band strikes up again.

Chase nudges me. "You having fun yet, New York?"

"Yes, Chief," I respond. "I'm having a ball. It's so nice being home, connecting. Seeing you again after all this time is amazing. It's nice seeing so much of where I grew up—the things I forgot I missed, being so busy with my career and all."

I feel the blood rush to my face.

"Well, you have truly been missed, Miss Dee," Chase says.

"Well, I thank ya, sir," I jest, mimicking his distinct cadence.

Then suddenly, there's a loud *boom*! And the night sky is filled with brightly colored ribbons of fire. Farmer Jones's famous fireworks show has begun. Chase and I laugh and nudge each other, gawking like children at each brilliant blast.

When the show ends, Chase offers to walk me to my car.

"Chase, why did we call you Chip back in the day?" I ask. "And when did you become Chase?"

"Well, it was just a nickname. You know, like, 'Chip off the old block'?" Chase explains. "That was till I grew up and wanted nothing more to do with my old man, who started using me and my mom as his punching bags. He was one mean, alcoholic son of a bitch."

"And one mean racist too, I hear."

"Yep. That too." Chase shakes his head and looks down at the ground. "He certainly was that too. He was a lot of things, Dee. He did and said some terrible things to people, including to my mom and me. But when I came of age, I swore I'd never be like him. And after he got so drunk that he beat my mama to the point of death, I swore it'd be the last time. After that, I wouldn't have anything to do with him. That's when I switched back to my real name, the one my mama gave me: Chase Monroe McKenzie."

We stand here looking at each other in pregnant pause.

"It's been a long time, hasn't it?" Chase asks in a hushed tone.

"Yes, it has been," I reply. "Way too long. I hate that I have to leave in the morning. There's so much more of the island I'd like to see. It's been so long."

"Listen to me." Chase takes a deep breath and a step closer. "I want you to know that I never really forgot you, Dee. I don't know what all happened way back when—what all our folks and the world did to keep us apart. All I know is that one day we were finally getting close and then you were just gone. You stopped coming back. Miss Joy said you'd gone away to college, then grad school, and then you went off and got married. I thought I'd never see you again. You have no idea how many times I have thought about you over the years, passing by your beach house, wondering where you were, how your life turned out."

"I wish I could say it turned out fine, Chase. But it hasn't." I'm taken aback by how easily my mouth spewed out my sad truth.

Chase nods his head as if he understands. He purses his lips, perhaps detecting how jumbled up my feelings and life must be right now. I hang my head, unable to speak.

"So who's the other man making fireworks go off in your life, DeeDee? Still married to him?"

"Yes," I reply. "At least, I think I am. We're working on it."

"Yeah, I know what you mean," Chase says. He seems melancholy. "We're working on it too, I guess."

"You got married too?" I ask.

"No, but certainly being pushed in that direction." Chase releases a deep sigh. "Her name is Missy. We've been seeing each other for a little while now, but … well, she's a nice girl, comes from a good family and all, but I'm just not convinced she's the one I should marry."

"Why not?"

"Just not the right one. My detective head tells me she's got another agenda going on, but I just don't know what it is yet. Time is on my side right now. I just want us to get to know each other a lot better before rushing into marriage. Just don't want to make a lifelong mistake, you know."

"Trust me—I know. That makes a lot of sense. Take your time, Chase. Everything'll work out for both of us, I'm sure."

"Yeah, I believe you're right." Chase takes my hand and steps closer. "And Dee, you deserve a man who loves you and treats you right. You are a wonderful woman. Make sure that man of yours treats you right."

"I'll do my best, Chase. Thank you." If he only knew the drama that awaits me back in New York.

"I'm always here for you." Chase squeezes my hand. "Your mama may not like that, but I am. I promise I'll keep an eye on the house and your aunt Joy while you're up in New Yawk!"

"I appreciate that, my friend." I give Chase a warm hug. "And again, thank you for everything. This fish fry and this time to reconnect with you were simply wonderful."

"Get home safely now," Chase says tenderly. I can feel his energy radiating from his body through mine as he hugs me back. "Be careful up there in Sin City. And promise me you'll get back to Topsail real soon."

"I will. Good luck to you, Chase. Hope everything works out the way you want."

"Yeah, you too, lady."

"And promise me you'll get that wording right on your police car," I tease.

"Oh, you caught that, did ya?" Chase shakes his head and chuckles as his face turns a bright red. "I will surely get on that, Miss D, first thing in the morning!"

I have to force myself to unlock eyes and energy with Chase. Vacation is over. Time to get back to my work and the harsh realities waiting for me back home.

I pull out of the parking lot and turn onto the little highway, heading back to the beach house to pack up so I can catch my plane to New York first thing in the morning. While I'm sad to say good-bye to my family, Chase, and Topsail Island, I must return to another island—the island of Manhattan, where the looming mysteries surrounding my life, career, and marriage remain unsolved.

Chapter
Sixteen

ARRETT AND I ARE BACK IN THE NEW YORK CITY NEWS RAT RACE AGAIN. I am looking for another big story, as the one about Thomas has long been buried by other breaking news. Garrett and I have barely spent any time together since we got back earlier this week. He seems to be avoiding me, always racing off to get to the assignment desk. We still have not talked about the distance between us and the future of our strained marriage or about all of the family tension we experienced at the beach. Perhaps we will make the time to be together this weekend to make things right. I'll get off work and get home early this Friday night, just as Garrett's waking up to a new weekend. I plan to steal some time with my man.

Garrett is whistling his own rendition of "Volare" when I enter our home. The television is blaring, and dirty dishes are piled in the sink. The scent of the fresh Irish Spring from his shower and the Polo cologne still hangs in the air, and I know my husband is up and running.

"Hey!" I yell out as I enter through the door. "I'm home!"

"In here!" Garrett calls back from the bedroom. I drop my things by the door and pick up a pile of mail as I follow his voice. He is standing over our bed, packing a suitcase full of clothes.

"What are you doing?" I asked, stunned. "Are we going somewhere?"

"Didn't you hear about that riot in Boston?" His mind is already at work. "They say it's a race thing. The brass wants me to fly up there this weekend and check it out."

"Great," I say, disappointed that yet another weekend will come and go without our spending crucial time together.

"Baby, don't look so sad," he says, planting a hard peck on my cheek. Garrett grabs his socks off the dresser and turns back to his packing. "It's a big story."

"I know," I reply.

"So look," he continues nonchalantly. "I'll probably just stay up there over the weekend." Garrett flips his toiletry bag into his duffel, zips it closed, and prepares to leave.

I certainly was not expecting this.

"I've got a lot of work to do," he continues. "And then I thought I'd visit with Jen and her new boyfriend. She lives up there, you know."

"Yes, I know." Duh. Like I don't know where his sister lives?

"So, gotta go, baby. I'll call you."

And with that and another peck on the cheek, my busy husband is gone.

I refuse to allow my haunting suspicions to flare up again, so I try to consider the bright side. A weekend to myself might not be such a bad idea. I could always cook a big southern meal and invite my girlfriends over for a pig-out slumber party. I could take a long, luxurious bubble bath or catch up on my reading. Maybe I'll clean the house and get it shipshape before Garrett gets back. Maybe it's all for the best. Garrett needed a breaking story of his own anyway.

And perhaps he does need to bond with his sister. It's been a while since we've seen Jenny, especially since she met Bradley the Buppie, her new live-in lover. Maybe Garrett is just doing his big-brother duties by checking in on her to make sure she's picked the right guy. That's my Garrett. He adores his little sister, and I'm sure he's looking out for her. Let him be.

I feel guilty for feeling anything other than pride about Garrett's trip to Boston, especially after he was so supportive of me during my hostage story. We have both been under a great deal of stress and pressure lately. I will not take Garrett's sudden absence personally. Instead, I will make the best of this time alone—by not being alone. I'll call my girls.

I need the close comfort of my girlfriends. I miss their company, so I invite the girls over for a Saturday-night dinner and sleepover. I buy lots of wine and vodka, so we have plenty to drink to keep our spirits high and the conversation flowing. I figure I'll treat the girls to my famous fried chicken and whip up some collard greens, wild rice and gravy, my grandmama's melt-in-your-mouth sweet potato casserole, and a batch of delicious homemade jalapeño corn bread, and a pitcher of sweet tea with mint and lemon, just like we do it back home. My New York friends love it when I cook a big down-home country meal, and this Friday night will be the perfect time to forget about our hips, hounds, and husbands and just splurge over our friendship feast. In the spirit of letting it all hang out, I think I'll bake up a nice peach and berry cobbler too.

Perhaps it is in respect to that age-old adage about keeping your friends close and your enemies closer, but I have decided that I also want Eve here among our circle of friends. Eve, Kat, Hope, and me—the four of us, just like we were in the good old days. Maybe I have been hallucinating all this time, convinced that Eve is having an affair with my husband. I have hunches but no solid proof. I admit that I miss her friendship and the way things used to be among us four girls. I would hate to be so insecure that I am wrong about my suspicions and then lose her friendship forever. Maybe I can get a better read on what's really going on during dinner. Maybe it's just my imagination. Sometimes I feel horrible suspecting the two people I love most of possibly causing me the most harm. What if I'm wrong? Even worse, what if I'm right?

Kat sounds so excited over the phone as we make our plans for our four-girlfriend weekend.

"Let's start early," she suggests. "I love your fried chicken, and the sooner I get to it the better!"

"Garrett's out of town, so come any time. Wanna say four o'clock cocktails and dinner at six?"

"Very cool. I'll beat the drums and let Hope and Eve know. See you early for cocktails tomorrow, snookums! Can't wait!"

"Neither can I," I reply. "I so need some girl time."

I hang up the phone and start the plans for our all-girls feel-good southern feast.

Chapter
✦ Seventeen

I AM PULLING OUT THE LAST BATCH OF FRIED CHICKEN WHEN THE doorbell buzzes. I take a quick look around the room to make sure everything is right. The tulips and tuberose I purchased from the corner bodega are opening up nicely. The first round of martinis is waiting. The dinner table is set for the fabulous fearsome four. We are about to have a blast!

"Hurry up!" an impatient Kat demands as I hear bustling at the bottom of the stairs. "Open up that door. I smell something *good!*"

Kat is a woman who knows what she wants. I chuckle at her demanding yet delightful antics, race to the door, and swing it open.

"Hey, girl!" We squeal our delight and excitement that our special night has officially begun. Kat squeezes past me and heads straight to the kitchen. "Where's that fried chicken, girl?"

Hope and I laugh as Kat scurries by. Eve must be coming late—as usual. Hope and I hug each other tightly. Oh, how I have missed these good girlfriend hugs.

"Come on in, Come on in. Dinner is just about ready," I say. "Put your things down over there." I motion toward the "briefcase place" next to the couch.

The girls make themselves at home, pouring themselves some stiff martinis before settling down, barefoot and cross-legged, on the couch in front of our bay window. We chitchat about the latest fashions and the cutest movie stars. We dog-out men, share our latest bargain-hunting heroics, and laugh until our insides hurt. Kat spills the beans on her latest date from hell, as I continue stirring the pots, preparing our thanksgiving dinner. I glance at the stove clock once again. It is almost six o'clock now—two hours after start time—and Eve is still not here. She hasn't even called to offer her typical explanations.

"Well, where in the world is Miss Eve?" I finally ask. "I'm worried about her. She's really late."

"Oh?" Kat looks up at me from her *Essence* magazine. She looks puzzled. "Didn't she call you?"

"Call me?" I shake my head. "No."

"Hmpf. That's funny. She said she'd call you. She leaves tonight."

"She leaves? Tonight?" I spin around, surprised and confused. "Where's she going?"

"To Boston," Kat replies.

"*Boston?*" I ask.

"Yeah, Boston. She said something suddenly came up."

Yeah, like my husband's dick?

Kat has no idea she just dropped a bomb.

"Eve is in Boston?" The words are still stinging and ringing in my ears. "Is that what you said?"

"Yeah, that's what I said." Kat is looking at me like I'm nuts. "She said she was going to call you before she caught the last flight out tonight."

"Well, she didn't!" I angrily snap back and slam my wooden spoon down on the kitchen counter.

"Whoa!" Kat puts up a defensive hand. "Don't get mad at *me*. I wasn't the one who stood you up for dinner. I'm here and I'mma eat *my* chicken." She rolls her eyes.

"She still should have called, Kat," a more level-headed Hope chimes in. "That's just plain rude, especially if your girl went through all the trouble to do all this cooking." She motions toward the dinner table, decorated for a feast for four friends. "Honey, did you check your machine? Are you sure she didn't leave you a message? She said she was going to call you."

"No, she didn't." I am still in shock. "Eve is really in Boston?"

"Yes. Yes. Yes! *Eve is in Boston.* Eve is in Boston. Big deal—let's eat." Kat swoops up her martini and heads for the dinner table.

"Eve is in Boston." I shake my head in utter disbelief.

"How many times are you going to say that?" Kat snaps. "Let's just eat, *please*! That fried chicken smells so good."

The pieces of the puzzle are suddenly starting to fit.

"Garrett is in Boston too," I say.

"And?" Hope doesn't get it.

"Garrett and Eve are in Boston together," I reveal, slowly and surely. "They are having an affair."

Hope's and Kat's heads snap back at the same time. Hope drops her fork. Startled by this sudden revelation, Kat puts down her martini.

"Whoa! Hold up—wait a minute," she says, squinting at me with her head cocked to the side. "*What* did you say?"

I nod my head slowly and stare at the hardwood floor. "Eve and Garrett are having an affair. It's been going on for a while." I look at each of them for any possible signs of their knowing.

"Please don't say something like that if it's not true," pleads Hope. "Are you absolutely sure? I mean, really, do you have any proof?"

"Hope, I found her red hair in my bed, okay?"

"Oh my God!" Hope and Kat gasp, understanding the severe and horrible implications of such a find.

"I found another strand of her red hair in my bathroom—in my tub, no less!"

As my emotions begin to percolate, Kat and Hope sit there, wide-eyed and slack-jawed.

"*And* Maxine told me that Garrett has been giving Eve gifts. I think I even saw some lingerie he gave her. Shit! I just *know*, y'all. To tell you the truth, I have always felt there was something more than an 'old friendship' between Garrett and Eve."

Hope looks shattered, as if she is about to cry. "But, honey, do you really think Eve—*our friend*—would …" She gestures her hands around in circles in the air, unable to speak the words that will annihilate what we have believed to be reality up until now. This particular truth will surely and severely hurt us all. Life, as we know it, will never be the same.

"Everything seems so clear now as I look back. Garrett has changed. Our marriage has changed. I have changed. There are actually times when I feel like I'm dead."

"Oh, honey …" Hope and Kat try desperately to comfort me. I confess to Kat and Hope that I feel that I have truly lost myself and am on the verge of losing my mind. At the same time, I sit here wondering if maybe I'm just hallucinating. I know where everything is in our beautiful brownstone— the clothes, dirty and clean; the bills, paid and unpaid. I even know where Garrett can find his misplaced socks, his golf glove, or lost keys, but ask me where I am, and I could no more tell you than the man in the moon.

The only place I feel alive and important is at work and out with my camera crew, chasing the news of the day through the fast-paced, hard, and dangerous streets of New York City. Here, I'm an eyewitness to the best and the worst of human nature. Funny how I can witness the same things in my own home, behind closed doors that seem so strong, solid, secure, and impenetrable, but, in reality, are not.

Having finally spoken my truth, releasing my worst nightmare and secret to my best girls, I burst into tears. I wail and sputter and cough my way through this heavy burden and unrelenting pain of finally facing my new reality.

Hope and Kat run over and grab me, just before I sink to the floor, wailing aloud like a desperate, wounded animal. My two best girlfriends hold me, locking me tightly within their loving arms, as together we drop to our knees. They will not let me go. They squeeze me even tighter, surrounding me with their love.

Kat keeps repeating, "I got you. I got you, baby," gently whispering the words into my ear so they drum home her message of care and concern and support. I know it is not easy for Kat to surrender to such a caring place. I know it deeply pains her to see me so weak. I know it scares her when it is not her time to be tough.

"Let it out, baby girl." Hope rocks me as I bawl in pain. "Just let it all out. We're here with you. We got you, Des. Just let it *all* out."

And I do, for what seems like days.

Once I have finally calmed down, Kat and Hope move me over to the couch, stretch me out, and cover me with an old quilted throw from back home. We say nothing. We just sit and think in silence, staring out the bay window, as the candles burn down to melted stubs, and our special feast of friends turns cold. We have all lost our appetites.

Finally, Hope breaks our silence. "What are you going to do?" she asks gently. "I don't know, Hope," I reply weakly. "I know I'm not happy. I believe this thing with Eve is Garrett's way of getting even with me for some reason. We are so distant these days." I start to cry again but fight through the pain to continue. "I truly believe in my heart that Garrett has always had a thing for Eve. This is like their unfinished business from college. I don't think I could have stopped them, even if I was aware that something was going on."

"That motherfucker," Kat hisses. "Men are going to do whatever they're going to do, honey. Even if you confront him about it, he's still gon' lie to you right there in front of your face."

"Hey, have you confronted him—or Eve, for that matter?" Hope asks.

"After Maxine told me that Eve said she was feeling uncomfortable with Garrett hitting on her and giving her gifts, I asked her about it."

"Eve?"

I nod.

"Well, what'd she say?" Kat sits on the edge of her seat.

"I asked her if Garrett was doing anything to make her feel uncomfortable, and she said no."

"Did you ask her specifically about the gifts Maxine claims Garrett's been giving her?" Hope asks.

"No," I admit, realizing now that I was afraid of the truth. It hurts too much to know the whole truth sometimes. But perhaps it hurts even more when you don't.

"Well, why the hell didn't you ask?" Kat demands as she stands up, hands on her hips. "I don't know why you didn't bust that bitch's ass right then and there."

"Why not bust Garrett's ass?" Hope throws back at Kat. "He's the one who stepped out of their marriage." She turns back to me. "Oh, how could they do this to you—to us? Garrett should know better. They both should ... oh, dear ..."

"Yeah," Kat agrees. "First rule—you never shit where you eat."

We sit again in silence that speaks so many words. "C'mon, y'all, tell me—you really saw no signs?" I'm desperate to know if I am the last to know. "Please, tell me the truth."

Kat and Hope look at each other and then to me.

"Well? Did you know all along?" I continue to press the question, looking back and forth at my two best friends for anything close to a clue.

"Well, we have noticed that Eve has been acting strange lately, you know, canceling on us at the last minute a lot," Hope says.

"She has also become unusually secretive," Kat adds. "We just figured she had another private dancer. We had no idea the dancer would be Garrett."

"Hm-hm-hm." Hope shakes her head in disbelief.

"But to tell you the stone-cold truth," Kat suddenly pipes up, "I honestly thought the bitch was fucking Maxine."

Hope and I almost fall on the floor.

"*What?*" we respond in unison.

"Seriously. That's why I think Maxine told you that shit about Garrett. She wanted you to get all upset 'cause Garrett's getting in her way."

"Oh, Lord." Hope exhales as she lifts her palms to heaven. "This is too many things."

I sit here simply dumbfounded, speechless, and confused.

"Yeah, honey, Maxine is an old dyke from way back," Kat continues. "She runs a lot of product for Fritz down in the Chelsea projects, and that's how she hooked up with Eve. Eve delivers the goods, you might say."

Hope and I glance at each other for a quick reality check and then turn back to a babbling Kat as we hang on every word.

"You see, Fritz made Maxine like a little kingpin down in Chelsea. She gets a little power, a little extra money for that lazy kid of hers, and she also gets Eve, who of course wants to keep all her meal tickets happy." Kat delivers the punch line with the dramatic flourish of a great gossipmonger.

"Kat," I say, fearing we have gone from bad to far worse. "What in the world are you saying? Frankie and Maxine are sharing Eve—and now with Garrett?"

"I'm just sayin' that as quiet as it's kept, a lot of those nice furs and jewels ain't from Fritz, honey. Huh-uh. They're from Big Momma Maxine."

"Aw, c'mon, Kat," I say.

"Well, we know they ain't from Garrett with his cheap-ass!" Kat snaps.

We all agree.

"Y'all remember that time that asshole gave you them zircons and made you believe they were real diamonds till Hope and I got you to take them fake shits to my jeweler boyfriend, who laughed and told you to get some new earrings *and* a new husband. You should have known something was up with that dickhead then." Kat sucks her teeth and rolls her eyes.

But Kat was right; Garrett had led me to believe that those fake diamond earrings were actually real. They turned out to be just as fake as our marriage.

"I need a drink," I say, exasperated.

"Me too," Kat and Hope chime in and the three of us head off to the kitchen to mix up some very, very strong martinis.

"Have you talked to an attorney?" Kat asks as she pours our drinks. "You know you may need more proof of this affair than just your gut. Any letters, phone calls, pictures of the motherfuckers?"

"No," I sadly reply. "I just can't believe this, y'all. I am so embarrassed. How has my life gotten to this point?" I start to well up again.

Kat throws out a batch of tough love as she hands me a drink. "You'll get through this, girlfriend," she says as she lifts her martini glass. "You gotta get through it to get to it! Here's to gettin' to it. Cheers!"

"Cheers!"

Hope places her cold martini on the table and her warm hand on my shoulder. "Forget about feeling embarrassed in front of us," she reassures me. "We're your girls. We got you. Remember, we're not here to see through each other; we're here to see each other through."

"What have you guys been doing, reading a bunch of self-help books or something?" I tease.

"After it's all said and done, I guess I'm not really all that surprised," Hope admits with her head down. "We all saw from day one how much Eve drooled over Garrett and his big TV position."

"You think all of this is for a TV job?" I ask incredulously.

"Maybe for Eve. She has nothing else," Hope replies.

"'Cept ho-ing," says Kat. "And we still don't know why your idiot husband would risk everything he has by doing something and someone so stupid and so close to home." Kat bites her martini olive and chews it up. "I'm sorry, but you don't work out your problems with your wife by sticking your dick in another woman's pussy!"

"*Kat!*" Hope snaps.

We take long sips of our drinks, staring off into space, in wonder of what we're all now aware of.

"What are we going to do now?" asks an exasperated Hope.

Kat looks up, waits a beat, and then turns to me and says, "Wipe your tears and dress to kill, honeybunch. We're going to Boston."

Chapter
★ Eighteen

THANKS TO HOPE'S JOB AS A FLIGHT ATTENDANT, WE ARE WELL ON our way to Boston after she finagled three last-minute buddy passes on the shuttle from New York. I admit that we are still a bit tipsy from our martinis back at my house, but we've had just enough of the liquid courage to get us on that plane by 8:00 p.m. for our one-hour trek north. We should beat Eve there—but only by an hour or two. We've got to move fast.

I called Garrett's assignment desk before we left for the airport to ask Garrett's boy, Stevie, where they were putting up my husband in Boston for the big race riot story. The girl who answered the phone informed me that there was no one named Stevie on the desk, no one named Stevie in the entire newsroom, but because she knew I was Garrett's wife, she would give me the information. Garrett's staying at the Ritz-Carlton. Once in Boston, we plan to race over to the swanky hotel, all in hope of storming my husband's room, where we highly suspect we'll find him fucking my best friend.

Oh, this'll never work.

"Y'all got your tickets? We've gotta board the plane," Kat barks as we march down the long LaGuardia Airport hallway leading to the shuttle gate. Kat is acting as if we're on some kind of military war mission. Perhaps, in a strange way, we are.

Finally seated on the plane, Kat, still breathless, holds an emergency strategy meeting across the aisle.

"Look, we'll just tell the guy at the front desk that you came to the hotel to surprise your husband for his birthday or something. Hell, you've got proof you're his wife. Wave the ring."

"Okay, Kat," I say, totally exasperated. "This is crazy!"

"No, it's not," Kat spits back in a harsh whisper. "Not if you want that bitch to stop fuckin' your husband."

"Be brave, girl," Hope offers as she gently pats my hand. "We're with you on this. Plus, you need to know once and for all what's really going on between Garrett and Eve—if anything. We're here to support you. Do not worry."

I am less worried about the plane going down.

"What if he's there alone?" I persist. "What'll I say then?"

"Well, then, say you came to surprise him, that you love him, and then you jump his bones, and get your husband back." Kat's cocky smile says she has it all figured out.

"Wouldn't that be a blessing?" Hope always imagines good things. "I mean, I really pray she's not there, and this is all a big misunderstanding."

"Me too," I say under my breath. I look out the window and down at the bright pinhead lights winking from the ground below. These may be my last moments of solitude. We'll soon land in Boston, where I may face one of the biggest challenges of my life.

The tall, slender flight attendant speaks with a silky voice through the airplane's PA system. "Please fasten your seatbelts and prepare for landing. Gather your belongings, and please be careful when opening the overhead bin, as stored items may have shifted during the flight."

Lady, my whole life has shifted during this flight.

We beat the crowd to the taxi stand and hail a cab. None of us says a word as we make our way through the streets of Boston, silently preparing for what, we do not know.

The Ritz-Carlton reeks of elegance. We drive up to the five-star hotel, where a smiling uniformed gentleman with a bright red face approaches our cab and swings open the door.

"Welcome to the Ritz Cah-lton," the man exudes in his Boston accent, which only reminds me of how far away we are from Harlem. "Can I gah-ther your bahgs, ladies?" He offers his impeccable white-gloved hand to help us out. Although the man has a round pouch of a stomach, the brass buttons on his jacket still lie uniformly neat and flat.

"We don't have any bags," Kat replies matter-of-factly as she slowly steps one of her long cocoa legs out of the cab. She lifts her skirt just a bit, and then, with a coy smile, she offers the man her hand. Quite pleased, he helps her out of the car, stealing a quick glance at her lithe legs. As Kat stands, she moves in closer to her unsuspecting prey. With a sexy lift of her eyebrow and a naughty twinkle in her eye, she seductively slips the man a hefty tip inside his left breast pocket. She smiles again, serving the man a sweet little pat-pat-pat on his pocket and then winks as she turns and smoothly floats away. "Thank you, sir," she purrs.

The man's eyes follow the slow and purposeful sway of Kat's voluptuous hips as she saunters her way up the long marble staircase leading to the world-famous Ritz. The uniformed man with the big brass buttons admires Kat as if she's a delicious piece of chicken.

Hope suddenly jabs me with her skinny elbow and together, we swiftly follow our Oscar-worthy girlfriend across the red carpet, up the marble stairs, and through the revolving door. From the scowl on her face, I can tell Hope is annoyed with Kat's bellhop theatrics.

"I do not believe you actually flirted with that big fat man!" Hope snaps at Kat as we tumble out of the revolving door and into the marble lobby. "You looked ridiculous out there, winking and rubbing on him like that."

"Hey, look." Kat spins around to face Hope. "That big fat man might be able to help us later. You never know. Now, let's move. We've got business to handle." Kat turns and struts away toward the front desk.

Hope and I, growing even more nervous, follow Kat.

The hotel lobby is simply breathtaking, with thick, ornate, gilded molding wrapping around the tops of the high marble walls. Angels in white flowing gowns and chubby blushing cherubs in baby-blue sashes gracefully fly around overhead in the oil-painted fresco on the ceiling. Posh Elizabethan furniture, selectively situated on Persian rugs scattered throughout the area, create conversation pits where well-dressed, well-mannered, and surely well-invested guests comfortably lounge, enjoying polite exchanges.

This is amazing. I am shocked that ABC would send my rookie-producer husband to the glitzy Ritz-Carlton Hotel just "so the people shall know." I wonder why he didn't invite me to come along, especially over the weekend, particularly since we're going through this difficult time.

"Good evening, ladies."

I snap out of my awe-induced stupor as an olive-colored man with a thick French accent greets us from behind the mahogany front desk. "May I help you with your reservations?" He grabs a leather ledger, flips through the pages, and then looks up at us with elegant anticipation.

"No," Kat replies sweetly. You could squeeze sugar out of her tone.

"We don't have any." She bats her big brown eyes as she leans in closer over the desk, as if she's letting the man in on something, like a peek at her bosom. "You see, we are actually here to surprise Mrs. Nelson's dear husband, who is staying here at your fine hotel." Kat smiles as she wraps her arm around my shoulder as if to prove that I am really Mrs. Nelson. For some odd reason, I instinctively flash my wedding ring.

"Ah, I see," replies the man, though he is still looking at us with a hint of reservation as we don't have one. I pray he doesn't take us for call girls.

"What is your husband's name?" the man asks.

Kat squeezes my shoulder, jolting me to answer the question.

"Oh, Garrett. Garrett Nelson," I quickly insert. My heart is pounding wildly. Why do I suddenly feel as if I'm lying?

"Mr. Nelson?" the man asks with a raised brow as he shuffles through the pages of his ledger. "Mr. Garrett Nelson?"

I nod as the three of us rise up to peer over the tall desk at the big book, as if it holds a treasure chest of secrets.

"Ah, yes!" the man suddenly exclaims, his eyes lighting up with swift recognition. "Of course, of course, Mr. Nelson. Such a nice gentleman," he says. "But madame, I do not believe you have surprised your *tres intelligente* husband this time." He waves his long index finger at me and smiles. "*Non*, in fact, Mr. Nelson was holding a very special table for the two of you in our main dining room. He told me specifically to make everything this weekend 'very special for Mrs. Nelson.'"

Hope, Kat, and I are shocked. We look at each other, blinking through blank stares, our minds and thoughts racing, while trying not to show our mass discomfort. My throat has turned to sandpaper. This is one surprising twist that even our brave Sherlocking strategist Kat had not figured out.

"He just left a message, however." The man snaps back into his elegant, professional tone. He squints at his ledger, reading some small print. "Ah, yes." He turns around to the dark wooden chest of mail cubbyholes behind him and pulls out a shiny room key dangling on a gold tassel. "Mr. Nelson asked us to inform you that he is held up at work and will, unfortunately, not be back in time for the special dinner he had planned for the two of you. However, Mr. Nelson asked that we give you the key to your suite, where you can go inside and make yourself comfortable until he arrives. I think you will be very happy with the accommodations, Mrs. Nelson. Your husband left no detail untouched." The man beams brightly.

I feel a strange sense of doom.

He hands over the key, holding the gold tassel between the long slender fingers of his well-manicured hand. I stare at the dancing metal before me and want to throw up. Nervous, speechless, and paralyzed by the shock of it all, my eyes won't stop blinking. It's as though they are trying to wipe away the harsh and brutal reality hanging right here in front of my face, dangling right before my eyes, dangling its promise to Eve.

"Thank you very much." Kat abruptly snaps the gold tassel from the man's hold. "Mr. Nelson is such a thoughtful man, isn't he?" She fakes a charming grin through rising venom. "Which way to the Nelson suite?"

"Just through the archway there." The man behind the desk directs with his graceful hand. "Emilio will gladly show you the way."

"Thank you," we three respond in unison.

"Just go with the flow," Kat assures us in a tight whisper, with a dogged determination under her brow. I am literally shaking, my nerves are so shot. This little sojourn of ours has just gone from really bad to even worse.

"Right this way, beautiful ladies." An energetic Emilio sweeps us across the gilded lobby toward the bank of polished brass elevators. "Floor twelve," he jovially announces as he pushes the up button with his gloved hand.

We stand here together, not daring to speak a word in front of this short, jolly stranger. I stare at our reflections shining in the polish of the brass elevator doors. We are each in our own deep abyss of heavy thought and grave contemplation, all except for the cheery little man standing here dutifully at our service. The heavy doors of the elevator clank open. We step in. The stocky bellman pushes the button for the twelfth floor, and we begin our slow, smooth ascent to anywhere but heaven. I think of all the frescoed angels soaring above the guests in the lobby below, and I pray that at least one of them is following us up to the twelfth floor.

The elevator bell rings, signaling our arrival. We walk out in silence and into the long, winding carpeted hallway that leads to my husband's love den. "Ah, suite 1207!" Emilio hastens to the door. "This is one of our best." His pride shines from underneath his little round hat and bushy brows. "Your husband is one of our best too. Mr. Nelson has climbed mountains to make sure you are comfortable in his absence, Mrs. Nelson."

Emilio sticks the key in the door and turns the lock. It opens with a hushed click.

"Here you are, ladies. Suite 1207," Emilio announces as he politely escorts us inside the cozy yet opulent suite. "I think you will enjoy the many amenities Mr. Nelson has ordered for your comfort." Emilio smiles without looking at me. "Please do not hesitate to ring us if you require anything else during your stay. We only aim to please." Emilio's smile lingers. So does he.

Kat is on it in a snap. With a crisp twenty-dollar bill neatly folded in the palm of her hand, she takes Emilio by the arm and escorts him out the door.

"Thanks, Emilio," she gushes as she seductively presses the bill into his waiting glove. "I see why the Nelsons always insist on staying at the Ritz. Ta-ta," she coos, playfully tickling her fingers at him as she pushes the poor soul back out into the posh hallway.

"Phew!" Kat exhales with her back to the door. "That little man is a little too happy."

"Now what do we do?" Hope looks as if she's about to cry. We both turn to Kat for direction and strength.

"Well, let's think," We follow Kat deeper into the suite.

It is one of the most lavish rooms I have ever seen. The large luxurious living room is decorated in deep shades of forest green, with inviting lounge chairs upholstered in rich, luxurious fabrics. I can't help but run my fingers along their textured backs and arms. Coffee tables with intricate inlaid wooden patterns hold porcelain lamps, painted with scenes of geisha girls dressed in brightly colored silk kimonos.

"Whoa, look at these." Hope is gawking at a ginormous bouquet of red roses in the center of the dining table. Carefully positioned in a sparkling crystal vase, the bouquet sits there like a pretty lady-in-waiting.

"There's got to be more than a dozen roses in there," says Hope.

The bloodred buds sit in silent preparation of their blossoming. These beautiful roses, however many, are sure to be a divine joy for the one so beloved as to receive them. Sadly, we all know, they are not for me.

"Yeah, looks like about two dozen." Kat circles the table, scrutinizing the bouquet with a frown on her face. "Is there a card anywhere?"

"One, two, three ..." Hope counts. "Yeah, at least two dozen. They only come by the dozen, right?"

"Or half dozen," I interject, remembering the six little pink roses Garrett slipped from behind his back as my first-date surprise. Six roses on the first date to me implied there would one day be more to come. Those six droopy baby-pink roses, sitting atop their short stems, meant the world to me. They made my Garrett a rich man in my young eyes. He told me that a half a dozen roses were worth more than a dozen.

"They're cheaper by the dozen," he explained.

And I actually believed him.

In one fleeting moment, this bunch of blooming red flowers has told the entire story. Garrett has made me feel cheaper by the dozens of sweet-smelling roses sitting right up here under my nose, sitting right up here in my face, standing here in all their blazing red glory.

Just like that red hair in our bed.

Seething and becoming overwhelmed with nausea, I make a fast move for the door, but Kat jumps in my path before I can reach the knob, blocking my exit.

"You can't chicken out on us now, girl." The words sear deep into my soul. "We've come too far to turn back now."

"But Kat, what if we get caught?" I spurt, fighting back tears. "What if he walks in here right now and catches us?"

"So what if he does?" Kat demands in a stern, urgent tone. "We just walked in here and caught *him*, didn't we?"

My stomach is in knots. I can't breathe. My eyes are stinging. A lump grows in my throat. I feel a heaviness overcome my chest. My heart remains shattered.

"Oh, my God," Hope whispers from across the room. She is looking through the double French doors leading to the suite's master bedroom. She stands there, staring, mouth open, eyes wide, hands still gripping the brass French doorknobs. "Y'all better come see this," she says, leaving the double doors to slowly swing open on their own, revealing a dream, a truth, and a nightmare, all at the same time.

Kat and I slowly and cautiously walk over to join Hope at the threshold of my husband's reserved bedroom. There, strewn gently across the king-sized bed, already turned back for the night, are at least another two dozen worth of ruby red rose petals. Each one thoughtfully, carefully, artistically, and most lovingly sprinkled across the stark white Egyptian sheets. I do not know the count, but I do know that this is the second time I have seen red in my husband's bed.

"Here's the card." Kat walks over to the bedside table, where a bottle of Moët & Chandon champagne sits chilling in a silver ice bucket. Next to it stands two long-stemmed fluted crystal champagne glasses. They each have fancy little doilies tied to their bottoms.

Oh, how the Ritz thinks of everything.

Kat snaps up the card, nestled between two bedtime Godiva chocolates wrapped in gold tinsel, and reads the note.

"Welcome to my world, my love." Kat rolls her eyes in disgust and looks up at me. Shaking her head, she takes a long, deep breath and continues reading. *"Have this on when I get home, and in my rose bed we shall roam.* Oh, give me a fuckin' break," Kat spits. "That's disgusting!"

I snatch the note from Kat and stare down at its loopy little letters.

"That's not even his handwriting," I sneer.

"He must be talking about this." Hope points at something on the opposite side of Garrett's rose-petaled bed. It lies there amid the scattered flowers, appearing silky and shiny in the soft, warm light of the Oriental bedside lamps.

It is a lovely piece of lingerie—a sexy little teddy of a very fine silk—part of Garrett's special party planning. This spicy little number is a distinct periwinkle blue, a color Garrett and I share—one color we, together, know all too well.

It was the color we chose for our wedding.

Chapter
★ Nineteen

"WHAT THE HELL IS PERIWINKLE BLUE?"

I remember the incredulous look on Garrett's face when I first suggested the color three years ago as a possibility for our wedding.

"And why do we need a color anyway?" He scrunched his face into a scowl and turned back to his televised football game.

Garrett seemed so agitated with the whole idea of a big wedding.

"Because it's tradition, honey. It's what people do." I looked for the scowl to melt. It only tightened.

"I don't care," he barked, his cold eyes never leaving the football game.

"How could you say that?" I was crushed.

"Say what?" Garrett shook some peanuts in the palm of his hand, popped a few into his mouth, and then reached for his beer.

"That you don't care." Hurt and angry, I started to well up. "It's our wedding, Garrett! Everything's important! And you *don't care*?"

"Geez, can't I watch the game?" Garrett whined.

Furious, I ran into our bedroom, slammed the door, flung myself across the bed, and bawled like a baby. Garrett finally came in and apologized. We made love all night—mad, passionate make-up love—and by dawn had agreed on periwinkle blue.

It was the first big fight we'd ever had. I knew he didn't know any better. He was probably more upset over Mother's sudden intrusion into our wedding plans than anything else. Just a year earlier, my parents had stopped speaking to us. They had vowed that they'd have nothing to do with our union or our wedding. They hated Garrett for no apparent reason, hated the fact they had no control over either of us, hated the fact that we were living together "in sin" for a year without being married, and *now* they hated the fact that we were getting married. We couldn't win.

It was way too much drama and mostly from Mother, who was finally forced against the wall by a call from my aunt Edna, her best friend from college. From her poolside mansion in Baldwin Hills, California, an area known as the black Beverly Hills, Aunt Edna shot from the hip and somehow managed to speak some sense into my stubborn mother. I truly appreciated her for that and for every other time she had done something similar to help Mother and me soothe our difficult relationship.

Free-spirited and blessed with a hilarious sense of humor, Aunt Edna was very much unlike Mother. She was a spunky woman of small dimensions, who laughed a lot, cursed a lot, and dressed in cool, hip, bell-bottomed jeans and big brass hip-hugging belts. She didn't care what people thought about her or her social status in life, although she happened to be married to a prominent and wealthy Los Angeles surgeon. She swore she hated socializing with phony people. She must have made a huge exception, befriending my mother.

One day, after talking with me for an hour on the phone, Aunt Edna called Mother and calmly yet firmly informed her that she'd better get with the program and quick. She went on to explain that whether she and Daddy liked it or not, Garrett and I were getting married. She even tipped her off that we had already started making wedding plans without her. And that was true. We had scraped up enough money to reserve Columbia University's Little Chapel for our big day. Aunt Edna told my folks that they had every right to like or dislike whomever they wanted, but the fact still remained that their only daughter was about to marry Garrett, whether they liked *that* or not. She warned them that they could keep their heels stuck in the ground and their noses stuck in the air if they wanted to, or they could swallow their pride and support us like a real family should. But whatever they decided to do, she further warned, they'd have to live with that decision for the rest of their lives.

That advice apparently worked, as it always did when Aunt Edna got going. She knew just how to push Mother's buttons, and she knew my father would obediently follow suit in hopes of avoiding any kind of conflict with his temperamental and demanding wife. I am sure that Aunt Edna's call got Mother thinking about the ramifications of her noncompliance; mainly, that everyone in our small southern community would be whispering behind her back, wondering why in the world

Garrett and I eloped up North. It just wouldn't look right. It would appear as if something was gravely wrong with *her.* Plus, knowing Mother, she realized that by not giving a proper southern wedding to her only daughter, she'd be missing out on one of the most important social and political occasions of a lifetime. And everyone knows Mother loves a good social and political occasion.

So just as we were about to put the down payment on Columbia's Little Chapel for our intimate candlelight wedding, with only a handful of very close friends and professors, my folks came through—and with a vengeance, as I found out when I flew home for a weekend of wedding planning with Mother.

By the end of it, there were eight bridesmaids, eight groomsmen, and an invitation list of more than a thousand guests and dignitaries. The long list included presidents of prestigious colleges; politicians; the great people's poet, Dr. Maya Angelou; and the town's mayor and the governor of North Carolina. It was quite the affair. I barely knew a soul on that list.

This humongous wedding was sure to be the talk of the town, maybe the nation, as folks across the country were into lavish fantasy weddings after Princess Diana had just floated down those cathedral steps in the longest train any of us had ever seen on TV, much less in real life. Glued to the international news, people all across America and the rest of the Free World dreamed of the "perfect wedding." My mother was determined to throw one.

"Oh, they are going to be talking about this one for years!" she gushed one day over her morning coffee and her forever-growing invitation list. "It's is going to be the talk of the town, I tell you."

Mother was dressed in a flowing lavender caftan, her thick black hair tied up on top of her head and wrapped inside an elaborate silk scarf, making her look like a bold African queen. Sitting at her throne at the end of the family breakfast table, she was using a no. 2 pencil to modify my wedding registry list.

"I marked off those silly pottery plates you listed here," she said as she struck another line through the word "pottery." "I listed a beautiful set of china for you instead—Wedgewood. It goes with everything."

"It doesn't go with burgers, Mother." It was too early in the morning for the you-are-a-lady-and-don't-forget-it speech. "Garrett and I don't need china. We like pottery. You know, earthy stuff."

Mother jerked her head up, staring me down with dogged disdain. She pushed down the sides of her mouth into a deep frown, as if something smelled bad.

"Well, then eat off the ground, for God's sake!" she snapped. I could hear her mumbling something about us being a couple of heathens as she shook her head, pursed her lips, and returned to slaughtering my registry.

"Mother," I pleaded, "please don't turn this into a circus. Garrett and I envisioned a small, intimate wedding with just a few close people we love and lots of candlelight and bunches of roses." I could feel myself float out of my body on my bubble of a dream—until Mother popped it.

"Well, that's ridiculous." She looked up from my list. "You come from a prominent family, remember. Your father is a doctor. We are not a bunch of hippies, for goodness' sake."

Had Mother heard one thing I'd just said? Did she even care? Did it always have to be about her? How did I suddenly become so insignificant in my own wedding?

"No, Mother, *this* is ridiculous," I proceeded with caution as I noticed that "you'd-better-watch-yo'-step" look come across her face. "It's *my* wedding, Mother, and you don't even acknowledge that. It's *my* day, you know." I prayed she wouldn't shoot off like a ballistic missile.

"Look, I am doing this for you." She whipped off her reading glasses, scolding me with one of the stems. "Your father and I worked too hard around here and doled out too much charity money not to have this whole damn town come out and support you."

Clearly, this was no longer about Garrett and me.

"But they don't have to give us china, Mother; that's all I'm saying. We don't need china."

"Well, what will you serve your guests on when you have dinner parties and such?" She looked at me like I was crazy. "Now look, you have eaten on china from birth. I will not even consider your not having a complete and decent set for your wedding." She snatched a frilly floral hanky out of her watchband, blew on her reading glasses, and started wiping the lenses clean.

"Trust me; you'll need a touch of class, living with that beast you're marrying. I bet he's the one talking about 'pottery.'" She popped her glasses back on top of her nose and peered over the rims at me. "Don't you let that man make you less of yourself, now. You hear me?"

"Mother, please ..."

"I'm serious. Don't you let that man turn you into a heathen and take away all your father and I have taught and given you. We fought for that. Sacrificed everything. You are *pedigreed—of a certain class*—and don't you forget it."

"Yes, ma'am." I bowed my head in my usual obedience.

"Oh!" Mother snapped her manicured fingers into the air. "I thought about the wedding march too. 'Trumpet Voluntary' by Purcell. It was the same one Princess Diana used for her wedding. Oh, you will *love* it," she gushed. "The piece is so full of grandeur—simple but elegant." Lost in the moment, Mother circled her hand around in the air like a musical conductor. Then, with a squint of her nose, she went back to my registry.

"China, a thousand people, and, now Princess Di's wedding march? Mother!" I wailed. She was barreling out of control. "What are you doing?"

"I am giving you the gift of a lifetime, madame." She glared across the table. "And you will shut up and appreciate it, and put on a good face for this family as you go ahead and marry that man you know your father and I do not approve of! It might as well be a good show."

"A good show?" I couldn't believe the coldness of her remarks. This is not what a mother is supposed to say about the best day of your life. "It's not about you, Mother," I said sadly. Her words hurt beyond belief. Was this beast in a caftan really my mother? I sat there staring at what I swore were two horns growing out of the top of her head.

"Not about me, you say?" she scoffed. "Not about me? Oh, yes it is! Ha! When you come home crying to me when he screws this thing up, I bet you it'll be about me then, won't it!"

"Excuse me," I said as I lifted myself from the table. I knew there was no need to reason with her. Mother was on a wedding-day mission—her own—and no one was going to stop her, not even the bride.

"You didn't eat anything," Mother said.

"Not hungry," I replied. I headed back to the safety of my childhood room, where I was staying for this "wonderful weekend of wedding planning." I suddenly had a rushing feeling that no place in this house was safe. I thanked God again and again for allowing me to forge a new family for myself and to move on with my life. It was the most important thing in the world to me. I survived that weekend with my mother just out of knowing that finally my family life was going to change and for the better.

"I tell you what ..." Mother's suddenly cheery voice stopped me in my tracks. I slowly turned to face the monster.

"How about I list both the china *and* those pottery plates you like. You can use one for your burgers or whatever and the china for special occasions." She sat there so confident and satisfied and pleased with herself. Even though I thought this too was a bit much, I could not take such glorious elation from Mother at that moment. More important, I needed peace.

"Not too much, you sure?"

"Oh no, no, dear. Not too much at all." She smiled her reassurance. "We've invited a thousand people, for God's sake!" She chuckled. "You can surely have two dinner sets." She settled back in her chair with the satisfaction of a fat cat. Periwinkle blue was one of only a couple of ideas that Garrett and I suggested that actually made it into our wedding. It didn't matter what we felt, as long as Mother was happy. Our wedding was a huge political and social success for her. Daddy, naturally and obediently, agreed, although he was so drunk when he walked me down the aisle that he almost danced a jig. I'm not sure he even remembers it. I know he was drinking to forget I was marrying Garrett—and who knows what else.

Old Miss Coon directed the wedding. Folks say it was the only one in town that year that started on time. In fact, we had to beg Miss Coon not to start the nuptials ten minutes early. God knows I needed that time.

"There's a lot of fancy white folks sitting out there," she whispered to the wedding party as we waited in the church vestibule. "We can't start this wedding on CP time!"

I remember at that very moment, wondering if I was doing the right thing. Perhaps all jittery brides go through second thoughts just before the wedding, but I recall all of a sudden remembering Chip, the golden boy from my childhood who stole my heart. I felt a deep sadness at the unfairness of it all. I could never have been with Chip, never imagined him waiting for me at the other end of the altar like this, and only because the boy was white and poor.

Why would I wonder about that boy on my wedding day?

While my parents were still not happy about my marrying Garrett, they pretended to be elated as they floated through the wedding crowd, accepting praise and congratulations. The champagne reception was held at the Little Theater, where years ago as a child, I had performed in my first play. It took more than an hour for everybody to get through the receiving line. Garrett and I cut the cake. I fed him a piece as we posed for the cameras. We laughed at how much our jaw muscles ached after all of that smiling. We could barely flex our faces for the photographers.

Back at my parents' home, company came from all over the southern region just to gawk at my high-falootin' wedding and our hundreds and hundreds of exquisite gifts. Mother's helpers—women from her bridge and social clubs—had erected long folding tables along the walls of our basement, covered them with the family's finest linen tablecloths (handed down over the generations), and placed each wedding gift on display with a name card noting the giver. Everyone could see who was invited and what gift they gave the happy couple. Mother designed this to be the wedding of the decade. You would have thought it was hers.

We received a sterling silver serving tray from Dr. Maya Angelou, with an elaborate "N" for Nelson engraved in the middle. The president of Duke University gave us a beautiful porcelain Swiss clock, and we received so many place settings of Wedgewood china (thirty-six to be exact) that we had to take some back to the store in exchange for the practical things a young couple needs—like a toaster, a blender, a frying pan, and wooden spoons.

"Look at all of those gifts." Garrett stood wide-eyed and open-armed in the middle of my family's basement. He was grinning from ear to ear at the expensive wares. Garrett never again complained about Mother having invited a thousand mostly unknown guests to our wedding. As far as Garrett was concerned, her involvement finally paid off.

We made *Jet* magazine—a huge honor in the black community, as the historic magazine sits on just about every black family's coffee table around the world. Our wedding news also hit our hometown newspapers, the *New York Times*, and some of the tabloids as well.

I have not thought about periwinkle blue since our wedding day. Have not even considered the color—until now, as I stare down at this piece of periwinkle lingerie that my husband has lovingly selected and laid out on a rose-petaled bed for his girlfriend—his lover—my so-called "best friend." He clearly knows what periwinkle blue is today.

I stand here, once again, seeing red.

Chapter ★ Twenty

"I THINK YOU SHOULD PUT THAT DAMN THING ON AND LIE ACROSS THE bed and surprise his ass when he walks in here," Kat hisses as Hope and I huddle around her. We all stare down at the lingerie as if it's some kind of strange fish that washed ashore.

"That would sure surprise him all right," Hope adds with a squinched-up face as she imagines the sordid scene.

"Fuck that!" I spit, not even sounding like myself. "I'm not stooping that low."

"No, you're right." Hope waffles back to my side. "But what are we going to do?"

"I don't know," I confess. "But Eve could be downstairs right now, telling that man behind the desk that *she* is Mrs. Nelson."

"Okay, okay, just hold up." Kat begins pacing the plush carpet like a panther. "Let me think."

"Well, we better do something fast," Hope urges. "If Eve is coming, she'll be here any minute. We're running out of time."

"And ideas," I interject. I am really scared now. At any moment, anything could happen. And whatever does is probably not going to be pretty.

Kat snaps her finger. "Okay, here's the deal."

Hope and I huddle back around her, eagerly anticipating our next game plan.

"Remember my fat friend downstairs at the curb?"

"Yeah, *your boyfriend?*" Hope rolls her eyes to the heavens.

"Yeah, well, I'm about to ask Big Boy for a little favor." Kat flashes a sly smile.

Hope and I lean in closer.

"I say we ask the nice gentleman if he would be so kind as to ask 'Mrs. Nelson' to go directly to her husband's suite instead of stopping at the front desk as planned. I'll put the key in an envelope, leave it with the fat guy, and have him give it to her as soon as she steps out of the cab."

Hope sighs heavily, losing patience and faith. "What? And what are we supposed to do then, Kat? Let her in?"

"How will he even know it's her?" I ask, not completely sold on her plan.

"Oh, he'll know," Kat says. "Who could miss all that red hair?"

Of course. The red hair is what started this whole thing in the first place.

"I know that doorman will be all over that girl *and* her booty with his big ol' fish eyes." Hope exaggerates the man's lusty look and bulging eyes.

"Okay, then what?" I ask, getting back down to business.

"Hope and I will wait around the corner just down the hallway, and you ..."

"Yeah?" I ask.

"We're putting you in the closet," Kat says matter-of-factly. "We came here to catch a cheat, and that's just what we're going to do. Proof, plus two witnesses!"

"What?" I am about to explode. "You have *got* to be kidding me! Have you lost your damn mind?"

Kat crosses her arms and looks at me. "Well, do you have a better idea?"

I stand, mouth open, looking back and forth at my two best girlfriends. But the truth is—I don't have a better idea, and I have to know the truth. Leaving is not an option. We have to do something fast.

"But what if he opens the closet door, Kat? What then?" I ask.

Kat swoops over to the double closet doors and swings them open by their elegant brass handles. Inside, Garrett's garment bag hangs down to the floor. Next to it hangs a plush terry cloth robe, compliments of the Ritz. He has a couple of suit jackets lined up—the green one his folks brought him back from Paris two years ago and the one his eldest brother handed down to him. It's his favorite—chocolate brown and green tweed with leather buttons and suede elbow patches. It smells like Garrett.

"Here. Stand behind the asshole's garment bag," Kat firmly directs as she pulls it back. I dutifully step behind it. "He's already emptied it, so chances are he won't even come over here. Just don't move anything.

You don't want him getting suspicious by seeing something out of whack."

I stand still, stuffed in the back of the closet. I can't believe we're doing this. My mind is twirling around so fast, I can't even think. I'm becoming claustrophobic for the first time in my life. I have to get out of here.

"How about I get under the bed instead?" I plead. "They wouldn't think to look there, would they?"

"I already checked under there," Hope chimes in. "Not enough room."

"Dear God," I say, slowly shaking my head. "Has my life really come to this?"

"We don't have time to talk about that right now," Kat says as she slams the closet doors shut in my face, leaving me in the dark. "C'mon, Hope, *let's move*," she orders. "Wait down the hall around the corner. I'm going downstairs to talk to Big Boy."

"Kat …" I hear Hope's voice crack. "Are you sure about this?"

"No," she snaps. "But it's the best stuff I got right now, and I don't hear nobody else coming up with any ideas. So let's *go*."

I'm left in the closet behind Garrett's garment bag, in sudden and deafening silence and fear. I can smell Garrett's cologne. It's that new one he bought himself just a few weeks ago. I loved it—until now. Tonight, it is the stench of my husband's illicit love den.

I feel sick at the thought of all that Garrett has planned for this room—not for me but exclusively for my best friend who is literally playing me. I'm dizzy at the thought of all the special things my husband has planned to do with and to Eve tonight. I think of how she lied to get out of dinner with us girls, just so she could instead have dinner and "dessert" with my scheming-ass husband behind my stupid-ass back.

That skank ho!

I want to jump out of this closet and annihilate this room, throw those roses out this twelfth-floor window, and rip that goddamned periwinkle teddy to shreds. I want to shove that cold bottle of Moet up Eve's ass and all of these fucking red petals down her throat. How dare she make fools of us like this? How dare she use our sacred friendship to deceive us all? And how dare my husband let her?

I suddenly jump at the sound of two loud pounding thuds on the door.

"Heads up!" Kat calls, breathing heavily. "We're all set. Red should arrive at any moment. *Stay cool!*"

I hear Kat scuttle down the hallway where Hope is waiting. The two will stand by for whatever is bound to happen next.

I am counting on my legs to hold up; it's as if I'm covering another long, grueling hostage situation. If I suddenly have to jump out at somebody, I don't want to do it from down on the floor, so I continue standing behind the big garment bag, happy that I am only five foot four, so if I bend my legs a bit, the top of my head won't show above the bag, and I can easily spring into action. I see a dirty towel thrown on the closet floor. I stick out my foot to pull it in closer, forming a high pile underneath the garment bag to hide my feet.

I am ready. So now, I wait. I take a few really deep breaths, fearing I may not get to breathe very much when they get here, as I might be heard. I wait and I wait. I hold my breath and release. Hold. Release.

Suddenly, my whirling thoughts are chased away by a sound at the door. I hear a key slowly sliding in the lock and then the hushed click of the door opening. I freeze. I tremble. I am scared.

I hear someone entering the suite as quiet as a cat. I hold my breath, carefully straining to hear every move. Whoever it is now fumbles for the light switch. Is it Garrett? Or is it Eve? I hear a soft gasp.

"*Oh my gawd!*" It's a woman's breathy voice. "Aww ... how *sweet!*" I hear her purr.

I know it's her.

She giggles uncontrollably, and then I hear her inhale deeply, apparently tickled pink by the sweet smell of her red roses. I hear her now moving toward the kitchenette. She pulls open the refrigerator door with a jerk.

"What? No champagne?" she says in a pouty voice. "Tsk-tsk-tsk. Ba-ad boy," she scolds an imaginary Garrett.

The spoiled bitch hasn't even looked in the bedroom, where her bedside bottle of bubbly is waiting.

She starts humming a happy little la-de-da-de-da tune as I hear her making her way toward the bedroom, through the opened doors, and then—"*Ahhhh!*"—she squeals like a surprised little girl on Christmas morning. "*Oh my God!*" I suppose all of those rose petals glimmering in the soft yellow lamplight and the periwinkle blue lingerie has caught the bitch's eye.

"How beautiful," she purrs. "Oh, oh baby."

She is still. I cannot hear her movements anymore. This scares me, because I don't know where she is or what she might be doing. I pray she isn't coming toward the closet to hang her coat or something.

I cautiously move my head out from behind the garment bag, straining my neck out so I can hear clearer. I try peeking through the shuttered door and catch a slight glimpse of her through the slats. I watch intently as Eve gets up from the bed, holding her new lingerie against her body. She is smiling, clearly adoring her lover's outpouring of gifts. She gently lays the sexy piece on the bed and begins peeling off her clothes—first her short trench coat and then her blouse, loosening the garment from around her perfectly round breasts, button by button, revealing a bright red bra. The seductress appears to be in a mental waltz with herself.

She is beautiful, and while I hate to reveal my own gross insecurities, I can see why Garrett craves her. Her supple brown skin looks soft and flawless, her muscles lithe and toned. She unhooks her bra and carelessly lets it fall to the floor. She has big dark brown nipples that are standing erect upon her voluptuous breasts. She kicks off her four-inch pumps and unzips her skirt. Her waist is slender. Her hips are shapely and round.

She carefully slides off her skirt, steps out of it, and then slips out of her red panties, wiggling them down over her hips. It seems she's anticipating all the imagined sweetness to come. She picks up the teddy and stands there, completely naked. I am surprised that even the tufts of curls between the tops of her long, muscular thighs are as red as those on her head. I have never seen anything like it. She looks like a black-Irish bitch goddess.

Eve slips on the teddy and admires herself in the mirror. She runs her fingers all over her body, feeling her smooth curves comforted in the coolness of the fine silk. She turns around in front of the mirror, admiring every angle of herself and her brand-new lingerie. Her fingers move down, down to her sacred place. She touches herself in a slow, deep, and sensuous way and then suddenly giggles like a little girl caught sneaking. She licks her fingers as if to erase her own sins. She leaves a naughty smile in the mirror, spins around, and belly flops on top of her lover's—my husband's—bed.

I squeeze my eyes tightly shut in hope of stopping this sordid scene. There is no denying the growing rage inside my gut or the wrenching pain inside my heart. Still, I can't stop watching. I want to finally witness for myself everything I have needed to know—and probably already did.

Suddenly, I am startled by the sound of the champagne cork popping.

I can't believe she is pouring herself a glass without Garrett. *That selfish bitch.*

I hear her pick up the phone and begin to dial. I wait.

"Hey, girl! It's me," she squeals through the receiver. "I finally made it. And, honey, you are not going to believe what my baby did for me this time."

This time? I wonder. How many of these expensive little trysts have these motherfuckers enjoyed? And who the hell is Eve talking to anyway?

"Uh-uh-huh." She is beside herself with pleasure. "Girl, he gave me roses, and I mean a *bunch* of them, all over the bed and everything. My baby got me champagne and chocolates and ..." She giggles again as she rolls over on her back and kicks her legs up in the air, like a giddy teenager. "Oh, Maxine!" she squeals.

Maxine! I am stunned.

"He gave me the most beautiful little light purple teddy."

It's periwinkle, you stupid slut.

"And he left me the sweetest little note asking me to have it on when his fine ass walks in here." She seems thrilled beyond her own belief. "He's still at work. Uh-huh ... Yeah, I'm just going to lie right here and pretend that I am already Mrs. Nelson. Girl, I *know* he's already married! I know his wife, remember?"

Oh, no, she didn't! I feel Eve's dagger digging deeper.

"I know you don't like what I am doing, Maxine, but I love him. I really do love Garrett."

I think I am going to pass out. I cannot believe I am listening to my best friend carrying on with my other friend about my husband and how much she loves him. I want to run out of here like my hair is on fire.

"Yes, yes, you know I'll be careful, even though I may just forget my diaphragm tonight. Oh, c'mon, calm down, Maxie, I'm just kidding. Honest. No, no, I said, I'm *kidding!*" I can see that coy grin on her face as she twirls the telephone cord around her perfectly manicured fingers. "Look, better go, sweetie. My man is on his way, and I want to be wet and ready when he gets here. Love you. Mwah" She blows a kiss through the receiver and hangs up.

There is dead silence again. I try not to move. I try not to breathe. I try not to jump out of this closet and kill her.

Then, there is another hushed click at the door. Eve and I both jump.

"Hellooo." It's Garrett. "Honey, I'm ho-ome."

I could slit his throat.

Eve giggles and remains on the bed. I see her pushing herself back through Garrett's rose petals as she seductively leans up against the mountain of plush pillows.

"In here, sweetie; *come and get it!*" she sings, waving her long, brown thighs back and forth.

I hear Garrett putting his things down in the front room. I hear him taking off his jacket and see his smiling face through the door slat as he enters the bedroom, loosening his tie.

"Ah, I see you found your champagne," Garrett croons in a low, deep sexy voice, one I have rarely heard.

"Yes, I did," Eve purrs back at him, arching her back.

"And your lingerie."

"Mmm-hmm." She has a mischievous look on her face as she playfully dips her finger in her champagne and then sticks it in her mouth.

"Do you like Daddy's surprises?" Garrett teases as he confidently saunters closer to the bed.

"Yes, I do, Daddy," she purrs in a baby voice. "I like them very, very much."

Garrett does not take his eyes off her as he impatiently yanks at his tie. "You look *good*, baby," he whispers in a gruff voice, with one knee on the bed.

She moans and giggles.

"Give me some of that champagne," Garrett orders.

She looks at him and flashes another naughty smile. She then wraps her big red lips around the rim of the champagne flute and takes a long, deliberate sip, locked in his gaze. Eve then reaches up and grabs Garrett's tie, pulling him closer, until their mouths meet. She moans again as he drinks the champagne straight from her mouth.

"Mmmm," Garrett hums sensuously. "Now, that's what I'm talkin' 'bout."

Garrett wraps his burly arms around Eve's slender waist and holds her tightly against his body. He rubs his big hands all over her back, her ass, and her thighs as his hunger grows wilder. Eve writhes underneath him, moving her hips around and around in the sensual private dance between lovers.

"I want you to do that again, baby," he demands through heavy breaths as he entwines his fat fingers between her long thin ones. He dives in for her neck.

She rolls over and takes another long sensuous sip of champagne, and he again drinks from her mouth, except this time, instead of swallowing, he roughly grabs her by the top of her thighs and yanks her down on the bed, squirting the bubbly liquid from his mouth all over her body—her pussy, her inner thighs, her ass, her stomach, neck, and breasts. He is completely lost in her and all of their wetness.

"I love you, baby, I love you," he mutters as he rubs his wet face into her glistening breasts, cupping them into his hungry mouth between his two big hands. My so-called best friend is giving herself to my so-called husband freely and fiercely.

"I love you too, Daddy," she moans.

Love? What are they talking about? He can't love her.

Garrett moves down her body as she spreads her legs. I lose sight of him, but he must be plunging his tongue deep inside her body from the sounds of her guttural moans. He must be melting her down, sucking and drinking her up, going deeper and deeper.

Just like that dagger in my back. And again, I want to die.

Knowing my husband is having an affair with another woman is hard enough to swallow. Learning that the other woman is my best friend makes it twice as hard. But to watch my man humping away on the girl with whom I have shared my deepest, darkest, and most personal secrets, some even about my husband, is the most outrageous experience I could have ever imagined. Sadly, it is all too real today.

I remain in this bedroom closet, peeking through the slats of the door, as my husband and my best friend lick, suck, and touch each other—everywhere. Not one place on either body left untouched or unmoaned about. Even when I close my eyes to shut out the horrific truth playing itself out right there before me, I can still hear Eve's deep guttural groans of pleasure as my husband thrashes his tongue deeper and deeper inside her holes, folds, and crevices. I am sick from watching, yet I cannot stop.

Even worse, Garrett and Eve seem to really be into each other. I watch them breathlessly sharing their deepest longings. They roll across the bed, wrapped in tight embrace, expressing whispered words and primal sounds of love. Garrett and I have never made love like that, rolling around, clinging, and spewing all kinds of passionate and dirty words. I am devastated.

My husband seems wilder, freer, and far more satisfied with his redheaded lover than it seems he has ever been with me. He talks dirty to her, and she likes it, responding with even more animalistic heat. He turns her over and smiles, smacking her ass, and then squeezing her buns with a lusty grin. He kneads them like dough between his fat fingers. She delights in every second. He plunges his hungry fingers inside her. She squeals with surprise and excitement.

In all that they are doing to each other, do they have any idea what they are doing to me?

Eve lets out another high-pitched squeal as Garrett flips her over and pulls her underneath him by her tight ass. She is giggling and moaning and arching her back in what is sure to be only seconds before she gives herself to him completely. Her cocoa legs jet out on either side of Garrett's big body in playful kicks. He climbs up closer to the head of the bed with Eve holding on underneath him like some kind of primate offspring.

They collapse, grabbing each other by the head and hair, locking lips in a hungry and desperate embrace. Garrett reaches down and fumbles with himself between his big thighs. He lifts his hips to better position himself.

"Ready for this, baby? You ready for some good dick?" Garrett taunts.

"Aw, yeah," Eve purrs. "Yeah, I'm ready.

And then with one fell swoop, Garrett plunges his long, thick love stick into my best friend's throbbing, glistening love snatch. She throws her head back and lets loose in a low, deep, and guttural groan.

"Oh my ghaaaaa-aaaad!"

Garrett is pumping himself inside of her like a wild dog.

"Open those legs, *wider.* Open up them damn legs!" he orders his love slave.

"Yes, Daddy, here it is—yes, yes—take it, Daddy, take it all. I got whatchu need, baby. Take it ... mmmm-mmmm-mmm," she pants.

Garrett pounds her body, up and down, up and down, and then swivels his hips around and around, digging deeper and deeper. She is holding the back of his neck and riding my husband like an upside-down jockey. They both have a look of excruciating pleasure on their faces, which on any other day could be easily confused with looks of excruciating pain.

"Oh, baby, lift your leg," Garrett gruffly orders as he keeps pumping Eve's pussy. Without missing a beat, he gets up on his knees. He slaps Eve's ass. She squirms but still begs for more. He slaps her ass again.

Suddenly, Eve screams at the top of her voice. Her eyes roll to the back of her head. She claws the wet sheets, her head thrashing back and forth, from side to side. "Aaaaaaa—aaahh-ahh-ahh—aaaahhahhah!" She looks possessed.

"C'mon, baby. Yeah, gimme that good cum. I got you, I got you. Cum for Daddy now," Garrett coos as Eve jerks around in epileptic movements, as if she's been zapped by a bolt of electricity.

Eve's orgasm turns my husband on even more, as he picks up the pace of his pumping. He is going for the gold.

"Okay, baby, okay … here it comes … awwwwww … here it comes … oh … yeah … yeah … yeah …" He pumps and pumps. Garrett's dropping beads of sweat. "Gimme that wet pussy, baby, give it to me—shiiiit!"

"Take it, baby. Take. My. Pussy."

"*Give it to me!* Yeah … yeah … aye-aah aaaaaaaaaaaaahhhh-ahh-ahh—aaaahhahhah!"

Eve swoops down and wiggles both of my husband's balls into her mouth and sucks them wildly as he cums. Garrett goes ballistic, screaming, groaning, crying, and wailing at the top of his lungs. Eve's head and tongue circle around and around.

Garrett can't take anymore of the pleasure he devised and grabs his lover's head.

"Okay, baby, okay, tha's enough. Damn!"

"I just want my baby happy." Eve pants as she hugs Garrett tighter, kissing him with an open mouth.

"Oh, I'm happy, baby. Shit." Garrett smiles, overheated, sweating profusely, and out of breath.

"Don't have a heart attack, now," Eve teases as Garrett rocks her in his arms.

They lie there, tangled into one amid the sheets soaked with champagne and their love juices. He plays with the curls of hair just above her right eyebrow. She inhales deeply and buries face in his hairy chest. She then looks up at him and smiles the smile of a woman in love. She lightly kisses my husband's nipples and then fingers his brown tufts of chest hair with her long red nails.

"I enjoyed that, Daddy," she purrs with eyes half closed. "You are so wonderful."

"Ah, baby," he sighs as he pulls her in closer to him, kissing the top of her red head. "I am always happy to please you."

They lie there still for another moment, apparently soaking up the afterglow of their illicit lovemaking.

"How about some more champagne," Garrett offers as he untangles himself and reaches for one of the fancy-bottomed flutes.

"I'll watch you drink it," Eve flirts.

Garrett pours the champagne to the top of the glass, in what Mother would refer to as a "vulgar portion." For the first time ever, that description makes perfect sense.

Garrett suddenly glances at his watch and then sighs.

"I better call home," he says as he sits on the side of the bed next to the phone. He hangs his head a minute, perhaps trying to compose himself and clear his voice, his mind, and his dick, and then figure out what the hell he's going to say to me.

Heavily, he picks up the telephone and begins to dial. He looks so overburdened and unhappy. Nothing like the cast-all-cares-to-the-wind guy who was humping my best friend only moments ago. I guess there is truth to the thought that men have affairs, not only for the sex but more often for the way the other woman makes them feel. Eve clearly makes my husband feel happy, confident, and alive.

"She's not there—machine," Garrett whispers to Eve. "Hey, honey, it's me," he speaks into our answering machine. "Had a really rough one today." He tries to sound tired. "Worked late. Headed to bed—exhausted. I'll try to catch you tomorrow. Love ya." Garrett hangs up the phone. He sits there a minute, head hung.

"What's wrong, baby?" Eve moves in closer to Garrett, rubbing his back as she sweetly leans her cheek against his big shoulder. "Everything okay?"

"Yeah." Garrett sighs as he rolls over on top of her. "I just thought she'd be home. It's late."

"Well, you know the girls were going over to your house for dinner tonight."

"That's why I was sure she'd be there." Ironically, Garrett acts as if he's worried and concerned about me.

"Well, you know those gals," Eve adds. "Maybe they're having too much fun—*too drunk*—to answer the phone. They probably went out."

"Went out?" Garrett sits up and looks at her.

Eve chuckles. "You don't know your wife very well, do you?"

"What's that supposed to mean?"

"Well, let's just say no moss grows under that girl's feet. I am sure she's glad that you're in Boston. So relax, honey."

I am about to jump out of this closet and beat that black bitch down. Not only is she fucking my husband, she's bad-mouthing me too?

"Yeah, trust me, honey—she's having her fun while we're having ours." Eve leans in toward Garrett. She smiles coyly as if she knows some dirty little secret.

"What? She's not having an affair, is she?" My cheatin'-ass husband actually has the nerve to ask that stupid-ass question and look like he's upset.

"Well, let's just say if she hasn't already, she just might very soon."

That bitch!

"With who?" Garrett persists, like he's going to do something. "Is there somebody else? Tell me, Eve."

The nerve!

"Well, there're always a lot of guys sniffing around her, and for the most part, she's pretty cool with them ... but ..." Eve teases Garrett like she's not going to tell him.

"But what?" he demands.

Eve lowers her voice and leans in a little closer, finding the power not only in her pussy but also in her fabricated, manipulative gossip. "Well, every once in a while there's one who catches her eye. She's a busy one, that one."

I have got to jump out of this closet and kill that woman.

Garrett jumps out of the bed, buck naked, and starts pacing the carpeted floor, his dick wagging in the wind. "I can't fucking believe it!" he exclaims, rubbing his forehead back to the crown with his big hands, as if his brow just burst another sweat leak.

"Well, baby, it's not like you're at home taking care of her." Eve drops a bomb. She is going in for the kill.

And so am I.

"Okay, bitch! That's *enough!*" I blast past Garrett's garment bag and kick my way through the closet doors. They fly open so fast they slam against the back wall with a bang so loud it scares the wits out of Garrett, Eve, and me. We all jump at the same time.

"*What the fu—*" Garrett looks at me like he's seen a ghost.

"*Oh shit!*" is all I hear from Eve as she grabs the sheets and pillows and dives off the other side of the bed in a mad attempt to hide herself and her nakedness. I am standing here in the middle of the floor, looking back and forth at these two assholes, panting like a thief, and not at all sure of what to do next. Do I show my pent-up rage and beat both of these motherfuckers to a pulp? Or do I remain calm and just walk out of here with all of my hurt, pain, evidence, and witnesses and have, at least, my dignity left intact? I am astonished at how calm and calculating I am right now, despite this chaos.

For the first time in my life, I know I can kill.

"What are you doing here?" Garrett's voice cracks. He is trembling. His once strong, erect dick looks shriveled, pink, and puny now. Eve is peeking out from underneath the covers on the other side of the bed, her eyes as wide as saucers.

"It's not what it looks like," the bitch has the nerve to say.

"You must be kidding me," I respond as I look at her like the whore she is. "Oh, honey, it is *everything* it looks like."

"I'm so sorry," Eve whispers, barely able to speak through her cloud of shame. She hides her eyes underneath her long red bangs that have fallen down over her sorry red face.

"Why?" I spin around to face Garrett. "Why *her*? Of all people, Garrett!"

Garrett blinks, looking profoundly ignorant.

"Answer me!" I scream. *"Don't I at least deserve that?"*

Garrett folds his hands in front of his limp dick and looks like a pale, sick little boy. His high-yellow skin looks pasty and sweaty now. He looks weak. I hate him. I cannot believe I was once so in love with this man. He has the pathetic look of a coward.

"I once loved you, Garrett—the best way I knew how—and you disgrace our marriage, me, and everything we promised each other for a piece of shit like *Eve!*"

"Hey, wait a minute!" Eve tries to stand up in protest, but the sheets are wrapped around her so tightly that she tumbles back to the floor.

"Girl, don't even get me started," I say in a slow, steady, threatening voice, my eyes locked into a death stare with hers. "'Cause right now—I swear I mean it—I will beat the shit outta you."

"Look ..." Garrett tries to act calm, but his voice and hands are still shaking. He clears his throat, covering his mouth with his fist, exposing his droopy balls. He looks like he's about to make a big speech in his birthday suit. "I never meant to have an affair, but you weren't home a lot. You were always working. Eve was just … just persistent, and it just … *happened*. It doesn't mean anything—I swear." Garrett puts on the puppy-dog eyes.

"Say *what*?" Eve makes it to her feet this time, her bouncy tits exposed. "What you mean—I was *persistent* and *it didn't mean anything*? You said you *loved* me, Garrett! *Lots* of times!"

"Well … I do—I mean—I … I … huh … huh."

"I heard you say it myself, you ass!" I scream at Garrett. "I heard you confess your undying love to this ho while you had her leg flung up in the air, and you were hitting it from the side!"

"*Damn*," Eve exclaims. "So it's like *that*, Garrett? You don't *love* me anymore? What the fuck does that mean? You ain't gon' take care of this *baby*, motherfucker?"

The whole world suddenly stops. I feel as if I have gone deaf, and my whole head is filling up with thick cotton. I slow down as a part of me dies.

"*A baby*, Garrett?" I can barely speak.

Garrett doesn't take his eyes off mine as he makes a punk dive for his pants, lying in a crumpled pile on the floor. He has this sorry look stuck on his face as he hastily struggles to pull up and fasten his trousers. He has not one ounce of power left. No "Big Daddy" antics to rely upon now. In fact, he looks damn pitiful.

"You and Eve are having *a baby*, Garrett?" I feel my nose sting as my eyes fill up with hot tears. I want to explode, but I have no strength left.

"Yes, *a baby*!" Eve snaps. "And Garrett and I are happy about it. He was going to tell you anyway. Tell her, Garrett!"

"How could you do this to me, Eve?" I look at her, wanting a true answer.

"I didn't do anything to you," she hisses, rolling her eyes. "You did it to yourself, always talkin' 'bout how unhappy you are. Shi-it, I thought I was doin' you a favor!"

I look at her and am even more disgusted over the fact that she is rattling on like some kind of ghetto ho with no regard or one bit of remorse that she has helped destroy my heart, our friendship, and my marriage. Hell, what friendship?

"It was easy." Eve lobs another verbal grenade my way. "You were always out chasing the 'next big breaking news story.'"

"That is my *job*, Eve!"

"Well, that *was* your man," she retorts, "who just happens to be *my man* now."

I can't help it, but Satan takes over, and I jump across the bed, grab Eve by the throat, and slam her head against the wall. She is screaming and gagging and spitting and spewing pleas for me to let her go. Her long thin arms are flailing in a fierce fight to survive, but I only tighten my grip around the base of her neck and continue to squeeze, pounding her red head against the white wall again and again. I squeeze and squeeze, wanting to squeeze the life out of her the same way she squeezed the life out of my marriage.

For the first time in my life, I know I can kill.

"Hey, stop that!" Garrett shrieks as he tries to grab my arms, but I beat him back with the same elbows that he once sucked, one of them crashing him hard across the nose.

"Yeee-oow!" he yells as he grabs his face. Blood is spurting everywhere, bright red splattering the stark-white Egyptian sheets. Eve is screaming while Garrett wails in excruciating pain.

There is a loud pounding at the door. I come to my senses and let go of Eve's throat. I jump across the bed and make a mad dash for the door, purposely stomping on Garrett's bare foot as I dart past him.

"I'll deal with your ass back in New York," I warn him, "*with* my lawyer!"

I swing open the door and am happy and relieved to find Kat and Hope standing there, ready to roll. They grab me by my arms as we tear down the long hallway, around the corner, and down the emergency steps to the eleventh floor, where we race over to the elevator banks and punch the button to the lobby. Hope is smoothing down my hair and shaking her head. I must look like a hot mess. Kat points to the ripped underarm seam of my blouse and the wad of bright red hair still clenched tightly in my hand.

"Are you okay?" Kat asks with deep concern. For the first time in all of this drama, she looks worried.

"Yeah," I answer as I shake off Eve's red hair from between my fingers into the ashtray bin between the elevators. I don't even remember ripping it out of her head. "I'll be all right."

"You look like you've been in a fight." Kat looks concerned. Hope frowns.

"I have," I respond as I slip off my wedding band and throw it in the ashtray atop Eve's patch of red hair. "I have been in one helluva fight, but I think I won that round."

"Well, then, that's all that matters," says Hope as she gives me a big hug. "You made it out A-okay."

"Yeah, 'absolutely zero killed,'" Kat emphasizes as she wraps her arms around the two of us. "And now that everything's outta the closet, so to speak, let's take our happy asses home."

None of us says a word on the long trip back to New York City. None of us even mentions that I removed my wedding ring and left it in the ashtray back at the Ritz.

There is nothing left to do, nothing left to say.

We saw and heard and left it all in Boston.

Chapter
★ Twenty-One

AT HOPE, AND I ARE MEETING THIS MORNING IN A NOISY LITTLE coffee shop just around the corner from Dr. Roberta Katzenberg's office. She is the counselor my best friends are insisting I see after witnessing weeks of my wallowing in extreme depression after we busted Garrett and Eve in Boston. Only adding to my deep despair is the sudden death of my aunt Joy. Just as I feared, she was not at all well when I last saw her on Topsail. Her heart—as big and full of love as it was—finally gave out from an undetected heart condition. I wish there had been something I could have done to save her life.

Chase came to Aunt Joy's funeral in North Carolina, which I truly appreciated. He did his best to console me, telling me how much Aunt Joy meant to him and so many others on Topsail Island. But no amount of consolation could soothe my soul that day. I was mentally off somewhere else, trapped inside a deep and unrelenting pain.

Mother, Daddy, and I sprinkled Aunt Joy's ashes along the shore, just as she had requested in her will. She also asked that I take good care of Tranquility, in hope that I would always find a peaceful home there. In a small purple-velvet pouch, she left me the key to the beach house.

Garrett called to give his condolences. But I refused to speak to him. I couldn't bear the pain of that too.

It is an early July morning on Manhattan's West Side and the sticky feeling hanging in the air tells me that it's going to be another hot and humid day, as spring quickly gives way to summer. The cool breeze from the coffee shop's old air conditioner feels good, despite its deep, constant, baritone humming above the crowd. I figure that with the change of season might also come a change in my depressed mental state, feeling paralyzed and stuck in this depression, overwhelmed by so many sudden and horrific losses. Distraught for weeks now, I have not been eating, or sleeping, or motivated to do anything. Even Grossman is ordering me to take more time off the news beat to get my head together.

The girls believe that Dr. Katzenberg might help me push through my transition of disposition, so here we sit, readying me to see a shrink for the first time. They know that I really don't want to be here, but they are determined not to let me back out of today's appointment with the doctor.

"Call us as soon as you're done," Hope says as she squeezes my hand. I take one last gulp of coffee and check the clock above the register again.

"Yeah, we want every sordid detail," Kat teases.

"Okay." I struggle to hold a smile as I grab my bag and scoot out of the tight booth.

"Do good!" I hear Hope calling out behind me. "We'll be waiting right here when you're done."

I head out of the coffee shop door. Its tinkling bell announces my departure.

Out on the street, I again face harsh reality as I stand out here alone on this filthy sidewalk, bustling with stone-faced Manhattanites. Scores of pedestrians flow around me like a school of fish. They move in a solid stream of unconsciousness. Not one of them seems to notice that I am here.

Have I disappeared from the world that much?

My friends promise me that these next steps I take toward my counselor will be steps toward a better life for myself. So I walk. Step, by step, by step, and in between steps, I hear my heart pounding. I become anxious, feeling a cool sweat burst out on my brow. My throat is suddenly dry. I take deep breaths, trying to relax, my head swimming, and I keep hearing Hope and Kat promising that this is going to be good for me, so I keep on stepping. I keep on moving down the long block of busy, bustling people, remembering Kat's excitement weeks ago ...

"There's a lady I want you to call today. Her name is Dr. Roberta Katzenberg. She's a women's counselor on the Upper Westside." Kat was at the end of her patience with my depression. "She's a bit quirky, but she's really cool. I think she can help you. Insurance should cover it. I just read about her in *Cosmo*, so I went downtown to her seminar where she was talking about the effects of divorce on women."

"Oh, yeah?" My interest is perked a bit.

"Yeah. From the article, she sounds like just the kind of shoulder you need to lean on right now. She *gets* it."

"What'd the article say?"

"Divorce sucks."

****

Dr. Katzenberg's building is in the middle of Seventy-Third Street, a nice escape just off Amsterdam Avenue. It's a quiet, tree-lined street, where the prewar buildings are covered with ivy, and doormen smile at babies from their doorway perches.

"Good morning," the doorman greets me as I walk under the awning.

"Good morning," I reply. "I'm here to see Dr. Katzenberg."

"Yes, of course." He smiles as he swings open the glass door by its polished brass handle. Then he says, "Hey—wait a minute." I can feel his excitement behind me. "Hey, aren't you that news lady." He squints. "Yeah, yeah, that's you. Destiny … Destiny Newell—the one from Channel 4. Yeah, that's you! You negotiated that hostage situation up der in Harlem. Yeah. That's you. That's you. Good job on that der."

"Thank you." I smile and take a deep breath, wondering if he's wondering about me. I've told him I'm here to see Dr. Katzenberg. He probably thinks that I cracked under the hostage pressure, or maybe he knows that I'm really just another crazy woman going through another crazy divorce who has lost her ever-lovin' mind.

"Right this way." The man makes a dramatic motion toward the door. "It's the last door on the right." He winks with a smart little cock of his head.

I nod my appreciation and slowly walk across the large marble lobby, up three short steps, and follow the melodious sounds of classical music echoing from the end of the dark hallway. The burgundy-and-gold runner, tattered in some places along the edges, looks as if it came from the castle floors of old Europe. Scenes of peasants pushing wheelbarrows of grain capture my attention, as they are beautifully hand woven inside the plush carpet canvas.

I hear a woman's vibrato voice humming along with the flute in what I believe is one of Mozart's concertos. She sounds more like a chef preparing for dinner than a shrink preparing for a session. Who is this person my friends have so adamantly recommended?

I hate to interrupt her classical musing, but I know that time is money and that this is business, so I push the doorbell. It blares a long, loud buzz, like a metallic bumblebee. I hear some shuffling inside, and then the slide and click-click-click of her unlocking her door.

"Ah, yes," says the woman peering around the door. "You must be my ten o'clock. Please, come in."

Dr. Roberta Katzenberg is not at all what I expected. Then again, I'm not really sure what I expected since I've never been to a shrink before. She is a short and mousy woman in her early forties, with blonde hair piled in a neat bun on top of her head and gold-rimmed glasses perched just above the tip of her nose. She is stylishly dressed in a mustard-colored pant suit, with a scarf of soft green and gold carefully tied around her neck. Supple and well worn, her brown leather flats look as if they were finely handcrafted in Italy.

Her apartment/office harbors shelves of important looking books, large-framed diplomas from Dartmouth and Yale, and richly upholstered furniture. The beauty of the room is enhanced by the quality pieces she has carefully placed—a vase of floppy white French tulips on her desk, a Lladro statue of a little boy holding a bird on the windowsill, and what looks like a pink Baccarat swirling crystal ashtray on a side table. Everything about Dr. Katzenberg and her professional space speaks of elegance.

"Tea?"

"What?" I am startled.

"Would you like some tea? I always like to sip on a little tea and enjoy classical music in the morning. 'Music soothes the soul of the savage beast,' they say." And with that, she disappears into the kitchen. "Did you say you wanted tea, dear?"

"Yes, please," I reply, hoping she's not thinking I'm a savage beast.

"Your friends told me just a bit of what you're going through. I am so very sorry."

"Thank you," I reply, feeling odd. I'm not completely sold on the idea of sharing my life and depression with a complete stranger, even though I know I need help.

"One of them—Kat, I believe—attended my seminar." Dr. Katzenberg reenters the room carrying a wooden tray with a china teapot and two cups on saucers. My eyes zero in on a small plate of delicate cookies. "She is quite a go-getter, that one, no?"

"Oh, yes, yes, she is," I respond, a little embarrassed, knowing how pushy and persistent Kat can be. I'm also not sure what my big-mouthed girlfriend might have told this little doctor.

"She is the one who insisted on your being here, isn't she?" Dr. Katzenberg hands me a teacup by the saucer.

"Who? Kat? Well, yes, both Kat and Hope did," I say and carefully take the teacup and then a small sip. "They both think it's important that I see someone."

Dr. Katzenberg peers at me over her fancy gold bifocals. "What do you think?" she asks.

"Me?" I blink, staring at this strange woman as I feel a blank, lost look blossom over my face.

She leans in closer, nodding. "I want you to check in with yourself right now and make sure you are here because you truly want to be here. In these sessions, we're going to stop doing everybody else favors, my dear." She settles back in her chair, closes her eyes, and inhales her lavender tea. The lenses of her bifocals fog up in the hot steam.

I'm starting to like this Dr. Katzenberg.

"Sit there, or you can stretch out on the couch and talk to me, if you like, but I must tell you"—her big blue eyes pop open—"things get very emotional that way." She wrinkles her nose, pushes back her glasses, puts down her tea, and then reaches for her pen and pad.

I reach for a cookie.

"You know, I always wondered why you see people in the movies lying on the couch in the shrink's office," I say, nervously trying to make conversation.

She remains undisturbed, staring down at her Persian rug with a thoughtful frown.

I nibble a bit off my cookie.

"First of all, I am not a 'shrink,' my dear. I would never dare shrink you in any way." She chuckles at the thought. "But it has been proven that lying down on the couch more deeply unlocks the emotional cavities of your mind."

"I see." I blink.

"No shrinking of the mind here, dear. We only hope to expand your thinking, so your mind can cope with your life."

I accidentally slurp my tea.

"Okay, let's get started, shall we?" She gets up and clicks off the stereo.

Then she returns to her perch on her burgundy leather wing-back chair. "Now ... why are you here?"

"I'm here because I guess I need help."

"You guess you do? Do you think you need help?

"Yes. Yes, I do."

"What kind of help do you think you need?"

"I don't know. I've been extremely depressed ever since I found out about my husband's affair with my best friend," I feel involuntary tears welling up behind my eyes. "Then I lost my great-aunt who was so, so special to me. I either sleep too much or not at all. I can't remember when I eat. Sometimes I can't move. My job is suffering. My health is suffering. Everybody is worried sick about me. And I ... I have been having thoughts ... really bad thoughts ..."

"Thoughts of hurting yourself?"

"Yes."

"Maybe even thoughts of suicide?"

"Yes," I say, ashamed. I look down into my teacup and want to drown.

"Don't worry. You have done nothing surprising or new, considering your extremely depressed condition right now. In some cases, it is almost expected and quite normal for one with a drastic hormonal imbalance, or a sudden death, divorce, or other traumatic change in her life to consider suicide when sometimes just waking up feels like enough of a burden."

I can certainly relate to that.

"But suicide and maiming ourselves is certainly not the answer," Dr. Katzenberg continues with a shake of her head. "No, it is not even an option. We have to find other ways to cope with life's tough realities."

"You're right." I don't know what else to say.

"Now, one reality is that women these days are getting divorced all the time, but they survive. They move on. Why do you think you are having such a difficult time accepting this breakup with your husband?"

"I don't know. Maybe because it hurts so much, that's why. Maybe because I feel like I've failed, like I didn't even see it coming, wasn't paying enough attention. I knew there were basic problems in our marriage, but I thought they'd go away with time. I never dreamed things would turn out as bad as this."

"You say you knew there were basic problems in the marriage. What kinds of problems?"

"I don't know." I look down, wanting to dive into my teacup again.

"We just never spent enough time together—you know—valuable time. We were always so busy, each of us with our own careers and everything."

"Yes, but your *husband* obviously had time to develop a relationship outside your marriage."

Ouch. Now that hurt. I think long and hard, desperately searching for an escape, but I can't find one. "I guess, I ... I guess I didn't spend enough time at home."

"Did he?"

I am totally deflated.

"Yes, these are the kind of hard questions that are sure to come up in these psychotherapy sessions. Oftentimes, we are not reacting to what seem to be the obvious issues in our lives. Sometimes our reactions go much, much deeper than that, only serving as the backdrop—the canvas, so to speak—to magnify our real issues and what's *really* going on."

"So what I hear you saying is that this divorce, this depression I'm going through, is really my reaction to something else much deeper than my husband dumping me for that whore, Eve?"

"Perhaps we are dealing with far more going on inside you than you realize," Dr. Katzenberg responds with a gentle voice. "Your past is what has brought you here, my dear. My job is to help you unlock its challenging mysteries so you can prepare and protect your future."

"Okay," I whisper, a bit overwhelmed. Dr. Katzenberg is starting to sound more like a spiritual healer than a psychologist. I just hope and pray that this psych is not psycho as she continues her diligent and persistent dive for answers.

"What we call 'talk therapy' is not just talking about your problems. It is also working hard toward finding solutions, encouraging you to look at things a different way or discover new ways to react to people and the things that happen in your life."

"I am right now scared to death to even think about getting that close to another person—or ever being in another relationship."

"Yes, my dear." Dr. Katzenberg shakes her head and raises her eyebrows. "You have certainly been served a double-whammy of pain here. But that can change. Remember, it's not what happens in life; it's how we react to what happens that matters. We can get through our pain, Destiny, as difficult as it is."

I exhale. "I hope so." I think I'm beginning to see the light. I lie back on Dr. Katzenberg's couch and stare at her crackless ceiling.

"Earlier, you told me that your parents strongly disapproved of your marriage to Garrett. Why?"

"Because he's arrogant and defends himself against their bullying. But they wouldn't have approved of anybody anyway."

"Oh? Why not?"

"They fear losing me—losing control. I guess anyone who threatens that, threatens them." I shake my head, roll my eyes, and feel my cheeks flush. "You know, they really know how to push buttons."

Dr. Katzenberg chuckles. "You know why parents know how to push our buttons, don't you?"

"No, how?"

"Because they *installed* them," she emphasizes with wide eyes.

"Ah, yes." I smile, appreciating her humor.

"What is your relationship with your mother like now?"

"Well ..." I sigh and stare at a large black fly that's landed upside down on the high white ceiling. "My relationship with my mother? Well, it's hard, you know."

"Why?" Dr. Katzenberg continues scribbling on her yellow notepad.

"Well, I'm not convinced she always wants the best for me. I think she wants the best for herself. She never thinks I'm good enough ... or anybody else, for that matter. She's a mean snob. We're very different people, and we've struggled to make peace all my life, something I think really affects my confidence and relationships."

"Oh? Not feeling good enough?" Dr. Katzenberg looks up over her bifocals.

"I know she's proud, but she gave up a lot of her own dreams to have me. I think she resents that sometimes and tries to live through me. She married a prominent doctor when she could have become one herself."

We sit in silence. I stare at the stubborn fly now circling the ceiling. I hear a clock ticking.

"How do you think the relationship with your mother has affected your life as woman now?"

"Well, she certainly made an overachiever out of me; that's for sure. I guess I just wanted her approval for once." I can't stop a sudden rash of tears from falling down the sides of my face. Dr. Katzenberg hands me a box of tissues. "I never told anyone this before, not even my best friends," I confess as I dab my snotty nose and struggle in desperation to inhale, "but I was pregnant just before Garrett and I got married." I sob. "We were very confused and not sure of what to do. I was scared to death of the grave responsibilities of motherhood. Afraid I couldn't handle it. I was afraid I might turn into her. I didn't want to be a mother because I might turn into my mother."

"What happened?"

"We decided not to have the baby because it would get in the way of our careers." I feel a deep, dark emptiness and betrayal. "Garrett escorted me to the local clinic, and we aborted our baby, already well into its first trimester. I felt it was a little boy ... a little boy. We both cried like we were babies ourselves that night. We held each other and cried and cried. I don't believe either of us ever got over that. How could we so easily abort our child? Maybe that was the first sign that we had no business getting married in the first place. I still don't know if that was the right decision. I think maybe I choked out of fear and insecurity. Mother always insisted I have a career, not a man and a baby. I believe that was truly her dream for herself. That's why my heart breaks at the thought of Eve now carrying my husband's child. She gets that chance with Garrett—not me—and I truly regret that. Truly regret that. Maybe I didn't fight harder for the things that I truly loved and wanted."

"Are you sure having children with Garrett was one of those things you truly loved and wanted?"

"Wow ..." I am startled by the severity and sting of Dr. Katzenberg's barrage of questions.

"I'm asking if you're sure you wanted marriage and children with Garrett to begin with."

"I think so. I think I loved him that much."

Dr. Katzenberg shifts in her seat. "You think?"

"Maybe I was more in love with the idea of freedom, a peaceful family life, and getting away from Mother than I was in love with Garrett himself," I confess. "Maybe he was the easy choice to avoid ever having to go back home."

"Is there somewhere you can go for a while? Spend time? Regroup? Is there any place that gives you solitude and tranquility so you can think about what it is that you truly want for your life? And then, together, we can start your new journey from there."

"*Tranquility?*" I repeat Dr. Katzenberg's word slowly, finding joy in the way the word rolls around on the sides of my tongue. I wonder, even more now, whether the good doctor is psychic. How did she know how much "tranquility" means to me? It is far more than just a word; it is the name of the one home I have loved and felt love all my life. And Tranquility now belongs to me.

"Home, wherever you find it, is a healing place," Dr. Katzenberg says. "Go home—wherever that 'home' is for you, and go wherever that home takes you." Dr. Katzenberg's clock cuckoos. "Well, our time is up today." She gently removes her bifocals and carefully places them inside a cat-embroidered cloth case. "You did exceptional work today, my dear. You dug deep. But be prepared to go even deeper, Destiny—much, much deeper."

I nod my head slowly, feeling the gravity of all I must do. As I gather my belongings and say good-bye, I feel a strange sense of wonder and excitement growing inside of me. I cannot wait to move on with clarity and occasional help from Dr. Katzenberg. But the first step is to book another flight home to my Tranquility—my dear Topsail Island—my home away from home. My salvation.

As I walk down the padded runner in the marble hallway, I hear Dr. Katzenberg humming once again as she cranks up her stereo and replays her Mozart concerto.

"Music soothes the soul of the savage beast, they say ..."

And I know, deep down inside, I am one of them.

Chapter
★ Twenty~Two

IT IS HARD TO BELIEVE THAT I HAVE RETURNED AGAIN TO TOPSAIL Island. I have traveled here more in the past few months than I have in many years. But I am always comforted by what I have always felt and known as home. Topsail seems the most likely place to retreat, especially under these grim circumstances of feeling so hurt, lost, and broken, especially my heart, which sinks at the thought that Aunt Joy is not here and never will be again. Though not in the flesh, hopefully in the spirit. I will miss her more than I know. I lovingly recall her greeting me with squeals of delight at the top of our beach house steps with her shrimp deveiner in hand.

I hear the familiar crack and squeal of the salty hinges as I push open the door of what is now my beach house. I am taken aback once again by the familiar smells that rush around me. It is the smell of home, of my ancestors, of my life and me. The smell of my grandparents and Aunt Joy. The smell of the straw rugs and driftwood on the shelf. Of Grandpa's pipe. Of fish frying and grits bubbling and biscuits dripping with butter. The smell of love and being loved, all locked up in this one little house. It is the smell of home. It is me.

I swing open the shutters, and the ocean is out there all around me again. She is boisterous today and her tide is rushing in. I feel her electricity and her invitation to take a swim or a long walk along her beach.

The phone rings. It has to be Kat or Hope. They're probably checking in on me, just as I am sure my parents will be doing soon, making sure I arrived safely and am not still considering suicide.

"Hello?"

"Hey, girl! What's happ'nin'? You got in okay?" It's both Kat and Hope on the other end of the line, with a lot of concern, energy, and a host of questions.

"Hey, yeah, I got here safely. It was the perfect choice," I say as I catch my breath, wipe my brow, and look out over the stretch of dark blue ocean.

"You all by yourself? Why you breathing so hard?" Hope asks. "What've you been doing?"

I chuckle slightly. "Flinging open the shutters, that's all. I just got in. It is so amazing out there. The ocean is so blue today—just beautiful. Nice to be isolated from the rest of the world, you know?"

"Seen Adonis yet?" Kat asks.

"Ah," Hope replies. "Yeah, that fine police chief?"

"I just got here! And his name is Chase," I say, and, once again, I feel a jolt of electricity at the simple mention of his name.

"Well, nothing wrong with knowing the police chief," says Hope. "You never know when you might need him one day down there on that island all by yourself."

"Yeah," Kat chimes in. "You might need him down there for lots of things!"

"Girl, please!" Hope snaps. "Stop that nonsense! Destiny's supposed to be trying to heal right now. Dee, unlike our sister here, I think it's really important to let go of one situation and deal with the aftermaths of that one before moving on to the next one. You're very sensitive right now."

"And that is why it is even more important for our sister to get laid," Kat argues. "Especially since you are totally through with that asshole, Garrett. So when are you gonna see Adonis?"

"I don't know," I answer. "Soon, I hope. He's a very special man and has proven to be a good friend. I really appreciate that he was there for me when we lost Aunt Joy."

"Be careful, Dee," Hope warns. "You know you're on an emotional roller coaster right now. You have come so far with Dr. Katzenberg, this trip to Topsail, and all. We just don't want to see you have an emotional relapse or anything."

"Yeah, and as much as I do believe that you really do need a good lay, Hope may have a point," Kat reluctantly admits. "Girl, I never want to see you looking like you 'bout to jump off a bridge again. That was not pretty, girlfriend. Uh-huh, that is *not* allowed. Not a good look." Kat shakes her head.

"Hey, listen to us, y'all—it's not even that big a deal. He was just a guy I used to know at the beach, right? No. Big. Deal."

Silence.

"O-kay," Kat starts. "First, it's a big deal; then it's a not-so-big a deal. Girl, you are truly *sprung*!"

Hope chuckles. "All I can say is, thank God we can halfway laugh about something. We haven't done that in while. Cheers to Police Chief Adonis!"

Hope is right. It's good to connect with my girls, dreaming like teenagers again.

"Wouldn't that be something if Chase turned out to be your neighbor again? But this time, instead of the trailer park, he lived in a mansion by the sea? Wouldn't that be the bomb?" Kat muses.

It would be quite the irony if things really changed that much. Back in the day, the only reason Chase was then my neighbor on our segregated island was because his family was poor. Poor white folks were just as ostracized as blacks folks by other whites, particularly the rich ones, so they had to live on our side of the island, their tin trailers lined up and parked across our one two-lane highway by the sound. The white kids weren't allowed to play with us because we were black. We weren't allowed to play with them because they were poor.

It was just understood. That was the way things were. But so much has changed. Or has it?

"You sure you won't be lonely down there?" Hope asks, concerned as always.

"I'll be fine, Hopey," I reassure her. "I'm home. I feel much safer here than anywhere else right now. Don't worry."

"Well, at least you're out of that brownstone of doom for a while. Have you even heard from that motherfucker, Garrett lately?"

"No," I reply. "I think he's too ashamed. It doesn't matter. As Dr. Katzenberg says, it's time to move on with my life. I have no control over what Garrett does anyway. I only have control over myself."

"Clearly, you can't control Garrett," Kat hisses. "Garrett can't even control Garrett! Dr. Katzenberg is right. Move on with your life."

"And you are doing it very nicely," Hope adds. I can feel her warm hug through the phone. "We are so very, very proud of you, Dee."

"I love you guys," I gush into the phone, at the point of tears. "Thanks again for checking in on me."

"You be good!" Hope says. "Call us if you need anything."

"I will," I assure her.

"Call us if you *get* anything!" Kat teases. "And kiss Chief Adonis for us!"

And with that, my angel girlfriends are back to their busy lives in the bustling boroughs of New York City. Another place, another home that already seems so far away—light-years away from where I am today.

I wonder what Garrett is doing back in New York—what my husband might be thinking, what he talks about with his lover, Eve, these days after they practically destroyed my life. Those worrisome thoughts slowly dissolve as the image of a golden and glistening Adonis glides across my mind. He smiles. I melt. And that one dream alone makes me feel far better than any of the realities of Garrett.

Chapter
☆ Twenty~Three

I AM NOT IN THE MOOD TO GROCERY SHOP, SO I DECIDE TO HAVE DINNER at the Mainsail Restaurant, one of the more upscale offerings on the island. Locals boast about the Mainsail's great seafood, steak, and pasta menu. It's back-porch dining area is considered by many islanders as the best spot on the sound for watching the sunset, to enjoy a good meal, and to watch an occasional crane mate. The sound scene is lovely in its serenity—tall cattails waving in the soft breeze, a mosquito creating a ripple on the smooth water, a hungry fish splashing in the distance.

I decide to have dinner on the popular back porch. I plan to enjoy a cold, crisp glass of wine while contemplating my future. I need to check in with myself as my soul rests in the bosom of Topsail.

"Hi, there. Here's your menu. What can I getcha ta drink?" A robust waitress with a strong southern twang stands there before me, pen and pad ready.

"I'll have a chardonnay, please," I answer.

"Coming right up, hon. Oh, and our special today is crab and shrimp stuffed flounder with a special sauce."

"A special sauce?" I am curious, remembering that old saying that if you stand still long enough down here, they'll either fry you or pour a sauce on you.

"I think it's a butter-and-lemon–based special sauce."

Ah, yes, and they'll pour butter on you too.

"Sounds good. I'll try it."

"Alrighty then. Your chardonnay is coming right up."

I settle back into the country porch chair that faces the sound and smile as I welcome the sun as my guest. She is just settling down after a long day of shining. She is such a warm friend. I close my eyes and let her baste me in her golden rays as she keeps me company.

The restaurant is quaint and country—lots of decorative blue and white china plates hung and displayed on the walls, with preppy-dressed patrons wandering in for a nice supper after a long day at the beach. The walls are painted forest green with dark wood accents, surprisingly different for a shore restaurant. Seems that Bobby Lee Martin, the Mainsail's owner, wanted to offer a more elegant alternative to the typical seashells-and-nets beach decor. He achieved a special look for his restaurant that separates his from the others, as does the sound from the sea.

"Well, it's 'bout time you got a day off there, Chief!"

I jump when I hear the waitress say "Chief."

"What happened? Missy not cooking for you again tonight?"

"Aw, now Laverne Jones, you know Missy and how she feels about the kitchen. Naw. She and her sister ran off shopping in Charlotte again this weekend."

"You tell that girl that she don't keep a man by shopping in Charlotte. She better start cooking on Topsail. Not that we mind feedin' you, Chief. C'mon, I got you your favorite table just in time for the sunset. Getcha a cold beer?"

"Sure, Laverne. Thanks."

Chase sits at the table opposite me on the other side of the porch. I feel like I am going to melt into the wicker of this chair. He is in civilian clothes—khakis and a light green cotton shirt that shows off his brilliant sea-green eyes. It must be his day off. It looks like he just had his sun-kissed hair cut into a cool military crew-cut look. His face is tanned and glows a bronze sheen as he takes his seat, closes his eyes, and, just like me, inhales the sunshine. I sit here, suspended in time, staring at the man who takes my breath away. The sun has even kissed his eyelashes.

Laverne bursts through the door with a tray holding two ice-cold glasses—one of chardonnay and the other filled to the brim with tap beer.

"Here ya go, darlin'." She smiles as she places the chilled wine in front of me. She is blocking my view of Chase. "That special is on the way too. Can I getcha somethin' else?"

I'm thinking, *Uh, yeah, I'll take that fine—and very alone—police chief over there. He'll do.* But I just smile and say, "No, thank you," and pray I know what to do when she moves her round body and Chase finally sees me.

"Okie doke. Well, you just let me know," she offers. "I'm Laverne."

"Thank you, Laverne."

She turns and walks away to the other side of the porch, where she plops down Chase's beer and starts up another conversation with him about the crab-and-shrimp–stuffed flounder with the special lemon-butter sauce. Laverne's aproned body is still hiding me from his view, but I can hear him and their conversation. He updates her on his mother, who's doing well and busy in her tomato garden, and Missy, who I remember is the girlfriend, and her never-ending shopping sprees. He marvels at the sound, which Chase proudly claims is the best-kept secret in the Carolinas. I have to agree.

Laverne blushes and giggles, obviously another doting fan of our very handsome police chief.

"I'll try that special," he decides.

"All right, Chief," Laverne gushes. "Let me go put your order in. That's two specials, comin' up, and—" Laverne suddenly stops short and playfully points to both of us on either end of the porch. "Y'all are just gonna love Bobby Lee's special today! And that sauce—mm-hm! It's gonna make you swaller yer tongue!"

Chase and I both laugh at Laverne's passionate testimony as she walks back into the restaurant, leaving us alone and finally face-to-face. Our shared laughter slowly melts into the recognition of our shared truth. We are alone again together.

"Destiny?" Chase looks surprised. "What are you doing here?"

"Yep, I'm back." I blush.

"Well, what … what in the world are you doing back here so soon? I thought you were up North in the big city, fightin' crime." Chase's eyes light up. "You didn't let me know you were coming back."

Chase starts to get up from his table. As much I want to see him, I cannot possibly tell Chase how screwed up my life is right now.

"I just needed a break," I say as I stand to greet my old friend and neighbor.

"Well, welcome home." Chase hugs me, and I feel a strong surge of electricity between us. "You mind if I join you? I'm eating alone—you're eating alone."

"Sure," I reply. "No need in our yelling across the tables at each other, huh?"

"Nope, no need." Chase grabs his place mat, beer, and utensils and sneaks over to my table. "Let's see if Laverne notices," he whispers.

I chuckle as he takes a seat. "I am sure she will."

The sky is turning orange as the sun starts her sunset symphony. Everything seems to come to a sudden stillness, including Chase, me, and the other patrons of the Mainsail. We all sit in our special spaces, suspended in silence and time as we stare at the sunset, each of us in awe of her majesty. I marvel at how close we are to God in this moment and to our ancestors.

I break the silence. "I remember sitting on my grandpa's porch, watching the sunset over the sound with Aunt Joy." I feel my eyes well up with tears. I miss her so much.

Chase takes a long, hard look at me. His eyes are full of concern. "Destiny," he starts, "I want to tell you how sorry I am that you lost your aunt Joy. She was a great lady. I know how hard it was for you. She loved you very much. If I can help you in any way—"

"Chase, you have already helped me in more ways than you know. Thank you so much for being there for me at the funeral and for all of your calls. It meant so much to me."

"I didn't hear back from you. I was worried about you."

"So much in my life is falling apart right now, Chase. Aunt Joy's passing certainly didn't help."

"Well, Dee, I will always be here for you. I promise." It was the same promise this man named Chase made to me when he was a boy named Chip, and sadly, I barely believe in promises anymore.

"Thank you," I reply, fighting back tears.

"Destiny," Chase interjects, "why do you suppose I keep running into you?"

"I dunno. Maybe it's—"

"*Destiny?*"

I feel my heart drop twenty stories as I fall deeper into Chase's spell. Perhaps he is right. Maybe it is our destiny to be here at these moments, time and time again, together. All I know is that there's no place in the world I'd rather be right now than right here on Topsail Island with my long-lost childhood friend. Maybe we are right here again because we prayed for each other.

Chase and I spend the next three and a half hours talking about our lives—how he is still holding off on an engagement with Missy, how I discovered Garrett's affair, and how much has changed on Topsail Island since the childhood friendship we had to share in secret, not so many years ago, under this very brush where we sit together now by the sound. It was the one secret place we could play together without reprimand or consequences for being together—black and white.

"Do you remember that strange little cabin that used to sit right back there in the sound on the water?" I ask Chase. "I think we used to call it 'the old potato house' 'cause somebody left a sack of potatoes in there. Why somebody would just leave a sack of potatoes, I have no idea!"

Chase chuckles for a long time, shaking his head. He smiles a mysterious smile and leans toward me. "Yes, I remember that potato house very well, Miss Destiny. I'd really like you to see it today. How's your morning looking tomorrow?"

"Oh, I'll have to check my busy schedule." I tease.

"How about I pick you up at 10:00 a.m. sharp? I have something I'd like to show you—a little tour of your old stompin' grounds. How about that?"

"That would be wonderful."

Chase insists on picking up the check and then escorts me out to my car.

"Yeah … well …" Chase sighs and kicks at the gravel. "Well, I'll see you in the morning."

"Okay. Sounds good to me," I say.

"Hey, in fact …" Chase flashes a mischievous grin. "You can join me on assignment."

"Wait a minute," I reply as I hop in my car. "On assignment? What assignment?"

"Just be ready tomorrow, girlie," he teases.

"Sounds like I'm back in the newsroom."

"Naw, little lady," Chase says with a snicker. "You're a *long* way from that newsroom. See you in the morning, New York—bright-eyed and bushy-tailed."

"All right, I surrender." I feel myself blushing. "See you in the morning."

I honk my horn good-bye and pull out of the Mainsail's driveway. I am simply dumbfounded by all that has happened over the past few hours—how much Chase and I have finally caught up and how much we still share, despite our many years apart, living tremendously different lives. I also find it promising that I will see my old friend again in the morning sun. And I cannot wait. For the first time, in a long time, I sing my heart out to the radio all the way home.

Chapter
★ Twenty~Four

*I*HAVE NOT BEEN THIS EXCITED ABOUT ANYTHING IN A LONG TIME, BUT I admit, I so anticipate Chase's Topsail tour this morning that I get up at the crack of dawn. After checking in with Mother and Daddy, convincing them that I made it here safely and am doing much better, I take my coffee and a walk on the beach to get my head together. The cool sand beneath my feet feels invigorating; the new day's sky, inspiring, as it's going to be another beautiful day on Topsail, especially spending this morning with Chase.

I decide to wear my yellow sundress and white sneakers. I grab my straw hat and sunglasses and toss them inside my beach bag. I have no idea where Chase is taking me, much less what my "assignment" might be, but I am ready and excited for this unexpected adventure with him.

Ten o'clock sharp, I hear wheels crunching down the driveway. It is Chase in a big red pickup truck. I feel a rush of heat as I watch him getting out of his vehicle. Tight Wrangler jeans. Cowboy boots today. I see why they say, "Girls go nuts for Wrangler butts."

"Good mornin'. You ready to go?" Chase asks as he opens the passenger door for me.

"Yessiree," I reply. "And you sure picked a nice day for a Topsail tour."

"Any day's a nice day for a Topsail tour," he replies. "It's a southern paradise we have down here. I think you're in for some real surprises today, lady."

I need this pleasant escape more than Chase knows.

We hop in his truck and head out for our day of sightseeing. We visit the historic Jolly Roger pier, the refurbished marina, but it is when we head toward our favorite marshes from childhood that lead to the sound that I become anxious. Chase turns the truck onto a dirt road leading underneath the dense marsh trees. I remember running barefoot down this road as a little girl, many moons ago. The bright sunshine gives way to shadow now. Then Chase stops the truck and cuts the engine.

"Okay, you gotta close your eyes before we go any further," he says.

"What?" I ask, a bit flustered by the request. "Where are you taking me?"

"Just close your eyes, you'll see. I have a nice surprise for you."

"I can't close my eyes and see at the same time," I joke.

"Aw, c'mon, girlie, just close your eyes."

"Okay, okay." I surrender.

Chase starts up the truck again and begins driving deeper into the marsh woods. The road is bumpy and the shade and breeze are cool. After a few minutes, he stops the truck again.

"No peeking, now," he sternly warns as he helps me out of his truck, holding me gently by the elbow and leading me to somewhere mysterious. I sure like him holding my elbow like this.

"All right, here we go. You can open your eyes now."

I slowly open my eyes and start to focus. I cannot believe what I see. There before me is what looks like the old potato house, except is has been renovated into a beautiful waterfront home, complete with a huge wraparound porch.

"Oh, my God!" I exclaim. "Oh, Chase! Is that really the old potato house?"

Chase is standing there quite proud, as well as amused by the absolute shock, awe, and surprise on my face.

"Yep, that beauty right there was at one time an old abandoned shack fulla taters." We both laugh till it hurts at the absurdity of it all.

"But who lives here now?" I ask, still awestruck. "Who turned our potato house into a home?"

"I did," replies Chase. "As soon as I had some savings put together, I bought this land. They asked me if I wanted them to tear down the house. I thought about all the good times I had back here as a kid and how I'd always imagined it being a real home one day. I couldn't let anybody destroy it. This little ol' shack holds too many memories for me. Too many hopes and dreams."

"Well, it's certainly not a little ol' shack today, Chase. Look at it! It's so cool you even got that wraparound porch you dreamed of."

"Yep." Chase chuckles and shakes his head. "Sure did. And I got you. Come on. Let me show you inside."

Chase takes my elbow again as we climb the stairs to the house. With each step we take, I feel that much closer to Chase. Being inside his home, I get even more of an insight on who this marvelous man is. His heart and soul are in this house, and he takes tremendous pride in having restored it himself. It is a wide-open space with light oak floors and two small bedrooms off to the side. The kitchen is located behind a bamboo bar, and from the number of pots and pans hanging overhead, the man obviously cooks.

"Would you like anything? Something to drink, maybe? I've got some sweet tea."

"Sure," I say. "I'd love some sweet tea. We don't get a lot of that in New York. I miss it. Thanks."

I watch Chase as he moves around his kitchen, preparing our refreshments. He is so drop-dead gorgeous. He pays the greatest attention to even the smallest detail. With two tall glasses brimming with sweet tea and clinking with ice, Chase leads me out to the front porch.

"Wait just a minute, before you take a sip," he says as he turns to hop down the front porch stairs. I can't take my eyes off those jeans. Chase walks down the side of the stairwell, stops, stoops, and then disappears from view. *What in the world is he doing?* Suddenly, Chase's head pops up, this time sporting a wide grin as he joyfully dangles a clump of freshly picked mint leaves.

"Now, you didn't go up there to New Yawk and get so citified that you forgot about this fine southern touch of mint, did ya?" Chase rinses his nosegay of mint and then playfully hops back up the stairs. Still grinning, he saunters up to me, swipes the glass of sweet tea out of my hand, and then dramatically spears its surface with his stem of mint.

There goes that smile again.

On him.

And on me.

Chase and I sit in his two big wooden rocking chairs, sipping on our freshly minted sweet teas, telling our funny and most familiar stories, and looking out over the settling sound from underneath the marsh trees. I enjoy him so much, and he seems to enjoy my company as well. I wonder if I ever could have had a real future with Chase.

"If you could have any dream come true, Chase, what would it be?" I ask.

"Wow." He seems taken aback by the question. "Any dream?"

"Yes, any dreams come true."

"Well, ah … hm … let's see … Well, I'd love to live right here with a good woman who truly loves me, this island, this sound, and this sea as much as I do. How's that?"

"Sounds good to me," I agree. "If you and your girlfriend, Missy, work things out. Don't you think you'd live here together one day?"

"Oh, I don't think so." Chase shakes his head and looks out over the vast sound. "For some reason, Missy don't like my potato house."

"What? Why not?" I am shocked at Chase's answer. "You have built a beautiful home here."

"I dunno the answer to that one, Destiny, and there's a lot I don't know the answer to right now." Chase looks sad.

"I'm sorry. I just thought—well, it really is such a beautiful place, Chase, I just thought … well, I just hate to see you have to leave your home—a dream home that that you built and all."

"And a home that I love," Chase interjects. I recognize the deep passion in his voice, and I know how much this house, this structure, this sound, and this sacred strip of land mean to Chase. All his life, this was his escape; Chase's no-man's-land, where he was safe from his father's brutal beatings, his family's racial prejudices and fears, and the taunting bullies who picked him to pieces every day because his family lived in a trailer park and was poor. Chase told me he always imagined the potato house was a real home where he also imagined he was happy.

"Missy wants to live in a big castle off the island," Chase explains.

"Oh, I see," I reply, but I don't see.

"Her dad is one of the biggest contractors around, and he wants to build his baby girl a great … big … house—with columns." Chase motions with his arms. "Yeah, he wants baby girl's palace to be a shining example of what 'McKay Construction can do for you.'"

"McKay Construction?" I ask. "They advertise on that big billboard just off the island, right?"

"Yep, that's the one. '*Let McKay Construction build your dream home!*'"

"Oh, I see," I say, afraid to push the issue much further.

Chase stares out over the water. He looks as if he is deep in thought and those thoughts have taken him far away. I feel for him because those thoughts do not look as if they are soothing ones.

"Hey, come on, it's time to put you on assignment." Chase snaps out of his pensive mood with a loud slap on his knee.

"Okay, here we go again with this assignment thing. What do you want me to do? I'm on leave, you know."

"Just follow me." Chase grins and extends his strong hand to me. I gladly take it and tumble down the stairs after him as we head toward the water. "C'mon, hurry up now."

Still holding my hand, Chase leads me down what looks like a hidden path through the gnarly marsh trees so dense they form a living tunnel. The marsh's forest-like floor is of deep, cool sand, so Chase and I bumble and sway, gently bumping into each other as we trudge down the path toward the sound.

"Where are you taking me, Chase?"

"On assignment. I told ya."

"What assignment?" I ask again, tugging on Chase's hand, as we break into the clearing.

"That one," Chase replies with a big smile as he points toward the water. "That one right over there."

My eyes follow Chase's finger offshore. There, sitting in the sunlight, bobbing on the water, is a charming little shrimp boat. The bold letters painted on the side sport its name: *On Assignment*.

"You are kidding me!" I squeal with even more surprise and delight. "Is this what you were talking about all this time? Aw, I can't believe you, Chase."

"Come on, Dee, whatcha say? Let's go on assignment."

"Oh, my God! I wish all my assignments were like this!" I laugh.

Chase helps me onto his boat, carefully taking my hand and ushering me aboard what turns out to be yet another one of his great refurbishing projects. It's a funny little boat, but I can tell that Chase takes an enormous amount of pride in it, as he has redone her insides in a beautiful golden wood and painted her outside in a stark white with a deep-red trim.

Chase takes me through the sound, and we spend the day traveling up and down the intercoastal waterway. It is a glorious afternoon, full of sunshine and wonder. We laugh and joke and talk about the many dart games we played as kids, playing at the piers, how many sour pickles we ate, where we crabbed under the little drawbridge using rotten chicken necks, and that we watched sea turtles lay their eggs. We learned that each of us grew up counting the tide tables, noting the ever-changing colors of the ocean, and loving the art of fishing, especially with a friend.

On Assignment carries us gently down the waterway. We pass some children playing together on the banks of the stream. They are black, white, and brown.

"Don't you wish we could have played together like that as kids—all out in the open instead of hiding in case somebody saw us?" I ask.

"Yeah. Sure do. I have often wished that things could have been very different for all of us back then."

Chase looks at me, and I feel a sudden surge of energy so strong that it feels as if the wind was just knocked out of me. I am so attracted to Chase that I can't help myself. And by the way he's looking at me, I believe that something is stirring inside of him too. I feel weak and alive and paralyzed all at the same time. I don't know what to do.

"You know, Destiny, I can't make up for all the time lost between us, but I am so happy that we found each other again."

"Me too, Chase. I mean, who'd believe that after all this time we'd be sitting here together—*On Assignment*."

"Yep, pretty amazing, right?

"Pretty amazing."

We sit here in momentary silence as the little boat continues her placid cruise down the water.

"Destiny …" Chase turns from steering the wheel and looks my way. "I don't think you have any idea how much I have thought about you over the years." Chase smiles that special smile again. I admire the laugh lines growing around his eyes.

The look on Chase's face says his thoughts have drifted to days gone by. "I'll never forget the night we first kissed. Remember how we used to dream we lived in the potato house together?"

"Yes," I say, remembering his sweet kiss. We hid in the moonlight for hours, despite our folks forbidding our even seeing each other.

"I swear I would look out for you every summer," Chase humbly confesses. "You just stopped coming to Topsail."

"I stopped coming because I had moved on, Chase. I think you know how much I wanted to be with you too. It seemed so impossible at the time to believe that we could have anything real."

"Hm. I know your folks weren't happy about us."

"And neither was your mom."

Silence.

"Destiny, I never stopped hoping you were okay or that one day I'd see you again—and look, here you are."

"Yes, a broken woman whose husband left her for her best friend."

"That isn't what I see," Chase replies. "I don't know how anybody could ever leave you."

"You did." I hit Chase hard with the truth. "You stopped meeting me in the marshes after that night—after you got me all stirred up inside. You acted like you didn't even know me when I saw you at the pier."

Chase turns away and sighs. He gazes out over the rippling water. The man I know I love looks deflated.

"Dee, you know how different things were back then. Folks down here just aren't as progressive as they are in your big city. Heck, your folks told me I could never see you again—my mother threatened to send me to live with my dad if I did—but I never ever stopped thinking about you, not ever."

It is the first time I have ever seen Chase so agitated, so upset. He scowls out at the sound, his face red. Then, finally, he breaks his simmering silence.

"So, tell me ... what the hell was *he* thinking? Who in the dickens would ever let you go?"

"Garrett," I reply matter-of-factly. "Hey, look, I don't even know why I got married in the first place, Chase. I know I wasn't ready."

"What? Buckled under the pressure?"

"No, not at all. In fact, my folks warned me that I was making a mistake, that I wasn't ready, and that Garrett wasn't the right man for me. But I think I was really just running away from home, to tell you the truth."

"Hm. Just seemed like the thing to do at the time, huh?"

"Guess so."

"I don't know. Maybe everything'll work out for both of us, somehow, Dee."

"I hope so, Chase. I sure hope so."

"Well, we'd better head back now." Chase starts turning his boat around.

"Yeah, sure," I say.

We travel up the waterway back to Chase's house, mostly quiet, just enjoying the scenery and these precious moments together. Finally, we reach Chase's slip, and he docks his boat.

"Chase, thank you for sharing this day with me."

"You are mighty welcome, Miss Dee. It's meant a lot to me. I enjoyed this time with you."

Chase hops off the boat, ties the ropes to the dock, and then offers me his hand.

I graciously take it, but as I am preparing to disembark, the little boat drifts farther from the dock, and I almost tumble into the water—until Chase grabs me by the waist and hoists me over the lip of the vessel and onto the dock. I look up at Chase, who is looking down at me—and something happens; something electric and magical and crazy happens. Our eyes lock, and suddenly I can't move. I smell him and feel his muscles flexing and his eyes staring down into mine—and something happens. Chase pulls me closer to him, his eyes locked into mine, and suddenly, he kisses me—a long, hard, deep and desperate kiss, just a hint of the boy I embraced before. This kiss is the kiss of a man. I swoon under his being, not sure whether to hold him closer or push him away, but my body and soul are so wrapped up into Chase that I just surrender into his kiss, into this feeling so strange, confusing, and welcome. Yet I feel that I am right where I am supposed to be. Where God has somehow led me after all of this time apart. Chase's body molds into mine. I feel so happy, I want to cry.

I am feeling that Chase and I can stay like this all day, until the persistent honking of a car horn breaks our bliss, abruptly snapping us back into reality.

Chase steps back, looking out of sorts. I stand back, breathing hard, just as dumbfounded and looking to Chase for direction. What were we thinking? How did this happen? Why did it feel so good—so right? We stare at each other, knowing why.

The car horn blares again in the background.

"We better go, see who that is," says Chase. "Could be an emergency."

I follow Chase back through the marsh trees, toward his house, and there, standing on the porch, tapping her espadrilled foot, is a tall, willowy blonde woman. Surrounding her feet are a half dozen shopping bags. This must be Missy.

"Hey, honey!" she calls out to Chase with an excited wave. "I just knew you'd be out there on that silly boat again today. Come on and see all the pretty thangs I got for Sissy's party." Missy begins gathering her bags but stops short when she notices me also coming out of the brush behind Chase. She squints. "Oh … hello. I didn't know you had company, honey."

"Missy, meet Destiny," Chase says with a warm smile.

"Chase was nice enough to show me the waterway today," I answer.

"Well, how nice." Missy looks back and forth at the two of us. "I didn't see your car anywhere."

"Well, actually—" I start.

"I picked her up this morning," Chase finishes.

"Well, bless your heart. So y'all been tooling around since this morning?" Missy checks her watch. "Well, y'all've been on that water a good little while, hadn't ya? I tell you, Chase could float on that water for a lifetime. I guess you could too, Melody."

"Destiny," I correct her. "And yes, I love the water very much."

"How sweet," Missy gushes. Then she turns to Chase. "Honey, I picked up a lot of pretty party thangs today. I wanna see whatchu think."

"Well, good," Chase responds. "Missy's little sister is having a big engagement party at the country club this weekend."

"Oh, how nice," I reply.

"I'm praying one day Chase'll give me good reason to throw a big party like that at the club. Right, Chase?" Missy elbows Chase, and then she turns to me and says in a stage whisper, "Maybe when I show him all this pretty stuff, he'll get the idea." She winks, giggles, and then nudges him again.

Chase entertains her thoughts. I want to disappear. Better yet, I wish Missy would.

I start looking for an exit. "Well, I really need to get back home."

"Oh, don't go so fast," Chase says.

"Now, honey," Missy chimes in as she reaches out and grabs Chase by the bicep before he can take another step toward me. "Let her go, if she has to go. A girl's gotta do what a girl's gotta do."

"Okay." Chase detects my growing discomfort. "I'll grab the keys."

Chase runs up the stairs and disappears into the house, leaving Missy and I standing outside alone.

"Well, it's nice to meet you," Missy says, saccharine-sweet.

I nod. "Nice to meet you too."

"So, now, how do you know Chase?" Missy squints.

"I grew up here on the island. I recently inherited our family beach house from my aunt, who just died, and I'm here trying to pull everything together."

"Oh, I see. I'm so sorry for your loss. I do remember Chase mentioning something about a colored lady dying. Maybe that was your aunt."

"Thank you," I reply.

"So you mean to tell me that your family owned a whole beach house down *here*? On *this* Island? *Topsail*?" Missy squints in disbelief. "You sure?"

"Of course I'm sure." I've had about all I can take from this sugar-coated bimbo.

"Well, now, who were your people?" Missy presses harder, as if she thinks she might actually know my "people."

"The Newells," I reply. "My grandfather, Dr. Maurice Love Newell, and my grandmother, Garnelle Smith Newell, helped settle Ocean City in 1948. We've been here a long time."

Missy looks as if she smells something funny. "Oh, I see," she says. "Well, I know that area you're talking about. I'm just really surprised you know Chase."

"Well, actually I called him Chip back then." I chuckle.

"Oh, I see." Missy looks stung by confusion.

"Hey, what are you two gals chitchattin' about?" Chase returns to the scene, dangling his truck keys.

"Destiny was just telling me she grew up here. Says y'all knew each other as little kids." Missy has not taken her eyes off me.

"Yep, we sure did." Chase smiles at me.

"Well, since you're visiting us down here and you're such a dea', dea' friend of Chase, why don't you come to our little party for my sister, Sissy, tomorrow at the country club?"

You mean there's a Missy *and* a Sissy? In *one* family? You have got to be kidding!

"It's gonna be so much fun," Missy continues babbling on. "There'll be lotsa real nice local ladies to meet, good food, great piano music. Don't you think it be nice if she joined us, Chase?"

"Lovely," he complies.

I look at him like he's crazy.

"Okay, so, I'll see you tomorrow at 4:00 p.m. at the country club, Chastity."

"It's *Destiny*," I correct her again, even though I know this passive-aggressive bitch knows my name.

"Oh, I am so sorry. It's just such an unusual name. I've gotta learn to remember it." She playfully wrinkles her nose at me.

Like "Missy" isn't a strange name for a grown-ass woman, I think.

Chase drives me home, and I am still trying to figure out why he is with Missy.

I don't know what he's thinking or feeling as we drive back to my beach house in silence, but it is clear to me that Missy is not where he belongs.

"I want to apologize to you," Chase says as he pulls up to my beach house. "I didn't mean any disrespect back there when I kissed you on the boat like that. I just—"

"No problem," I say quickly. "We can act like it never happened, just like before. It's okay."

"No, it's not okay, Dee, that's not what I meant. And it *did* happen—just as we wanted it to, didn't we?"

I start to get out of the truck.

"Destiny, please," Chase pleads, but I feel as if I can't breathe, like my head is about to explode. I fumble with the door handle to escape Chase's big red vehicle and all the confusion inside it.

"I have to go, Chase. I am so emotionally messed up right now. I just have to go."

Chase jumps out of his truck and comes around to help me out. I feel the warmth of his body as he takes my hand and looks me in the eye. I cannot help it. I am enraptured. He leans in and kisses me again, but even deeper this time, and I know I belong to him and that this is where I am meant to be—where I have been always meant to be. Is this my long-awaited second chance at love?

Life is far more complicated than that. We will have to wait and see what tomorrow brings, as time moves on, one day at a time.

Chapter
★ Twenty-Five

I AM BREWING SOME TEA AS EVENING FALLS. THE TELEPHONE RINGS, AND I figure it's Mother or one of my wonderful, meddling girlfriends, checking to see whether I'm flirting with the deep end or the handsome police chief. I wipe my hands and answer the phone.

"Hello?"

"Hello, baby."

I am startled by the sound of Garrett's deep voice on the other end of the receiver.

"Destiny, it's Garrett."

"I know who it is. What do you want? How did you know I was here?"

"Smart guess."

"Dumb-ass," I snipe.

"Look, dumb-ass or not, I just want to talk to you. Try to make—"

"*Talk* to me? *Now*, you want to *talk* to me? Why didn't you want to talk to me back in New York, months ago before you started fucking Eve?"

"I'm sorry things went down this way. I don't know what else to say, except—"

"You weren't sorry when you were deceiving me every day of our marriage. And a *baby*, Garrett? My God! *A baby?*"

"I didn't know that part either, until—"

"Until she blurted it out, standing there buck naked in front of us, claiming she's having your love child!"

"I swear I didn't know."

"And you know what makes it even worse, Garrett? You didn't even have the balls to tell me first—to keep me from being humiliated and annihilated right there in front of everybody. In fact, how many people knew about you and Eve?"

"I don't know. I swear I didn't know she was pregnant!"

"I bet you still don't!" I snap. I want to hurt him so badly, to see him suffer and be deceived the same way he did me. I wish I had held a gun to his head and made him fuck Eve again right there in front of me. The intense and growing hatred I feel for Garrett and Eve is pumping madly through my veins as my blood pressure rises, and I feel a powerful surge of adrenaline, energy, and a desire to push them both off a cliff. I am panting like a wild animal. I am so angry that I have no fear.

"Do you love her?" And still, as much as I hate him right now, I do not want to hear the answer.

"Yes. Yes, I ..." Garrett takes a deep swallow. "I do. I love her."

"Well, then enough said, you sorry piece of shit!" I slam down the phone, and I am so furious at Garrett's unyielding nerve that I throw the jar of instant coffee across the room. It slams against the wall and rolls under the table. The waves now fiercely crashing ashore reach a crescendo with the ones now crashing in my head. How did I get here, with a husband in love with my best friend and now the mother of his bastard child?

I think about the trip that Garrett and I made together to the abortion clinic that rainy day just months before our wedding. The pregnancy was so far along that I had a small pooch of a tummy clearly visible as I tried on wedding dresses. I even suffered from morning sickness, becoming faint and woozy as I stood there dripping in lace, as an older Spanish saleslady tailored my wedding gown for our big day. At the start of every day, like clockwork, my body regurgitated foul yellow bile that sent me retching over an open toilet. I became nauseated at the smell of cigarette smoke and fish. And I even felt the fetus flutter, like little butterfly wings inside me, while chasing breaking headline news stories throughout New York City.

I still remember the night we conceived and knew the moment we both reached orgasm that we had created life. It was one of the strongest feelings I ever had. It was the feeling of being a woman—a mother. There was so much tender love between Garrett and me then, or so I believed. I was certain God would give us a baby. I think back now and wonder if we should have kept it, even while knowing full well that that was definitely not the right thing to do. We were broke and just starting our careers and a new marriage. We were convinced that we were in no way ready to handle parenthood. I wish we had been as clear about our marriage.

The devil makes me wonder if Garrett and Eve lay around in posh hotel suites, planning their pregnancy, while Garrett and I were doing everything we could to avoid having one of our own. I clearly don't know Garrett at all. And I am not sure that I really know myself right now either. I know I don't know Eve, but the bitch must have a platinum pussy.

The phone rings again, and I'm convinced it is Garrett, calling back. It amazes me how arrogant he is to think that he can continue to invade my sacred space like this after he created this hot mess to begin with. I grab the phone.

"*What?*"

"Look, we don't need to make this any nastier than it already is, okay?" Garrett starts in. I want to explode. "Can we just talk for a minute like adults?"

"Why now, Garrett? Why *now?*"

"See, there you go, not listening again! I'm trying to talk to you, woman—trying to make some sense and peace of this."

"*Sense* and *peace?*"

"Look, I know the way I handled everything was really, really wrong, but—"

"No, it was downright shitty, Garrett! Why *Eve*, Garrett? *Just fucking tell me, goddammit!* Why my best friend of *all* people? Huh? What, was our marriage *that* bad?"

"*You were never there!*" The truth stings, and I wonder now if it might have been better had he instead said something gross and cavalier like "Shit happens" and then walked off. Instead, Garrett blasts off with, "You were so busy out there, trying to be Barbara Walters, that you were never at home. You didn't take care of your man, Destiny, Eve did."

I roll my eyes to the ceiling and count to ten. I don't know whether to burst into tears or cuss out this motherfucker. I listen as my fool of a soon-to-be-ex-husband rattles on and on, digging a grave with his words and revelations.

"But why *Eve?*" I press the question.

"Eve is always there for me. She loves me. She takes care of me. She cooks for me."

"*Cooks* for you?" I snap. "So, if I'da popped a fat Virginia ham in the oven for you every night after busting my ass covering rapes, murders, and hostage situations all day, we'd still be married? Is that what you're saying? Jeez, Garrett! What do you want?"

"I want a *wife!*"

It feels like somebody just plunged a hot steel pole through my heart. As much as my folks never thought Garrett was enough for me, Garrett obviously thought that I was never enough for him either.

"What did you expect me to do, Garrett? You have always known that I'm never going to be anybody's 'little wife.' I have a career. I love you, but I swear I will not get lost in your fantasy of what a woman is *supposed* to do and be. You can save that shit for Eve."

"All you think about is your career. It's like you're obsessed or something. It's all you talk about."

"And what is wrong with that, Garrett? What? It's not okay for me to want success like you, to make money and have my dreams come true too?"

"*I* want to be your dream come true. As your man, I needed that."

"And I needed you as my husband to sit down with me and talk this thing out, instead of screwing my friend! Where was the dignity in that scene in Boston—for *any* of us? It's a shame we were all brought to such a level."

We hang on the phone in pregnant silence. Then he says, "Look, Des. I'm staying with Eve. You can keep the apartment. Call me if you need anything. Really. I mean it."

"Fuck you, Garrett!" I slam down the phone.

I would strangle that man if I thought I could get away with it. What he has done to our lives and my heart is a travesty and a shame—our marriage was nothing more than a charade. And for what? To look like the perfect successful news couple when we're not.

I bolt out of the door in a desperate race for fresh air. I feel as if the walls of the beach house are starting to close in on me, as if Garrett has left his foul scent lingering amid the rafters. I have to have the strong sea wind blow his lame-ass energy off me. He makes me want to puke right now.

The sea seems to sense my distress, as she has turned a dark, almost black-blue. The waves are choppy, and the whipping wind seems to have shifted and is now picking up force. I feel the sharp sting of sand on my cheeks. The sun's warmth is threatened by huge, puffy clouds blowing in from the south that seem to be gathering. Maybe an angry storm is heading our way.

I walk along the beach, pushing my body through the winds, hoping it will blow away my frayed nerves. I refuse to plunge back into that self-pitying funk I went through in May. It is a new season, and I have promised God, my two best girlfriends, my parents, my late aunt Joy, and myself that I will get through this emotional storm okay—and maybe be even better for it.

It takes so much work.

The sand dunes' tops are swirling with sand trapped in the wild, frenzied dance of the wind. The sea grass sways in mass confusion. The sandpipers dart across the beach in what seems to be mad scurries for a last-minute meal. The gulls seek refuge from the relentless wind and darkening sky.

I head back toward the beach house, feeling somewhat relieved of my emotional stress. I stretch my arms toward the cloud-filled sky and exhale a long, loud sigh to the whipping wind, praying to hold fast to any glint of hope for better days to come.

Chapter
Twenty-Six

AFTER THAT EXHAUSTING PHONE CALL WITH GARRETT, ALL I WANT TO do is climb into bed and go to sleep, pretending that the cruel joke called Garrett never happened. A hot bath and a hot toddy might help me fall into a deep sleep. I just want to escape this feeling that my depression is coming on again.

I get home to a dark house and flip on the light as I open the door. I feel uncomfortable in my own skin, tired of carrying this heavy load of disappointment on my shoulders. Is this what I am bound to face for the rest of my life in love—one disappointment after another? What did I do to piss off the gods?

I find nothing in the kitchen except an old bottle of Pinch scotch in the cabinet under the sink. I am so happy to see this shapely bottle of mercy that I help myself to a big pour, believing it might calm my nerves, settle me down, and help me get a good night's sleep so I can forget about everything for a while. I drop in a couple of ice cubes and walk out on the screened-in porch. I choose Aunt Joy's chair; the big wicker rocking one with the tattered cushion that faces the sea. This was her throne. I fold my legs up under me and nestle into what is now my throne. I listen to the ocean waves crashing against the shore.

Even with the gusting wind, humidity hangs in the air like a strong smell. I rub my eyes, realizing how physically and emotionally exhausted I am. I take another long sip of the scotch. It goes down smoothly, warming my insides, soothing my tension and my mind, helping me escape thoughts of Garrett and his lame excuses and Chase with his lame girlfriend, Missy.

I take another sip. While the scotch may lessen my tension, it only magnifies my emotions. I begin to cry, pitying myself for my many failures in love. I take another sip of my liquid relief, feeling a bit light-headed and loose as the alcohol gently seeps into my system, taking me away to a place of no pain. I look out over the darkness, imagining walking into the deep black ocean, disappearing beneath its stormy waves and the howling wind, where no one can hear me crying.

Blindly, I fling open the porch screen door and take off down the steps and across the dunes, onto the beach, and up to the churning water's edge. Hot tears stream down my face. I begin to wail. Why do I have to constantly have my heart broken?

"I don't deserve this!" I shout into the whipping wind.

"And when you truly believe that, kiddo, it will stop happening." Startled, I snap around, expecting to find someone there, but I see no one in the darkness.

"Hello?" I call. "Who's out there?"

The only answer is the howl of the wind.

I know it was Aunt Joy's voice I heard. Those sounded like her words of wisdom. Is it the alcohol, or is my dear aunt speaking to me in the wind from heaven? I know she loves me enough that I can count on her anywhere—even after life—and Lord knows I need her now, perhaps more than ever.

"Aunt Joy!" I cry out to pierce my voice through the wind. "If you are here … p-pl-*please* show yourself." I keep screaming out for her as if my life depends on it—and maybe it does. "Aunt Joy, if you can hear me, p-pl-please help me. I need you."

I wait for an answer, swaying and crying in the wind, looking for some kind of sign that I am not alone. I hear nothing but the pounding of the waves. I walk deeper and deeper into the water, staring into the empty blackness of the sea. I feel the warm water whooshing around my ankles … calves … thighs. I move deeper into the churning waters, the salt of my tears mixing with the salt of the sea. I keep walking, waist deep now, being tossed back and forth by the strength of the swirling currents and waves. But I don't care; I just keep walking as if there's a huge magnet in the ocean drawing me deeper and deeper into her hypnotic grip. I don't know why, but I just keep walking.

"How will you ever find love if you give up?"

There's that clear voice again. But I stumble and turn again in a desperate search for Aunt Joy, but again, no one is there.

A huge wave crashes on top of me and knocks me down. I am tangled in the ocean's relentless control, until finally, she spits me out onto the shore. It's as if she's rebirthing me back into my own life. Trembling and clawing at the sand, I drag myself across the beach and stumble back to the house. I finally make it. The telephone rings. Should I even pick it up? Take the chance that Garrett is calling back with more of his nonsense? Or maybe it's my girls.

"Hello," I answer through breathless panting, expecting Hope and Kat on the other end of the phone. I'll be so happy to hear their voices once again, ensuring me that I am cared for, loved, not alone, and most of all, alive.

"Where have you been?" It's not Kat or Hope. "I've been calling that house for more than an hour now."

It's Mother.

"I ... I was out on the beach." I struggle to sound sober. I find myself instinctively straightening my back, my hair, my voice.

"On the *beach*? At this time of night? What in the world were you doing out there?"

"Well, I was talking to Aunt Joy."

"Say *what*?"

"I was ... I ..." I am fighting to focus through my fog.

"DeeDee, what's the matter with you? You don't sound like yourself. What's going on down there?"

"I'm fi—I am fine. I f—"

"Destiny? You don't sound well. Are you okay? Hold on. I'm going to put your father on the phone."

"I gotta go, Mother," I say.

"Destiny!" Mother snaps, but I am fading far away from her. "Don't you go anywhere!"

"Gotta go." I struggle to hang up the receiver, but it crashes to the floor.

I feel dizzy, so full of emotions and scotch. I lie down on the couch and close my eyes, but the room keeps whirling around me. I feel like I am going to be sick, but I can't lift my head. Oh God, don't let me throw up all over Aunt Joy's rose-covered couch. I know how much she loved her roses.

I feel horrible, lying here listening to the wind, and the waves and with my heavy heart pounding. And now, I also hear my mother's questions still pounding in my head. Am I losing it again? I just keep losing it as the phone keeps ringing.

I pass out and slip into a dream that I am floating on top of the sea, my long waves of brown hair furled into the curling waves of the sea. Little cherubs surround me blowing their sweet melodies through conch shells. They have smiles on their plump little faces. Their cheeks and bums are cherry red. They make me smile as I drift along on the ocean's surface, floating away in a peaceful slumber. And then Aunt Joy gently floats by, dressed in a long and flowing purple gown. I smile, remembering how much she loved purple. Her silver hair is styled in the same bun-in-the-back beach look she wore each summer. I can even smell her gardenia perfume once again as she floats closer and closer to me. I am afraid to wake up, to open my eyes, because she might float away as quickly as she appeared. So I remain very still and keep my eyes closed. Aunt Joy hovers above me. I can feel her there. Then she leans over and kisses me just above my right temple and lovingly speaks into my ear.

"I love you," she says. *"And I am very proud of you. And I'm going to have a talk with that police chief. You two belong together, kiddo."*

And then she disappears into a cloud.

I sit up, wide awake and heart pounding. I am in shock—stymied and startled because the dream was so real. I'm not sure whether Aunt Joy was really here, and even if she was, whether a talk with Chase right now would really make difference. I roll over and bury myself under Aunt Joy's comforter. It still smells like her. I pray to God that when Aunt Joy talks to Chase, she's not too late.

Chapter ★ Twenty~Seven

THE LOUD AND PERSISTENT POUNDING AT MY FRONT DOOR STARTLES me awake. Whoever is there is also ringing the doorbell with annoying repetition. Who the hell could it be at this time of the morning? My head is also pounding. I reach for my watch on the bedside table—and I realize I never made it to the bed and am still sprawled across Aunt Joy's couch, smelling like scotch and suffering from a splitting headache. I drag myself off the sofa and make my way into the kitchen to find that it is eleven in the morning! I cannot believe I slept so late, but then again, with this brutal hangover, I see why my body was taking its sweet time facing this morning.

Bang! Bang! Bang!

I am going to kill whoever is beating on my door like that. I stumble my way to the door and swing it open, ready to lay one on the big banger—and much to my shock and surprise, there stands Mother.

"You look horrible!" she exclaims as she pushes her way past me and inside my home. "What in the world has happened to you?" Mother looks me up and down.

"Why are you here?" I ask.

"Because you didn't sound right last night, and your father and I were worried sick, that's why!" She moves into the kitchen.

"Did Daddy come?" I ask, looking toward the car. My heavy and hurting head is still in a fog, but I would give anything for a hug from my daddy right now.

"No." She shakes her head and sighs while peeping into the kitchen cabinets. "He had patients to see today and thought it would be best if we had a little mother-daughter time"—whatever that's supposed to mean.

"I see ..." I say, but I don't.

"My God! Do you eat?" Mother has made her way to the empty refrigerator, where there's nothing in it but the light.

"I just haven't had the chance to shop, that's all," I explain.

"You may not eat but clearly, you are drinking." Mother raises the half-empty bottle of scotch to my eye level, peering at me with a raised brow through the pinched glass.

"So I had a drink," I say.

"A drink?" she asks incredulously. "Not the way you smell today and sounded last night. You had a lot more than *one*. And you had us worried stiff! So I jumped in the car and headed here first thing this morning. The last thing we need is for you to go off the deep end again."

My head is throbbing even harder now. I wish that she would stop making me field all these questions and get back in her car and go home. Somehow, having her five hours away makes my life a lot easier.

"Let's go shopping," she suddenly chirps. Mother loves to shop. To her, the thrill of buying things seems to solve every problem. "Well, you have to have groceries in here. You can't survive on scotch alone."

"Mother, I can't make it," I confess, knowing there is no way I can handle being cooped up in a car with Mother right now.

"Well, I'll run to the market. You jump in the shower and be ready for lunch when I get back. And comb your hair." Mother grabs her keys and her Hermes purse and is out the door.

I drag myself upstairs, pop a couple of aspirin, and jump in the shower; the cool water is soothing. How in the world am I going to deal with my mother today? I do need groceries, and I do appreciate her wanting to feed me, and maybe once she sees that I'm okay with a house full of food, then she'll leave.

I move out of the shower, feeling a bit better. By the time I get dressed, Mother is in the dining room, putting the finishing touches on our mother-daughter brunch table. She has broiled salmon, boiled rice, and tossed a fresh salad. I can't possibly be mad at her today. We get through lunch with a long talk about my future—whether I've chosen the right divorce lawyer, and Mother wants to make sure I get every set of Wedgewood china we got as wedding gifts. She also presses the point that alcohol is never going to solve my problems, so I should lay off the bottle, since I apparently don't handle it well anyway.

I would love to escape from my mother—take a walk on the beach, clear my mind, clear the air, clear the area—but it has started to rain, so I make a cup of tea and sit here on the couch where my day began, listening to the brawling brook that is my mother. While she talks on and on, I stare out over the stormy sea, thinking about Chase and the irony that we have known each other most of our lives and have waited for this moment of rediscovered friendship for a lifetime.

"Thank you for sharing lunch," Mother says as she clears the last dishes and crumbs off the table. "I'm going to take a nap now. This day has exhausted me."

You? I think, but instead, I say, "Good, Mother, that'll be a good thing to do." I'm happy to finally get a break.

I turn on the television and am watching a late-afternoon soap opera when a tropical storm warning scrawls across the bottom of the screen. I hope this nasty storm passes. It's a bear being trapped inside this house with Mother, even when she's sleeping.

The sky has turned gray, and the wind and rain are whipping through the sea grass, tossing it into a wild and frenzied dance. The waves crash violently against the shore. I snuggle back underneath Aunt Joy's old throw, dreaming of falling asleep in Chase's arms to the pounding ocean and rain. I am snuggling in deeper, readying myself for my much-needed slumber, when the doorbell rings. Who in the world could it be now? In the middle of the afternoon? And in this bad storm? Annoyed, I drag myself to the door and impatiently swing it open.

There stands Chase. Is this a dream? Was he reading my mind?

"Chase? Hey, how you doing? This is a surprise," I say, just as a fierce, wet gust of wind blasts through the doorway. "Oh, please come in." I fumble nervously, fighting through my daze, exhaustion, overwhelming surprise, and embarrassment. "Come in and get out of the rain, for goodness' sake." I pray he doesn't smell the scotch and hope my face isn't green. I quickly rub my hand over the back of my hair just in case of bed-head strays.

Chase politely wipes his thick black leather boots on the doormat and enters. He removes his police hat and rubs his thick fingers through his sun-kissed hair. I am taken by how incredibly valiant, gentle, and handsome he is. Even in a drenched police slicker and rain-soaked boots, he is still my golden Adonis.

Time stands still.

But why is he here?

"May I take your coat?" I offer.

"Oh, no," he says. "I'm on official business today. Just wanted to stop by and warn you to avoid driving tonight until this storm passes. We've got some nasty hurricanes headed this way and just want everybody to keep an eye on the weather reports in case we have to evacuate the island."

"Evacuate? Chase? Are you serious?"

"Yes, it could get a lot worse. It's a tropical storm; it's hurricane season. You never know what Mother Nature might do, so make sure you batten down the hatches."

"I will. Thank you, Chase."

"But be on the safe side. Keep an eye on the news," Chase says with a paternal yet genuine concern. This only adds to my all-the-great-things-I-like-about-Chase list. He reaches into his pocket and pulls out a business card with his name embossed in gold: *Police Chief Chase Monroe McKenzie.* I rub my finger across the raised letters and silently swoon.

"That's my number if you need me. This'll put you right through to the dispatch, and they'll radio me in the patrol car. I'll be right here."

"Okay, thanks. I'll be all right."

"Well, Miss Dee—*Miss Destiny*—I better be moseyin' on along now. Got some elders, babies, and pregnant ladies out there to calm down in this bad storm. Hope this puppy clears soon. I want to see you back *On Assignment.*" Chase winks.

I blush.

I know he cares because it's his job to care, but I also feel his deep and loving concern for me and the other islanders. He'll probably spend this rainy night stopping door-to-door, checking on each and every resident and renter. I hope he cares as much about himself as he does for others. And I pray he'll continue to care this much about me.

"You be careful out there too," I warn him.

"Will do. Bye now, Miss Dee," he calls over his broad rain-drenched shoulder as he grabs the brim of his hat and ducks and dashes through the rain to his waiting patrol car.

"Good-bye, Chase," I call after him through the howl of the storm.

I stand here in the threshold of my home, getting splattered by the wind-driven rain. I watch Chase sprint to his patrol car, agilely trying to dodge the raindrops. I could have sworn, as perfect as he is, he could have just walked between them.

Chapter
★ Twenty-Eight

WAKE UP THE NEXT MORNING AND CAN SMELL COFFEE BREWING AND bacon frying. The sun is bursting through the windows, the sky is clear, and I can hear the playful cries of seagulls as they scurry along the beach, happy to have discovered a windfall from the sea. Interesting things always wash up on the shore after a major storm has churned up the ocean. I can't wait to get out there and scavenge along with the seagulls, but first—Mother and breakfast.

I walk into the kitchen, and Mother is setting the table.

"What's all this?" I ask.

"Go wash up. Breakfast is almost ready. I wanted us to start this day fresh."

Mother has no idea how beautifully my day ended. And I take a certain pride and delight in holding this secret from her. She would fall into the coffee percolator if she knew that Chase McKenzie was actually in this house and that we enjoyed a wonderful reunion right there in my doorway last night. I look in that direction, remembering yesterday, hoping to find any trace of Chase still standing there. I smile a secret smile as I remember how sweetly he looked at me and how surprised and happy we both are to have finally found each other again.

"Well, don't just stand there with that dumb look on your face. Wake up, girl! Go wash up now. We'll have breakfast, and then I'm going to hit the road."

"You're leaving?" I try not to sound too obviously happy.

She sighs. "Yes, it's time to go. No need in prolonging your misery, dear." She raises an eyebrow and a slight smile in my direction. "Plus, the storm has passed, the sun is out, and you seem to be back on your feet. You have plenty to eat here now, so go wash your hands."

It amazes me how my mother still orders me around, even in what is now my own house. She rarely spent a moment here throughout my childhood, and now she just shows up, starts shopping and cooking and ordering me around as if she lives here. I bite my tongue and count to a million, longing for the moment her Louis Vuitton overnight bag is back in her car, and she's pulling out of my driveway. I do appreciate that she is at least trying. She has prepared a wonderful breakfast of waffles and strawberries, bacon, and scrambled eggs. She has even decorated the fluffy yellow eggs with pieces of fresh green parsley. *"Presentation is everything, my dear!"* she often reminds me.

"It looks delicious, Mother," I say as I sit across the table from her with cleaned hands.

"Well, I hope you enjoy it," she replies over her coffee cup.

"Oh, I'm sure I will," I say as I dig into Mother's scrumptious peace offerings.

"So, how long do you think you'll be here?"

"I dunno," I reply truthfully. "Until I feel better about my life, I suppose, and in which direction I want to take it. I really don't know right now."

"Well, what about your job? Your father and I are very concerned about what the station might think about all of this. I mean, how in the world are you going to bring home an Emmy if you're down here crying all the time?"

As harsh as her logic may be, I can't argue with Mother. I have spent a lot of my days here crying from a broken and confused heart. But maybe that will change as time moves on and especially now that there's an exciting chance to get to know Chase all over again. Suddenly, I can only feel tears of joy, as I am falling into the fantasy that fate is our friend. I desperately want to get to know my new home, my island, and my Adonis even more.

"Mother, there is so much more to life than winning an Emmy," I try to reason.

"Like what?"

"Well, like being happy. Like taking a second."

"You've taken *weeks*."

"No, Mother, I mean taking a second to take a second look at your life—the decisions that you've made. Have you ever wondered if the life you chose was really the life for you? The life you really wanted for yourself? Or were you in some way pushed into believing that that was the life you should live?"

"Oh, Destiny, the questions you ask."

"Mother, look—Ralph Waldo Emerson says, 'A life not examined is not a life worth living.' And I really need to examine my life right now and see if this is really what I want, if I am heading in the right direction."

"Your father and I told you a long time ago that Garrett would one day lead you to all of this misery and confusion."

"Well, Mother, if it took Garrett to get me here to Topsail again, then so be it. Maybe it's not misery you see. Maybe it's just regrouping, catching myself turning around, taking a second chance, and starting over."

"Well, Destiny, I wish you luck," Mother says as she shakes her head. "I have no idea what you're talking about or what you see on this little country island when you have the whole island of *Manhattan* at your fingertips. But you have always been a romantic thinker."

"And thanks to dear Aunt Joy, I have a place to live and money from the generous trust she left me. I am set for quite a while, Mother. So please, don't worry."

"Well, take your time—but not too long. You should put the bulk of that money into a savings account for your retirement, unless, of course, you're claiming it now." Mother rolls her eyes.

"I don't know, but what I do know is that I haven't really spent time here since childhood. I want to take this summer to get to know this place again, to get to know the people here."

Mother stops her piddling around her plate and slowly looks up at me. "What people?" she asks suspiciously.

"The island people."

"The island people? Oh, Destiny, how do you sound? You have no intentions of getting to know these sandy country bumpkins down here. It's that *Chase* you're after, isn't it?"

"Mother—"

"Ohhh, you're not fooling me, young lady. In fact"—Mother leans back in her chair and folds her arms—"I heard a man's voice at the door yesterday afternoon. From all of your giggling, I could tell it was somebody you liked—*a lot.* I was curious, so I looked out of the window. I saw the patrol car."

I suddenly feel blood rush to my face, leaving me standing here blushing like a teenager caught in the backseat of the car.

"Really!" I say, but it sounds so dumb.

"The police chief," Mother slowly articulates as if I'm deaf. "He was here yesterday, wasn't he?"

"Yes, he stopped by. He was on official storm duty. He said he was just stopping by to check things out."

"Hmpf. I bet he's 'checking things out,' all right." Mother darts me a look. "You be careful, Dee. Leave that man alone. His family is nothing but trouble, and he has no good intentions of letting you be a part of it."

"But Mother, Chase is not like the rest of his family. He has been nice to me and shown me nothing more than kindness and respect."

"*Nice* to you? *Respect*?" Mother persists with an incredulous look on her face. "Destiny, he's the *police chief.* He's supposed to be nice and respectful to you!"

I stand here, hurt, looking at the woman who refuses to like anybody but herself.

"Okay, Mother," I say, trying to hold back my exasperation. "Here— let me take your plate. I know you must be in a rush. Want me to help you with your bag?"

"Please."

Mother has already packed and placed her Louis Vuitton travel bag by the door.

"Tell Daddy I love him," I say as I help her out to the car.

"I will," she replies with a light smile as she starts the engine. "Your father loves you very much, you know."

"I know." I nod.

"We both worry about you a lot, though, Dee. But we know you're a big girl now. You can take care of yourself—I hope. You call us if you need anything, you hear? And please, Dee, your father and I want you to leave that police officer alone!"

"Police chief, Mother. Have a safe trip home." I blow Mother a kiss and wave good-bye. She honks her horn a couple of times, signaling her grand farewell, and slowly pulls out of the driveway, back onto Highway 1, heading home.

Today is such a beautiful and clear day it's hard to believe there was actually the threat of a dangerous storm here just last night. The gentle breeze smells as pleasant and fresh as just-cleaned laundry. Everything seems happy, from the blades of sea grass dancing on the dunes, to the sandpipers zipping down the beach. And as I check into my emotional self, I find that finally I am happy too.

I can see for miles up and down the beach and way out offshore. The ocean is frisky, but nowhere near the pouty little girl she was last night, sporting her dangerous riptides and angry waves. No, today she is simply a saint.

I walk along the shore, dreaming of days gone by when I'd take my grandmother's hand, and we'd comb the beach for interesting keepsakes, particularly after storms like the one last night. I instinctively hunt for a sand dollar, once so plentiful along this beach that you had to hopscotch to avoid cracking them under your bare feet. They were large and small, cracked, chipped, and whole, each of them extraordinary and beautiful in its own way.

"Do you know how you can tell these are gifts from God?" my grandmother would ask me as she kneeled on the sand, speaking to me eye-to-eye. "You know how you can tell?"

"Uh-uh. How, Grandma?" I would ask, filled with a child's wonder.

Then she would gently turn the sand dollar over in her delicate hand and softly brush away the white sand. There, in the middle, appeared a cross. "You see that?" Grandma would smile. "That's how you tell." As a curious child, I later discovered that if you break the sand dollar in half, like a cookie, a white dove also appears out of nowhere. Indeed, glorious and curious gifts from God on Topsail Island by the sea. Tranquility. I would give anything to make such a find today. I find a piece of twisted driftwood here, a barnacle-covered conch shell there, clumps of red and green seaweed strewn about, but rarely a sand dollar. Like a child, I search for them anyway.

There is so much of this island that I have yet to see. So much that has changed, while so much remains exactly the same. It is ironic that I left here to grow up and now, here I am again, to grow up in yet another way. So much of my past and now so much of my future is right here— right now.

This might have been God's plan all along.

Chapter
★ Twenty-Nine

NO MATTER HOW MUCH I FEEL ABOUT CHASE, THE FACT STILL REMAINS that Missy is the lady in his life. While he is for some reason still unsure about marrying her, she is clearly pushing extremely hard for at least an engagement. I am very sensitive to the damage another woman does when she falls in love with another woman's man. I don't want to be that girl who destroys people. But I know Missy is not the right woman for Chase. He knows it too. We want to be together. But we also want to do what's right. I tell him Missy may get messy either way.

Maybe just the act of my going to Missy's sister's prewedding party will serve as a good conduit to help me deal with the harsh reality that the man I love is, once again, forbidden. But Chase is also my friend, so I will put on a proper outfit and a happy face and will force myself to accept Missy's party invitation and with gratitude—if for no other reason than to see what this Missy is all about. No matter what, I will remain Chase's friend, so I will attend out of respect to our friendship.

I decide to go into town to find a nice gift for the bride-to-be. I have no idea what Missy's sister would want, much less need. I travel to the other side of the island to the small shopping strip. I see a nice beach home-furnishing store and decide to go in. The place is full of gift items, most of which are made of seashells or carry a beach theme. There are wind chimes and candleholders, tablecloths, and lamps with decorative shades, salad bowls, vases, and beautiful crystal and porcelain figurines. Any girl would love anything from this shop.

"Hi there," the chipper voice of a preppy brunette greets me. "Can I help you find anything?"

"Oh, I'm just looking right now," I reply with a smile.

"Well, all right, but you let me know if I can help you, okay?"

"I sure will. Thank you," I say, deeply appreciating the woman's southern charm.

My hungry eyes gobble up just about every beautiful and shiny piece in the store. I remember my own wedding and all the wonderful gifts we received and how much each one meant, so I want to be extra thoughtful, even in the face of doubt. I am trying to decide between a silver-plated photo album, an ornate gold letter opener, or a set of pewter salad forks with seashelled handles, when two chatty white women whisk through the door, deeply lost inside their own world and conversation.

"Lord, I told that girl her father would kill her if she backed out of this thing now. And he's such a nice fellow too. I don't know why she's so smitten over that other one."

"I don't know why either, Clara." The woman's friend shakes her head. "But you know how impressionable your daughter can be. Looks like the bride wants to trade in a badge for a bank account, if you ask me."

I really don't want to eavesdrop on their conversation, but they're both so loud and shrill that I can't help but hear them. And the more they blab, the more interesting the story gets.

"I keep telling her that cadet is about to go into service overseas. She needs a man who's right here and in a good position. And Jesse Mae"—the woman suddenly stops in her tracks and turns to face her friend with a worried scowl over her plump, red face—"you know I would just die if my baby girl left this country and had to live around a bunch of foreigners. That's my baby, and I would just die, I tell you."

"Aw, Clara, it's all gonna work out, honey. Don't worry yourself to death."

"Jesse Mae, now you know how Dean wants this police department connection more than he gives a crab's ass about his own daughter's happiness. 'It's good for the family business,' he keeps telling her."

"Ugh," Jesse Mae shudders. "That Dean …"

"Dean's got it in his head that having a cop in the family is going to save his ass on a lot of his construction sites, whatever that means."

What does that mean? What cop are they talking about? Chase mentioned that Missy's father is a contractor—Missy McKay. McKay Construction—oh, no.

"So now, Jess, you have to promise me that you will help me convince her to try to marry the *chief*, not the cadet."

No way!

"I'll do my best, Clara," the other woman promises with a deep sigh. "Well, one thing's for sure: Missy loves men in uniform."

This cannot be happening.

"Aw, Jesse Mae. It would just kill that poor man." Clara shakes her head again.

"Yes, it would." Her friend shakes hers. "Chase is a very nice fellow."

"No, I mean my husband, Dean!"

"Uh!" The woman rolls her eyes in disgust. "Yes, of course, *Dean.*"

They cannot be talking about Missy and Chase. My ears must be deceiving me. What am I hearing here? The man I love is being set up to marry a woman who's more interested in helping her father's business than being in love with him? I am stuck, stunned, and frozen right here behind a rack of lacy place mats as I listen to this woman, who is apparently Mrs. Clara McKay.

"Well, it is Missy's decision," Clare says, as if she is still trying to convince herself that Missy will make the right one.

"Hmpf!" scoffs Jesse Mae. "Sounds to me like it's *Dean's* decision."

"Well, let's just get that cake cutter and get on out of here." Clara glances down at her watch. "Man alive, it's getting late. Sissy's engagement party starts at four, and I need to get there early to make sure those darkies at the country club got everything right—*for once.* I tell you, they make me so mad I could—"

But before the woman can say another word about "darkies at the country club," I step out from behind the rack, my dark self slap-dab in the woman's view. She takes one look at me and almost chokes.

"Excuse me," I say with a sly smile. I brush past her wide body and make my way up to the counter, where a very red-faced saleslady awaits. She takes my choice of the pewter salad forks with the seashell handles and fusses with the price tag.

She tries to remain chipper. "Did you find everything okay?"

The two old hens, quiet now, shuffle their way to the back of the store.

"Yes, I did, thank you," I say. "I found even more than I was looking for."

"Would you like these nice forks wrapped?"

I take a second and think. While my natural instinct is to throw these gift forks across the room, refusing to even attend the racist witch's daughter's party, I decide to attend it anyway. Suddenly, forks seem to be an appropriate gift. Plus, my journalistic curiosity is getting the best of me. I want to do a little background research on this devious McKay family and their plans to marry off their daughters, seemingly for more position, power, and protection in the construction industry. Why would they need a police chief in the family? Sounds as if there may be more a lot more to Daddy McKay's story than just building. As Mother would say, "Best way to know thy enemies? Go to their parties."

"Yes," I reply. "Please wrap them. That would be nice."

"By the way ..." The saleslady leans in, cautiously checking the back of the store. "I apologize for that lady. She's said a lot of crazy things lately. Her daughter's getting married, and sometimes all that pressure can bring out the worst in people. Please don't hold it against our store. Please come back and see us again."

"Thank you," I say. "I will. Next time I may choose the knives."

The woman giggles.

My heart goes out to Chase. Now I understand why he looks so sad and confused when he speaks of Missy. He knows in his heart and soul that it would be a disaster to go any further with her. He deserves another chance at love too.

The nice saleslady hands me the exquisitely wrapped salad forks that I would, quite frankly, rather stick into Missy's mom right now. How dare Missy be in love with another man, while selfishly using the man I love and keeping him away from me? Why?

And who is this other man, the "bank account cadet"? The one who wants to sweep Missy out of the country? I don't know whether to shame the suitor or kiss him on the mouth for his timely intrusion. Chase said something was missing. It's called love.

On the way home, the radio DJ is rocking beach music, until he suddenly interrupts the program with a special weather bulletin, warning of a huge hurricane, packing super-high winds and possibly heading our way as it barrels out of the Caribbean. Looking out the car window with the brilliant sun shining in my eyes and the warm summer breeze in my hair, it's hard to believe that a storm could possibly be coming our way. It's too beautiful a day. In fact, it's a perfect day for a party.

Chapter
✦ Thirty

"BIG GIRLS DON'T CRY, BIG GIRLS … DON'T CRY-YI-YI-YI, THEY DON'T CRY." FRANKIE Valli croons on the radio as I shower and change for the big prewedding party. It will be interesting to be there, not only to check out Missy, her sister, Sissy, and the rest of the McKay clan, but also because it wasn't that long ago when blacks and Jews weren't allowed in the Onslow County Country Club. So yes, this is going to be very interesting indeed, and I will be right there, representing change and Chase, as I check out the happy crowd.

I decide on a simple light-blue linen dress, a sweater, and flat sandals, since most parties at the country club are traditionally held on its rolling, perfectly manicured, azalea-lined grounds. I turn off the radio just as the disc jockey jokes that big girls may cry when a harsh rain blows in later today. He can't be serious. There's not a cloud in the sky. It's a glorious day.

I grab Sissy's gift and head off to her party, which turns out to be quite festive. Giddy girls donned in pastel sundresses and wide-brimmed sun hats are scattered throughout the luscious green grounds, chatting and laughing and oo-ing and ah-ing each other's latest summer fashions and latest news. Other than the help, I am the only black person in the club. Something tells me that most of this crowd would probably like to keep it that way. I don't know any of these ladies and while I may get an occasional smile, I still feel like an outsider. I receive a cool reception as I make my way through the sounds of their girly squeals and chitter-chatter.

I have slipped away to the bathroom to check my makeup, patience, and composure, when an elderly white woman walks out of the stall and asks me for a towel. When I politely explain to her that I don't work at the country club, she asks if I might be related to "one of the nice colored helpers" who does.

"Your people do such a fine job here, you know," the old lady insists. "Which one of 'em do you belong to?"

I want to strangle her. "Well, actually, I'm here for Sissy McKay's prewedding party," I inform her. "I'm a guest."

"You don't say?" The woman looks shocked. "Well, how in the world do you know Sissy?"

"I know Missy, actually."

"Well, how in the world do you know her?" The nosey and persistent old lady squints at me.

"I met her through my one of my childhood friends," I say, now feeling defensive.

"Who?" she presses on without shame.

"Chase. Chase McKenzie."

"The Topsail police chief?" She steps back. "Well, man alive! He's a nice fella, that Chase, and a good-lookin' one too."

I smile. "Yes, he's a really nice guy."

"I hear Missy and Chase may be the next ones walking down the aisle, if Miss Missy has her say," the woman muses as she turns to peer into the mirror.

"Oh, my," I say. "That's a lot of weddings in one family. Well, have a nice day!" I quickly make my way out of the bathroom and back into the giddy crowd.

Under white canvas gazebos, dotting the vast and lush green grounds, the champagne flows and the gifts pile up on decorated tables, carefully organized by some of Sissy's friends. The country club's perfectly manicured lawn and sprawling gardens are some of the prettiest and most talked about in the area. The azaleas are particularly outstanding this time of year, as they are bursting in color, with hues of fuchsia, lilac, and pink. I spot Missy chatting it up with a group of girls across the way. She looks in my direction, notices me, and starts to head over.

"Well, I'm so glad you could make it!" Missy oozes as she saunters across the grounds toward me with a hand of welcome up in the air. "I'm so glad you're 'one of the girls' today."

"Thank you. It's nice to be here, Missy. Everything looks so beautiful."

"Well, I appreciate that. The workers here at the country club did a good job, but I was cracking the whip the whole time." Missy laughs. I wonder if she also refers to them as "darkies," like her mother.

"Ooo!" she suddenly exclaims. "Is that pretty gift for my Sissy?"

"Of course it is," I say, handing over the goods.

"Oh, thank you so much, Destiny. I just know whatever it is, she'll love this gift from you!"

"I hope so." I feel uncomfortable talking to Missy, knowing her real story now.

"I'm so glad you came," Missy gushes again and throws her blonde curls over her shoulder. She cocks her head to the side. "Chase just loves you, you know. He talks about you *all* the time."

"Really?" I say. I am surprised by Missy's admission.

"Yep. And I'm getting a little jealous," she teases. "Destiny, Destiny, Destiny!" She rolls her eyes to the sky. "That's all Chase talks about lately."

I'm not sure where Missy is going with this, but she's intent.

"You two seem to be happy," I offer.

"You really think so?" Missy asks. "'Cause I wonder if I'm making Chase that happy, ya know? He's just moving so dang slow, and hecky poo, I want a wedding! Now Destiny, you're his friend. What does he say to you about me? What can we do to make him marry me? Tell me."

"What makes you think you need to do any more than what you're doing?"

Missy squinches up her nose and looks away. "I don't know," she admits. "I don't know. He's just such a good catch—good-lookin', powerful in a down-home sorta way, and he wears a uniform. I just love a man in uniform. I have to have him. I have to make him my husband."

Missy looks so desperate that had I not heard the truth from her own mother's mouth about her deceptive plot, I might have given the bitch a second chance. But now I see why Chase is so hesitant. He can sense game when he smells it.

"You can't make anybody love you, Missy," I tell her, because it's true.

"Well, honey, I'mma do everything I can do. I'll change his mind, you'll see. And I might need your help, just between us girls."

"Yes, of course," I reply. "Just between us girls."

I hope Missy can't see my face burning from the inside out.

"Come on and meet my girls." Missy takes me by the arm and escorts me toward her posse. "Y'all come on over here and meet Miss Destiny," Missy calls out. "This is Chase's friend I told y'all about."

Missy then turns back to me with a big beauty-queen smile. I wonder what she told them. She begins her introductions, complete with a little morsel of information about each one of her girlfriends—from the ones she went to high school with, to where they held a job in town, to how many children they have. Some of the group I'd already met with Chase at the fish fry earlier this summer.

"How do you know Chase anyway?" one girl asks.

"From childhood—growing up on Topsail," I reply.

"Oh, I see." She looks taken aback. "You grew up in the *trailer park?*"

"Funny. Chase has never mentioned you," adds another.

"No, I grew up across the street from Chase in Ocean City."

"Ah-h-h-h," the girls express in unison and surprise, eyebrows raised. They don't seem to know what else to say, since they were probably forbidden to venture into either neighborhood. So they stand there blinking at me with those fake smiles on their faces. I feel like a fish out of water.

"Ladies! Ladies!" A woman's voice over the loud speakers grabs our attention. "Welcome to Sissy's prewedding party! We are so glad y'all are here. Now, come on around 'cause we got some wonderful entertainment for y'all today."

The pastel-painted crowd politely applauds and with delicate oohs and ahs, the ladies move toward the main gazebo, where the entertainment is about to begin. Missy walks to center stage and patiently waits for the crowd to settle down as she prepares to sing. Her accompanist is a tall and handsome man in a military uniform. He is a cadet. The smiling women whisper and point at the man whose back muscles seem to ripple underneath his uniform as he prepares his sheet music at the piano. Could this be her dashing cadet?

"Good afternoon, everybody," Missy greets the crowd. "As most of you know, I'm Missy, and I'd like to dedicate this song to my sweet sister, Sissy, who is about to get married."

The crowd claps, with some shouting woo-hoos and congratulations thrown in. Missy and the cadet begin their love song.

Love, soft as an easy chair
Love, fresh as the morning air
One love that is shared by two
I have found in you ...

I suddenly feel faint, as if I am watching this whole scene in an out-of-body experience. Everything seems so surreal. Is another truth playing itself out right here before my eyes? Is Missy, who is now singing to the handsome pianist, really the one destined to be with the man I love? Shouldn't a song called "Evergreen" be sung for Chase and me?

Like a rose under the April snow
I always knew our love would grow
Love, ageless and evergreen
Seldom seen by two.

I watch Missy closely. She is making constant eye contact with the cadet, who is coyly smiling back at her as he plays his heart out on the piano. Doesn't anyone else see that she is clearly not thinking about Chase right now? She is the imposter. Both Chase and I know it.

Time, we've learned to sail above
Time, won't change the meaning of one love
Ageless and evergreen …

The crowd bursts into applause as a teary-eyed Sissy runs across the stage to hug her sister.

"Thank you, thank you so much, Missy. I love you. I just love you so much. Wasn't that wonderful, y'all?"

The gathering of women applauds.

"And let's hear it for the handsome gentleman at the piano," Missy announces. "First Officer Derrick Bradford." The flock of infatuated females claps in adoration, each girl admiring the striking man in the military uniform, now standing and taking a bow.

"Nothing like a man in uniform, huh, y'all?" Missy playfully cajoles the crowd. "Thank you, Cadet Derrick, you played beautifully."

The way these two smile at each other, I bet he's played more than her piano.

"Please grab a glass of champagne as the waiters come around," advises a round woman who has joined Missy, Sissy, and the cadet on the stage. It is the same round, red-faced woman from the store earlier today, who calls black people "darkies"—Missy and Sissy's mom.

"It's time to toast my Sissy!" she grins. "Oh, y'all, I'm so proud of my girls!" She squeezes each daughter on either side of her rotund body. The happy crowd applauds again for the girls as the two admire their gushing, teary-eyed mother.

Bile rises in my throat, so I reach for a glass of champagne from a passing waiter to wash it back down. The older man suddenly stops in his tracks and nearly spills his tray of flutes as he looks up in surprise to see me, his dark eyes shining through his even darker skin.

"Well, how you doin' today, Miss Lady?" he politely asks.

"Fine, thank you," I reply.

He chuckles slightly and then lowers his voice. "We don't see too many of *us* 'round here. Mighty nice to see *you*."

I chuckle too. "I know what you mean, sir. I know just what you mean."

The man smiles and moves on.

"All right, y'all. Everybody got your champagne?" Missy's mother is holding up her flute. "I'd just like to toast my dear daughter Sissy. I am just thrilled about her upcoming marriage to a big ol' real estate agent. Big Daddy Dean sure is happy. We say, 'We got one sold off at the auction block; we're working on number two!'" The red-faced woman turns to smile at Missy, who is all smiles.

The women laugh in agreement and point at Missy, who blushes and mimics praying, "Please, please," to the heavens. I make eye contact with the old black waiter standing at service in a corner in the back. He just shakes his head and looks down. So do I, as the guests continue to cheer on the McKay mess.

I have to get out of here, but just as I turn to walk away, I run smack dab into Mrs. McKenzie, Chase's mother. She looks just as surprised to see me as I am to see her. It is the first time we have ever made eye contact. We both stand here blinking at each other, like two wide-eyed deer caught in headlights.

Mrs. McKenzie gives me a shy smile. Among those squealing rich girls, she seems out of place here in her simple cotton dress and her simple country manners. It's the one thing that we have in common right now: we both seem out of place. She seems totally overwhelmed by this perky, preppy crowd.

"Hello," she finally says.

"Hello, Mrs. McKenzie," I reply. "It is nice to see you again."

"Yes." She nods and smiles a faint smile. She seems planted in the manicured grass, not knowing which way to turn, until Missy swoops down and wraps her long, toned, and tanned arms around Mrs. McKenzie's red neck.

"Hey, Momma McKenzie." Missy swoons over the woman she is

plotting to make her mother-in-law. "Can I get you something? I see you've met Destiny."

"Yes, I have." Mrs. McKenzie smiles again, although she still looks uncomfortable.

"Well, you let me know if I can get you anything, you hear?" Missy kisses Mrs. McKenzie on the cheek, throws a smile at me, and then disappears as quickly as she came.

"Destiny," Mrs. McKenzie says, looking hard at me. "That is the girl I want for my Chase."

"I see," I say, but what I really see is a mother who may be willing to join in on a plot against her son just to get her own country leg up in society. "But what about Chase?" I ask. "What does he want?"

"He wants what his mother wants," she answers. "What is best for him."

I smile. "Are you sure? That he wants what you want?"

Mrs. McKenzie stares at me with a frozen smile.

Suddenly, the sky begins to darken, as if it's reflecting Mrs. McKenzie's mood.

"Well, we'd better go in," Mrs. McKenzie says as she frowns up at the darkening sky. "Dear God, this looks like a bad one."

"Mrs. McKenzie! Mrs. McKenzie!" As if on cue, even before I have a chance to offer my help, Missy reappears. "Let's get you inside, for God's sake!" Missy's once perfectly coiffed hair is now blowing in the wind, which is now picking up even more speed.

"Lord, I pray it's not going to rain on Sissy's party," Missy whines as she looks up to the sky. "Please, God, don't let it rain."

For such a deceptive girl, she certainly does ask God for a lot.

A crack of thunder breaks, and a bolt of lightning streaks across the sky.

"Oh, my God!" Sissy screams. *"Mama!"*

Squealing girls run everywhere as the wind gusts and blows. The dainty pre-wedding decorations begin to come unhinged. The tents sway under the force of the wind. Guests and waiters frantically run across the large lawn in hope of beating the rain and getting inside the country club. It suddenly begins raining so hard that most of us don't have a chance of making it to shelter dry. Some tables and chairs have blown over and tablecloths are strewn across the ground. Everyone is scrambling and fighting the wind and driving rain.

A water-soaked and tear-drenched Sissy is crying uncontrollably, her hair wet and her perfect makeup now streaming down her cheeks in black streaks. Her sodden friends and family flutter about her, patting her back in an attempt to soothe her frayed nerves.

"It's ruined!" she cries. "Everything is just ruined!"

The weary, wet women gather inside the country club lobby, wondering what in the world to do next. The bad weather, messed-up hair, wet clothes, and ruined makeup have certainly put a damper on the spirit and mood of Sissy's big celebration. Some guests are leaving, in a hurry to get home before the storm gets worse.

"Well, we were about done anyway," Missy's mother says, trying to find a rainbow in the storm. "Thanks so much for coming, everybody. Be careful getting home; it's really bad out there."

Everyone rushes to say good-bye to a sad, disappointed, and pouting Sissy.

"I just want to go home," she whines.

"Well, honey, we can't just leave right now. We got a lot to do. I've got to settle up here." Mrs. McKay pushes her rain-drenched hair off her face.

The good-looking cadet steps up. "I'll be happy to take her home." Missy looks up with surprise, as a bright smile blossoms across her face like sunshine.

"I'll go with you," she offers.

The dutiful cadet beams. "Be glad to give you both a lift."

"Derrick, you are so sweet," Missy oozes, slightly touching the cadet's strong arm, as they prepare to leave. "Sissy and I thank you so much for your nice offer."

I can't believe this is happening right before my eyes.

"Go straight home now, Missy," her mother warns. "It's very dangerous out there."

"Of course I will, Mama. I'll be there in a jiffy." A suddenly perky Missy bounces out the door with the handsome cadet. She didn't even say good-bye.

I can't take anymore of this deception. I can't witness anymore of this shameful lie or this looming disappointment. Someone has to alert Chase. But who? I've to get out of here. Like the darkening skies over Carolina today, I too am about to burst.

Chapter
⭐ Thirty-One

MAYBE IT WAS ALL OF THOSE TEARDROPS I CRIED AGAIN LAST NIGHT that has brought on even more rain this morning. I peer through puffy eyes to see that it is still pouring, with the ocean and the sky as dark and gray and tormented as my soul. The wind is still as ferocious as it was all throughout the night, hurling masses of raindrops against the doors and windows, riddling and rattling them like shotgun bullets. If I weren't so emotionally despondent this morning, I might actually be afraid. Instead, I stand here, fearlessly staring out the window, watching rivers of rain streaming down the windowpane, as rivers of tears stream down my cheeks.

Whatever happened between Chase and me on his boat has emotionally wrecked me. Whatever it was between us unlocked something buried, hidden, and frozen deep inside of me—something that I tried hard to ignore for years; something that I buried so deep in my soul that I simply forgot, ignored, and dismissed it. This is love.

But how can God be so cruel as to deny me Chase for a second time? What if Missy convinces Chase to be with her? Could I handle that pain? We are finally living in a day where we are able to go public, out in the open, freely expressing our love and commitment to each other, despite our racial and cultural differences. Finally, after all of these years of hiding, we can be free. Except Chase is not totally free. Someone else beckons his love.

Is God playing a mean trick on me?

A loud and powerful thunderclap startles me out of my self-pity with a crushing boom. It's as if God has just answered my question—or maybe He was offended by it. Another huge bolt of lightning strikes out over the sea, followed only seconds after by a deafening clap of thunder.

As kids, we used to count the number of seconds between the lightning and thunder to serve as a gauge of how far away the storm was. Based on nature's flash-and-boom performance just now, the storm isn't far away at all.

The telephone rings, as it has been all night and morning, but again, I refuse to answer it. I don't want to talk to anybody. I am not in the mood, but that damn phone keeps on ringing and ringing, and it's starting to drive me crazy. I want silence. I want to be left alone. I just want to keep standing here, staring out the window, watching raindrops through teardrops through the pain, as I question God, love, and myself.

Is it so wrong to want what feels true and right? Is it such a crime to continue loving the same man I have loved all of my life?

God, am I too late?

The telephone rings again. Exasperated and agitated, I surrender and answer the damn thing.

"Hello," I hiss, my voice searing the telephone line.

"Destiny?"

I melt.

"This is your father. Are you okay? Your mother and I have been trying to get hold of you all day."

I have rarely heard Daddy so concerned. "Yes, Daddy, I was just tired, that's all." I try to sound chipper. "I was sleeping all day."

"Sounds like you've been crying all day," Mother chimes in, having picked up the other line.

"I'm okay. Really."

"Well, have you been watching the news?" There's urgency in Daddy's voice. "The weather service has issued a hurricane warning, and we think maybe you should get out of there and come on home before this thing hits."

"A hurricane warning?" I am dazed.

"Yes, they're reporting that it's going to be a pretty big one this time." Daddy has clearly been glued to the news all day. "Right now, she's off the coast of Bermuda, but they're saying that by morning, Hurricane Belinda might be slamming into Topsail."

Daddy's words seem pressing, and I know the information is vital, but his voice becomes a muffled sound in the howling rain. It is hard for me to focus on whatever he's talking about right now. I couldn't care less if a hurricane is heading this way. I don't even care if it hits this house. In fact,

Hurricane Belinda can take the whole damn island if she wants. But I'll be right here with it, going nowhere. Nothing matters more to me than staying exactly right where I am. Right here. In Tranquility.

"Destiny, are you there?" Now Mother sounds concerned.

"Y-yes, Mother, I'm here."

"Do I need to come back down there?"

"Oh no!" I blurt. "You don't have to do that. Look how bad the weather is."

"Is it raining there?"

"Pouring," I confess. "But I'm sure it'll pass. Y'all know how those weather reports are. Every year this time, they warn about some hurricane hitting us, but it never does. Chances are it'll just blow over again. Please, don't worry about me."

"We always worry about you, Dee," Mother says with a sigh.

"Yeah, honey, you don't want to get caught down there on the ocean in a bad storm and a high tide."

"I'll be okay, Daddy. Promise."

"Well, call us later. You might change your mind. We'll come get you if you want."

"Thanks, Daddy. I'll be fine."

"And turn on the TV, for goodness' sake."

"I will, Mother."

I hang up the phone and look out the window at the torrential downpour again. The sea grass is blowing and bending so hard in the ferocious wind that the tips are about to touch the sand. Mother Ocean seems agitated and angry, churning and hurling her huge gray waves so fiercely against the beaten shore that big, fluffy patches of white sea foam are now blowing down the beach, like tumbleweeds across the sand.

The telephone rings once again, but this time, without hesitating, I pick it up, expecting to hear Mother with one last thing she forgot to mention.

"Ye-es?" I answer sarcastically. "Wha-at else?"

"Destiny?"

My heart suddenly skips, sinks, swells, and swoons. I feel so discombobulated that I swear my bottom just dropped out. I am nervous. I am scared. I am completely lost for words. It's Chase.

"Destiny?" And there, in the midst of this violent storm, is the sweet sound of his voice calling my name once again—in that same cautious and careful way I remember him calling my name so many times before. I remember the sound of his voice, even as a child, whispering across the sound, through the darkness, where he would invite me to share the moonlight with him. We shared stories, and secrets, and special collections, and, as we got older, we shared our dreams, fears, and hopes for the future.

"Destiny? It's Chase. Are you all right?"

"Yeah …"

"I'm worried about you, Dee. I've been trying to reach you since last night." I can hear concern and care in his voice, which only makes talking to him more difficult.

"I'm okay. Just trying to stay out of the rain."

"Oh, it's more than just rain, Destiny," Chase warns. "Hurricane Belinda is heading directly toward us. We're keeping a close eye on the storm, praying that she decides to change directions and heads out to sea, but if it gets any worse—if Big Belinda gets much closer—we're going to ask everybody to evacuate the island."

"Evacuate?" I ask in disbelief. "Are you serious?"

"Very serious. Aren't you watching the news, 'Big City'? They say it's going to be pretty bad. We haven't had a hurricane hit in almost fifty years, but that doesn't mean this one won't. Keep an ear out, okay?"

"Okay," I promise, fumbling to turn on the television.

"And Destiny?"

"Yeah?" I am distracted, waiting for the picture to come into view.

"Again, about the other day—I swear I meant no harm. I just—"

"You what, Chase? You made a huge mistake? Yeah. We both did."

Silence.

"Well, that's not exactly what I was going to say," Chase says in a low and humble voice. "I was going to say that I really, really do care about you, Destiny. I always have. Always will."

"Chase—"

"Hold on; hear me out. Just lemme finish. Destiny, I just don't want to lie any longer."

"Lie? About what?" I am not sure what Chase is referring to.

"I don't want to lie about us, about how I feel about you. I didn't get a bit of sleep last night, thinking about you, about what you might be thinking about what happened between us. I want us to sit down and talk about everything, like adults, just as soon as this storm is over and everything calms down."

"Maybe it's too late, Chase." I have to face the reality that I'm afraid. "Maybe too much time has passed."

"And you're going to try to convince me that that'll make you happy? You're going to try to tell me that you didn't feel something between us? That what we've felt since the day we first laid eyes on each other isn't real? You know and I know that this special thing between us is not a lie, Dee," Chase says, his voice cracking.

"Then are you going to marry Missy? Huh? Answer that? Are you?"

"No, Destiny. I am not going to marry Missy. I want to marry you. Can't you see?"

A loud clap of thunder sends static through the line.

"Chase, I'm already hurting from one man who claimed to care about me and then changed his mind. I can't take another blow to my heart like that."

"Destiny, I would never hurt you that way."

"I don't know, Chase," I say, feeling overwhelmed by the storm at sea and my own private storm of emotions.

"Look, Destiny, I've gotta go. There's a lot on our plate today with the storm and all. But please, let's take some time and talk about all of this, once everything settles down, okay? I don't know what to do, but I know I don't want to lose you again."

And I don't know what to say, so I just stand here holding the phone and staring at the TV screen. The continuous crawl at the bottom warns viewers that a serious hurricane is packing winds and heading our way. I have never seen Topsail Island on a weather map, never even heard the tranquil little island mentioned in the news, but today, it's threatened by a tropical storm and is headlining the national news, with people all over the country taking bets on whether she'll actually slam our little island.

Somehow, the storms of life seem far worse right now.

"If we get another chance, I think we should take it, Destiny. I think that we should grab it with both hands and not let it go."

Another loud clap of rumbling thunder interrupts before I can respond.

"Let me think about it, Chase," I finally answer. And as weird as this situation is, in this one divine and unexpected second in time, I actually do believe in something. I believe in—

"Destiny ..." I hear a soft whisper. "Always believe in Destiny."

And I know that deep in my heart, that is the spirit of my aunt Joy, talking to me. She is right here with me. *"Never give up on people,"* I hear, as she often reminded me. *"Never give up on love."*

So I make a new promise to be more open today, to believe in destiny, love, and never giving up on people—not even myself. I have also learned to never underestimate the power of pain or the tremendous power of love.

Chapter ★ Thirty-Two

ESPITE THE LIFT IN MY MOOD, THE FURIOUS RAIN REFUSES TO LET up. It continues to beat down relentlessly on the beach house, as the strong ocean winds from the south continue to blow. There appears to be no end in sight to the storm. As the tide rises and the tumultuous sea creeps dangerously closer to the steps of my home, the weather reports I see through occasional static on the TV are dismal. Hurricane Belinda is steadfast in her determined trek across the Atlantic, heading straight toward us right here on Topsail Island. Still, most are hoping that at the last minute, she might show mercy and change her direction.

Despite the evacuation order, crashing waves and whopping winds, I refuse to leave. While I admit that the thought of riding out the storm is both exciting and adventurous to the journalist in me, I am also staying put because I feel I have nowhere else to go. I don't want to go to my parents' house. I surely don't want to go back to New York to Garrett. This is the only place I want to be, at whatever cost. I will stay right here in Tranquility, close to Chase, determined to ride out the storms of life and sea.

The phone rings again, and I pick up.

"Hello?"

"Girl, you better getcho happy ass off that island!" It's Kat. I must admit I'm relieved to hear her voice.

"Are you okay?" Hope is also on the line. Her voice brings comfort too.

"Hey, y'all!" I can't hide the happiness in my voice. "I'm okay, just under a lot of water, that's all. But I'll be okay."

"Girl, your mother called us, talking about you refusing to evacuate the island. What's all this about?" Kat demands.

"Oh, girl, it was just for precautionary measures," I reassure her. "I'm going to stay right here until it passes."

"But why, Dee?" Hope asks, genuinely concerned. "If they say it's so dangerous, then why in the world would you stay down there all by yourself?"

"Because I don't want to go anywhere else, Hope. There's nowhere else to go anyway. You know how much I love this place. The hurricane'll probably pass anyway. They always do."

Kat is not having it. "Girl, get your ass off that island. Go to a shelter, get a hotel room, do whatever you got to do, but get your ass off that island!"

"She's right, Dee," Hope adds.

"I'll think about it," I say, knowing I already did.

Meanwhile, the storm is steadily growing worse. The rain spews horizontally. The horrendous wind shakes the house. The ocean licks my front stairs. I wonder where my Chase is and if he is okay out there on patrol in these fierce and dangerous elements. I know he is thinking about me and praying for me too. I feel his energy inside me.

"You seen that police chief?" Kat asks, as if she just read my mind.

"Yes," I answer. "And a lot has happened since I last talked to you guys."

"*Yes?*" Their interest is piqued.

"Well, we spent a whole day together. He showed me his new house, which is actually an old house we used to play in as kids. He refurbished an old boat and named it *On Assignment!*"

"I wonder why," Kat muses.

"We talked a lot about the past—our lives, our feelings, and our regrets."

"*And?*" Hope and Kat are both clearly hungry for information.

"*And* he says he wants a second chance."

I hear them both gasp on the other end of the phone.

"As well he should!" Kat bursts, as does another huge rain cloud. "*A second chance?* Nothing wrong with that. Hell, if we all got a second chance, I bet most of us would snatch it right up."

"What do you mean, a second chance?" Hope asks. "He wants a second chance at what?"

"He said ... he said ... he wants me in his life."

"*What?*" the girls cry out in unison.

"Y'all must think you're going to die down there," Kat snaps.

"I know, you think it's too much too soon. I know. But I do love him. I really do."

"Girl, listen to me." Kat sounds intense. "You and I both have been through a lot of heartbreaks—sadly, by them fools we married. If there is ever a time for happiness, Dee, it's now. That man can't help it if he loves you. If you hadn't gone back down there after all these years, he might have married Missy and lived a long, unhappy, and very boring life. But you came back down there, and he started rethinking things. Let him rethink! He's just lucky your ass got back down there before he took any wedding vows, and you're about to get out of yours. I call that the perfect storm for love."

"So what are you guys going to do?" Hope asks.

"I don't know," I say truthfully. "I'm a little overwhelmed and confused right now."

"Confused? Oh, no, you're not," Kat insists. "You may be many things, girlfriend, but 'confused' is not one of them. Not when it comes to how you feel about this policeman and how much he obviously feels about you. Girl, if there wasn't some kind of true love in there, you would have forgotten about Chase's ass long time ago."

"What about Missy?" Hope asks.

"Well, he's not completely broken off all ties with her yet, but I have a strong feeling he will."

"Are you sure?"

"Yes, I'm sure."

"Okay, in your heart, Dee, what do you want to do?"

"I don't know. Maybe I'm just too scared to enter another relationship right now. I don't know what to do yet."

"Yes, you do," Kat insists. "You have another chance right in the palm of your hands, Destiny, and you are a fool if you don't at least explore your options here. Take it slow, but definitely explore your options. Live up to your name, girl! You have loved that man all of your life. You better wake up. Life is too short, and this is not a dress rehearsal."

"Yeah, Dee, you deserve to be happy," Hope interjects. "But first, just promise us—"

The line suddenly goes dead. The lights flicker. The house quakes. The wind, rain, thunder, and lightning continue their chaotic dance. It is the first time I feel cut off from the rest of the world. I am anxious. I tap the telephone receiver, hoping in vain that the line will come back. I push the zero button on the phone again and again, thinking that an operator might suddenly appear. But I am cut off from all communication—from everyone, even Chase.

Be careful what you wish for.

The static has picked up on the television, but I can still hear the news reports through the crackle—most residents have long evacuated the island. The newsman speaks of about a dozen or so "stubborn stragglers," and I realize that I am one of them, as the ocean steadily licks the steps of my beach house.

There is suddenly a loud banging at the front door. I nearly jump out of my skin.

I look out of the window, and I see a police wagon and Chase's big red truck parked outside my house in the pouring rain. Relieved, I race to the front door and swing it open. There stands Chase, rain pouring off the brim of his hat.

"Chase!" I want to run into his arms.

"Destiny, are you all right? Why haven't you boarded up your windows?"

"I … dunno." I feel so stupid. I never even thought about the damn windows.

"Well, before you get a house full of broken glass and water, we'd better get those boards up. Where are they?"

"Down in the storage room, I guess. I've never been through a hurricane before."

"Even more of a reason why you should evacuate, Destiny!" Chase's harsh police chief tone catches me off guard. He seems exasperated. "Look, we're dealing with a very short window of time here. I can't force you to leave the island, but I sure wish you would."

"I'm not going, Chase," I say. "I want to stay."

Chase takes a deep breath and then expels a long sigh. "Okay, but you got to get those boards up. My men, here, can help you." Chase motions to the police van, and about six big guys in rain gear eagerly jump out, ready for work.

I don't like the look on Chase's face—he tries to remain professional and calm, but I know that in his heart, he is truly concerned about me, as stubborn as I am. Chase's men scramble in the pouring rain to board up the windows of my home.

"Thank you, Chase. I appreciate everything you and your guys have done. I'll ride it out. You'll see—it'll be okay."

"We'll see," Chase says with a worried look. "Well, we've got to drop by some other homes. Things are pretty crazy right now. You stay inside and away from the windows. The phone lines are down, so I'll check back in on you later. Be careful, Dee."

"I will, Chase. You be careful out there too," I say as we lock eyes. He is the only peace in the midst of this raging storm.

Chase and his crew pull out of the driveway to continue their rescue mission. I go back into the house and play the waiting game, waiting for this hurricane weather to end. The windows are boarded shut. The light comes from the television that drones on and on about Big Belinda. The weatherman reports that she remains unyielding, continuing to inch her sadistic way closer and more directly toward our helpless little island. I cuddle myself underneath Aunt Joy's patchwork throw and pray that this storm too shall pass.

Chapter
★ Thirty-Three

NIGHT HAS FALLEN. THERE IS NO LIGHT ANYWHERE ON THE ISLAND. IT sounds as if my tiny beach house is being attacked by wild, hungry, howling demons.

I am suddenly frightened and all alone.

I have never heard a house moan and creak and bang about so. I can actually feel the house sway and rock in the violent force of the reported one-hundred-mile-per-hour winds. The ocean, now swirling beneath the house, continues to surge over the dunes that were once my home's sole protection from the powerful sea. Tranquility stands tall upon stilts dug deep into the sand, as it has for fifty years and three generations of my family. Now, Tranquility must once again withstand the surging sea.

I can hear the planks of my bottom steps clacking and whining as the wood warps, contorts, and shrinks to make way for the force and constant flow of the raging water. I peer through the slats in the boards on the windows and in the moonlight, I can see that the ocean has completely surrounded my house. Every time I look, it has risen higher. Fluffy puffs of sea foam churned out of the pounding sea litter the entire area, flying in the wind and rain and moonlight, as if it's snowing outside. I see rooftops, cars, big rafts of wood, and old tires zooming by in the swift currents—a sign of the destruction of homes, boats, and possibly lives also tortured by Hurricane Belinda's deadly storm.

The house continues to moan, croak, rattle, and shake. I hear the mighty ocean waves creeping higher around my house. I have no idea what to do. I realize that as the water is rising, the chances of my escaping the house—much less the island—are now impossible. I feel as if I'm shipwrecked at sea in my own home. Trapped. Thank God for those stilts. I may have a chance.

The thunder claps so loudly this time that it scares me to tears. This has not turned out to be the exciting adventure I had once imagined that had my adrenaline surging like the raging sea. As bad as Garrett is, he's at least not life-threatening.

Mother Ocean is angry, unforgiving, disturbed. So I do as I did when my own mother was in a ferocious mood—I remain quiet and pray. I pray that she will let me live.

I scramble around the house in a desperate search for flashlights and batteries but soon realize that they are probably in the storage room downstairs, which is now submerged in rushing ocean water. I am so afraid that I feel dizzy and sick to my stomach. What was I thinking when I made the decision to stay? Has my life gotten so far off track that I don't think it's worth saving any longer?

Suddenly, there's a loud bang on the right front side of the house, as if something heavy plowed into it through the crashing waves. The house squeaks and sways, and I am terrified because I can hear the water further rising around the house, as if it's after me. I run into the bathroom. I slam the door shut, as if there's some mysterious safety waiting here. I am heaving sobs. I can't see through my tears or the darkness. I fear I will drown in my own home. How could I have come this far, only to die?

And if I die, I will never forgive myself, because I would have never gotten that chance at a second chance to see what might have happened— what might have been between Chase and me. He will never hear me say the words "I love you," which right now I would give my life to say.

The house rocks and shakes and sways. What do I do? Where is my Chase? Is he even thinking about me, or is he comforting Missy through this storm right now? Dear God, what have I done?

The thunder roars and sheets of wind and rain blanket the windows. Full of fear, I climb into the bathtub and close the shower curtain. I ball up into a fetal position and pretend that I am crying into Aunt Joy's lap, and she is gently rubbing my hair, just the way she always did whenever I felt alone and afraid and heard scary sounds in the night.

Aunt Joy and I, together in my bathtub, drift off into a stormy sea of darkness.

Chapter ★ Thirty-Four

I AM AWAKENED BY THE SILENCE. I STEP OUT OF THE BATHTUB IN WHICH I shamelessly sought safety and comfort last night and go peek out the door. The rain has subsided, but the sky is still gray. The ocean has receded now, leaving scattered debris behind. I am left here all alone and stranded, with no telephone, no electricity, no radio—no way to communicate or call for help.

The house is already full of the damp smell of molding ocean water. I cannot escape, as the beach house steps have been totally ripped from the porch and washed away, leaving me stranded in a house on stilts. Tranquility sits here above the ruins and destruction, like a battered matchbox on toothpick legs.

I am so overwhelmed and hungry, tired, alone, and afraid. I'm overcome by heaving sobs again. I know that as calm as it looks right now, the hurricane is anything but over. After hours of enduring the violent storm, this is only its eye, and in just a short time, I will have to endure the back end of Big Bad Belinda's raging vengeance. How can I survive the tempest again? As far as I can see, there is not another soul around—no one to rescue me, no one to call for help. I don't know what to do.

I have been waiting and worrying and wringing my hands for hours, mostly watching the clock and the skies and dreaming of something to eat. I am totally helpless and wonder if I might not also be a bit crazy for having been so defiant with everyone who practically begged me to evacuate.

"We do live by our decisions, don't we?" I can hear Mother scolding.

But no matter how crazy it was, no matter how life-threatening, I know I stood by my conviction by standing by my Tranquility. But things will be all but tranquil in just a few hours.

Suddenly, the faint puttering of an engine out at sea captures my attention. Is it a rescue boat—or maybe pirates or thieves coming to pillage the island, maybe take advantage of a woman alone? I look out over the vastness of the blue ocean to spot a single little boat tugging its way across the waters. It looks so diminutive on the big, wide ocean.

This could be my only chance.

"Oh, my God! *Help!*" I yell, leaning out of the screened porch door. I wave wildly. *"Hello! Help!"* I race into the house and grab a white beach towel. I run back to the door and start waving the towel madly. Please, somebody see me. See this frantic sign of life.

The little boat keeps chugging my way. As the vessel moves closer, a man steps out of the captain's quarters and waves both of his arms over his head. My heart skips a beat. I have never been so happy to see another human being. I remember Aunt Joy's binoculars and grab them from the hall closet. I focus on my rescue vehicle, which is picking up speed. And to my surprise, painted on the side of the boat, I see *On Assignment*. I cannot believe my tear-filled eyes.

"Chase!" I scream, waving my arms wildly. "Chase! Chase!"

The sweet little boat creeps closer and closer. I see the golden hair of my Adonis standing there at the helm. He takes off his shirt and waves it madly toward the shore. I pray he will take us out of here to safety, as the sky is already beginning to spatter more rain, turning back into a dark and angry gray.

Chase pulls the boat as close to shore as he can, then jumps out and wades waist-deep to the beach, muscles rippling as he trudges through the waves. I am so happy to see him that I could burst. He runs across the beach to the house—to me.

"Destiny, are you okay?" His voice cracks as he shouts up to me. He is out of breath. He looks even more worried than before.

"I was scared to death, but I'm okay now that you're here. Oh, Chase, thank God you're here."

"Okay, Dee. Get me a rope or something, so I can climb up to the house. We need to secure those boards while we have this break in the storm. We don't have much time."

"Shouldn't we leave?" I ask.

"I don't think we have time, Dee. We'd probably get caught in the storm, trying to get the boat around the island. As bad as it is—and I know it's scary—it's better to be on land than out to sea. The storm is already picking up."

I doubt I can find a rope anywhere, so I grab a bed sheet and tie it to one of the boards left behind when the ocean took the staircase. Chase hoists himself up to the porch, his big arms bulging. I finally feel safe.

As Chase climbs upon the porch, I drop to my knees and wrap my hands around his face. I desperately want to look into his eyes, to know he is really here and that God surely heard my prayers. I notice one of his eyes is swollen and bruised.

"What happened to you?" I ask.

"Oh, it's a long story," he replies as he stands looking out over the stormy sea. He then offers me his hand, and I stand alongside him. We grab each other and kiss deeply and eagerly. I'm not sure if the salty taste is from our tears or the sea, but I drink him up, every drop.

I gently run my fingers over Chase's bruised eye. I stand on my tiptoes and kiss it. I kiss his strong jawline. I kiss down the side of his neck, hoping to soothe my hurting hero. Chase suddenly breaks away.

"Let's get those boards checked," he orders. "Storm's blowing in."

Chase and I go around, checking the boards, rehammering the nails that have come loose in the monster storm's unrelenting grip, as the wind and rain begin to pick up again.

"What are we going to do, Chase?" I ask. "Can't we leave by land?"

Chase shakes his head. "The bridge has been destroyed. Too many live electrical wires down, plus a lot of dangerous debris flying through the air like torpedoes. There are poisonous snakes and other vermin roaming around on ground out there. No, it's way too dangerous to go by land right now. They'll have to bulldoze us outta here by the end of this storm."

"Well, we could go *On Assignment*," I reason.

"And get shipwrecked at sea? No. We'll just have to ride it out, sweetie. At least, this time, you won't be alone. I'll be right here with you till it's all over. We're going to be just fine."

Chase reaches out, pulls me closer to him, and then wraps his strong arms around me as I nestle down deep into the hollow of his chest, embraced inside his deep hug. He smells like the sea.

"Let's get back inside now," Chase says as he kisses the top of my head. "We've still got a few more hours left of this madness, good God willing.

"You think it'll be worse than the first half?" I'm sure Chase detects the fear in my voice.

"That's up to Mother Nature," Chase replies.

We go inside, double-checking the windows and securing the doors. It's as if we're in the middle of a horror story, where there's a wild, invisible monster out there chasing us, and we are frantically trying to batten down the hatches before her second round of attacks. My biggest fear is that when that mighty monster moves ashore, she might take my Tranquility, my Chase, and my life in her deathly path—everything I finally have, everything I have always treasured. What if those stilts don't hold up this time around? What if we collapse into the churning sea?

I try to snap out of it. "I'm going to run the hot water and maybe make some tea. It might help soothe our nerves. I can't believe we have to go through the same storm again."

"Yep, same storm, except the wind will shift to blow in the opposite direction."

"Dear Jesus," I say and head to the kitchen. Chase follows. The water comes out of the faucet in spurts, spewing and sputtering. Finally, it flows. I wait as the water gets only slightly warm. I take two mugs and fill them up, dropping in tea bags that barely steep. I probably won't even taste it anyway.

Chase is grateful for his lukewarm tea. We stand in the kitchen, looking in silence out the back window that overlooks the sound, waiting for the onslaught of the next stage of Hurricane Belinda.

Chase has an intense look on his face. He seems far away. I wonder if it's that black eye.

"You gonna tell me how you got that shiner?" I finally ask. "Were you out there rescuing somebody and got hurt?"

"Pshaw! Funny you should say that," Chase says with a peculiar look on his face. He walks out of the kitchen. Curious, I follow him into the living room where we both take a seat on the couch and quietly sip our lukewarm tea.

"You want to talk about it?" I finally ask.

"Well …" Chase hesitates, as if he's figuring out how to say whatever it is he has to say. "A funny thing happened when I left you yesterday afternoon." He lets out a long sigh and slaps his knee. "The department got an anonymous call about an abandoned car hidden way back out in the marshes." Chase exaggerates the distance with both arms. "My partner and I were working late on emergency hurricane duty, so we checked it out. We located the vehicle and saw that the windows were all fogged up. The car was rocking back and forth and we heard moanin' and groanin' goin' on inside. We figured it was a couple of frisky teenagers exploring their sexual energy during the storm." Chase hesitates.

"Okay, go on," I encourage him, wondering where he's headed with this story.

"Well, we got up closer to the car, and we saw the girl's legs come flying up in the air, and the guy just pounding away on her. And you know what's funny? Get this—he's still in full regalia, a complete military uniform. So we figure the guy's just trying to get laid before he has to hightail it back to the Fort Bragg military base. Still, we gotta get 'em outta there, because there's a hurricane coming. So, I knock on the car window with my badge. The cadet jumps up, all startled and surprised, you know?" Chase chuckles and looks down at the floor. He shakes his head as he takes a long sip of his now-cold tea. Finally, he looks at me with a squinted black eye. "But then, when the guy turns around, there's Missy lying right there under him, spread-eagled for all the world to see—lying there as my spreadsheet of evidence." Chase spreads his arms wide in description. "I knew she was up to something."

"Whoa!" I am shocked, not surprised, yet still sad that Chase had to find out the horrid truth in such a graphic way.

"Well, dumb me—I'm standing there thinking the soldier's gotta be raping her. So I go after him, and he starts punching me. I swear, it never occurred to me that … that he was willing to fight a *cop* for her. This dude is claiming all the while that he loves her. I tussle with him a bit before my partner pulls me off the guy. Even he said it wasn't worth it. So, that's the story. That's how I got the black eye."

"Jeez! What about Missy?"

"What about her?" Chase snaps. "She couldn't even look me in my swollen black eye!" Chase shakes his head and wipes his lip as if he had dirt on it. I can only imagine what that scene was like. Chase now sits here in the middle of another disaster, hurt, deceived, and angry. I know how he feels.

"Oh man, Chase, I'm so sorry that you had to find out that way."

"I swear, I always knew in my heart that Missy might not be the one. I always felt something was missing. She always seemed distracted and distant. No wonder I could never get close to her."

"I know, Chase," I say soothingly. "I know."

"I think that girl just likes men in uniform or something," Chase jokes.

We share an uncomfortable but welcome chuckle.

I reach over and touch Chase's hand. "Well, the good news is you weren't in any deeper than you needed to be. You found out the truth before you went too far. You get a second chance—a get-out-of-jail-free card, my friend."

Chase takes my hands and pulls me closer to him. "Everything's going to be all right, Destiny. You know that, don't you?" Chase looks deeply in my eyes. "Do you believe that, Destiny?"

"Yes ... yes, I do now, Chase," I admit.

"Call it divine intervention or divine planning or whatever. I know it might not look like it now, but God is working everything out for us, Dee. It's our chance now, and I know He's not going to let anything get in our way this time. Nothing is going to happen to us in this storm. We are not going to die. We've got too much living, too much rebuilding, and too much loving to do."

Chase plants a deep sweet kiss on lips that have been craving his touch for years. We kiss so hard, for a minute I forget we are trapped in the eye of a life-threatening storm.

The wind begins to roar as the storm rages once again. Chase pulls me closer. He stares into my eyes. I can feel his breath on my face as he draws his mouth closer to mine. He kisses me—gently, lovingly, softly. "It's going to be okay, Destiny," he coos. My lips part to find his. We bring our mouths together closer and closer until the frenzied dance between our searching tongues begins—dancing in the freedom of finally expressing our true love, plunging in with passion. There is no way we could stop the floodgates from lifting now. We have waited too long. We have fought too hard for this love.

"I love you," Chase whispers as he kisses me all over my face and my eyelids, nibbling on my ears and neck, and running his fingers through my hair. "I have loved you all of my life."

"And I love you," I whisper between his kisses, surrendering to his passionate touches, with his strong fingers entwined in mine. "Forever."

"Forever."

"Forever."

Chase takes my face in his hands and pulls it close to his. I see his beautiful green eyes as the lightning strikes. He continues to kiss me deeply and sensuously, looking at me longingly all the while, as the thunder roars outside. I pray that this kiss and that look lasts forever. I totally surrender my heart, body, and soul to this one man.

Crack! Crash! Boom!

I shudder in sudden alarm and fear, grabbing Chase's strong arm. The sky explodes with a spectacular show of thunder and lightning. Chase holds me tightly, rocking and soothing me while the wind whistles through every crack and crevice of the beach house. Sheets of rain continue to pour. The ocean swells and surges, sending powerful waves pounding the shore like monstrous fists of fury. The second stage of Big Belinda's wrath has begun.

"Don't be afraid, Destiny." Chase soothes me with a soft kiss on my cheek. "I'm right here, baby. I'm right here."

I bury my head in Chase's chest. I inhale deeply, trying to capture every single molecule of his being until we become one. *If I die today, please, dear God, let me have this moment now.* It's as if we have no choice. We are driven by our love and nature. We are grabbing and pawing at each other as if we'll never see each other again or as if we may not survive this brutal night. The lightning bolts above the beach house continue to crack, while the thunder consistently booms outside. The wind has a horrid howl, but neither of us is focused on the life-threatening storm right now. We are far too focused on each other, as if we are discovering one another for the first time. The electricity surging through the air only heightens the electricity surging in our souls. While Hurricane Belinda wreaks havoc, we make love as if our lives depend on it.

I take my lover's hand and lead him to my bedroom, where we continue our mad, passionate lovemaking, promising in deep, breathless whispers to never leave each other—not ever again. Chase's tongue travels all over my body, kissing every inch of me with intention and purpose, as he peels off my clothes and takes me in his arms. I love him more with every passionate kiss and whispered promise of loving me and caring for me forever.

I cling to Chase as our bodies mold into one, grinding and sliding, feeling skin to skin, chest to chest, tangled into a love knot. I feel his sigh on my neck, his hand on my thigh. I am tangled into one with Chase.

"Oh, Destiny," he says, panting.

"Yes, my love?" I whisper deep into his ear, as he rolls over on top of me. "Talk to me."

"No talking." Chase pants as he takes his muscular thighs and separates mine.

I open myself to him, both of us wanting and waiting for this moment forever. Chase slides his big strong hand under me and pushes his long, thick, hard love into my deep, wet softness. I lift myself to him as he digs into my soul, deeper and deeper, until I can't hold it anymore and burst into tears of happiness and ecstasy. Chase kisses me through my emotions, while he loves me deeper, harder, working into a frenzy of desire and need.

We cum at the same time, screaming, moaning, and panting in ecstasy over the pleasure and release that blocked out the raging storm at sea. It is the best love I have ever had or made. I want Chase McKenzie for the rest of my life. I want this love to last forever.

While the hurricane rages outside, here inside Tranquility, there's only the warmth of spirit and the golden glow of love. Chase and I fall asleep in each other's arms, knowing that God, the angels, and Aunt Joy are watching over us. For the first time in a long time, and despite the storms of life and sea, I feel, safe, loved, and alive once again.

Chapter ★ Thirty-Five

I AWAKE TO THE MANLY SMELL OF CHASE MCKENZIE AND THE FEEL OF his strong arms still wrapped around me. The birds are tweeting happily outside my window, as if nothing at all unusual happened last night. Despite the horrendous storm, I finally feel a sense of happiness and peace, a cleansing and safety that I can barely describe. I feel like a survivor, and I can do anything.

"Good morning, sunshine." Chase smiles down at me and kisses my forehead.

"Good morning, my darling." I smile back up at him.

"Well, we're still here," he teases.

I chuckle. "Yes, and thank God we are."

"Let's see what awaits us."

The storm has passed. The wind and rain have stopped. Outside the sun is shining brightly again. There's not a cloud in the sky. The ocean is blue, calm, and gentle, with barely a wave licking the shore. She is as glassy as a lake and as innocent as a lamb. If not for all the debris scattered around—the mass destruction left behind, some residents' homes and longtime businesses now missing—we wouldn't guess a vicious hurricane just struck. We still don't know how many injuries or if any lives were lost. Looking at the calm seas and skies right now, one would never believe a horrendous hurricane had brutally battered this area. How in the world did we survive?

A military evacuation chopper, surveying the area, spots us and makes an emergency rescue landing on the beach.

"Everybody okay?" shouts a soldier over the loud thump-thump-thumping of the helicopter's propeller. "Y'all are lucky to be alive! You okay? Any injuries?"

"No, we're just happy to be here, man," Chase says.

We board the emergency aircraft. Chase holds me closely, warding off my fears. We fly away to safety, together preparing to rebuild our lives and the little island where our love began so many years ago in a very different time.

Chapter
★ Thirty-Six

CHASE WAS RIGHT WHEN HE PREDICTED IT WOULD TAKE WEEKS FOR workers to bulldoze the huge piles of debris out of the way before the rebuilding crews could get back on our devastated little island. Emergency crews eventually evacuated everyone safely. There were some minor injuries on the mainland and a few babies born a lot earlier than expected—a natural phenomenon during these times—but fortunately, no deaths to report in the area. Many homes were badly or completely damaged, leaving residents stranded and struggling to find emergency housing, food, and insurance representatives.

Chase and I are working hard around the clock, volunteering for the emergency relief efforts. Topsail Island is hurting badly, and we are staying here to help rebuild our treasured home.

Chase's potato house fared well in the storm, perhaps protected by the thick marsh trees. He insisted I move in with him after the hurricane, at least until my beach house is restored. It may seem strange, my living with another man so soon, but it doesn't feel strange at all living with Chase. We blend and harmonize well together, as if we have known each other all our lives—and quite truly, we have.

Grossman gave me a chance to report about the hurricane disaster, live from the island, even using my battered beach house as the backdrop for my reports. Whether I meant to or not, I witnessed this news, upfront and personal, and again my big lead story made the national network broadcasts. Mother and Daddy were again relieved that I survived another big news story and once again were extremely proud.

While out in the field, gathering interviews on the hurricane relief efforts, a cameraman from our local affiliate in nearby Wilmington, North Carolina, told me about a job opening in the station's Investigations Unit.

He encouraged me to call the news director myself, saying he'd probably be happy to have an experienced New York City reporter, who's also a native North Carolinian, on his investigative team. So in a tremendous leap of faith, I called the news director to inquire about the job and just as the cameraman predicted, his boss was thrilled about my inquiry and hired me on the spot. After Grossman realized he couldn't talk me out of transferring to North Carolina, he called our sister station himself to put in a good word for me. He also told me I always had a place back in New York City, if I ever changed my mind.

Mother was not at all happy about my decision to remain on Topsail Island. "Are you *crazy*? You got a master's degree in journalism from Columbia University *in New York City*. You are breaking your teeth in the *number-one market*. We've always had big dreams of your winning that Emmy one day, and you're just *that* close to going network, and *what*? You blow it all for *love* with a *white boy*—on a tiny, little countrified island?"

"Mother, I'm not blowing anything," I say as I patiently try to explain the situation and my choices to her, but she just rambles on and on about what a tremendous mistake she thinks I'm making. I know in my heart that while this may not be the decision Mother would make, it is the only decision for me. "Look, I am with the man I love, on the island I love, and still able to pursue the career and the passions I love. What's so wrong with that?"

"But there's so much more out there for you to accomplish, Dee."

"Mother, listen to me—you have always pushed me to be the very best at everything I do, and I deeply appreciate that. I tried it your way, but my dreams are not your dreams. My choices aren't yours. Mother, can't you see how happy I am—for once? Again, this is not about *you*. I want a much simpler life for myself than maybe you would choose. Just let me be happy, Mother, please? Can you please just be happy for me for once? Please?"

Mother is quiet. I'm not sure whether she's sincerely contemplating my words or about to blow a gasket. But I rest in my finally knowing what I want for my life and for the first time, I'm determined to get it, not craving anybody's approval or caving under anybody else's pressure. I am destined to be happy, fulfilled, and—as Aunt Joy always reminded me—I promise not to give up on love. I will truly, deeply, forever love Chase Monroe McKenzie, as I always have, all my life. And I will never second-guess our love again.

"But, where are you going to live, Dee?" Mother asks. "The beach house needs so many repairs."

"Chase has asked me to live with him, at least until Tranquility is ready."

"Dear Mary, Mother of God! Your father is going to have a fit."

"I know," I say, resigned to the fact that Daddy will only see my living with Chase as shacking up. "He'll come around. After all, I could still be living up in 'the ghetto' with Garrett. I really do need your support right now. Chase and I both do."

"Well," Mother says resignedly. "I don't know what we would have done without that Chase. I must say, that young man does stand by you during the worst of times, doesn't he? He seems to be there for you no matter what. That's very important, Dee. I guess that quality in a person is admirable—in any color."

"I appreciate that, Mother."

Life keeps getting better every day.

While I have this break from my volunteer work on the island, I decide to do some more hurricane cleaning around Chase's house while he remains on around-the-clock duty. So many things need to be put out to dry before they mold and mildew inside. Other than some flooding and lots of dampness, the good news is that Chase's dream home turned out to be stronger than we imagined. Flooding or not, it feels wonderful being in the house that Chase built. Something deep in my heart tells me he built this home with me in mind.

I am hanging Chase's kitchen rug over the front porch banister when I hear a vehicle slowly creeping up the long driveway through the marsh trees toward the house. I know it's not the familiar rumble of Chase's big truck, and we're not expecting anyone, so who in the world could it be? The car gets closer, slowly entering the clearing around Chase's home. I have never seen this car before. The car slowly grinds to a halt. I cannot see the driver's face from up here on the porch because of the sun's bright reflection.

The shadowy driver sits there. He does nothing, which gives me even more of an eerie feeling. I stand on the porch and wait for this unexpected intruder to make a move. I remember Chase left an emergency radio sitting on the kitchen table. I will use it if I have to. Maybe it's just my New York instincts that have me on edge right now, but I feel there is something weird about this approaching car.

"Hello," I call out. "Can I help you?"

There is no movement.

"Hello?" I repeat. When still no one budges from the car, I storm into the house, grab Chase's emergency radio, and then march back onto the porch, preparing to recite the car's license number to the radio dispatcher. Finally, the car door slowly opens, and to my shock and surprise—out steps Garrett Nelson.

"Hey, baby," he says smoothly as he slides his sneaky way out of the car. "Don't get all excited now. It's me. *Surprise!*"

"Yeah, some surprise, all right!" I am livid that Garrett has the nerve to resurface on Topsail. "Why are you here and what do you want?"

"Hey, hey, easy, Dee. I come in peace," he teases as he saunters closer to the house.

"Garrett, get right back in that car and drive straight back to New York where you and your mess belong."

"Dee … Dee, look, hold up," Garrett says, making his way toward the steps.

"Stop it right there, Garrett! Don't you dare come a step further. You are not welcome here. Go home!"

"Not welcome here? Wait. Hold up." Garrett kicks the sand. "I come all this way to see you because I was worried about you, baby. I heard you got caught on the island down here in that big hurricane. I heard you were homeless. Then I hear you're living back here in the woods somewhere with some white dude. I was just worried about you, Dee. I came to take you home."

"Take me home? What home? We don't have a home, Garrett. You destroyed that months ago, remember? Around the time you were impregnating Eve!"

"Baby, please, listen to me. Let's talk." Garrett walks up the first few steps.

"Back up, Garrett! Get off the steps!" I feel as if I am shouting at a bad dog. "Go home! Now! It's over between us. I want nothing to do with you."

Garrett looks like I just knocked the wind out of him. He gives me one of those puppy-dog looks. I will never ever buy into that look again.

"Destiny, please, just listen to me for a minute. Baby, I made a big mistake, and I know that now. I took you for granted, and I think I was angry that married life wasn't as easy as I thought it would be. I started believing you were more in love with your career than with me. Eve was just there, baby. I swear I never stopped loving you. I want another chance, Destiny. I swear I'll work harder."

"Garrett, you sound ridiculous. And does your pregnant girlfriend, Eve, know you're down here groveling in front of me like this? You can't just waltz into my life whenever you feel like it. It's over, Garrett. It can't be more over, and no amount of begging and looking at me all sad like that is going to change the circumstances or the situation. I have already moved on!"

"But I want us to try one more time, Destiny. Honey, please, I'm begging you."

Then the fool actually starts to cry. Something horrible must have happened between Eve and him, something so horrendous that it made him drag his pitiful ass all the way down here to Topsail Island and track me down with some big old crocodile tears to plead for a second chance. Garrett might have lost Eve and me, but he still hasn't lost his nerve.

"Okay, what happened, Garrett? What happened to you and Eve and the baby?" I wait at the top of Chase's stairs, staring down at my pitiful soon-to-be-ex-husband.

"There is no baby," he mumbles.

"Excuse me? What did you say? I didn't hear you." I can't believe what I really heard. But then again—yes, I can.

"I said, there is no baby. Eve was lying all that time. Can you believe that?"

"What do you mean, can I believe it? You lied to me all that time too!"

"Yeah, but to lie about a *baby,* just to *trap* me into leaving you—that wasn't right."

"Oh, Garrett, it happens all the time." I sigh and muse that for a smart man, Garrett can be so stupid.

"Hey, and get this—Eve was cheating on me too." Garrett looks up at me in wide-eyed hurt and disbelief from the bottom of the stairs that I will not let him climb. He has been hoodwinked and bamboozled by a stone-cold perpetrator. Eve duped us both. "Dee, I swear she was fuckin' Maxine behind my back. She left me for fuckin' ghetto-ass Maxine—a *woman.* Damn! I still can't get over that shit!"

"Well, too bad," I say.

"Plus, she was a slob, Dee. All she wanted to do was lie around all day. She didn't want to get a job, but she always wanted presents. And she couldn't touch you in the kitchen, baby."

"Why are you telling me all of this?"

"Baby, Eve always accused me of one day going back to you. She never completely trusted my love for her. She said I'd always love you, not her completely, and it's true. She was real insecure about you. She knows you're the better woman."

"Garrett, go away. It's over between us," I say, exhausted. What did you really expect from me when you came here today?"

"I don't know. I wanted to check in on you, surprise you, and make sure you were all right. But baby, I really wanted to see if maybe we could get back together, you know—start all over again. I admit I made a mistake, and I am here to say I'm sorry, and I want you back, Destiny. Heck, I was thinking maybe we'd go to the movies tonight."

"Funny, I was thinking we wouldn't see each other anymore."

Garrett scowls.

"It's time for you to go home now, Garrett. It's over. I'll call and have my attorney draw up the divorce papers tomorrow."

"*Tomorrow? Divorce papers? Whoa!*" Garrett hops up the steps, coming face-to-face with me. "Can't we talk about this, baby?"

"What is there to talk about, Garrett? You fuck my best friend and destroy our marriage, and you want me to act like nothing ever happened. I swear, you have a lot of fucking nerve, Garrett!"

"Destiny! I said I was sorry. Damn! Gimme a break!"

"Oh, I'm going to give you a break all right!"

Garrett looks desperate. "Okay, I made a mistake," he says. "But what? You can't forgive me?"

"I forgive you. I forgive myself for marrying you. And mostly, I've moved on, Garrett," I say firmly.

"Moved on? What the hell does that mean?"

Suddenly, I hear the deep rumble of the engine of Chase's big red truck. He is coming down the driveway to the house. Garrett looks in that direction, raises an eyebrow, and then looks back at me.

"You better go now," I advise. The last thing I want Chase to see is Garrett standing outside his house, begging me to get back with him.

"Come on, Destiny. I'm taking you home with me," he says as he grabs my wrist and starts pulling me down the steps. "Enough already!"

"Let go of me!" I yell, but Garrett maintains a firm grip on my wrist and continues yanking me.

"We'll talk when we get home, Destiny!"

Chase's truck slams to a halt. Chase jumps out and races over. "Hey, hey, hey, buddy, what's going on here? Destiny?"

"None of your damn business, and I ain't your goddamn buddy!" Garrett spits at Chase, barely looking at him as he keeps pulling me toward his rental car.

"Hey, hey, hey—slow down. Let's talk a minute, Let the lady go." Chase is in civilian clothes, but I know he still carries a gun somewhere. I pray he doesn't have to use it on Garrett today. I have never seen Garrett like this. As arrogant as he is, he has never touched me so violently before. But he's desperate, and humiliated, and he's doing whatever he can to save whatever little is left of his manhood from even more self-inflicted shame.

"This is my *wife!*" Garrett retorts.

Chase remains professional. "Yes, sir, but I'm still asking you to let her go."

"Fuck you!" Garrett spits and tugs me harder down the stairs. I am desperately clinging to the banister with my other hand. At the bottom of the stairs, I finally start beating on his hand to let me go.

"I said, let her go!" Chase demands as he rushes over and grabs Garrett's upper arm. Garrett lets go of me and takes a swing at Chase, who ducks and head tackles Garrett to the ground, where their mad tussle continues. I am screaming for them to stop, afraid that someone is going to get hurt, and we all make the evening news. Haven't we all been hurt enough?

Garrett is cussing and fighting back hard as Chase punches him hard in the gut. "Owwww, man!" Garrett yelps. Chase then flips the doubled-over Garrett on his aching stomach, twisting his arm behind his back.

"Let me go, motherfucker," Garrett spews into the dirt. "Let me go!"

"Settle down, or I will arrest you!" Chase demands.

"What the fuck you mean, arrest me, motherfucker?" Garrett squirms to free himself.

"He's a cop, you idiot!" I scream.

"And I will arrest you for assaulting a woman *and* a police officer, you keep it up!"

Garrett freezes. "A cop?" he says. "What the fuck? Dee? Is he really a *cop?*"

"No, Garrett, he's really the Topsail Island police *chief!*"

"Holy shit!" Garrett exclaims as he breaks free from Chase, rolls over, and painfully scrambles to his feet. "Hey, man, look, I didn't know who you were. I—"

"Now, *you* look," Chase says as he gets up. "You don't need to cause any more trouble to Destiny or yourself, for that matter. She'll be okay right here, where she wants to be, where she belongs."

"Where she belongs?" Garrett looks back and forth at the two of us. "Oh, so it's like that?" Garrett asks, finally putting all the pieces together. "You fuckin' a *cop*? Holy shit! You fuckin' the white po-po?"

"It's over, Garrett. Just leave and sign the divorce papers as soon as you get them."

"You *love* this dude?" Garrett points at Chase with an incredulous look on his pitiful face. He looks confused but finally resigned. "Fine, Dee, if that's the way you want it. But we could have worked this out, you know."

"Good-bye, Garrett," I say.

"Get off this island and stay off," Chase warns. "You leave Miss Destiny alone, and you won't have any problems with me. But you step one foot back here—you get anywhere near this lady—I promise you, it's another story altogether. Are we clear?"

"Yeah, no problem, man." Defeated and deflated, Garrett walks to his car and opens the door. Then he stops and turns around to me. "You know that little blonde flight attendant with the big tits? She gave me her number this time. I wasn't going to call her—till now."

"Do whatever you want, Garrett. You're a free man."

Garrett looks like a pimp rolling off in search of another pussy adventure. As he drives away, I shake my head in utter disgust. How could I have ever married that man?

"Destiny, you okay?" Chase asks in a tender voice. He lovingly kisses my temple. I nod my head, though I am still shaken. Another storm just ended in my life.

Chase takes me inside the house that we shared as children and now share again as lovers. He cranks up his little cassette player up on a shelf that somehow also survived the storm.

"I was meaning to play this for you before the hurricane." He pushes the button on the player and walks over to me. "May I have this dance?"

"Yes, Chief," I reply, with tears in my eyes and even more love for this man in my heart. "I want to dance with you forever."

"Me too, Destiny. Me too." Chase leans in and kisses me as our song begins, with Johnny Hartman crooning, *"It's very clear, our love is here to stay—not for a year, but ever and a day ..."*

Chase and I slow dance right there in the middle of the mold and mildew, holding fast to each other, happier than ever before. I don't know how we ended up here together, after all this time, but I have to believe the fates, God, and good old Aunt Joy had a lot to do with it. We vow to let nothing keep us apart ever again. Yes, time moves on, but destiny lingers. Chase and I are proof of that. And we both know that neither our lives, nor our beloved island, will ever be the same again.

"Are you ready to start a new life with me?" Chase asks as he squeezes my hand.

I smile. "I have been ready all my life."

"Me too," Chase replies as he dips me like a prized dancer. "Me too."

About the Author

For more than three decades, Rolonda Watts's name, face, and distinctive voice have been known by audiences of all ages everywhere, thanks to her many award-winning works in television, radio, digital media, magazines, and film. Watts is the CEO of her Watts Works Productions, as well as an Emmy- and Cable Ace Award–nominated journalist, TV and radio talk show host, executive producer, actor and voice actor, novelist, speaker, talent manager, and humanitarian.

Most know her by one name—Rolonda—under which she launched her own internationally syndicated talk show, produced by Watts Works and King World Productions. *Rolonda!* ran for four seasons: 1994 to 1998. Ro has not stopped talking since! Today, she continues as creator, host, and executive producer of *Rolonda On Demand*, a one-hour lifestyle, current events, and celebrity interview podcast heard weekly on Play.It, the new CBS local digital media platform: RolondaOnDemand.com or Play.it/Rolonda.

Rolonda began her television career as a local CBS news reporter in Greensboro, North Carolina, before joining New Jersey network WNBC-TV, and later WABC Eyewitness News in New York as an investigative news reporter and anchor. She hosted Lifetime television's talk show *Attitudes* before joining *Inside Edition* as weekend anchor, producer, and senior correspondent, and then she launched her own internationally syndicated TV talk show. Rolonda's deep, rich, and raspy voice is one of the most recognized in the business, serving as announcer for *Divorce Court* (FOXTV) and *Judge Joe Brown* (CBS).

In animation, Rolonda stars with Tyler Perry in his first animated movie, Tyler Perry's *Medea's Tough Love* (Lionsgate). Ro also voices the role of Professor Wiseman in *Curious George* (Universal) and Warrior

Priestess Illoi in the *League of Legends* game. In movies, Rolonda stars in *American Bred, Sister Code,* and *House Party: Tonight's the Night* (WB), *Broken Roads, House Arrest,* and *A Mother's Love,* which won the highly coveted Five-Star Dove Award. Ro's other movies include *Second Chance Christmas, Christmas Mail, Soul Ties,* and *25 Hill.* She stars as Hollywood legend Dorothy Dandridge in *Defying the Stars* and Josephine Baker in *Return to Babylon.* In television, Rolonda's extensive acting credits include *The Blexicans* sitcom pilot and *Light Girls,* both directed by Bill Duke (OWN). She also has played recurring roles in *Love That Girl!* (TVOne), and *Mann & Wife* (BOUNCE).

A committed philanthropist with an honorary doctorate from Winston-Salem State University for her humanitarian efforts, Rolonda supports Our Children of Our Troops, her charity drive for military families. She has served on the board of directors for Literacy Volunteers of New York City, the board of advisors for the Rahway State Prison's Lifers Group, and the board of advisors for the United Negro College Fund. The Spelman College Alumna Association awarded Ro for her community service and contributions to the entertainment industry, and the McDonald's Corporation honored her as "a Broadcast legend." *Facebook & Business* magazine calls her "the queen of all media."

Rolonda holds degrees from Spelman College, where she was graduated magna cum laude. She holds a master's degree from Columbia University's Graduate School of Journalism, where she served as president of Sigma Delta Chi, the Society of Professional Journalists. There are official "Rolonda Days" in New York City and Newark, New Jersey. Ro is single and lives in Los Angeles, California.

CPSIA information can be obtained at www.ICGtesting.com
Printed in the USA
BVOW02*0943181115

427519BV00001B/1/P